i

WESTERN NOVELS
BY G. R. HOWE

Fiction

NO TIME TO TRUST

DRAGONS OF FIRE

CROW WOMAN ON DEADMAN

TEQUILA PROMISES

NO CHANCE

Short Story Collection

SHORT STORIES OUT OF KANE

RUMORS

G. R. HOWE

Published in the United States by Allied Publishing, a Wyoming corporation.

This is a work of fiction. Names, characters, and incidents are either the product of the author's imagination or are used fictitiously. Any resemblance to actual persons, living or dead, events, or locales is entirely coincidental.

Acknowledgment

Thanks to the following individuals who have contributed so much time and effort in the editing and creation of this novel: Joy Howe, and Rachel Montgomery. These individuals were marvelous and free with their time, generous suggestions, and comments.

For Joy

CHAPTER 1

June 5, 1886
Sage Creek, Montana Territory

I can't stand it. I really can't. So I wrote a letter. That's it. Nothin' more'n that. I got a knucklehead for a husband. Makes me wonder, he does. It ain't like I don't love him plumb to death 'cause I do. It's just sometimes he don't make a lick of sense. It's usually when I need him to be makin' sense that he ain't about to do it. Why do you think that is?

It's been more than a month and Petey just sits on the porch wrapped in a buffalo robe. He don't say much; watchin' everythin' goin' to hell. He won't ask for help, like it's a snake 'bout ready to reach up and bite him. So, I writ' a letter. One to each of his brothers. Same letter. There ain't nothin' wrong me writin' letters. Don't know why it upsets him so. They're his brothers and when you get hurt, you're hurt. That's when they's supposed to come and help. It ain't like they got a choice. That's what brothers do. Leastwise, that's what they're supposed to do if they got a lick of sense and any raisin' at all. I figured one of them letters I writ' might get through. No tellin', considerin' a letter travels by horseback, stagecoach, the Union Pacific, and the Chicago, Burlington And Quincy. One gettin' through will do. Just one. We need help. We need it 'fore there's nothin' left to be helpin' with.

This predicament got started when Petey got himself all buggered up: broke his leg 'cause the horse he's ridin' rolled on him. Truth is he might of fell off. Lordy, we got a thousand head of cows. Well, we had a thousand head. Ain't got 'em no more. 'Bout the same time Petey has his little set-to they just disappeared. That day he didn't come home so I wants to ride out there to find him. I can't go a hundred yards, what with the cold and the snow and two kids in the house. I was sick worryin'. Only thing I could do is wait.

Late that night, me walkin' the floor, these Absaroka Crow, friends of his, they come ridin' in, one holdin' Petey in the saddle, his

1

leg off to the side, unnatural. They bring him into the house; he ain't himself, not at all. Mostly he's just groanin', ragin' with a fever. Lucky to be alive. Anyway, I got Petey all settled, set the bad leg. Doc O'Martine, he comes from Kane and fixes up Petey's bad leg. Says I did okay. In April, soon as the weather turns a bit I got him sittin' on the porch, a jug of water near to hand. Still cold. Snow ain't melted. We're sittin' our backs agin' a mountain. Lots of snow in the trees. After that, with Petey sorta settled, I fork the little paint pony and I ride out to the south pastures to see what it is I'm gonna have to do. I find there ain't nothin' I'm gonna do. Don't know why I even thought it.

Nothin'. There ain't a single head grazin' out there on the Reservation. Same for the west pastures that follow along Sage Creek with the canyons on one side and the Crow on the other. Nothin'. Not one head. Not a cow, not a calf, nothin'. It's clear what's happenin'. Someone, seein' Petey's all laid up, come and picks us clean. It was a pretty soberin' moment in my twenty-two year life. What with my man laid up, and two kids, three and five years of age. There's only so much I can do. That's when I starts to askin' for help. 'Cause I can't do this myself. How am I gonna go up against those filthy, rustlin' bastards? How? There's just me.

I don't tell this to Petey. I daresn't tell him 'cause if he gets an inklin' me askin', then he's gonna do somethin' crazy. Him havin' that broke leg. It'll be broke again in the same place and Petey will be crawlin' on his belly for the rest of his worthless life and I'll for sure be packin' him around, a broken down man. I surely don't need that. I can't see me tellin' a story like that, what with us havin' two young'ns, Josh and Katie Sue. That Katie Sue—she's as cute as a red button. She's the oldest. Smart. Lordie, is she ever smart!

I know'd better. I got back late evenin' from lookin' at the south and west pastures and fixed Petey somethin' to eat. I'm feelin' low, a snake's belly in a wagon track low. So I suggest to Petey that maybe we oughta be writin' those brothers of his askin' for help, seein' how we need it.

Me mentionin' the word 'help' and Petey blows the lid right off that black kettle thick skull of his. He's a sayin' maybe we won't be doin' that, that he ain't wantin' to bother 'em none, that they

2

won't wanna be comin' all this way just 'cause he has a broke leg.

"'Sides," he says, "in another three or four months, I'll be up and around." Three or four months. Listen to him.

He says that it's best we don't be askin' for help. That's what he says. Frankly, I don't get it. Him not askin' gets my dander up. Too much pride. I'd ask my sisters 'ceptin' they're takin' care of Daddy. They's got their hands full with all they're a doin'.

Petey goes on and and on how he's just fine. After listenin' to that I go in the house and I set on the kitchen chair and I rested my arms on the table and I said, "God, what are we ever gonna do? We're in a fine fix. Petey bein' stupid and we ain't got no cows. I can't do the garden with all of this goin' on. It just got worse. We got two hungry kids and I got a husband that ain't of a mind to be askin' for no help and he himself bein' as helpless as a one-legged critter can be. For some reason known only to him he says I sure as hell ain't gonna write his brothers and do no beggin'.'"

Beggin'? Is he an idiot? Askin' family ain't beggin'!

"That ain't gonna happen," he says.

"What?" I says. "Those boys, they got consumption? What's wrong with 'em?"

"Nothin'," he says. "There ain't nothin' wrong with 'em."

"Well, then why ain't we askin' for help? We need it."

"I don't wanna explain it," he says. "Trust me. It's for the best. They ain't too good at gettin' along."

"You ain't told them 'bout Pa, has you? You ain't writ 'em like you said, has you? You promised me you'd tell 'em. You ain't done it."

"What?" he says. "Why can't you leave that be? They don't need to know."

"That's what this is all about. You ain't told 'em Pa gots himself kilt. You said you would. It's just a little ol' letter and you ain't writ' it. Some gutless wonder you turned out to be. It's somethin' that has to be done, like askin' for help when we need it. Sometimes you just gotta do it, Petey. What's wrong with you? They's just men. They's doin' the best they kin and you ain't tellin' 'em? They need to be here. They need to be doin' what's right and you ain't lettin' 'em. You're a fool. That's what you are."

I ain't never been so angry. I just stared at him like he's out of his mind and I drop it. I shouldn't have but I did. What's the use? I gotta live with him and he's gotta live with me. I had to have the last word on this one, though.

So I says, "Petey, things are gonna get a helluva lot worse 'fore they get any better and you waitin' around not tellin' your brothers ain't helpin'."

He says, "I don't wanna talk about it. Not another word," he says. "We'll handle it ourselves. I ain't gonna be sick forever. I'll do it, myself. I don't wanna talk about my brothers ever again. Ever!"

That ended that.

Two weeks later I'm sittin' at the table, work's stackin' up: hay's growin' like crazy, needin' cuttin' soon, fences to fix in the corral, brandin' to do--though that ain't gonna be much 'cause there ain't no cows and there ain't no yearlings to put the mark of Texas on. I'm feelin' pretty low. So I finally figure I really ain't got no choice. I decide I'll write his brothers, do some "beggin'," lay it all out there and get some help 'cause if anyone be needin' help, it's me. They can't be all that bad. Petey ain't a bad man himself. They're outta the same litter. I'm hopin' that maybe one of them letters gets through to just one of his brothers. Maybe one will come and give us a hand.

I just don't get it. I ain't never met his brothers all grown up. Knew who they was when I was a youngster. I'm twenty-two and Petey, he's the youngest of his kin, and he's six years older than me. My sister Claire, she's twenty, Betsy is eighteen and Sally, she's sixteen. Petey and me, we sorta grew up together, meetin' in the fall at round-up ever since I can remember. Them boys would come help and collect any cow wearin' the MT brand.

I decided not to tell Petey that I was goin' to his brothers beggin'. I know he can't stand it, won't stand it. Well, I can't stand it, either. Except I figure I ain't got no choice. Like I said, I never met his brothers 'cept when I was a little girl. There's the secondborn, name a Syrus; there's Riles, he's firstborn, and there's the thirdborn, whose name is Far, short for Forest. Petey be the youngest and Far is two years older than him. Those boys left home 'fore he was runt-sized, hardly twelve. His pa was still alive. His mother, she died in

Seventy-nine. Got pneumonia, poor lady. Coughed her lungs out.

From the beginning little Petey was raised on Sage Creek, a little east of Indian Springs. We lived forty miles north of Kane, maybe fifty, maybe more, sittin' right up next to the big mountain on the other side of the West Pryor. The way I hear it, Petey's pa left the place to him 'cause the other boys was done gone. I ain't seen no papers. Petey never talks about 'em. There weren't no pictures, no tintypes. Petey just don't have much to say on the subject. I was fresh eighteen when we married. I didn't ask. Figured it wasn't my place. I had Petey to figure out. That was enough to my way of thinkin'. With all the work, there wasn't much time for wonderin' 'bout papers or his pa's intentions.

It was around the first of May when I writ' those letters askin' for help, past desperate. Figured that Petey can get angry if he wants, then he can just get over it. I was down to no choice. Me and the box elder bugs was 'bout to be livin' on the crumbs at the bottom of the bread box. Like I say, it didn't look none too good.

A skunk got into the chickens and damn near kilt all my layin' hens. Pigs got out. I can't get 'em in. They don't drive. Always cuttin' back on you. Like pushin' a string 'cross the dinner table. Didn't take 'em long to set up house down on the creek: rootin', tearin' the trees up. Bastards. I'm 'bout at wit's end. Josh fell in the yard, cut himself on somethin'. Don't know what. He couldn't tell me; a three year old ain't got much to say: don't know a lot of words. Hard to tell what he has on his mind: him cryin', tears runnin' down his checks and blood runnin' out the bottom of his foot.

Petey's still laid up. Leg's swoll up where it was broke. Don't know if that's natural. Don't look good.

I sent them letters a travelin' to where they're goin' on the fifth of May, 1886. On that day I caught a fellow comin' through, ridin' out from Red Lodge: first traveler I'd seen this year. Truth be told, I didn't have any hope. I knew I waited too long. I posted my husband's brothers' three letters, one each, and went about my business best I could. I asked him to post those letters in Kane since he was goin' there. Said he would, bein' most grateful, for Petey and I fed him proper, let him sleep in the barn. Didn't have much, mostly venison and potatoes, and a bit of ground flour.

As I said, I'm the oldest of the Stafford girls. My name be Diana. That Diana was originally a Roman gal. Someone special. A goddess. I ain't no goddess but I was named for one. I'm the oldest, goin' on twenty-three years. There's four of us kids and we hail from behind Little Mountain where Deer Creek drops into the Porcupine and Porcupine loses itself in the canyon. That'd be forty or fifty miles from here, ridin' east 'cross the canyon. Quite a ways 'cause you can't get there straight. Don't work that way. It'd take a fat man ridin' a skinny horse four days just gettin' there. Ain't been home in a while 'cause it takes so long comin' and goin'. And I've got plenty to do with Petey bein' laid up. It's been gettin' on eight months since I seen my family. Come fall, 'fore the snow starts on the Horn I'll get over there and see Pa and the girls. Been thinkin' on it. Gotta do it. Told Petey I'd need to do it and he said he'd go with me. Sometimes I gotta love that man. The way he looks out for me.

It's been four weeks since I posted them letters. Ain't right me callin' 'em letters. More like a note, a real short note. Nothin's happened. I figure nothin' is gonna happen. I figure it might take a month for them letters to get to where they're gettin' and then, if his brothers are comin', maybe another three or four weeks. I'm thinkin' nobody's comin'. Nothin's happenin'.

CHAPTER 2

Date: July 2, 1886
Forty miles east of Bend, Oregon Territory

"Hey, Slim Jangles, y'all got yourself a letter. Got a lady's hand, it does. You all sweet on some gal? Well, she's writ' you. It's right there sittin' in the mail can waitin' for you. Red Olson brought it from the post office three weeks ago. You see it? Damn. That's what I say. Nobody gets theyselves a letter. Not often. I ain't never seen it, myself 'ceptin' once when I was a kid, livin' with my folks."

Riles Stockton had ridden in from the high mountain pastures, from the line cabin above Strickland Canyon. He'd wintered there and he'd spent most of the spring playing nursemaid to three hundred fifty-six head of stock cows and forty-six head of green horses belonging to the Cross W. That number didn't include an onery five year old mule, two saddle horses and an ugly, long-haired, one-eyed dog. Those were his.

The grass was green on the high ridges above the timberline. It was during the advance of the spring rains when he decided he had had enough. That had been four or five weeks ago. He was not exactly sure. It had felt like it was time: time to move on: time to draw his accumulated pay.

Three days earlier Buck Jackson found him catching up his sorrel mare. Catching the sorrel wasn't odd except he'd already saddled the Buckskin. Riding two horses at the same time probably is odd.

"Where you goin' with two saddle horses?" Buck asked.

"Ah," he responded, "I'll be callin' it quits."

Buck had leaned up against the horse corral gate and nodded. "'Bout had enough, have you?" he said.

Riles Stockton didn't answer him, concentrating on coiling his rope, noting the sorrel's feet, reminding himself to check her shoes. One looked a little loose on the left front hoof.

"Where to, you figure?" Buck had asked.

Turning his back to the sorrel, he'd glanced at Buck who had started rolling a cigarette and offered a paper to his companion. Riles nodded, took the paper as well as the sack of Bull Durham Smoking Tobacco.

"Don't rightly know," Riles answered. "Figure I'll go west. Ain't never seen the ocean. Thought I'd give her a look-see."

Wetting the tobacco filled paper with his tongue, Buck wrapped it tight, twisted the ends, and stuck the cigarette between his lips. He struck a diamond tip on the worn sole of his boot. The match flared. A few strands of tobacco fell out of the end of the rolled and twisted concoction onto his shirt. He held the fire to the end of the cigarette and sucked air through it, causing a bright glow of embers. Satisfied, he offered the flame to Riles, cupping his hand around the glowing match to prevent the breeze from extinguishing it. Leaning down, Riles drew on the cigarette, watched the end catch, glowing red. Casually, he stood straight and blew smoke through his lips and nostrils.

"Well," Buck said, "I'll leave you to it. When you leavin'?"

"Thanks, Buck," Riles said. "Today. Maybe tomorrow. Sorrel needs a little work on her feet. I'm gonna take a look at the north pasture this mornin'." He nodded. "Keep the wind at your back, Buck."

"I'll do it," he'd said. "You, the same."

Those were the last words he ever heard Buck Jackson say. Riles was standing in the early morning cool examing the sorrel's feet when Buck disappeared around the corner of the horse corral. Moments later, Riles took the Buckskin horse and checked the livestock in the north pastures; a mountain lion had been feeding on a dead cow. Riles thought he'd put an end to that before "eatin' cow became a habit the lion didn't wanna break."

Later, midafternoon, Riles Stockton tightened the cinch on the sorrel, tied the Buckskin's lead to the back of his saddle, then started down the mountain. He wondered what the blue ocean looked like. *It looks blue*, he thought, laughing at himself. *And it's big. How big is big? How blue is blue?* It was a good feeling, quitting, going somewhere he'd never been. Seeing something he'd never seen. Not like leaving his home on the creek when he was seventeen, leaving his brothers, his mother, glad to be gone, glad to be away from the Old Man and his unending observations. He'd headed west, looking at the land from between a horse's ears. That was twenty years ago.

At first it was a little frightening, for there was no going back. He'd had enough then, too. No more, he'd thought. "I ain't puttin' up with no horse shit." And he hadn't. Recently, he'd grown as restless as he'd been at seventeen. Maybe it was too much of the same thing. And for the hundredth time he wondered what the "it" was that he couldn't put up with.

Behind him the mule and dog trailed like they always did. In the end, the dog would be in the lead, the mule walking free alongside the saddle horses.

"Ya hear me, Slim Jangles? I said y'all got yourself a letter."

"I heard you," Riles Stockton replied. "Everybody heard you. You're actin' like nobody ever got a letter before."

"Well, they ain't. They ain't and I ain't."

"They ain't?" Stockton stared at the skinny cowhand. For a moment, he wondered if this kid, this cowhand from Nebraska, wasn't the "it" that he'd gotten tired of. *Sometimes*, he thought. *Sometimes*. Stockton had been thinking about drawing his pay. It had been a year ago June when he'd last done that. One year and one month, give or take a day. He never saw the point; there wasn't anything to spend his money on. The Cross W's main buildings were forty miles east of Bend and that meant it was a forty mile ride to waste your money on women and a banjo-driven song, neither of which he cared for. So he left his money with the paymaster. He was owed three hundred thirty-five dollars.

Dropping his saddle at the head of an empty bunk, he laid claim to it, making it his because it was empty and because no one was using it. It was a three day ride from the line shack on Strickland Canyon, and he was exhausted. In spite of his tired muscles and the need to sit down, the skinny, excited cowhand made him smile. Personally, he didn't care whether he received a letter or not. What he wanted was a hot bath, something warm sitting heavy in his stomach, and a place to lay his aching bones, a place to sleep and not wake up until the day after tomorrow or, maybe if he was lucky, next week.

Who'd write me anyways? Whatever it is...it sure as hell ain't good news. Why hurry grief?

"Where's it from?" Riles asked.

"Where's what from, Slim Jangles?"

"The letter. Does it have a postmark? You must of looked at it. Tell me. Where's it from?"

Stockton wouldn't admit it but the conversation suddenly grew tiresome. The cowkid, his rusty hair dropping into his eyes like a duck blind, glanced at the envelope he'd retrieved from the mail can, then back at Stockton without saying anything.

"I dunno," he said. "How's I supposed to know that?"

"The upper left hand corner of the letter. Does it have an address?"

"Let's see. It does," the cowkid exclaimed. "There's some writin' right here."

"Read it to me."

The rider looked up from the battered, ragged envelope at Riles Stockton. "Y'all better read it yourself." He handed Riles the envelope. "Here," he said, offering it to him.

Stockton took the envelope.

"You can't read," Stockton said. It was more of a statement than a question, an observation, the words falling to the floor in a single room log cabin dominated by a fireless pot-bellied stove. The front door was wide open, sunlight streaming through it. Outside, the cottonwood trees that followed the creek were dark green. Their leaves fluttered in the breeze. The one-eyed dog, tongue lolling to the side of his mouth, sat in the doorway, catching Stockton's attention as he lay down, stretching his long frame partly into the room.

Shouldn't have fed him when I did. A little late now. Damn dog. Hadn't fed him, he wouldn't have followed me. It hadn't been that much. Some rabbit bones. Now he won't let me out of his sight. Knows the value of a free meal and he ain't givin' up on it.

The cowkid shook his head in answer. "Ain't learnt. I sure ain't. I knows it's special gettin' a letter. My mother got one once. Sure did. She musta read it a thousand times. 'Til it was fallin' 'part."

10

"You ought to learn. It'd serve you well."

"I know I ought to. So where is it comin' from? Your letter?"

Riles Stockton glanced at the envelope, turning it over. The return address said: Sage Creek, Montana Territory. "Canceled stamp says Kane, Wyoming Territory. That's what it says. So the letter was written on Sage Creek and then mailed at the U.S. Post Office in Kane, Riley Kane, Postmaster."

"You know somebody in this Kane place?"

Riles glanced again at the envelope and at the prim, rounded, ladylike script, plain and clear.

"Not right in Kane. Outside of it forty-fifty miles. Up in the Pryors. North to the other side of the mountain, down on Sage Creek. My brothers...." Stockton paused, looking at the kid. *He don't really wanna know all that bullshit. I'm just jabberin' to hear my teeth click together.* "My folks live there. I'm pretty sure my youngest brother still lives there. I think he stayed. The rest...I figure we all left. It's been a goodly while since I've been there."

"What's it say?"

"You're a bit nosy, don't you think?"

"I sure am. But I ain't know'd nobody to get hisself a letter. Just my ma and she surely liked it."

Riles Stockton smiled. "How do you know I can read?"

"Only folks that can read gets letters."

"That some sort of rule?" Stockton asked.

Ignoring him, the rider said, "So what's it say? My mother got a letter from her mother 'fore the ol' lady up an died. Letter told Ma that someone she knew croaked. Nothin' good comes from gettin' a letter, you know? Just bad news. Except my ma; she liked it plenty. It wasn't all bad. That's what I'm sayin'."

Stockton nodded. "I see," he said. "You think I ought to burn it without readin' it? Who needs bad news?" Stockton glanced at the skinny cowhand. Then he looked at the envelope, turning it over in his hand.

The cowhand laughed. "It's bad news, all right," he said. "So open it up and let's see who died. Might be some folks you know. Maybe you'll be lucky and someone will get themselves born. Or married. That could happen, you know. In that letter my ma got

11

herself she was told how her sister had herself a baby. Said her sis was doin' fine. Her pa, he died but the baby was doin' fine. Both doin' fine. That's what it said. Maybe that's what your letter will say. Could be."

"All right," Riles Stockton said, sitting down on the edge of his bunk. He glanced at the red-haired rider. The other two line riders had stopped talking and were staring at him. The one-eyed dog inched his way through the doorway, whining, unsure of himself. Hesitating, he laid down again, this time inside the doorway.

The red- haired rider was right. It wasn't often someone got a letter. The postmark was smudged. No readable date. The envelope was addressed to Riles Stockton, Bend, Oregon. It was a woman's hand, all right. *What woman do I know that would write me using a return address of Sage Creek? Maybe they just addressed the envelope and someone else wrote it.* Taking his pocket-knife from his pants pocket, he ran the blade slowly along the long side of the envelope, then removed a single sheet of folded paper.

The rider stood leaning against the top bunk. Stockton glanced up at him, amused at his interest in a letter written to someone else and at him wanting to hear good news. It read:

Dear Mr. Riles Stockton,

I'm your brother Petey's wife. We're in trouble. Petey done broke his leg. Horse rolled on him. I reckon he fell off. It's just me, Josh, and Katie Sue. They's young bein' they was born not long ago. They's no help. Their legs are barely long enough to reach the ground. They ain't grow'd. Somebody stole the cows. Can't find 'em. They ain't no more. Horses busted out. They's gone. Corral fell down and needs fixin'. Poles don't stay fit no more. Horse needs shoeing, anyways. Dog got into the chickens. They's mostly dead. Sucked them eggs dry. Would have shot the dog 'cept he keeps the skunks away. Hay's gonna need haying. Just started to grow. Up six or seven inches now. There's just me. Please? Kin you come? I'm Diana. I'm a Stafford. You know who I am. My folks, they live on the other side of the canyon. I writ your brothers. Hope you show up 'cause we need help real bad. Last fall your Pa died. Got kilt. Petey was gonna tell you. He didn't. Diana

"What's it say? Somebody died? That's terrible. That's what it is. I'm sure sorry."

"Says my pa died last year. It says my youngest brother got his leg broke. Needs my help. It says somebody stole his cows."

"That's a hell of a note. A broke leg? His cows stolen?"

"It says he fell off his horse."

"Fell off his horse? Your brother a tenderfoot?"

Now there's a question. Pistol fallin' off a horse?

"Naw, he ain't no tenderfoot," Riles Stockton replied. "Pistol ain't never fell off a horse in his life. Not Pistol."

"Then that'd be a damn lie. My ma didn't like no damn lies. Worst kind."

"A lie? Maybe. Bound to be more to the story. Makes me wonder."

"What you gonna do?"

"Don't know. I should go back to the MT. See what's goin' on. Between you, me and the gatepost, can't say that I want to. Guess I have to. Don't know."

"MT? What's the MT?"

"Trail brand. Came up the trail from Texas and it's a little spread in southern Montana on the edge of the Res where I grew up."

"That Texas trip's some trek."

"Sure as hell is."

"When you leavin'? You leavin' right away?"

Riles Stockton stood up, folded the letter and inserted it into the envelope. He nodded, grimaced, glanced at his saddle lying at the front of his bunk, and shook his head. "Reckon I'll get a bite to eat first. Maybe in the mornin'. Gotta convince myself that's where I wanna go. Haven't been there in some time. Maybe ten-fifteen years. Let's see I'm thirty-seven. Left when I was seventeen. Twenty years! Lord. Don't know. Hard to tell what's goin' on. Don't sound good. Somethin' real bad. The Old Man is dead. I never expected that."

"Hey, Slim Jangles, someone was lookin' for ya a while back. Askin' after you by name."

Riles Stockton looked at the rider. "For me? When was that?"

"In the fall...sometime after y'all left for the high winter country. That had to have been...." the rider glanced at Riles Stockton. "Well, it's whenever it was."

"Where was this?"

"Pendleton."

"Pendleton?"

"Yeah, Pendleton. He didn't look none too friendly. Skinny fellow. Narrow face. Big ears. Turn sideways, you'd miss him. Know what I mean? Carried a pistol in a shoulder holster. Dressed like he was a go-to-church gambler. Had a hideaway."

"A hideaway? How do you know?"

"I've been around. I know'd what a hideaway looks like. He had one."

"What'd you tell him?"

"I didn't tell him nothin'. Looked like trouble. Ain't seen him since. Told him I ain't never seen the likes of you nowheres. Ain't that right, Lasser?" He looked at the rider sitting at the card table. "Ain't that right?"

"Yeah, kid, that's right. He was trouble. See it a mile off."

Stockton took a breath and looked at the dog lying inside the bunk house door before turning to the rider. "Well, Rusty," he said, "I thank you. I appreciate it. You sayin' nothin'."

"Figured you didn't need no trouble. So we sent him on his way with nothin'."

"Thank you, kid."

"No problem. Sorry 'bout your brother. Sorry 'bout your pa. Sorry 'bout your trouble. Like your letter. It's a good one."

"Appreciate it. I do."

That evening Riles Stockton didn't leave the bunkhouse for long. Instead, he ate biscuits and venison drowned in venison gravy, loaded with Black Jack pepper. He took a bath in a round galvanized tub two thirds full of hot water and soap. He read Diana Stockton's letter twice more. Finally he went up to the main house and drew his pay.

He left the Cross W in the early morning, before sun up, before false dawn when the world was dark and quiet. There was a heavy dew, no wind, not even a breeze to rattle the leaves in the cottonwood trees. He rode the Buckskin and led the sorrel, a troubled man. What he couldn't believe was his pa was dead. He thought he'd never die, that it wasn't possible. Not knowing if he even liked him, he thought about the Old Man.

How could I? Damn his miserable hide. Damn his miserable, miserable hide. Pa. His formal name was Carl. The Indians called him Moose. How could he possibly be dead?

It was July 12, 1886. Riles Stockton started home.

It was dark. Several hours passed and the cottonwoods were still ghostly galleons against a dimly lit eastern sky. It was chilly, still no sun; a brisk breeze came up, blowing in from the west. He'd covered ten miles when the sun burst over the mountains in the east amid angry red clouds. The one-eyed dog was out front, his long-haired coat wet from the dew that clung heavily to the grass. A breeze came up, gusted, rattling the leaves. It felt cold. He buttoned his jacket against the chill.

Riles Stockton felt angry, agitated. *How could that miserable so and so be dead?* That knowledge bothered him the most, more than anything else. Maybe some of the agitation came from the fact he knew where he was going. He'd already been there: home. The memories he bore were heavy, black with suet, not good, not friendly. He didn't want to go. He didn't want to remember. It was like awakening the sleeping giant, kicking him in the side again and again, jabbing him with a sharp stick.

Riles Stockton carried a 44-40 Winchester in the boot, an SAA Colt 44-40 in a plain leather holster tied to his thigh, another stuck in his waistband, yet another in his saddlebags. Normally, Riles Stockton felt good, young, full of buckwheat and vinegar, looking forward with anticipation. Not now. Now he rode concerned, hesitant, the letter an agitation: Pistol with a broken leg, his father, dead. He had always figured he'd go home, yet never any time soon. Not yet. Later, certainly. It was later. Later had arrived and he wasn't sure he liked it.

Lord...the Old Man dead? How?

It didn't seem possible. It wasn't.

He stopped at a spring in a grove of quaking aspen to give

the sorrel and the Buckskin a drink and take a breather. Stepping down, standing next to the sorrel, he watched the mule and the Buckskin. He patted the Peacemaker on his thigh, checking the loop that encircled the hammer and kept the 44-40 Colt from falling out of the holster. Safety was a factor with him. It always had been.

Damn the Old Man. Safety.

The hammer of his Winchester did not rest on an empty chamber. It sat on a live cartridge. Not so with his SAA Colts. The Colt's hammer rested on an empty chamber, empty in that it didn't carry a live round. It did have a ten dollar bill wrapped up tight resting in its place. A ten dollar bill wasn't going to explode if the hammer was nudged a bit. It was the Old Man's thinking that being too safe could get you killed; best to keep a firearm loaded against the time it was needed. An empty chamber in a rifle wasn't a safety factor. It wasn't even an idea worth considering.

A hammer on an empty chamber in a Colt, on the other hand, was being safe. A hammer pushing a firing pin resting against a live round was subject to being inadvertently hit. It could easily strike the cap on a live cartridge. Bang, you either shot yourself or the horse you're riding, or both. That happened too often. The Old Man had reminded him of that over and over and over again.

If things were getting a little dicey, that was an entirely different matter. Flipping open the loading gate, inserting a cartridge in the place of the ten dollar bill might just be the thing to do: six live rounds are sometimes better then five. And a man needs to do what he thinks best. That was the Old Man talking again.

How could he possibly be dead?

Riles Stockton had money. That's not to say he was a Carnegie or a Vanderbilt, but on the morning he left Oregon Territory he carried two years, three months and one week of income earned from riding for the Cross W folks out of Bend, Oregon. He'd been earning thirty dollars a month, plus room and board. It was a lot considering that five American dollars would fill the back of a buckboard with a year's worth of groceries. He'd been saving for a while, not sure why.

He led a four year old, sixteen and a half hand high, fifteen

16

hundred pound Buckskin gelding, rode a six year old sorrel mare, and was sort of followed by a five-going-on-six year old ill-tempered mule he called Cecil. The mule was an oddity. *That damned mule!* For some reason two years ago the mule had gotten it into his head that he was being left behind and deeply resented it. The fact was, Cecil was in full blown resentment whether he was being left behind or not. As a result, he was always crowding, trying to go some place that necessitated being in front. It was the thought that bothered him. It certainly wasn't the load he carried. It wasn't how far he was required to travel. It was the idea of the Buckskin (and sometimes the sorrel or the one-eyed dog) going anywhere without him. Thus, he was always trying to establish himself in the lead and avoid being left behind. Most of the time he didn't know where he was going. He didn't care. He'd get out front, wait, and get nervous when he discovered he was alone. Alone drove him crazy, put him on the run.

Cecil liked the Buckskin the most, often staying at his side, sometimes a couple of feet in the lead and sometimes a step or two behind. It was an odd pairing: the halterless, no-lead-rope Cecil, the Buckskin, and the one-eyed dog. Once moving, the mule hung out in the vicinity of wherever the Buckskin happened to be. The mule made it easy; lead rope or no, he never ran away, and if he did venture afield it wasn't far and it was purely accidental.

The order of travel generally was this: out front walked the one-eyed dog; next came Cecil, the halterless mule, followed by either the Buckskin gelding or the sorrel mare. The walking order of the latter two depended on which horse Riles Stockton rode. The morning he started east, he rode the sorrel mare; he was heading for Idaho and a small, one horse settlement named Boise. From Boise, he'd follow the Snake River until it didn't suit him, then he'd turn north.

CHAPTER 3

June 22, 1886 to July 2, 1886
Big Horn County, Basin City, Wyoming Territory

Being the tightwads that they were, the Big Horn County Commissioners built the scaffold with one trap door. It wasn't big, the platform being a solid nine feet by nine feet. There was barely enough room to support five men standing, let alone three girls, hanging. It was not built in the same way the U. S. Government had built the one for the hanging of Mary Surratt and the men accused of assassinating President Lincoln. That scaffold had been built with federal government money. The Surratt scaffold was a four-holer, used once, then deconstructed before it could be used again. It was a huge monstrosity of death and no one wanted to look at it once Mary Surratt and company had fallen through the floor, their necks snapping, killing them instantly.

The Big Horn County Commissioners made a "reasonable," cheap, backroom decision, because, to the man, they knew--indeed everyone knew--the Stafford girls' hanging would not take place. Several of the thoughtful citizens asked why they built it at all. It made no sense. But then politics and elected officials never made any sense.

The common man, the man who fed his worn out Percheron draft horses in the morning, slopped his Berkshire hogs in the afternoon, and threw rolled oats to his Rock Island Reds several times a day knew those girls would be turned loose in a couple of days. Nothing more would be made of it. It was the generally held belief that they'd be released inside five days. Old man Meekers wasn't alone when he said, "What the hell's goin' on here? Don't those bastards know there's hay to put up?" Old man Meekers repeated himself, lifting a cold glass to his lips on the twenty-ninth of June, it being a week since the trial--a trial that should never have been conducted "in the first place." The bartender nodded, for he'd heard that sentiment repeated a lot. Folks were wondering when the

18

release would be and why it hadn't already taken place.

"Be patient," folks said, knowingly, nodding their heads. All the dangling, unanswered questions, the legal commotion--all the residual hubbub of trial--were caused by the turning of the slow wheels of the law, the mysterious workings of justice, of governmental protocol working itself out. If two men and a ruddy faced boy could do it in a day, the government would take a "month of Sundays" just to come to a decision.

"Yes, be patient," they said again and again. "Those girls will be released before first cutting is curing in the barn."

"Damn straight" they said. "Nothing to worry about."

On the appointed day for haying to begin, folks would gather to help, since the Stafford girls had no men folk, their fifty-six year old pa having been shot in the back by the cowardly Jed Mumford, using a sawed off twelve gauge Winchester shotgun.

Jack Peterson had wondered about the Winchester. "Where'd Mumford get such a shootin' iron, Jed never havin' two quarters to rub together?" That's what Jack asked. No one had an answer and the conversation drifted on to Buffalo Anderson, himself. Mumford worked for Buffalo for a while and more recently he worked for a man named Linderman. It appeared he was trying to take over the entire county.

"Didn't make no sense." That's what folks said. Old Buffalo owned the east side of the Big Horn and lived out on Crystal Creek below old Bald Mountain.

Sheriff Jason Gilson agreed with the Commissioners in their collective wisdom. Although he, too, did not see why the county was building a scaffold no one planned on using. It was sinful: spending county tax money on an apparatus that met no ongoing community need. After all, who in their right mind would hang three girls for finding the man that killed their pa and for sending him straight to hell courtesy of a Winchester 20 gauge? It was their pa. It was right.

There was an irony in Mumford dying by means of a smaller gauge shotgun than he'd used on their father. Still, it made no difference. He was tucked away in the damp ground where he "sure as hell" belonged. Those girls had set the world right. "Bless their hearts." As well they should. Hanging the girls for a "righteous killing was unthinkable and not just 'cause they was girls, neither. It was Mumford, if he was yet alive, who should be hung by the neck until dead for back shootin' their pa. The girls? They ought to get a gold minted medal for killin' him. Yes, bless their hearts."

If the county had spent the money on three trap doors instead of one, the expense wouldn't have amounted to much. The additional trap doors would have required a few extra nails, three twelve foot, two by six, pine boards cut in 24 inch lengths by Sawyer's Mill and Planing, twelve metal hinges purchased from the Crowley General store, and three common latches. By building the scaffold that never would be used with one trap door, the cost savings was four dollars and fifty-three cents. By hiring the manpower to construct this monument to community development, the cost over-run was eight hundred fifty-three dollars.

"Now thet's a damn sin if there ever was one."

The local *Basin City Rustler* newspaper declared it to be a boondoggle, making no sense. It was government and government spelled waste. People up and down the Big Horn River agreed.

"Sure as hell. And what's the Sheriff still got them in that jail for?"

"If he had a brain, he'd play with it for sure. Damn fool."

On June 22, a jury, under the specific directions of U.S. District Circuit Court Judge William "Bill" Kilpatrick, had found each girl guilty of murder, of knowingly shooting Mumford in the back, of killing him "dead." Before anyone could grasp what had happened, Kilpatrick had sentenced them to hang by the neck until dead. The finding, the judgment of the court, was absurd. Everybody said as much. Even then, no one thought they'd hang. Not really. If anyone had considered hanging a possibility, someone would have busted them out of jail and scurried them out of harm's way. That didn't happen. There was no need. Their release was imminent. Sheriff Gilson, himself, said, "No hanging would be happenin' and y'all could take that to the bank."

Folks figured that July 2, the day Judge Kilpatrick set for the girls' hanging, would come and go. Setting the day of execution was just a procedure he went through: something judges did, something he'd set aside later when he had a moment. It was judicial protocol and nothing more. He'd get it straightened out in due time. After all, no one had hanged "no woman" ever. Certainly not for doing what was righteous. Mary Surrat was forgotten by then. Besides, she'd helped kill Abe Lincoln and deserved the rope, if anyone did.

It was rumored that sometime after July 2 the county people would dismantle the scaffold and store it behind the jail in the makeshift woodshed the county kept. Come winter, they'd burn it, and use it for firewood should the need arise. Soon the scaffold would be forgotten. If it wasn't used for firewood, dry rot would consume it.

Though it was assumed the girls would be freed, folks for miles around planned to show up in Basin City on July 2 for the scheduled hanging. They'd come out of curiosity, do a little shopping, stock up with necessary supplies: wheat flour, cornmeal, 44-40 cartridges, and a twenty cent bag of salt to flavor their cantaloupe and watermelon. Coming to Basin City was what folks did on a holiday. It'd be a celebration that extended through the Fourth of July; there'd be fireworks, continuous drunken celebratory parties, a shooting contest, several horse races, and a spontaneous rodeo. Everyone was expecting a "hell of a good time." It was the right thing to do; guilty or not, those Stafford girls would be released and walking the streets with everyone else, doing what everyone else did. From one side of the county to the other, the girls' expected freedom was a forgone conclusion. Since before there was a judge, before Gilson was Sheriff--that had been the way matters were handled. It was a righteous killing. The girls had done nothing more than kill the man that killed their pa, and a man could damn well take that to church come Sunday morning and get himself a front row seat. The preacher had said as much from the pulpit on the Sunday of the week the trial had started and before the first witness was ever called.

On June 22, Sheriff Gilson sent a rider to Cheyenne to obtain the Governor's signature on a paper that would straighten out the whole matter. The Judge suggested that the rider be sent. The Sheriff had already arranged for the horseman before the suggestion was voiced. The rider left the very day the jury found the girls guilty, just as Judge Kilpatrick had told them to do. The rider Gilson selected was one of the Larson boys from up on Gyp Creek, reliable as rain. A man could certainly count on him, his pa being who he was.

Expected or not things, didn't work out the way everyone thought they would.

Eight days passed following the June 22 Basin City murder trial. The second oldest Stafford girl, the twenty year old Claire Stafford, marked each day off, scratching short lines on their cell wall with a bent nail. They wanted out, yes. Relying on the Sheriff's promise, they hadn't made any preparations. Betsy had asked whether they should send a message to Diana. Claire said "no" because they'd be out soon. While they waited for their promised release, the scaffold was constructed in the street outside their cell. Monitoring the progress of the county construction project was easy, though quite unnerving. The continuous hammering and sawing drove them crazy; rest was impossible, wearing their strained nerves ragged.

Betsy said it best, waiting in the cramped cell with her two sisters. "Why's they buildin' that thing when they's not intendin' to use it? Makes no sense. Do you think we should be worryin'?"

Claire Stafford, staring out the small window at the rising scaffold, nodded. "It is worrisome," she said. "It makes no sense." Still, day after day, they waited with hope, thinking their ordeal would be short-lived. There was so much that needed to be done at home.

In the midst of all of this sawing, hammering, and pounding, Old Man Time marched on, minute by minute, hour by hour, the long fingers of the calendar reaching inexorably toward July 2. All told, it was ten days from sentencing to execution of the sentence. Prior to their trial, in which they were convicted of murder, they'd spent six weeks in the center jail cell of the Big Horn County Jail in Basin City, Wyoming.

On June 30, 1886, Sheriff Gilson found himself standing in the street in front of the newly constructed scaffold trying to determine exactly what he needed to do to avoid using the ungodly contraption. *What a waste of time*, he thought. *And money.* He supposed he would need to get it to function properly within its obvious limitations. He didn't dwell on that possibility. After all, the accepted fact was it wasn't going to be needed. Still the established date for the hanging was a mere forty-eight hours away. There came a dawning, a mere inkling, the beginning of a thought the Sheriff did not want to accept; the hanging that wasn't supposed to happen would happen if he did not do something. The existing judicial schedule was on track and running like a down-hill locomotive, the engineer's hand pulling down on the throttle. *Damn. Double Damn. I've let too much time pass. If I don't get goin', the impossibility could become a possibility. Not like I've been sittin' around lettin' the dust settle on the tops of my boots, but I do need to get busy.*

He thought and thought and it occurred to him that the Larson boy he'd sent to Cheyenne couldn't possibly return in time. *Ten days to get there, one or two days to meet with the Governor, then ten days back. Three weeks if it was a day. Like that was going to happen!* "Shit," he mumbled softly. "I'm down to two days. I should have thought of this. I'd better get on it. No one would be riding in from Cheyenne with an order signed by the territorial governor in eight days."

Jason Gilson did not see it as an insurmountable problem. It would be solved by having the Judge sign an order continuing the hanging. A simple Order signed and he'd be off the legal hook from which he found himself dangling. To Gilson's thinking, this was one problem he could solve. After all, the Judge was in his office over at the courthouse, and if not at the courthouse, he'd be at the River Bar wetting his proverbial whistle. Certainly, he'd sign an order postponing the hanging he'd set.

Standing on the steps, staring at the stark, unpainted scaffold, Gilson prodded himself into action. He'd get on it now that he could see the problem. Fact was, if Gilson hadn't been so busy, the matter would have already been handled. Gilson thought about Kilpatrick and shook his head. Kilpatrick was no fool. Certainly, he was not easy to get along with. Judge Kilpatrick—"his Honor," as he liked to be called--created his own problems. Take this Stafford hanging. On June 22, the Judge had set the hanging for July 2, just ten days later. The rider he'd sent to Cheyenne would take over three weeks to ride there and back. *Why'd he do that?*

Thinking he had come up with the answer, Gilson rubbed his chin and smiled to himself. Looking at the problem, it appeared to Gilson that the Judge knew what he was doing. Gilson's left hand kept wearing at his two day old beard. He thought, *I'll bet that Kilpatrick just wanted to be the girls' savior--be the man who prevented the*

Stafford girls from hangin; by signin; an Order. All right, Gilson decided. He'd let the fool be the hero. It didn't matter to him at all. His left hand stopped wearing at his chin.

Still worried though, he thought, *Somethin' ain't right.* He didn't know what. That bothered him. To put the problem to rest, on the afternoon of June 30 in Basin City, Sheriff Gilson met with Circuit Court Judge William Kilpatrick at the Basin City River Bar and Hotel. What he wanted he knew the Judge would give him: a continuance of the hanging. He had confidence he'd get the Order. So much so, that he told the Stafford girls what he was doing: how he was asking the Judge for his signature on an Order. The Judge would be the hero; a few people would get drunk, throwing down shot after shot, in celebration. Next Tuesday, the Judge would get his name in the *Basin City Rustler* newspaper and that would be that. Next year, or the year after, the Judge would run for Territory Governor and get his name in several papers on how he stopped the hanging and saved the day.

Gilson prepared the proposed Order for the Judge's signature, folding it twice and putting it in his right shirt pocket. It took him a good forty-five minutes to painstakingly print it using a soft lead pencil and paper that the Territory purchased for court use only. Finished and walking east down the street toward the river, he felt good. There was the possibility the Stafford girls could be free by evening fall. He'd see to it. That'd be nice. He knew their pa; he went hunting elk with him several years back. They'd gotten themselves a big one, wearing a fine rack. The full spread of it was hanging on his dining room wall. Folks would drop by and comment on it from time to time; from tip to tip it was some sort of record.

Damn shame Jake Stafford got himself shot. That Mumford was some bastard, surely. Poor excuse for a man. Shot Stafford in the back with a Winchester shotgun. It would be good to remember old man Stafford by turning his daughters loose. That's what I'll do. Damned if I'm not the Sheriff for Big Horn County. I can do those sorts of things. Sure don't need to ask. After I turn them loose, I'll go down to the river and, while the ferryman is waiting for a fare, I'll fish off the end of the ferry. Me and Jonah Cardston will tell stories in the evening air, swat a few mosquitoes. It will be good. Real good.

Gilson seated himself at the Judge's table and waited for the bartender to bring him a cold draft cooled by ice from the ice house.

24

He was a little uncomfortable sitting in the hard oak chair with the Judge staring at him and smacking his lips as he sipped his iced tea. Gilson shook his head. How the Judge drank that Lipton tea, he never knew. It tasted awful.

The bartender arrived, setting a beer stein down in front of him. The Judge stared at it, then allowed his eyes to settle on Jason Gilson. "Jason," he said, "you've got something on your mind. What is it?"

He knows damn well what I got on my mind. How could he not?

Gilson cleared his throat and took a sip of the frothy beer. It wasn't bad but it wasn't good, either. Setting the mug down, he took the proposed court Order from his shirt pocket.

"Came to get an Order continuin' that Stafford hangin'," he said. "Thet rider I sent--he ain't back. Ain't due for another ten days. Figured we'd better do it before it's too late. Keep all things proper and in order." Reaching across the card table, Gilson set the prepared Order in front of the Judge, tapping it with his index finger. "I copied an Order that you signed before in another case several years back. Don't know if you remember it. I think it should work here."

Judge William Kilpatrick didn't immediately respond, nor did he pick up the proposed Order that Gilson had prepared for his signature. The silence made Gilson squirm uneasily in his chair. This fellow was a Federal Judge after all. To settle his nerves, Jason took a swig of the dark draft, swallowed hard, blinked his eyes, and forced himself to look at the Judge.

What the hell's wrong with you? he thought. *Sign the damn Order. Who the hell do you think you are? Starin' at me like some peacock?*

"Nothing doing," the Judge finally said, breaking the silence. "There isn't anything I'm going to do that stops that execution from moving forward. Short of an Order signed by the Governor or if not him, a stay Order from the Wyoming Territorial Supreme Court, there isn't anything that will stop it. Nothing. Saving their necks from the rope is the Governor's job, not mine."

"What?" Gilson stammered, not believing what he heard. "What did you say?"

"You heard me. I said no, Mr. Gilson. On July 2, they will hang by the neck until dead."

"No? Bill, stop joshin' me." Gilson sat up in his chair. "Judge, there never was any chance of an Order arrivin' from Governor Nelson. Cheyenne is too far from here. There ain't enough time for the Larson boy to go there and get back. At least suspend the execution until he can reasonably do so. It is the only thing to do. The rider will come. The Governor will sign the Order releasin' the girls. You know it. I know it. Hell's fire, everybody knows it."

Kilpatrick shook his head no. "I don't know it. I'm not signing it and that's my decision."

Gilson's heart began racing. *What was this son of a bitch doing?*

"Bill," Gilson argued, "they's three girls. No one hangs girls for anything, let alone what happened here. Good Lord, man! Mumford was a horse thief, a rustler, and he killed their old man. Shot him in the back, killed him dead. No one holds it against 'em for that, not at all."

Gilson was begging. *Let him have his fun,* he thought. *But, dear God, sign the order, you crazy son of a bitch!* Of course Gilson didn't say that to his face. After all, he was a Federal Judge.

"Sheriff, hear me. I don't want to repeat myself," the Judge said, "I'm not signing your Order." The Judge handed it back to Gilson. "I am not doing anything to stop the execution. They were found guilty of murder. The Order for Execution was signed by me. There isn't any legal reason to change it. The law must be served even when it isn't popular. Do you understand?" The Judge paused. "You damn well better." The Judge paused again, staring at Gilson, then he said, "You do your job. I'll do mine. I'll make myself available for a rider from Cheyenne."

"Yeah, hold yourself available. Lot of good that's gonna do. You son of a bitch. Why are you doin' this? No rider is comin'. He ain't due for another ten or fifteen days. It's impossible for him to get here."

"Sheriff, you be careful or I'll throw you in jail for disobeying my legal order. And you're right. Me hanging around here will do no good. At all. Frankly, I'm going to make myself unavailable. That's what I am going to do. I'm riding up Shell Canyon. Going to do some fishing. You know where to find me." The Judge stared at Gilson. "The fact is, Sheriff, there isn't any bonafide reason for you to even look for me." The Judge stood up. "Do your job, Sheriff Gilson. That's what you were elected to do and that's what I'm ordering you to do."

"Jesus, Judge. Think! You go through with this, you'll never be elected judge. Not ever again. Not in this territory. Not in your lifetime. This ain't right."

Judge Kilpatrick smiled. "Jason, I was appointed for life. No one is taking my job. Leastwise not for doing my job."

"Killin' three girls ain't your job."

"Sheriff Gilson, you're not listening. Pay attention. A jury found them guilty. You were there. You testified. One of them certainly knew what she was doing. The youngest, probably. The other two lied to protect her. They're all in it." Judge Kilpatrick sat back down and leaned back in his chair, staring thoughtfully at Gilson. "Setting fact and the law aside for the moment, they all admitted under oath to killing Mumford. Sure, two were protecting the youngest, but in doing so they admitted to killing the man and did so under penalty of perjury. They admitted it in open court in front of me, God, and everybody else, not to mention the jury."

"Judge, Mumford was hit by one shotgun blast. As you noted only one of those girls could have possibly pulled the trigger. Two of them are merely protectin' their sister. Two's innocent. You know that. I know that. The youngest shot him, not the other two. If you got to hang someone, hang her." Gilson could not believe he'd said that. He swallowed hard.

"One more time, Jason. All three admitted to killing him. Those are the facts the jury heard. The jury found all three guilty just as they were supposed to do."

"Just like you told them to do, you mean."

"Yes. Just like I told them. There is nothing I can do. The law is the law."

"Except go fishin', you son of a bitch."

"Except go fishing, and I'm doing that. I better not hear that again, Sheriff. Ever. Do I need to hold you in contempt to get your attention?"

"You'll go fishin' and all three will be dead when you return. They ain't supposed to be. All they did was kill the fellow that shot their pa in the back, right in front of 'em."

"Timing is everything, Jason. If they'd shot the man at the same time he shot their pa, that'd be one thing. They shot him ten days later. That's murder. They should have let the law hang him."

"Judge, it ain't right. You're havin' the law kill 'em."

"That's true. I am. Especially true given no one can make that trip to and from Cheyenne in less than three weeks. They only had ten days outside." The Judge paused, staring at Gilson. "Do your job, Gilson. Hear me. Obey the order. You know where to find me." Kilpatrick paused. He said, "Looks like you might need some help."

"I don't need no help."

"Looks like you do."

Jason Gilson stood before the Judge sitting at a table in the corner of the Basin City River Bar and Hotel staring at him. To his incredible surprise he had gotten nothing. To describe him as shocked was an understatement. He picked up the unsigned Order continuing the execution. If he had the time the Order provided for, the rider would make it back from the Governor with a signed Order and that would be that. A bewildered Gilson shook his head. What was going on in Kilpatrick's head? *Something. Yes, but what? It didn't make sense. Now what am I going to do?*

The Judge leaned back and started reading the *Basin City Rustler,* ignoring Gilson, dismissing him, ending the conversation. Julie Ann Mitchell, the resident bartender, bar girl, and piano player walked over to the Judge's customary table. "Bill," she said. "Sheriff. You two need anything? Somethin' to eat, perhaps? The cook is bakin' fresh corn bread. Perhaps somethin' to take your mind off law business and this infernal heat? I miss anything?"

"No thanks," Gilson said. "I've got enough trouble without borrowin' more. Promised Elsie I'd be home for dinner. She's got a venison roast bakin' in the oven, potatoes and gravy. I ain't gonna miss that if I can help it."

"Well, Julie Ann," the Judge said. "I haven't got a venison roast in the oven. No one is waiting on me. Besides fresh cornbread, what do you have in mind?"

She looked at the Sheriff, smiled.

"If you'll excuse me," Gilson said. "I'll be on my way."

Gilson turned toward the door and made his way around the tables. Behind him, Julie Ann Mitchell was leaning over; she and the Judge were engaged in a conversation. Gilson couldn't hear what it was. It crossed his mind that the Judge was married, had a couple of kids. He'd mentioned that in passing, weeks ago. They were in Philadelpia, if Gilson remembered correctly.

Gilson left the bar perplexed, bewildered, confused, and angry. Outside, he looked up and down the street. He shook his head. He thought of the three girls sitting inside the county jail not four hundred yards from where he was standing. Alone. Fatherless. With no one to help them. *What am I to do?* he thought. Those girls: they knew he was talking to Kilpatrick. He'd told them. He'd assured them he'd get the Order. He'd failed.

Now what? There was something that the Judge wasn't telling him. *What was it?* Obviously something. He didn't get it. Gilson looked eastward toward the big mountain. *Come to think of it, that damn Kilpatrick knew there was goin' to be a hangin' when he sentenced them "to hang." Nobody else did. Why? Why? What do I do now? I can't let this happen,* he thought, *but what do I do?* An Order was an Order was an Order was an Order. He wondered what would happen if he walked into the jail, opened the door, and just turned them loose. "That's what I ought to do," he said aloud. "That son of a bitch."

CHAPTER 4

One week earlier, on June 24, two days after the verdict had been rendered, Mrs. Maybell Karlinsey came to the Basin County Jail to speak to Sheriff Gilson. She was an older lady, in her late fifties, who lived on Fourth Street behind the old blacksmith shop that belonged to Magland, the blacksmith. She was one of Reverend Kimball Paul Wilson's flock. A busy woman, once a year she was in charge of the church bazaar down on Third Street. She headed all of the community dances. She served on the election committee board. She was into a little bit of everything of a civic nature. On the June 24, she sat across the desk from Sheriff Gilson. The three Stafford girls were in the back, secured behind iron bars, listening to the incessant pounding of hammers outside their window. He knew they could hear Maybell. *Hell, everybody could.* She had a loud booming voice that carried.

"Jason," she asked, "do you suppose I can make those poor girls new Sunday go-to-meeting dresses for their hanging?"

"Dresses?" he questioned. "What for? There ain't gonna be no hangin', Maybell."

"Dresses. They are going to meet their maker in those shabby ones they were wearing for their trial. They ain't had a change. They ain't had a bath. Let me make them something nice. Let me bring in a tub and make them a hot bath. We can do it right there in their cell. Won't have to go nowhere. They deserve that. A new dress. A bath."

"Mrs. Karlinsey..."

"Yes, Sheriff Gilson? I think it is a good idea. Don't you?"

"Maybell," he'd said, speaking louder than he usually spoke so that the girls could hear him over the pounding of the hammers. "There ain't gonna be no hangin'. I ain't asked him yet, but Kilpatrick will postpone it until the rider gets here from Cheyenne. You'd just be workin' yourself to a frazzle for nothin'. Kilpatrick is a good man. He'll come through for me. Always has before."

"Bill," she said sweetly, "they still need a nice, new dress, a hot bath, after all they've been through." She lowered her voice, lower than the steady drumming of hammers. "Sometimes things don't happen the way we'd like. Sometimes," she paused, "bad things happen. Let me make them dresses," she pleaded, looking Gilson in the eye. "Just in case things don't go the way you expect them to."

He'd laughed, nodding his head. "All right," he said. "All right, I don't see why not. Can't hurt none."

"Thank you. I'll need to take some measurements and bring in a tub. We'll use your stove right there to heat water. It'll be hot in here while I warm the bath water. You best plan for it."

"All right, Maybell. All right. Let Lloyd have a look at your basket there. I know you ain't got no weapons, but we need to be careful."

"Because it's your job."

Sheriff Jason Gilson had smiled. "Yes," he said, "because it's my job and as you know sometimes this job has me do things I don't wanna do."

"Sure, Sheriff. Sometimes.... The basket, it's just some warm biscuits, Sheriff, and some chokecherry jelly, some butter. I brought some for you and your deputy as well."

"Thanks, but no thanks, Maybell. Give them biscuits to the girls. 'Preciate it, though."

That conversation had taken place seven days before.

July 1, 1886

For the second time, Gilson stood in the street looking at the scaffold standing behind the jail and next to the County Courthouse. The girls' cell had a barred but open window. There was framed glass behind the bars. During the summer the window was left open for fresh air. It looked east toward the big mountain and, each morning, the rising sun. The scaffold was finished. Thirteen steps to the platform and one trap door.

Just in time, he thought, *for a hangin'. How am I goin' to solve this problem? I can't let this hangin' go on.* He thought of the clock in the foyer of the County Court house. Tick, tick, tick. The pendulum moved steadily back and forth. He shook his head.

"I gotta do somethin'," he muttered. "What? What am I gonna do? I oughta just turn them loose. What could the Judge do if

31

I did that?"

Glancing at the scaffold, he wondered how it worked. *Worked? It wasn't going to work.* He had to do something to stop it; to put it on hold at the very least. *What?* He stared at the newly constructed steps. *How would it work? Bring the girls out one at a time? Stop it, you ass!*

He tried to imagine it: all three standing on the platform in their new white Sunday-go-to-meeting dresses courtesy of Mrs. Karlinsey. *At least they'd be clean. How had Maybell known? Known? That damn Kilpatrick. I guess there was a possibility all along,* he thought. *There had always been a possibility. No. No, this hanging wasn't happening. Not if I believe in miracles. Do I?*

Gilson didn't. He slowly shook his head yet again. No matter what he decided to do it was going to be wrong. *Well, if I do get to a hanging tomorrow, I'll bring all three out at the same time; all three standing top of the scaffold, all three waiting their turn. Turn?*

"What the hell is wrong with me? There ain't gonna be no hangin'." He spoke in a whisper, mumbling to himself, then looked around to see if there was anyone who heard him talking to himself. "I'm surely losin' it," he said. "This is simple: turn 'em loose and quit. What could the Judge do? Re-arrest them, stupid."

It was early morning. The unsigned Order continuing the hanging was in his breast pocket.

Turns? God, what am I thinking? Turns? He studied the scaffold. *But there ain't no other way. Oh leave it be. Better yet, I'll join Kilpatrick on upper Shell Creek; the trout would be biting. They always were. And there won't be no hanging 'cause I won't be here. That's for damn sure. On the mountain the locust would be singing like some church choir. Yeah, that too. I sure as hell don't wanna be here tomorrow.*

It's my job, he thought. *I'm responsible. But I can't be murderin' no three girls even if it is my job. It ain't murder. There's a Judgment, there's an Order and twelve local citizens followin' the law had said so. They'd reached a verdict. Guilty is what they said. Just like the Judge told them to. That was the problem. Why'd he done that? He knew better.*

Gilson thought he'd go down to Maggies Café and have a cup of coffee, maybe some eggs and potatoes. *No. No, I ain't. How many times have I been asked, "Are you going through with it, Jas? You ought not do*

32

that, Jas. Wait for the rider. No one'll blame you." And he'd replied, *"No worries. It ain't gonna happen. Kilpatrick will continue it. The rider will come. I sent him myself."*

So many times he'd said that; he no longer kept track. He had believed it. He pulled the unsigned Order from his pocket and looked at it. The U.S. District Circuit Court Judge William Kilpatrick, one of the duly appointed Circuit Judges for the Territory of Wyoming--the son of a bitch--had refused to sign it. In his left pocket was the other Order. A Judgment. It was signed. Kilpatrick signed it on June 22. *I'm supposed to do that? Hang three girls?* He couldn't say it. Not out loud. *But I done took an oath to follow the court's orders.* He remembered, "Do you solemnly swear to uphold and execute the laws of the Territory of Wyoming... and those of the United States? An oath that he'd taken before God, Judge Kilpatrick, Minnie Gilson, and everybody. *Now what do I do? I surely can't hang no three girls. Oh, who gives a shit about some sheriff's oath taken in Northen Wyoming Territory in 1879. Yeah, who? That son of a bitch. Goin' fishin'? Probably already gone. Sally Stafford had shot the wrong person. Ah,shit. I'll postpone it myself. I'll do it in the mornin' first thing. Who's to stop me? That's what I'll do.*

Having decided, Jason Gilson turned and walked slowly back to the jail and into his office. He slouched into the oak chair and slowly rolled himself a quirley. Some of the tobacco shavings fell onto his shirt. He brushed them off on to the floor. He felt relief at having made a decision.

"Sheriff," a voice called from the corridor that led to the cells. "Sheriff?"

He recognized Claire Stafford's voice.

"Yeah?" he responded.

"Can you come here? We wanna talk."

"Sure," he said, standing, placing the hand-rolled cigarette between his lips without lighting it. He didn't feel like looking for a match.

The three girls were kept in the center cell. Sally and Betsy were sitting together on the center bunk, Claire standing closest to the iron door. The cells on either side were used for vagrants and drunks when the need arose.

"Sheriff," Claire said through the cold steel bars, "don't you have somethin' to tell us?" She paused. "Tomorrow is July 2. Have you heard anything? Has the Judge signed the Order continuin' the hangin'?"

"Nah," he said. "I ain't got nothin' to tell you. No rider has come. Not yet." *Tell them what you're gonna do.* "The Judge hasn't signed no Order movin'...you know, postponin' the hangin' to another date." *Tell them.*

"Have you asked him? You have asked him, yes?"

Gilson nodded. "I have."

"What did he say?"

"He said...he said no. That's what he said." Gilson lied when he followed with, "He didn't wanna postpone it until he had to. Until he knew the rider wouldn't be here. You know...." Gilson's voice trailed off. *She knows I'm lyin'. She knows. Well, tell them what you've decided to do, then do it.*

Betsy was sitting on her bunk when Sally stood up. She breathed in sharply. "Well," she said. "Well, what's gonna happen then? Tomorrow...tomorrow...tomorrow is the second?"

"Is...is there gonna be a hangin' or not?" Claire asked. "Is it goin' forward like the Judge said? You need to tell us, Sheriff. That scaffold's been built with you standin' there tellin' us there's gonna be no hangin'! What's with us takin' a bath, and gettin' new dresses? Every time you open your mouth you're sayin' no and you're sayin' yes." Her voice trailed. "Are we gonna hang tomorrow?"

"I'm workin' on it," Gilson said. *Tell them what you're gonna do. What's so hard about that?*

"Workin' on it?" Claire said. "Workin' on what? Either there's gonna be a hangin' or there ain't. You gotta tell us. We need to know. We don't have much time. If it's not gonna happen, somethin' has to happen now. Are you gonna turn us loose or not? Answer me."

Claire was pushing him and he resented it. Anger boiled up in his chest. He had enough problems.

"Right now...the hangin' is scheduled for tomorrow. Ten o'clock. Right now." He paused, taking a deep breath. "I'll do somethin'. I told you I'll do somethin'."

"What? What can you do? You keep tappin' your shirt pocket. Unless I'm mistaken, you keep thumpin' that Order from

34

Kilpatrick. It's right there in your pocket. That's it, ain't it? It's the Order to hang us on July 2. Yes?"

Sheriff Gilson nodded.

"What can you do? We need to know. Time is short. Somethin' needs to be done. It needs to happen now. Ain't there anythin' you kin do?" Growing impatient, she continued. "I'm beginnin' to doubt you. I don't think you kin do a thing. I think you've been lyin' to us. I think you're just a gutless wonder. If you could have done somethin', you would have. Am I right? Tell me I'm wrong."

All three girls were staring at him, waiting.

Gilson, stripped to the bone, looked at Claire, the second oldest daughter of Jake Stafford. "I don't know," he admitted. "I don't know what I can do. But I'll do somethin'." *Just tell them. You are a gutless wonder. Just tell them.*

He didn't.

"All right, Sheriff." She stared at him. "Let me tell you what I see. You've been kind but you're lyin'. Pattin' us on the head tellin' us everythin' is gonna be all right when it ain't. What you're sayin' is tomorrow you're gonna hang us for killin' Mumford. That's what you're sayin'. No rider is comin' from Cheyenne. He can't. That worthless Judge ain't signin' any Order, is he? We're in real trouble, ain't we?"

"That is where things stand right now." *Tell them you're turnin' them loose; then do it.*

Claire turned away, her back to him. She stared out the window at what she could see of the scaffold. Betsy was sobbing. Sally stared at him, swallowing him with her eyes. It was so unnerving. So pitiful.

And I am such a worm. So worthless. So indecisive.

"Sheriff," Sally walked across the floor and seized the grey bars between them. "Sheriff," she said, "I think what Claire is sayin' is that you need to tell us what is gonna happen tomorrow. It appears that we're gonna hang by the neck 'til dead. Would you....would you tell us what to expect? What do we do?"

"Sally, I.... I have several things that I am gonna do that affect what's gonna happen tomorrow. Might change everythin' altogether.

35

Let me go over this and answer your questions a little later today after I know more."

"Sheriff Gilson," Betsy said, her voice soft and low, "do we have any hope?" She stood in front of the center bunk. All three girls looked at him. "You said you'd get us out of here and try to set us free. But really, is there any hope? Please answer me. If we're gonna hang tomorrow we need to know. We need to get ready as much as we kin."

There it was. The question Sheriff Jason Gilson could no longer avoid, not with three girls staring at him from their jail cell. He answered, his words tumbling across his teeth and lips, lifelessly falling down his shirt, hitting the floor, rolling in the dust.

"Miss Stafford," he said, "right now, unless somethin' happens, there will be a hangin' tomorrow. Unless somethin' happens, that is. I'm workin' on it, believe me. I don't want there to be no hangin'. I do not."

"Thank you, Sheriff, for your tellin' us straight. Now, please go. We need to be alone,"Claire said.

Sheriff Jason Gilroy nodded, turned on his heel, and walked out. Escaping. He left the jail and his office and walked out of town, clear to the river. He listened to the rushing waters flowing north toward the Yellowstone River and the Missouri hundreds of miles away. He stayed there until midafternoon, then walked slowly back. He didn't know any more then than he had when he left the jail.

Midafternoon July 1, 1886, the Sheriff was sitting at his desk trying to busy himself. Lloyd had just arrived from the Picket place north of town and downriver. He was throwing his saddle in the corner when a skinny man, probably five foot nine inches, dressed in black broadcloth appeared in the door way. Gilson looked up, having shuffled a worn deck of cards for the ninth time.

"Sheriff?" the stranger said, directing himself to Lloyd, removing his sowbelly hat.

Lloyd pointed at Gilson. "That'd be him."

"Yes?" Gilson responded, setting the deck of cards on the worn desk surface. "How can I help you?"

"Name's Conroy. Hangman by trade. That's what I do."

Gilson didn't say anything, his office suddenly quiet.

"From Fort Casper?" Lloyd asked.

"I am. Left three days ago. Got here an hour ago. Stayin' at the hotel you got yourself here. Ain't been here before. Nice little town if I don't say so."

"Have a chair." Lloyd pointed.

"No, thanks."

"What can we do for you, then?"

"I'd like to see what I'm workin' with. See who I'm hangin'."

"Now? Right now?"

"Yes. Now, yes. I checked the scaffold a few minutes ago. Nice and new. Far as I can tell everythin' works. Don't expect any trouble. Before I go to my hotel I'd like to see who I'm hangin'. Don't want no surprises. Need to know weight and height so I can get it right."

Gilson looked at the skinny man. *Tell him,* he thought to himself. *Tell him there ain't gonna be no hanging. Tell him. What are you waiting for? What's the matter with you? Do it.*

Gilson thought he could just call it off. He didn't say what he was thinking. Instead, he stood abruptly, grabbed his hat from a peg driven into the wall, and seated it firmly on his head. "You handle this, Lloyd," he said and walked through the open doorway into the dusty street, not stopping until he reached the ferry.

Conroy watched him leave and turned to Lloyd. "What's ailin' him?" he asked.

"He ain't dealin' with this hangin' business," Lloyd responded. "Ain't dealin' at all. How kin I help you? I ain't much in favor of it, myself."

"As I said, I'd like to see who I'm hangin'. Get an idea of what I'm dealin' with. I understand there's three and they're women? I ain't done that before. Three women? In all my doin' that ain't never happened. Damn. What'd they do to get themselves here? Kill the Pope?"

"Naw. Nothin' like that. Seems one of 'em killed the man that killed their pa. Shot him with a shotgun."

"She did, did she? What's wrong with that?"

"Nothin' far as I can tell...except I guess it's agin' the law."

"I ain't ever heard of that law. Stealin' horses, maybe."

"Do you wanna see the girls?"

"I do."

"Follow me." Lloyd turned to the corridor that led to the cells. Conroy followed him.

"Ladies," Lloyd said, "would you all come forward? Stand shoulder to shoulder. This gent wants to have a look at y'all."

Claire, who had been sitting, stood. "Who is he?" she asked, approaching the front of the cell. Sally and Betsy joined her. Lloyd, the jailer, turned to the slightly built man.

"I'm the hangman," Conroy said. "Mike Conroy. That's my name."

"Oh," Claire said in reponse, staring at him. "You're a little early, ain't you?"

"Like the Sheriff, here, said, I'm here to have a look at y'all. Would you please approach the front of the cell. Stand so I can see you. Shoulder to shoulder would work fine."

The girls did as they were asked, standing in front of the jail cell, their hands on the bars.

Conroy, looked at each girl, finishing with Claire. "You're about one hundred thirty-five pounds?"

"Somethin' like that," she responded. "Don't know for sure. Why do you need to know that?"

"Make sure I got the right rope. Don't suppose it will be a problem here. You all don't weigh much."

He looked at Betsy. "You're about a hundred and a quarter, I'd say."

Betsy didn't respond.

"And you're about a hundred twenty?" He was speaking to Sally.

"Somethin' like that," Sally responded. "Why'd you say you need to know how much I weigh again?"

"So I can get the right rope. Don't want it to break. I haven't had that happen."

"Oh," she said. "Kin I ask you another question?"

"Surely."

"Is...is...is this gonna hurt? I mean hangin'?"

The hangman looked at the wisp of a girl. "Ordinarily, no.

38

You hit the end of the rope, your neck snaps. You're dead in seconds. No time to hurt. Course, I've never been hanged. So can't tell you personally. You're a hundred twenty. Fall eight to ten foot. You'll be dead when you hit the end of the rope. Don't see any problem. Not at all."

"Thank you," Sally said softly.

"You're welcome. Other questions?" He was looking at Betsy and Claire.

"No," Sally mumbled. "No, wait. Maybe you kin tell us how it's gonna happen? Tell us what's gonna happen. If you would? You ain't never been hanged before and neither have we."

Conroy smiled. "Yes, of course. I can tell you generally. The Sheriff will have to fill in the specifics."

All three girls moved closer to the front of the center cell, listening.

"I'll give you the short version. The way I see it is that all three of you will be on the platform at the same time. We'll hang you one after another 'cause there is only one trap door. When it's your turn, I'll situate you over that trap door. It's just an openin' in the floor. I'll tie your hands behind your back. I'll tie your feet to keep you from kickin' too much. I'll put the noose around your neck and tighten it up so your head won't slip out when you hit the end of the rope. Once I've done that, I'll man the lever that will open the trap door and send you to your Maker. Basically, that's it. All of this will be done at the direction of the Sheriff. He can stop it if he wants to."

"He kin stop it?"

"He could. But ladies, I ain't never seen that happen. Saw a man break out of jail once down there in Cheyenne. Got plum away. Nobody ever caught him that I know of. Heard he didn't stop runnin' 'til he was in Australia. That's what I heard. Damnedest thing. I got paid anyways 'cause I was there. Once it gets to this stage, the hangin' is practically a done deal. I wouldn't have any hope of redemption if I was you. I don't mean to burst any bubbles but us talkin' like we are...that means you're gonna get hung per what the Judge said. I hope no one has promised you any different. Personally, I can't stop it from happenin'. The Sheriff can do that, but not me."

Claire asked, "Does it matter the order? I mean which of us

goes first?"

"Not that I know, it doesn't. Makes absolutely no difference to me. I can't see how the law would benefit one way or the other. Any other questions?"

Claire shook her head.

"Good. See you in the mornin', then. Sheriff should bring you out of this cell around ten o'clock."

Mike Conroy turned and walked down the corridor, followed by Lloyd, leaving the girls standing in their cell.

"Jeez," Sally said to no one in particular. "Tomorrow it looks like we're gonna get ourselves hanged. I was hopin' someone would.... It's all my fault," she declared, her voice trailing off. "I'm sure sorry I got you into this. I am. I wish I could do somethin' to stop it."

"It ain't your fault," Betsy responded. "Any of us woulda shot Mumford if we had the chance. Any of us. You just happened to be closest to Pa's shotgun, so it fell to you."

"I'm responsible. If someone's got to hang it should be me. Not you. You two was inside when I pulled the trigger. You weren't even there. What are we gonna do? We have to stop this." Sally paused. "You know," she said, "Diana don't even know we're in this trouble. We ain't told her."

"You pulled the trigger twice. Both barrels. The bastard deserved it."

"That's right. I did. And that's right. He did. Near knocked me down. I didn't even have it to my shoulder. It hurt so bad."

Claire looked at her sister. "Sal," she said, "that's water under the bridge. The Judge cut us no slack sayin' we was all there, we was all to blame. To our way of thinkin', he should have. But we're in this together. To be real clear, I wish we wasn't. I wish none of us was."

"If it was to be anybody punished for killin' Mumford, I wish it was just me," Sally said.

Claire hugged Sally, all three standing in the center cell, quietly sobbing.

40

CHAPTER 5

It was late afternoon before Sheriff Gilson thought about returning to the jail and his office. Down amidst the solitude of the river, Gilson decided for the hundredth time to call it off. It was his decision to open the center cell door and let them walk out. It was the only thing to do. At first he thought he'd release them come morning but the more he thought about it the more he thought he'd do it as soon as he got back. *The Judge be damned!* Standing at the river's edge under the shade of a massive cottonwood, he listened to the murmur of the swirling water moving north toward the Yellowstone. In the damp, cool quiet he reached overhead and broke off a twig with five or six dark green leaves. Staring at it, he rolled the twig between his fingers, the leaves fluttering. He let the decision flutter like the leaves in his hand. Nodding, he thought, *I'll do it right now. Soon as I get back.*

Having made his decision, he felt good. A huge weight had been lifted from his shoulders. It was a cross he no longer had to bear. *Damn, damn, damn,* he thought. *Why'd I wait so long? Why'd I send myself through this torture? Never, ever again.* Mid-river a catfish leaped from the water's surface and fell back with a splash, disappearing beneath the surface of the moody river. "Good" felt good nonetheless. Twig in hand, he sat at the foot of the cottonwood, learning back against the trunk and watched Cardston pulling the ferry across the river to accommodate four riders who had arrived on the far bank. Two had dismounted. Not one of the four seemed to be in a hurry.

They were strangers, probably there for the celebrations, arriving for the hanging that had just vanished. *Sorry,* Jason Gilson thought. *That hangin' ain't gonna happen. I'm turning 'em loose. I'll just say,* "It's a bad decision, Judge, and I want no part of it. You know what you can do to yourself." Gilson tossed a small, smooth rock into the rolling water, pleased with himself.

Across the river, Cardston's ferry had reached the far bank. The four men were leading their horses on to the ferry, big horses

41

that looked to have come a long ways in a short time. They stood, not moving, heads bowed, spent. Cardston was readying himself to pull them across to the west bank. Overhead, lost somewhere in the leaves and branches of the cottonwood, a magpie complained. The leaves rattled as a gust of heated air swirled through the limbs, then moved off.

Freed of the weight of the impending hanging, Gilson decided it was time to return to his office and open the cell door. Only then would it be over. He would be done. Finally. Yet he lingered. Instead of getting to his feet, he picked out another small river rock and tossed it out into the swirling currents. Its entry caused small circles of waves to mark the place of its disappearance. He felt tired, almost giddy, as if he'd been working all day in the hot sun. *Time to get this done,* he thought to himself. Getting to his feet, he started the slow walk into Basin City, past the bar where the Judge liked to sit and drink, on to Third Street, and ultimately his office. It took the better part of twenty minutes, but he was feeling so good he hardly noticed the time.

A man's horse tells a lot about the man riding it. If, for example, the rider weighs two hundred forty-five in his stocking feet, built solid, and is a horse thief, it's a good bet his horse is also big, taller than seventeen hands, muscular with depth and endurance. Often this horse will meet the rider's defining need for speed. If a man's horse is big, lean, and muscular, with depth and endurance, it's a good bet the rider seldom stays anywhere long. The rider owns this particular kind of horse for a reason. That reason makes a particular horse a necessity; the necessity makes the horse expensive. Nine times out of ten, if a big, hard, muscularly lean horse is ridden by a big man, that man is a loner. His activities justify a compelling need to cover distance quickly, his life depending on it. Often those activities are illegal. If men are chasing him, it's a good bet they want to kill him. Their lives depended on their mounts.

The four horses standing at the rail in front of Gilson's office were all of that. All four were bays; seventeen or eighteen hands at the shoulders, lean and lank, with deep chests for the long haul, and hard sinew and muscle built for speed over short distances. They were bred for dependability, meant to outlast any other horse over time, and distance. These horses were coveted on sight, paid for with considerable gold coin. They were the exception. These were the horses whose riders depended upon them to carry the rider out of harm's way. They were meant to outrun and outlast whoever was chasing them from whomever they happened to be running. These horses were grained every day without fail, curried every night, rubbed down, babied, and trained until hell wouldn't have it. They were extraordinary specimens: horses owned by men in need of extraordinary performance at the tap of a spur.

Sheriff Jason Gilson stared. He'd seen horses like these, not these horses particularly, but others like them. He'd seen them in front of the Cattlemen's Bank in Wichita, Kansas, a bank being robbed. He remembered the men walking out of the bank easily, stepping into the saddle, and walking their horses down the road moments before a bank employee burst through the bank's doors screaming, outraged. He remembered similar horses ridden by calvary, raiders riding for William Tecumsah Sherman and George Armstrong Custer during the late Civil War. These men, whose lives literally depended on their horses, turned away the mounts supplied by the quartermaster and located and purchased their own. When those raiders rode at the front of a column of men, no one doubted who they were: just one look at the horses they rode and they'd know.

Once, outside the Dollar Saloon in Abilene, Kansas, he'd seen horses of this sort ridden by several Pinkerton Agents: men searching for the outlaws who'd robbed a train, the irony being they were tied up at the same hitching rail as the horses of the men they sought. The mixture brought about a lively discussion on whether or not trains should be robbed, as well as a funeral on the outskirts of town. That day the Pinkertons came up short.

Gilson studied the four horses. His conclusion was instantaneous. The four men inside his office owning these horses were either rustlers who'd never been caught, bank robbers seldom seen, stagecoach thieves, or desperadoes: men on the outlaw trail. These very horses more than likely had carried their riders out of harm's way repeatedly.

Gilson glanced at the wide open door to his office. Bright sunlight prohibited him from seeing inside and distinguishing the features of the men inside the dark interior. Loosening the leather latch from the hammer of his Peacemaker, he started toward the doorway, his heart beating rapidly, his body flooded with a sense of foreboding. The four horsemen could only be bad news: outlaws or worse. The irony was that they were standing in his office.

Passing through the door frame, he paused to let his eyes adjust. Lloyd was sitting quietly at Gilson's desk, his forearms resting on the desktop, staring straight ahead. The expression on his face was a composite of disgust, distrust, anger, and frustration. Lloyd sat looking at four men, not one of whom was physically forbidding. Gilson had guessed wrong. He had imagined men who were six feet five, weighing two hundred fifty eight pounds comprised of solid muscle and sinew. These men ranged in size: five foot ten inches to six feet: yes. Weighing one hundred eighty-five to one hundred ninety eight pounds: yes. Their squinty, hardened eyes rested on Gilson as he stepped inside the frame building that housed his office and the jail.

It doesn't happen often, yet every once in a good while it does: a man meets himself coming out of the same doorway he's going in. It is never a pleasant experience. It wasn't pleasant for Sheriff Jason Gilson, a man who, after hours and hours of soul searching, of beating himself up over the right course of action, had decided to do right, to be right. He had reached a hard fought decision to ignore the will of a federally appointed judge and the corrupt decisions of a spineless, misdirected jury who had been more concerned with pleasing that judge than with doing their duty as prescribed by the very law under which they had served. There Sheriff Gilson stood in his worn down at the heel boots, both a good man and a weak man.

"Sheriff," the man closest to him said, breaking open a brand new ten gauge sawed off Greener, purchased by the federal government's Department of Justice for the use of its deputies, "the name is Killmond Jacobson." He cradled the Greener, the breech still open. Jacobson opened up his sheepskin vest to reveal a shiny, new badge reflecting his status as a sworn U.S. Deputy Marshal. "We're Deputy U.S. Marshals," he said. "Here to aid you in the hangin' tomorrow. Judge Kilpatrick thinks you in need."

What the wizened, hard bitten man didn't reveal was that in his watch pocket rested a fifty dollar gold piece received from Kilpatrick himself as pay for what was determined to be one day's work. He didn't reveal that he was wanted in Kansas and Minnesota for robbing banks, trains, and shooting a conductor who moved too slowly for his liking. Nor did he tell the Sheriff that the horse he rode wasn't his, hadn't been purchased. In fact, his horse, wearing a box diamond on his right shoulder, was stolen from a horse barn in St. Louis. Its owner hadn't wanted to sell so Killmond Jacobson took it out the front door of the livery at four in the morning on a Sunday six weeks ago. The circular, one that Gilson didn't yet have tacked to his wall, revealed that transgression, in addition to others. It was only weeks later that Gilson received the circular picturing all four men, offering five hundred dollars a piece for each of the "deputies." Historically, the reward was never paid. They were never apprehended, never caught and never saw the inside of a jail.

"We don't need any help," Gilson stated. What he wanted to say and didn't was, *Now get the hell out of here.*

"Well, you're gettin' our help," Killmond Jacobson replied. "Whether you want it or not. Whether you need it or not. Kilpatrick sent us to make sure three convicted felons get what's comin' to 'em. We'll be stayin' right here 'til mornin'. You'll send out for beans and biscuits, somethin' for us to eat. We'll throw a bedroll on the floor. We'll need a couple of bottles of Walker's Kilmarnock Whiskey. You'll find it in a square bottle."

"I know what Walker's Kilmarnock looks like," Gilson said. "The county ain't buyin' you whiskey and you ain't stayin' here."

"Judge said to put it on the tab he keeps at the River Bar."

"That's between you and him. I don't want you stayin' here."

"Tough shit," Killmond Jacobson said. "We're here 'til this job's done."

Fifty dollars paid times four extrapolated to determine what would be paid to four deputies over a week's time comes to fourteen hundred dollars. Most cow hands make thirty dollars a month. The deputies were being, not only well paid, but over paid.

"Make your own arrangements for whiskey. Lloyd and I ain't your servants."

Killmond Jacobson stared at Gilson like he was a three legged cockroach that he was about to stomp on. "Let me make myself clear, Sheriff," he said. "Tomorrow there's gonna be a hangin'. You're gonna be the man. You do anythin' 'cept conduct a hangin' and I'm gonna take this Greener, pull back both hammers, and cut you and Lloyd here, in half. These boys here will swear it was an accident, the damnedest thing they ever saw. We clear?"

Gilson said nothing.

"I said, are we clear?"

"Crystal," Lloyd said from behind the desk. Gilson nodded, his face grim. He was barely able to breathe; he was so angry.

"Good. I surely don't want there to be no misunderstandings."

The fifty dollar gold piece settled comfortably into the lining of "Deputy" Jacobson's watch pocket as he closed the Greener's breech, the click falling flat within the walls of the room.

Gilson looked at the speaker and his three companions: three others of the same ilk: all heavily armed, dark, scowly men, pistols strapped to their thighs, pistols tucked behind their belts, all carrying new Greener ten gauge shotguns.

"Sheriff," the second man standing beside and a little behind Jacobson said, "you need to understand we're here from the Judge. Deputy U.S. Marshals. Judge Kilpatrick swore us in earlier this mornin'. He told us you'd need help with the hangin'. Thought you might back out of doin' what you're supposed to do. That's what he said. We'll be here through tomorrow mornin'. Keep things on track."

"Just the same, Lloyd and I can see it through," Gilson said in response. "We don't need no help."

"We're here, just the same," the man said, his voice low and gravelly. "We're here to see that no one stops you and to do the hangin' case you can't. If'n you don't do the hangin' you'll be dead. We expect no trouble, you do what the Judge ordered."

Standing next to his desk with Lloyd sitting in his worn oak chair, Gilson looked at the strange men. Jacobson stood with a loaded shotgun in the crook of his left arm. Gilson wondered what he could possibly do. In his mind, he could feel the unwanted hanging charging forward like a locomotive, its boiler hot with fire, steam gushing from the pistons, gaining speed: four U.S. Marshal deputies and a Federal Judge tossing in more coal, building the fire in the firebox until the boiler was ready to burst. Gilson couldn't help but wonder why the Judge was taking all this interest. *What had he to gain? Why was it so important? It was legal murder, that's what it was, but why?* He cursed himself for waiting too long, searching his soul for the impossible solution.

CHAPTER 6

July 2, 1886, 8:15 a.m.

Mrs. Karlinsey had not yet arrived to help the girls into their newly tailored dresses, dresses that she and her helpers had painstakingly pieced together. When Gilson walked down the corridor with Lloyd behind him all three girls were standing, staring at him without speaking, their eyes large in the dim light.

"No one's come yet," he advised them. Judging from their demeanor, they obviously didn't think anyone had.

Claire stared at Gilson. "No one is comin', Sheriff," she said. "No one will be comin'. The question is what are you gonna do? You might as well tell us what is gonna happen. Who's out there in your office? We heard some men come in yesterday. Who were they? Are they still here?"

"U.S. Deputy Marshals," he answered.

"Marshals?" she asked. "Marshals? Why? How many are there?"

Gilson nodded. "Four," he said. "Judge Kilpatrick sent 'em. They are here specifically to make sure the hangin' goes forward as the Judge ordered. Girls," the Sheriff paused, "I ain't got no choice here. I'm sorry. The Judge has taken it away from me." He paused again, then repeated himself. "Those men you heard are here at the Judge's order to make sure the three of you...." Gilson's voice dropped away to a mere whisper. Then he was silent, staring at Claire. "That the hangin' goes forward."

Claire's demeanor did not change. She said, "In a few hours, then? You can't stop it? That's what you are sayin'?"

"In a few hours. Yes. Yes, there is nothin' that Lloyd or I can do. It is completely out of my hands. I hope you understand. It's the law. The Judge is makin' it hard not to follow it to the letter. It's either Lloyd and I or those four. If we don't do it. They will."

"It might as well be you makin' sure we die," Claire said. "Least we know who you are...and who you aren't."

48

The Sheriff stared at her. Finally, he said, "All right. In an hour or so, at ten, I'm gonna come to get you. All three of you. When I do, we'll walk out of the jail together, single file. I'll be in front leadin' the way. Each of you will follow close behind. Lloyd will be last, bringin' up the rear. Together we'll walk out into the street. We'll proceed to the scaffold single file. You'll climb the steps. At the top, the hangman will tell you what to do. That's what's gonna happen."

He wanted to say unless someone came but he knew no one was coming. Claire was right. No one would. The Sheriff stared at Claire, feeling he should say something more, after all of the lies he'd told them. "I thought I could stop it," he said aloud. "I really did. But it turns out I can't. I got an Order. I have to follow it. Can't call it off. I want to but I can't. Those boys will kill me. I'm sorry," he said again.

Claire stared at him. He felt so small.

"Just to be clear," she said, "we're gonna hang this mornin'. You, the law, that man Conroy, is gonna hang us for killin' the man who killed Pa? That's right, ain't it? I've got it right? Yes?"

"Yes," the Sheriff said. "You have it right."

Standing in front of the three county jail cells, looking at Claire, her sisters beside her, he saw again clearly who he was. Finally, after all he'd said and done, after all he'd gone through and tried to do, with all of his thought and good intentions, Gilson was faced with the shadow of himself: with the man he was. It wasn't much. He considered Claire's question and nodded his head, yes.

"As of right now, no rider from Cheyenne has made it. Kilpatrick didn't sign no Continuance Order. He sent those deputies to make sure I go through with this hangin'."

"Sheriff," Claire said quietly. "There never was a rider comin'. If he left three weeks ago, maybe. But he left ten days ago. No one's comin'. There's just you. No one else. All along, you was our only hope. It didn't happen, that's all. Your fault, my fault, nobody's fault. It don't matter now. We're dead accordin' to the law. Right? That's what you're sayin'. The law demands we die."

Sally sniffed, trying not to cry. Gilson didn't look at her. He couldn't.

Claire asked, "So, how's this gonna work, Sheriff?"

49

Six eyes were on him.

"You'll hang one at a time," he said. "That's how it's gonna work. Sorry we can't do it at the same time. That's just the way the scaffold was built. No one thought there actually would be a hangin'. I didn't. There's only one trap door. It has to be done one at a time."

Claire took a deep breath and let it out before speaking. "Who goes first?" she asked.

The Sheriff stared at here momentarily before answering.

"Does it matter what order you hang us?"

There was a moment of extended silence. Gilson paused, finally answering her question."Not really." He hadn't thought that far ahead. *Youngest first? Oldest? Draw straws? He hadn't given it any thought. In the end they were all dead. And that was it. What did it matter?*

Claire volunteered. "I'll go first," she said. "That way you don't have to decide."

"No," Sally whispered, her voice barely audible. "It should be me," she said. "I did the killin'. I pulled the trigger. Triggers," she said, correcting herself. "I'll go first." She paused, looking at Gilson, begging, her voice grew louder. "Sheriff, you know my sisters lied to protect me. Let them go. Please? Hang me. I'm the one that pulled the triggers killin' Mumford. It was me, just like I said."

"Sally," Claire said, "it don't matter. Each of us was convicted. That's what he said."

Gilson shook his head. "No, Sally," he said, "no, no. and no. Claire's right. I told the Judge it was you. He said it don't matter who did what. I know your sisters lied for you, to protect you. Everyone knows it. The jury found you all three guilty because all three of you said you killed him at your trial. All three of you admitted to killin' the man. All three of you was there. There's nothin' I can do. The jury and the Judge believed you. I got the Order right here." The Sheriff patted his shirt pocket.

Betsy started weeping. Claire immediately put her arms around her, looking over her sister's bowed head at the Sheriff. "We understand, Sheriff. We ain't blamin' you. We're here of our doin'."

The Sheriff nodded slightly and looked at Sally. It didn't help how he felt. "Sally," he said, "respectin' your wishes, you come out of the cell last. Claire first. Betsy second. You'll be first. Understand?

50

That's the way we'll do it."

Claire stared right at him, her eyes starkly blue even in the dim, muted light. "Sheriff, we just wish you'd a told us what was gonna happen from the beginnin'. So we could get ready. Diana don't even know this is happenin'. No one ever told her."

"Who?"

"Our sister, Diana. She's the oldest. She lives over on Sage Creek. Her husband is Peter Stockton. When this is over, will you tell her? She needs to know. Please?"

"Sure," the Sheriff said. "Sure, I will."

Behind him, Gilson heard the front office door open. Women's voices carried down the hall. Jason Gilson turned to see Maybell Karlinsey enter the corridor carrying three white dresses draped over her left arm, holding them high to keep them out of the dust and dirt. Behind her were two women from the Basin City League of Christian Women. It was 8:42 a.m.

Gilson glanced at Maybell, then he said to Lloyd, "Lloyd, you stay here. You need me, I'll be out front." Gilson turned to leave, having a hard time reining himself and his emotions in; stoic, he had always been. Not now. Now he wanted to run and hide, a shallow man caught between right and wrong: a signed scrap of paper, the law, and four thugs in the outer office sent to him by the Judge. He wondered where they had come from. There weren't four U.S, Deputy Marshals in the entire territory. Now there were four in Basin City.

At 9:50 a.m. Sheriff Jason Gilson walked down the corridor and stood in front of the doors to the holding cells. He noted the results of the work of Maybell Karlinsey and the two ladies from the women's civic association. The three girls were stunningly beautiful dressed in white, their hair curled and put up on their heads as if they were going to a wedding or Sunday morning church. He wondered how it was done in such a short time.

"It's time," he said, his voice sounding hollow, forced. Claire turned to him immediately; the other two didn't, not at first. Then slowly they turned to his voice, their eyes on him, waiting. Ten seconds passed. He noted the floor length white dresses.

Maybell Karlinsey looked at each, nodded her approval at

51

what she'd created, then turned and hugged Claire, then Sally and Betsy. "God bless you," she said quietly. "You're all so beautiful." She patted their shoulders and touched their cheeks. She hesitated, overcome with emotion, not wanting to leave. Finally, she turned to the iron door and looked at the waiting sheriff

The door swung open. Maybell and her helpers walked through it leaving the girls standing alone in the cold brick room. Maybell and the two women with her disappeared down the short hallway and out into the Sheriff's office.

Lloyd joined the Sheriff. "All right, ladies," the Sheriff said, "it's time. We've done all we can do."

Turning to Lloyd, Gilson said, "Let's do it, Lloyd."

Lloyd stepped inside the cell.

"Ladies," Gilson said, his voice hollow, "it's time to go." His words sounded authoritative. Inside him they were everything but; Gilson's mind was unraveling. *I could quit,* he thought. *I should quit. Quit? Can I quit? Oh, shut up. Just shut up, you gutless wonder. There is nothin' you can do, not with four armed deputy marshals in the outer office waitin'.* He scrunched his eyebrows and pulled his Stetson down over his head, tighter than he wanted. He looked at the women standing inside the cell with Lloyd, their faces solemn, their eyes slightly red from crying. *Thanks to me.*

Gilson could no longer hear Maybell in the outer office. He looked at the three girls dressed in their simple finery: white broadcloth. Maybell had worked with what she had. The three girls stood in the center of the cell, their backs to the bunks where they'd slept for the last two months. They stared at him for a long moment Sally backed up and sat down.

"There's a lot of people outside," he said. "I mean a lot. More coming. We'll do exactly what I told you before. We'll walk through the office and out onto the boardwalk. I don't want anyone gettin' lost. Claire, you will be right behind me. Betsy, you come next. Sally, you will be last. Behind you will be Lloyd carryin' his shotgun. I don't expect trouble, not with four armed U.S. Deputy Marshals. Questions? I mean, do you have any?"

There were none. Sally stood up; her skirts swished. Gilson was relieved, wondering whether he'd have to drag her out to the scaffold. Apparently not.

"All right, let's go. Let's get this done." Immediately, Gilson hated himself for having said those last five words. It was so crass, so devoid of feeling. But there it was. *Me and my mouth. Forget it,* he thought. *No, I'm not forgettin' it. Why am I goin through with this hangin'? It's because I am goin' to follow the signed Order just like I am supposed to do, like I must do under the threat posed by the U.S. Deputy Marshals. They are not goin' to permit it being stalled. Do it and see. You idiot. I'm not goin' to buck those boys. They ain't takin' no for an answer. They'll shoot me. You gutless wonder. Yes. Yes, that is what I am.*

Once again, standing in front of the girls' cell looking at Claire for the hundredth time, he reviewed the tired, inadequate argument. *No. No, I'm not goin' to do this. I'm goin' to stop. I can stop. That's what I'm goin' to do.* Having said that, he turned and looked down the corridor, his mind continuing to roll in a dozen different directions. He thought about stepping inside, locking the cell door, locking the girls and himself behind the door, and waiting it out. *Why not?* he thought. *What can they do? What can those bastards do?* He didn't have an answer and that bothered him.

Claire started toward him. It was done. Gilson turned and began walking down the corridor, out into the office. He glanced behind him to see if Claire was following. She was close behind. It was all so surreal. *I can't believe this is happenin'. I can't believe I'm doin' this. You're gutless.... Yes, I know.*

In the outer office, Gilson proceeded to the doorway and the bright sunlight outside. Claire followed immediately behind him followed by her two sisters. The office was occupied by four newly minted U. S. Deputy Marshals. As soon as they saw the Sheriff coming towards them, they made their way to the front door and outside. The Deputy Marshals, armed with Greener ten gauge shotguns, started forward, clearing a path, pushing the spectators away and to the side, cutting a trail for Gilson and the girls to walk. The crowd, seeing Gilson, seeing the girls, stepped back to give them room. A shout of "Make way, make way" was heard.

Gilson glanced about. There were so many people. One of Judge Kilpatrick's deputies fired his shotgun into the air. The percussion was incredibly loud and sent people scurrying backwards and away. "Back," he yelled, pushing his double barrel shotgun into the air, waving it. "Make room. Make room." The crowd split, giving Gilson and the girls and Lloyd more space.

It was maddening; people were standing on every corner, in the middle of the street, in doorways. The bars and saloons were full. The general store was running out of rock candy and broadcloth. People were milling about the scaffold, standing, hands in their pockets, waiting, watching, wondering what the Sheriff had in mind by this grandstanding. They'd been gathering since sunrise. By nine o'clock, there were upwards of four hundred people, not counting youngsters; by ten o'clock, the number was closer to six hundred. Everything seemed upside down and sideways.

Before Gilson brought the girls out, the collective mood had been upbeat. Mostly folks were wondering why the girls hadn't been released and they fully expected it now. They were tired of waiting. Folks appeared in a festive mood, coming from far and wide, wondering what was going on. A scheduled hanging of three young women didn't happen. No one expected to witness a hanging that day, certainly not a hanging of women. Everyone knew Gilson would release them. They were here to celebrate an early Fourth of July. The shotgun blast brought more people into the street. No one wanted to miss out on the festivities.

The sun was warm on Gilson's face as he stepped onto the hardpack street but he didn't feel it. The crowd was surprised to see the three young women in pretty white dresses following him guarded by four U.S. Deputy Marshals, two in front and two behind. A rumor had run through the crowd that Gilson would release them from the top of the scaffold. "Good publicity, that," they said. Upon their appearance, an impromptu celebration started and a cheer went up as the word spread of their imminent release. "Happenin' now, right now." The word was passed along.

Hands reached out to touch the girls as they proceeded forward step by step toward the stairs leading to the gallows. Someone yelled, "Speech, speech." Claire stared in the direction the demand came from, her eyes wide with fear. Glancing at Gilson's back, she hurried forward. More people came running. No one wanted to miss this. It was anticipated that someone was going to be

54

giving a speech; the girls were being released, if they hadn't been already. A string of fire crackers burst into the morning air, exploding like popcorn, only much louder.

The U.S. Deputy Marshals moving forward pushed people aside, clearing the way to the foot of the stairs. They moved quickly. Crowd control wasn't difficult. No one was angry and loaded shotguns were frightening, especially if the barrel was pointed directly at anyone in their way. People just naturally gave way to a ten gauge. Even with the Marshals pushing the crowd aside, hands reached out to the girls, offering comfort. No one said anything to Gilson. The small procession walked through the multitude. It split in front of him and immediately closed behind. Three steps into the street, Gilson took Claire by the left elbow and guided her. It took several minutes to cover the distance from the steps of the County Jail to the bottom steps of the scaffold. The Marshals immediately secured the scaffold, the first two climbing the stairs The third took his position at the side of the scaffolding. Each took a position and stared out over the crowd, holding their shotguns at port, ready to use.

The edifice stood tall in the morning light and stark against the clear blue sky. Gilson noted the fresh smell of rain-scrubbed air. Somewhere it had rained. *God, I wish I was there. Anywhere but here.*

Claire offered no resistance to Gilson's guidance. Behind her came Betsy and Sally, close together, Betsy holding Sally's hand. Lloyd followed the girls, his double barreled twelve gauge shotgun pointed up. The last deputy stood behind him, facing the crowd. No one made an attempt to stop the procession. Not everyone had heard the rumor of their "release." Their negative voices were heard amidst the din and laughter.

"Don't do this, Jas," someone said. "It ain't right. Don't do it."

"Stop this, Jas. You don't have to go through with it. What the hell you doin'? That Kilpatrick is a crooked son of a bitch."

Gilson wondered about that. He glanced around to see who the speakers were; he was confronted with a wall of faces staring at him. Whoever it was that'd complained so vigorously was suddenly silent. *The bastards. What's wrong with people anyway?*

Farther away, away from the girls, a cheer went up followed

by a burst of raucous laughter. It was followed by a chant of "Release them, release them," then a call for "Speech, speech, speech." Someone was playing Yankee Doodle on a mouth harp. Another round of applause moved through the growing, unsettled crowd.

The procession of the County Sheriff, the condemned girls, and Lloyd, the deputy Sheriff reached the bottom steps of the scaffold. The County Commissioner, Randolph Fillmore, standing at the top of the stairs, raised his hands for quiet. Quiet came; the commissioner didn't say a word, although the crowd was expecting it. Instead, he stood looking down at the people who'd congregated at the bottom of the stairs. Claire stood beside Gilson in her new white dress, holding the hem up out of the dust with her right hand, her golden hair falling on her shoulders, curled. Gilson had her by the elbow. Amidst the noise, he glanced up the thirteen steps at Randolph Fillmore, then turned to Claire. She'd turned to him, questioning what he was doing.

"I'm stayin' here, Claire. You go the rest of the way." He released her elbow. "This is as far as I go," he said. "Go on. Up the stairs with you."

Claire nodded, trepidation in her glance, looking up the stair steps at Fillmore standing at the top waiting for her. She glanced again at Gilson, then taking a deep breath stepped onto the first rung, her left hand seizing the railing, her right holding the hem of her dress. At the top, next to Fillmore, the hangman, Michael Conroy, stood in his black broadcloth, waiting patiently, his hands clasped in front of him. Claire glanced back at Gilson and started climbing the stairs, making her way to the top. Gilson didn't move, stationing himself at the bottom of the scaffold, watching her ascent.

After Claire, Betsy and Sally followed, each glancing at Gilson as they passed. The fourth deputy followed close behind. At the top, Claire hesitated, unsure of where to go next. The hangman directed her to the back of the scaffold and into the corner. She nodded and started across the floor, followed by her sister, Betsy. Betsy looked back at Sally as she passed Conroy. Sally started to follow Betsy but was stopped by the hangman. He stopped her, taking her by the elbow. Startled, she glanced at him, questioning what was happening.

"Over here," he instructed. "You need to stand over here."

She nodded, looked to where he pointed, and allowed herself to be guided to the center of the platform, stopping over the newly constructed trap door. The wood creaked as it accepted her weight. A new hemp rope, a noose tied at its end, hung from a beam overhead. Sally stared at it, her eyes wide. Conroy had her take a step forward. Sally offered him no resistance. Unsatisfied, he took her by the shoulders and moved her several inches to her left. The noose hung slightly behind her where she could no longer see it without turning her head.

So very young, Gilson thought, his mind racing involuntarily, seeking a resolution, any resolution to a problem he didn't want to confront. *Stop this right now,* he told himself adding another line to the ongoing, internal argument that plagued him. *Do it. How? How can I stop it? I sure as hell have no business hangin' a child. How can I stop this with four armed U.S. Deputy Marshals watchin' my every move, insurin' I go forward? Would it make any difference if the Judge hadn't sent them? Maybe. Oh, shut up. I have to do it. I've got that gawdawful Order. Ignore it. I can't ignore it. It's an Order. It's signed. Stop it. Stop it. Stop it. You're drivin' yourself crazy. Stop thinkin'. This is like a runaway train. How do I stop it? How?*

From the street Gilson looked at the crowded platform above his head, then glanced behind him at the pressing crowd. There were too many people. Especially up there on the scaffold. He shook his head. Too, too many. In addition to the hangman were the three girls, three U.S. Deputy Marshals, Carlyle, the town mayor, Patterson, a County Commissioner, and Judge Kilpatrick's clerk, a young man named Holland, whose purpose it was to read the death warrant. Randolph Fillmore again raised his arms, asking for quiet. Ten in all.

Gilson was glad that he had decided to remain at the bottom of the scaffold with Lloyd and his shotgun. *Up there I'd have no place to stand. I'd be in the way. I am in the way. Oh, shut up.*

The crowd's mood changed perceptibly. Something odd was going on. No one knew what. The fellow in the black broadcloth, had positioned the youngest Stafford girl in the middle of the scaffold flooring. Why? When were they going to be turning those Stafford girls loose? What was going on? It did not look like they were turning that child loose.

Randolph Fillmore raised his hands above his head. He had the crowd's attention. It grew quiet as they waited for him to say something. He said nothing. The Court Clerk Holland stepped to the railing and started reading Sally Stafford's death warrant, the court's Order for her execution "to be hanged by the neck until dead." He read as loud as he could but his voice didn't carry far. Behind him Sally Stafford stood, saying nothing, listening to the words tumble from the clerk's mouth, biting her lip, waiting.

Gilson was very aware of the crowd, of everyone expecting the circus to be called off. As the clerk finished, all eyes turned to Gilson. The crowd watched him, waiting for what they knew would happen, had to happen. It was Gilson's turn to call the whole thing off. He would give a sign of some kind; say something. Surely he would release the girls and that would be that. But why was the clerk reading the girl's death warrant if they were going to turn her loose? This was all for show. It had to be. Surely they weren't going to hang her?

"Hey, Gilson, what the hell you doin'?" someone yelled. "Release them girls." A firecracker ignited, popping loudly. A woman yelled, "Hold on now, Sheriff! Ain't you gonna stop this?"

Lloyd raised his twelve gauge menacingly. The four U.S. Deputy Marshals who'd positioned themselves on all four sides gripped their shotguns and ordered people back. The restive crowd grew quiet, sullen, and now, apprehensive. Ten gauge shotguns do that to people.

On the scaffold the hangman had Sally by the right elbow. "Put your hands behind your back," he instructed. She paused, looked at him to see if she understood him correctly, then complied. The hangman looped her right wrist with the tied end of a small rope, then wrapped both of her hands together, securing them at her wrists, adding two half hitches for good measure. Standing in her new dress, Sally stared at her feet aware of a thousand eyes on her. Tears were crowding her vision. Her bravado had worn thin.

Below her Gilson was in the middle of his ongoing internal debate. *Stop it, right now. How can I? I got an Order. I got these U.S. Deputy Marshals, those damn Marshals. It ain't right, that's how. No, that's why. Someone will come and stop me. No, someone won't come. I have to stop this. It's*

58

me. Well, just call if off. Do it right now. Just turn and say, I'm callin' this off. How can I do that? I got a gawdawful Order. I got these, these men with their shotguns, waiting for me to screw up. Damn me. Damn me all to hell.

After Conroy secured Sally's hands behind her back, he knelt at Sally's right side. Reaching under her skirts he slipped a loop around her right ankle, pulled it tight, wrapped, then tied the end of the rope around her left ankle, pulling the slack out, testing it, adding two half hitches. He worked quickly.

Finally, the hangman stood, stepped in front of Sally, and, surveying his work, nodded his head slightly. He then glanced at the noose hanging behind her head and walked around her. Taking the noose in hand, he widened the loop, then worked it over her head, resting the bottom of the hangman's knot on her shoulder behind her left ear. Satisfied, he tightened the noose around her slender, exposed neck until the hemp strands dug into her skin. The oil he'd used on the new rope to ensure the proper slippage stained her collar and the lace of her dress. Lastly, he pulled the slack up on the rope, allowing it to drape behind her, almost to the floor, insuring the proper drop before her body hit the end of the rope, snapping her neck.

Watching the hangman work, Gilson shook his head. *Damn him*, he thought.

Standing on the platform above the trap door, Sally bit her lower lip, waiting for the hangman to finish. Tears ran freely down her cheeks. The hemp dug into the skin on her neck. It hurt. She glanced nervously at her sisters standing slightly behind her at the corner of the scaffold. She mouthed, "I love you. I'm so sorry. I love you." Sally turned away, looked for Conroy, not finding him, then she stared straight ahead over the silent crowd, beyond the buildings on Main Street to the Big Horn Mountain rising straight up in the distance. She imagined her chickens pecking at the dirt, doubting that anyone had fed them that morning or any morning since she'd been arrested.

The crowd standing in the street watched the hangman busy himself getting Sally Stafford ready. It began to dawn on the those standing on the edge that she wasn't being released, that someone…that they were hanging a sixteen year old girl…for nothing worth mentioning. Crowds are odd. They look for a leader, an instigator. And everyone in this crowd was waiting for someone else to do something. No one moved. No one said anything. Yet they seemed wary, full of distrust.

Then someone said, "What the hell's goin' on here? Gilson, you ain't supposed to be doin' this."

Gilson could feel the restive mood of those in the street.

He looked at Sally in her white dress. Something was missing. *Oh, my God*, Gilson thought. *I forgot a hood. There was no hood to cover the poor girl's face. Oh, shit. What should I do? How about a blind fold? Where will I get that? Can't get one now. It's too late. I should stop this hangin'. Stop it before it's too late.*

The hangman surveyed his work and nodded. He mouthed "good" to himself. Sally stood on the crowded scaffold, standing over the trap door, the noose pulled tightly around her neck. She waited fearfully, anxiously, her nerves raw. The crowd suddenly grew quiet. The hangman strode across the floor of the scaffold, his boots striking the flooring loudly, and seized the lever that would release the trap door. His fingers wrapped around the lever, his feet slightly spread. He glanced down at Sheriff Gilson in his chosen position at the bottom scaffold steps, and waited for his signal. Except for pulling the lever, he was done with the first girl.

Sally Stafford took a deep breath and waited. Her sisters were staring at her, full of apprehension, full of foreboding. Her last moment in time had arrived. Gilson merely had to nod and Sally Stafford would drop through the floor. Behind him the crowd waited, the collective belief still being that he'd call it off, that he'd suspend the court order, that he'd wait like he should for the rider. Someone, somebody should do something. The problem was that "someone" had not come to this hanging.

Gilson looked at the sixteen year old girl standing over the trap door, remembered her testifying in the hot June trial not two weeks ago, dabbing her cheeks with a handkerchief, sweating. It was so hot. He remembered her declaring emphatically, "I pulled the trigger on my father's twenty gauge shotgun. My aim was true. The blast nearly cut Mumford in two. He deserved to die for killin' my father. For shootin' him in the back." Her voice had been clear, steady. Gilson believed she'd told the truth.

Behind her and to the side, Gilson saw her sisters staring at him, waiting. Yes, Mumford had killed her father. That was weeks before. When she found him, she should have called for the sheriff. For him. She should have. She didn't. She hadn't. Instead, she'd shot Mumford dead. That was murder, or so the Judge said. That is what Kilpatrick told the jury they had to find if they found her testimony to be true. They did. That is what Kilpatrick saw also. Gilson envied that son of a bitch fishing on the upper Shell Creek leaving him with this mess. Gilson let the air whistle out over his teeth. It was now or never. She may be sixteen but she was a murderer. She'd killed a man, the wrong man, in cold blood, knowing what she was doing. *Shit. I gotta do this.*

Gilson nodded.

The hangman immediately pulled back on the lever, yanking it clear. The trapdoor sprang open.

Sally dropped through, her eyes suddenly wide as the floor gave way. She screamed as she fell through the hole. The sound was cut short, her neck snapping as her one hundred twenty pounds hit the end of the rope, jerking the noose tight, shutting off blood and air. Immediately, her body started swinging, turning, her feet coming up slightly, kicking. Her eyes remained wide open; she bit her tongue; blood trickled from her mouth. Her legs continued to kick spasmodically, jerking her body in a circle. Within seconds she was dead, her corpse turning slowly beneath the scaffold. The Sheriff glanced at Claire and Betsy. They couldn't see what he saw beneath the scaffold. The spectators did. Those poor girls could only imagine. He watched Claire hug her sister. Both were crying, sobbing.

Ah shit, Gilson thought. *I've sure done it. How can I stop this? I just can't, I mean. There ain't no way.*

The crowd, people coming from as far north as Fort Smith, was morbidly silent. No one spoke. Even the young ones who'd been running wild came to a stop. They were in shock. This hanging wasn't supposed to happen. It was supposed to have been stopped. Nobody was supposed to die. The girls were supposed to be released. The Sheriff had told so many people that it wouldn't happen. But it did. It was happening right now and the Sheriff was making no effort to stop it.

Beneath the scaffolding platform, Sally Stafford's body swung back and forth at the end of a hemp rope, her head canted off to the side, her neck broken. Her dying body jerked spasmodically, pee ran down her leg. It wasn't a pretty sight, even in a new white Sunday-go-to-meeting dress. Someone behind the Sheriff retched. He didn't turn around to see who.

Emery Smith and his brother, Cal lifted Sally's light body while Sam Joiner worked the noose loose. It had severely tightened around her neck when she hit the end of the rope. Loosening it took time. Emery Smith had the girl in his arms, her head lolling awkwardly. Finally, Sam worked the noose from around her neck and head. During his effort the rope had become tangled in her long hair. Now it was off. Finally. Emery laid Sally's limp body inside her waiting casket. Something about the way her body lay in the pine box bothered him. He reached inside to change something, perhaps move her head, an arm, a hand. Finished, he looked at Gilson, nodded his head, then turned and watched the rope as it was pulled up through the trap door. Cal placed the lid on the casket, then nailed it tight. Emery joined him, working a claw hammer. Behind him the trap door was re-latched so it would accept the weight of the next girl, the eighteen year old Betsy Stafford.

On the scaffold flooring the hangman inspected the rope, loosened the noose more, pulled it head high, then looked in the corner at the remaining two girls. Purposefully, he strode across the floor over what must have seemed to both girls a wide expanse. Reaching them, he took Betsy by the left elbow. She jerked away glaring at him, as if to say how dare you touch me. Claire whispered in her ear, holding Betsy's face in her hands.

Later, Gilson learned she'd said, "Betsy, go with him. Let's get this over and done. Sooner the better. You'll be all right. Go with him. I'll be right behind you. There's nothin' we kin do to stop this." Claire stopped talking, then asked, "Do you want me to go before you? I will."

"Oh, Claire, oh, Claire, I'm, I'm so scared."

"Me, too. Go. I'll be right behind you. Or if you like I'll go right now. You can be last."

"That's supposed to make me happy? I don't want to be last. I can't be last."

"No. No, Betsy, it's not. Betsy, I love you. It's just that there is nothin' we can do to stop this. Go with him, Betsy. Get this over."

Betsy stared at Claire for a very brief moment, nodded her head, then turned to the hangman. "All right," she said, to him, wiping her eyes and ruddy cheeks, dry. "Show me what I'm supposed to do." She allowed Conroy to guide her across the floor of the scaffold and place her in front of the noose, her feet over the trap door. She could smell the fresh cut pine and remembered in some odd way her father sawing pine logs for the winter fireplace. That was before he was dead. Killed.

"All right, my dear," the hangman said, explaining to her what he was doing. "I'm gonna tie your hands behind your back." He took her right arm by the wrist. "We'll get this over and behind you as fast as I can."

Betsy nodded, letting him pull her arm behind her. "Just promise me it won't hurt. Please promise me. Lie to me if you need to. Just promise."

He looped her right wrist, wrapping the rope around her left, and tied her hands behind her back at the wrist.

"I promise," he said softly.

"Thank you," she said.

Betsy's hands were secure. They wouldn't be flopping around. She wouldn't grab for her throat when the rope was jerked tight. He walked in front of her, tilting his head backwards to stare at her. "Almost done," he said. "Almost."

"Thank you," she replied again. Betsy glanced at him, finding some consolation in his words even if they were a lie.

Moving to her left, kneeling, he looped her left ankle, tying it to her right. Finished binding Betsy's ankles, he stood, moving slightly behind her and to her left. Standing, he spoke to her. "See, we're almost done. Almost there."

Betsy didn't reply, glancing at Claire, her lips trembling. Claire nodded encouragement to her sister. She couldn't the hangman without turning her head. She turned, but he paid her no attention. He glanced at the noose hanging behind her head. Taking it in hand,

63

he widened it, then worked it over her head, laying the knot on her shoulder.

"Oh my God," Betsy said. "Oh, please. You're frightenin' me."

"Sorry," he said, "Almost finished," he said as he tightened the noose around her neck until the fibers bit into her skin.

She winced. "That hurts," she said.

"Almost done," he assured her.

"It hurts. You promised me it wouldn't hurt."Betsy stood trembling.

Touching her back, the hangman offered words of encouragement, saying, "You'll be all right. This will take but a moment and it'll be over. Done."

Betsy mumbled something in reply. Gilson couldn't hear what she said and never did find out.

The hangman abruptly strode to the lever. The sound of his boot heels striking the planking was in her ears. Betsy sobbed, fear overcoming her. Her shoulders began to heave. She trembled, a leaf in the storm that blew around her, pushing her to the edge. Behind her and to the side, Claire buried her face in her hands, no longer able to watch.

The hangman glanced down at the Sheriff. Gilson's attention was on Betsy. She was barely able to stand, waiting apprehensively, her slender frame shaking, reminding him of leaves of grass tossed by the wind. Gilson realized again he'd forgotten a blindfold, cursing himself. He doubted whether Betsy knew about his forgetfulness. This girl who'd never killed anyone. She didn't have it in her. Sally had confessed first and repeatedly, but Betsy wanted to save her sister from the scaffold. Who could blame her? Certainly, she showed courage. But she'd admitted under oath, claiming she killed Mumford, that it wasn't Sally. Shot him with her father's shotgun. That's what she'd said. There it was. The jury had believed her. That was the fatal flaw: she said she killed him. She admitted it in front of everybody, and that admission made her a murderer. Plain. Simple. Clear. Betsy, was a murderer by admission. Except, it wasn't that simple.

Gilson swallowed hard, looked back at the hangman, then

against his will and his better judgment, nodded his head.

The hangman pulled the lever, the floor gave way, and Betsy dropped through. The bone in her neck snapped, breaking as her body abruptly reached the end of the rope, one hundred twenty-five pounds coming to an immediate and complete stop. The hangman hadn't tied Betsy's legs very well, for instantly they were loose. She was kicking and the kicking caused her body to twist around awkwardly. For a moment her body struggled, jerking spasmodically. A few seconds passed, thirty, and Betsy's body stopped struggling, her head resting awkwardly to the side. Emery glanced at Gilson. Gilson nodded. Emery and his brother went to work: Emery and Cal lifting, and Sam Joiner working the noose off of Betsy's neck. Once off, he released the rope.

Betsy's fall shocked the silent crowd. Suddenly outraged, the townspeople turned in horror to look at one another, mumbling their disapproval. Two dead girls and it was suddenly waking up, coming alive, no longer entirely afraid of U.S. Deputy Marshals or their shotguns or anyone else. The rumbling came from practically every quarter. All of this had happened quickly, too quickly. What they were witnessing certainly wasn't right. It was wrong. A good number of them had seen rustlers hang, horse thieves brought to a quick justice. They'd seen murderers get what they deserved. This hanging certainly wasn't what these girls deserved. This was dead wrong. Why hadn't the Seriff kept his word about releasing them? That lying son of a bitch. It was a gawdawful law that would kill three girls for killing the man that killed their pa.

Emery Smith carried Betsy's warm body to the second coffin, placing it gently inside. Immediately, the other two men hammered the lid in place, driving the eight penny nails into the soft pine wood.

By the time Gilson looked back at the hangman, the rope had been pulled through the opening and the trap door re-latched. The hangman tested the trap door with his weight. It didn't move. Satisfied, he looked at Claire who stood quietly in the corner, waiting. His eyes found her. She tightened her lips and walked straight across the flooring toward him. Without being asked, she stood over the trap door, holding her hands behind her back so that he could secure her wrists, one to the other.

Almost done, Gilson thought. *Almost. Done? This will never be done.*

The hangman grunted his approval and tied her wrists together, perhaps too tightly, for she winced but did not complain. Once her wrists were secure, he knelt beside her and tied a loop around her left ankle and secured it to her right, binding her ankles together.

Claire remained mute, waiting for him to finish his preparations. The hangman asked if she had anything to say, any last words, something that her sisters had not been asked, something they had not been offered. She shook her head no. "Please," she said to him, "let's get this done."

The hangman nodded. Moving behind Claire, he pulled the noose wider, then worked it down over her head until the knot rested on her shoulder. Then he tightened the noose quietly, swiftly, efficiently. Finished with the noose, he situated the slack in the rope behind the young woman's back, five feet of rope, the loop almost reaching her knees. Claire waited, knowing she was about to drop through the hole to her death. He stepped back and away from her.

"You finished?" she asked.

He nodded.

"Get this done. It's not good to keep people waitin'. They came for a show. Let's give 'em one."

"All right," he answered, reviewing hands, ankles, rope, slack. "I'm finished," he said.

"Good," she said. "Get on with it."

Abruptly he turned and walked four steps to the lever that would release the trap door. Claire took a breath, let it out, and waited. She'd seen what had happened to her sisters. She tensed her body, readying herself for the floor to open up beneath her feet. A breeze played with the curls in her hair, pulled at the folds in her skirts. She turned her head and saw the hangman standing, feet spread, his hand on the handle. "Come on," she said.

The hangman didn't reply. He was looking at Gilson.

"Cut 'er loose," someone yelled. Others joined in. "What the hell's goin' on, Gilson? You outta your mind?"

"This ain't right. Stop it."

66

One of the U.S. Deputy Marshals discharged his shotgun, broke it open, and immediately reloaded, his eyes on the crowd in front of him.

Standing in the middle of the scaffold, the blast caused Claire to jump. She turned to look in the direction of it, saw the officer reloading. The noose was tight around her neck; it felt raw against her skin.

From the bottom of the stairs, Gilson looked up at her, a statute in a white dress, a lovely princess standing quietly above the trap door, waiting for the nod of his head. Her eyes were on him. He could feel them boring into him. *Damn her.* She'd confessed to a crime she had not committed. Gilson knew she hadn't done the shooting. He knew it. He'd told the Judge so, repeatedly. There it was. Sure, she lied. Under oath she'd admitted she was a murderer, that she killed in cold blood. That was her admission; that was her word. Yes, she'd given sworn testimony to protect Sally. Stupid. So stupid. Gilson felt his pocket and the scrap of paper that was the Order of Execution, the court's Judgment following a jury's verdict. There it was: a piece of paper that sentenced Claire to hang until she was dead. The heaviest sheet of paper he'd ever carried.

He glanced at the hangman who was also staring right at him, waiting. Killing a beautiful twenty year old girl wasn't good policy but what choice had he? She had been determined to be a murderer by a jury, the very people who were complaining right now. He had the Order. Signed. And there were these gunmen wearing Marshal's badges. He looked at Claire, thinking about her predicament and his. Someone yelled for him to let her go. She'd closed her eyes, opened them, and stared at him again. Waiting. He brought his attention to the hangman. Their eyes met. Just as he had with Sally, with Betsy, he wanted to say no. He should say no. Instead, he nodded his head.

The hangman pulled on the lever in one swift motion, without hesitation. Claire dropped through the floor, emitting a brief abbreviated yelp which ended when she reached the end of the rope. Her neck snapped, her knees jerked upward, her body struggled for life. A minute passed. Her body ceased to struggle. Claire dangled from the end of the rope, a beautiful but dead creature, turning slowly beneath the cheap scaffold flooring.

Behind him the crowd stood in an ungodly quiet. The silence frightened him. There was no telling what an angry crowd would do.

Emery Smith lifted Claire's body. His brother removed the noose from around her neck. Emery carried her body to the last open casket, the only one remaining, and laid her limp body inside. For an instant, Emery stared inside the casket, shook his head in disgust, then stepped back. The lid was seated and hammers commenced driving nails into the fresh pine wood.

Gilson watched, listening to the sound of hammers falling on eight penny nails. He noted that the four U.S. Deputies were gone; they'd vanished into the July heat like a mirage.

My god, my god, what have I done? Gilson thought. *Well it's over. Is it over?* he asked.

Lloyd interrupted his thinking. "Jason?" he said. "Jason, let's get off the street. These folks ain't gonna be none too happy. Best not push our luck. We ain't got any. Where'd those damn Deputies go? They sure as hell didn't stick around. Bastards. Gave me the creeps. They sure had us."

Gilson glanced at Lloyd, nodded his head. Lloyd was right. Gilson glanced around him. No one looked at him. Suddenly he was a pariah: rotting flesh that should be shot, killed, and buried. *Now that ain't right,* he thought. *I got an Order. Signed.* Pulling his pistol, he eased back on the hammer and followed Lloyd to the door of his office. *Ain't too safe out here,* he thought. *Can't be too careful.*

CHAPTER 7

July 1886
Dakota Territory

"You Far Stockton?"

Forest Stockton stared at the fat man speaking to him.

"If you're Far Stockton, I have a letter for you."

"A letter? For me? I'll be damned. Who'd write me?"

The fat man nodded at the slightly built man standing in front of him, noting that his hat made him look tall, really tall. He reminded the postmaster of a dying willow tree, limbs blowing crazily in an ill wind.

Forest Stockton looked tall because he wore a tall hat and was skinny, sinewy, with almost no meat on his bones. Some of his height was due to the way the crown of the 10x Beaver fur felt hat jutted up and the brim was pulled down covering his eyes. A scowl hung on his narrow face. He took after his mother's side of the Stockton family: tall, thin people.

"That fellow over there said you'd be Far Stockton. That your last name? Stockton?"

Turning in the direction the fat man pointed, the tall, skinny man, all six feet of him, asked, "Which fellow would that be?"

The fat man glanced down the boardwalk, pausing, his eyes following the curve of the street, studying it.

"Don't see him right now," he finally said. "Name of Jasper Speakman. Told him 'bout a letter I got a month ago addressed to General Delivery, the Post Office. Right here in Johnsburg. That'd be me. I'm the post office. Strange thing was it was addressed to Far Stockton, Johnsburg, Dakota. Nobody else. No place else. I don't know nobody name of Far Stockton. Nobody I know knows no Far Stockton. Ain't been nobody askin' after Far Stockton. Then Jasp says he's heard of a Far Stockton over in some place called Single Tree. That be more northern Dakota than southern Dakota. Now that's a ways from here. Then Jasp is lookin' down the street and he

69

says, 'Well, I'll be damned. Speakin' of the devil, that be Far Stockton standin' right there. That sure be him...the skinny fellow.'"

"So I says where? He points out you. He says right there, pointin' at you. Sayin' the fellow standin' in front of the only appy at the hitchin' rail, lookin' sorta lost. Then he says he wouldn't bother you much if he was me. Says ya likes to be left alone. Says y'all are quick to stomp on snakes. And you're not too partial to what kinds ya stomps on."

"What?"

"Says ya likes to stomp on snakes. That ya ain't partial to what kinds y'all steps on. That's what 'ol Jasp says."

"Snakes? What about this letter? I don't give a damn about snakes."

"Over there in the post office. I'll be there in a few minutes. Drop over and I'll show it to you. I was about to send it back the way it came."

"Where'd it come from?"

"Some place called Sage Creek, Montana Territory. Postmark says Kane. Ya heard of it? I ain't never."

"Maybe. Where's this post office of yours? Where?"

"'Cross the street. Two doors down that a way. Says 'Post Office.' Not too clear but it says it right there on the wall. I'll be there in ten, fifteen minutes, y'all wanna wait? I got some business I gotta take care of. That letter, it's been there for maybe a month. Five weeks, maybe. Don't suppose it'll hurt to wait a few more minutes."

"Five weeks?"

"Yes, sir. 'Bout that. Maybe four. I don't rightly remember just how long since I got it."

"All right, Buster. I'll be there to see this letter. I'll be goin' there right now. It'd be right nice if you was to hurry yourself up with your business."

"No. No. It'll be fifteen, maybe twenty minutes. I ain't gonna be there right now. Like I said I got some business to take care of."

"I'll be waitin' for you, Buster. Don't let any dust be collectin' on your boots."

"You are? I mean you will?"

"That is what I said."

"All right. I'll be right there. Soon as I can."

"You do that. I'll be waitin' to see this letter of yours."

"Oh, it ain't my letter. You Far Stockton? Is that you?"

"Forest Eugene Stockton."

"Forest? Is that long for Far? Is that you?"

"It is."

"Well, then it's yours."

"That's what you said."

"Yes, I did, didn't I?"

The newly found postal patron turned to his Appaloosa, pulled the reins from the hitching rail, then looked at the Postmaster standing on the boardwalk. He said, "I'll see you in a few," then started walking down the dusty street, heat waves rising from the roofs of the crowded store fronts, the raw boned Appaloosa in tow walking behind him.

Damn. He's going to the post office right now. I'm not there. I told him fifteen or twenty minutes. I told him he'd be waitin' 'cause I got business! Don't anybody listen? The fat man looked longingly down the boardwalk toward the Skill Masters Bakery. *Dammit. I told him.* The Postmaster turned and looked in the direction of the United States Post Office. He saw Mrs. Feldman peering into the dark window of the Post Office, a white envelope in hand.

Dammit why does everything happen at once? I sure wanted one of them confections Mrs. Skillman makes on a Friday morn. Dammit. Guess I better get back before there's a crowd. I don't care for a crowd. Not one bit. There's already a crowd. Better hurry.

Forest Stockton stood in front of the post office in Johnsburg, North Dakota. In hand he had a battered envelope addressed to Far Stockton, General Delivery, Johnsburg, Dakota. It was postmarked Kane, Wyoming Territory. With a jackknife, he cut along the seam and extracted a single sheet: a note written in English starting with:

Dear Forest Stockton,

I'm your brother Petey Stockton's wife. I have writ' to Syrus and to Riles askin' for help. We need it. We are in plenty of trouble. Petey done broke his leg. Horse rolled on him. I reckon he fell off.

It's just me, Josh, and Katie Sue doin' the work. They's young, bein' they was born not long ago. They's no help. Their legs is barely long enough to reach the ground. Ain't grow'd. Somebody done stole the cows. Can't find 'em. They ain't no more. Horses busted out. They's gone. Corral fell down an' needs fixin'. Poles don't stay fit no more on account of the post done rotted away. Horse needs shoein', anyways. Dog got into the chickens. They's mostly dead. Sucked them eggs dry. Would have shot the dog 'cept he keeps the skunks away. Hay's gonna need hayin'. Just started to grow. Up six or seven inches. Need it come winter. There's just me. Please? Kin you come? I'm Diana. I'm a Stafford. You know who I am. You should. My Pa and my sisters live on the other side of the canyon. Hope you show up 'cause we need help plenty bad. Got bad news. Your Pa, he died last fall. He was kilt. Petey was to tell you but he ain't got it done. Don't know why. Diana

Forest Stockton read the letter three times. Finished, he inserted the single sheet back into the envelope, folding the envelope over, then placing it in his right shirt pocket, buttoning the flap. Stepping off the boardwalk, he approached the Appaloosa from the right side. For a moment he idly patted him on the shoulder. With the index finger of his right hand he traced the MT brand that decorated the hide on the right shoulder, looked at the horse, and nodded his head as if agreeing. He said to the horse, "Guess we're goin' home, Apples. Pistol has some problems. Done broke his leg and the Old Man's dead. Can you believe that? Who'd of thought that'd even be possible?" Forest ran his hand on the neck and mane of the Appaloosa. *Wonder what Riles will think of that? The Old Man ridin' him like he did. Bet that'll knock his socks off.*

Stepping into the saddle, he reined the Appaloosa around and, with the touch of the reins on the horse's neck, started him walking west down Main Street, Johnsburg, Dakota Territory. In ten minutes he was on to the open prairie. Johnsburg, not too big to start with, was getting smaller.

72

CHAPTER 8

July 15, 1886

It's been more'n two months since I writ' them letters. I'm close to givin' up. Don 't know why I still bother hopin'. Gonna take Petey to Kane to see Old Doc O'Martine. Gotta see if Petey's leg is gettin' on proper, and maybe get a sack of flour and some salt. We're near out of everythin'. Push is way past shove. I hitched the bays to the buckboard for the trip. The kids are gonna set up on the board seat with me and Petey will be in the back with down pillows under his leg to keep him from bouncin' too much. Would of had to turn the saddle horses out 'cept they was already out; the damn corral is fallin' apart. I let the milk cow go 'cause I couldn't feed her no more and for a week-ten days I ain't gonna be here to take care of her. We ain't got no more firewood for the cook stove. I find myself between that rock and a hard place the Bible talks 'bout. Don't know what else I kin do. I've done taken all that I kin take. I keep gettin' up every mornin' so guess I ain't done. 'Cept like I said the hogs got out. They's done. If I can get back here, I'll butcher a couple of 'em. That'll fix 'em good. Give me somethin' to eat, too.

Damn hogs. Know'd I was gonna have to shoot 'em sooner or later. Can't let 'em run wild. No tellin' what they's gonna do, they get real hungry. I ain't fed 'em in a month of Sundays. Not since they got out. They's on their own for now. Chickens survived the skunks twice. Down to five layin' hens and they's stopped layin'. Got one rooster. Awful lookin' specimen. No tail feathers. Looks to have the mites. He's sheddin' his feathers somethin' fierce. Naked in places.

It's gonna be a long trip over the mountain. We're sufferin' from the heat of summer. Boilin' is what it is. Them locust are roostin' in the cottonwoods singin'. Drivin' me crazy. Like they won't shut up.

These bay geldings I got pullin' the buckboard got a ways to go. I'm gonna be lookin' at their hind ends for the better part of six days, comin' and goin'. Much as I don't want to, I gotta get to town.

73

As I say more than two months since I writ' them letters. Nothin' in reply. Ain't nobody come. Don't know what we're gonna do, my man laid up like he is. 'Course I thought that two months ago and here I am..

Come winter, we're in trouble. I don't know how we're gonna make it. We're either gonna be lucky or we ain't. Told that to Petey and he said "luck ain't got nothin' to do with it." He's right. Still we sure gonna need a load of it if we are gonna make it to December. Guess we'll be livin' on venison, elk, and maybe an old buff and hog meat. Got some apples and some squash growin'. That'll help. Locust done ate the corn so we don't have any of that. Took it right down to the stalk.

Our outfit lies between the Reservation on the north and the Pryor Mountains on the south. From there it extends up and down Sage Creek. There's a West Pryor and a East Pryor, and right in the middle between the two, there's a low place. I'm takin' the wagon right between 'em, headin' down Crooked Creek past where old man Tenpenny and his family live.

Startin' out, I had to take the wagon back and forth until I got on top, then I just followed the Creek along the west side of the Canyon.It was in that wagon goin' to Kane I confessed to Petey that I writ' his brothers askin 'for help. For the longest time he don't say a thing. He shut right up. I figure it's gonna make him plenty mad.

In my defense I says to him, "It ain't like we got any choice, Petey. We done reached the end." I said, "Petey, we ain't got no cows. We got nothin'. They're gone to who knows where. The hogs, they's gone wild. I can't keep a horse in the paddock without hobblin' him. Petey," I says, "we're in trouble. We sure are."

I couldn't help it. I starts to feelin' sorry for myself and I cloud up, fixin' to rain. Don't like that sort of thing but sometimes I do come apart. Especially when my world starts to look like a horse wreck.

After I told him 'bout writin' his brothers, Petey looks at me and he can see I'm at wit's end. He says, "Dee, it'll be all right. If my brothers come, and, who's to say they won't, we'll saddle that horse. Sure don't make me happy,but it's done."

74

Petey looks at me, smiles, and tries to put my mind at ease. "They's normal people, Dee. I didn't mean to make 'em sound awful. They ain't. They's like spots on a appy. Except maybe my second brother. That'd be Si. He's...." Petey stopped talkin'. "And Riles? Like I said, we'll saddle that horse when it gets here. Fact be, Diana, I don't even know if Si's alive. 'Til he gets here we ain't knowin' he's comin'."

Petey shook his head. Seemed he was thinkin' dark thoughts. We made the head of Crooked Creek the first day. Stayed with ol' man TenPenny's bunch. They's good people.

CHAPTER 9

"Where to, Mister?"

"I hope to get to Kane, North Wyoming Territory sometime soon."

"Where'd that be exactly?"

"Wyoming Territory? I'm goin' to the MT on Sage Creek. Little outfit. Don't think you can get me there."

"MT?"

"That be located in Southern Montana Territory."

"And you are?" he asked. The ticket agent for the Wells Fargo Overland Stage Company out of Auburn, California was a fellow named Curious Matterly, itself a curious name.

"Name's Syrus Stockton."

"Mr. Stockton, lookin' at this here map, this Kane, you're talkin' Wyoming. Northern Wyoming. That right?"

"Nailed 'er right solid, sir. That's to hell and gone if you wanna know." Syrus pointed Kane out on the map. "Sage Creek ain't there. It's close. Close as you can get, I think."

"All right. That it? Just you?"

"Just me. I'd like to say it was my wife and a passel of kids. I ain't so lucky."

"You'll be travelin' UP to Green River. Stage north to Fort Casper. From there the stage to..... to... looks like Sheridan. Closest I can get you is Sheridan. You're on your own after that. This business or a vacation? Work or pleasure? Both?"

The stranger looked at the ticket agent; a smile formed on his mustached upper lip. He rubbed his chin thoughtfully. "Well sir," he drawled, "lessin' them folk at the the other end changed some, I'd say I was goin' to a righteous gunfight or two, for sure a funeral, maybe catch a cow rustler or two. There will be a hangin' or two, maybe a weddin', whose I don't know. A little of everythin'. I'll say that 'cause that's the way it always is. Gawd only knows. I'm hopin' for the best. Maybe I'll run across some lucky woman and sweep her plumb off her feet. Like I say, I'm hopin' for the best. The other part? The first part about gunfights, funerals, hangin's, maybe a weddin'-- that's a dead-for-sure-certainty."

The agent did some pencil work, looked up, and finally said, "That be twenty-three dollars even. Green River is a long ways. Once you get to Green River, you'll need to find the Stage Office. I can't do that for y'all. You're gonna be travelin' the better part of two weeks. A long ways."

"You sure as hell got that right. Thank ye kindly, Mister. Appreciate it."

The agent pushed tickets across his desk to Syrus.

"The Auburn Stage will be here in about two hours. From here you'll be goin' to Reno. There you'll catch the UP. Be here for an hour or so before it leaves goin' east. Those tickets will take you to Green River. Don't lose them. And you're most welcome," he said. "Have a nice trip. If it's possible."

The stranger who'd identified himself as Syrus Stockton touched his hat with two fingers, turned and walked outside onto the boardwalk, the ching, ching, ching sound of his spurs biting into the wooden planks followed after him. After Syrus left, Matterly got up, stepped outside and watched the stranger as he walked away, noting the broad Bill Hickock like shoulders. He watched him until he disappeared inside the Blakely Market and Way Station. Once the man was out of view, Matterly returned to his desk and shifted himself forward in his chair, enabling him to look up and down the street outside his office. There was no one. He waited to see if the stranger would return, thinking he wouldn't. Concentrating, he carefully uncovered the telegraph key, tapped to clear the line, then started tapping in earnest, once in a while slowing to glance at the Morse Code schedule to reacquaint himself with a forgotten letter. He wrote:

Eleanore Matterly Olson, Stop. Rodney Brooks, shootist, coming to Kane. Stop. Don't know what name he'll use. Stop. Claimed to be Syrus Stockton. Stop. Traveling alone. Stop. His picture is on a wanted poster. Stop. Bringing his guns. Stop. Expects gunfight. Stop. Going to a funeral. Stop. Notify Sheriff trouble coming. Stop. Curious Matterly. Stop.

Finished, Matterly re-covered the telegraph key and leaned back in his chair, thinking. *Those folks are in trouble and they don't know it. It's surely coming. Rodney Michael Brooks just bought and paid for a ticket. He's coming. That's for sure.*

Rising to his feet, Matterly stretched, then stepped outside his small office, closing and locking the door, then proceeded north down the boardwalk toward the Livingston Saloon. The stage wasn't due for most of two hours. Looking south, toward his office, Matterly saw the man he'd identified as Rodney Michael Brooks standing next to a slender, pretty, red-haired woman carrying a blue parasol. A boy ten or eleven years old stood by her side. She was engaged in a lively conversation with the man who'd called himself Syrus Stockton. Syrus caught sight of Curious standing in front of the Livingston Saloon. He waved at him, then turned his head to listen to the woman. The boy was standing, hands on his hips, staring at the horse and foot traffic moving up and down the street.

Curious Matterly shook his head. *Syrus Stockton? My foot. Him, you ain't. And you lied. You are traveling with someone: a woman and a boy. Yes, Rodney Michael Brooks, that's who you are. I've seen your picture at the post office, more probably at the sheriff's office. Why ain't you usin' your real name? You ain't no stranger to me. I know who you are. And I'm warning them. Not that it will do any good. I heard what you did to those Mormons out there in San Bernardino. Shame some brave soul hasn't shot you dead. Expect it's harder than it looks.*

CHAPTER 10

On July 18, 1886 we got to Kane to stock up while we could with what little money we had, and to have a conversation with Doc O'Martine. What we had wasn't much: four dollars and fifty-three cents to be exact. Out of it we had to pay Doc what we owed.

Petey seemed cheerful, probably 'cause not one of his brothers has showed. By the time we got to Kane, I'd given up on the possibility. It was easier. Like I say, it'd been a while since I writ' and now I don't figure there's anythin' they can do anyway. Truthfully, I'm just waitin' for my man to come to grips with the idea that we're done. He don't seem close. Quittin' ain't somethin' he knows about. Those two ain't never been introduced. I'd say they's about to get acquainted.

Kane has a Sheridan Avenue that runs north and south the length of it. There's the State Bank diagonally across from what we calls the Jingle Bob Hotel. Its rightful name is Big Horn Hotel and Café. It's more of a store on the first floor with a table or two, and a whorehouse on the second. No one complains on how folks keep themselves in bacon and beans and the stove warm in winter. Kane has a blacksmith shop, pool hall, and the Calico, which is another saloon. Brackston General occupies a lot across from the State Bank. Farther out of town on the east side of Sheridan Avenue is the Wilson Livery Stable and another bar--the Shoshone. Drinkin' is a all consumin' occupation in Kane. They get a lot of business from the ML. The Shoshone bar don't have a pool table, though a man can get himself into a card game or throw darts, if he's a mind to.

Up against the hill, north of a pointed hill called Katie's Nipple, there's a shootin' range. A mile north of the town there's a two room school, half for older kids and half for younger. One school marm does the teachin' on both sides. Next to the school is the Presbyterian Church and Bible Ministry. The preacher has a little frame house in the back; he's a squirrelly little man of God, who inherited a nervous tic. Keeps squintin' his left eye like it's got a hair buried in the ball. It's the damnedest thing you ever saw for a

79

preacher.

I left Petey, Josh, and Katie Sue sittin' in the back of the buckboard in the shade of the State Bank across from the Jingle Bob Hotel and Brackston General. As I said, the Jingle Bob is not its real name. It's just what I and everyone else calls it. I went inside Brackston General to do some shoppin'. I was hopin' I could restock a little so we could stay a bit longer on Sage Creek. At least to keep us from starvin' to death. We was in need of salt, flour, corn meal and such. Josh and Katie Sue need shoes. That will have to wait. I don't think we'll have enough for that 'cause Petey needs to see old Doc O'Martine to see how his leg is gettin' along.

We needed some 44-40 cartridges. I needed to buy a can of Black Beauty, a thick black wheel grease, to keep the wheels turnin' on their hub. The wagon wheels needed greasin' somethin' awful. That was the reason I brought the buckboard and not the wagon. The rims were a might loose and needed tightenin'. That could wait for we also needed several sets of horseshoes and the harnesses needed fixin' to keep 'em from fallin' off. Best I could do right now is soak some fresh bull hide, let it dry in place and tie it together. Not the best of repairs, but it'd do.

Fact is, we was on the low side of things. Normally we would have restocked when we sold the two year old heifers and steers. Since we didn't have any yearlings or two year olds, that four dollars and fifty-three cents had to last until we got some. I didn't know how I was gonna do that. A gal would need a couple of Colt Peacemakers and have the will to use 'em to stretch our money. I went into Brackston General to see how close to the impossible I could come. Like I said, I didn't have a lot of hope. None, is right close to what I had.

CHAPTER 11

July 18, 1886

    The rider, sitting easy in the middle of a Buckskin gelding, entered the north side of the town of Kane, Territory of Wyoming, at a slow walk, not appearing to be going anywhere fast. He was looking. He led a sorrel mare, lead rope around her neck and the other end tied to the back of his saddle. The Buckskin's head hung down in the afternoon heat; he looked to have been walking a long, long time over a great distance. In front of the Buckskin moved a halterless pack mule, loaded, a pack saddle on its back, his head canted off to the right enabling him to see the Buckskin. In front of the mule twenty paces was an ugly, one-eyed, dark, long-haired wolf hound. He walked right down the middle of the roadway, veering neither to his right nor his left, yet conscious of the rider coming behind him. Such had been the order of travel for three weeks. His practiced gait matched that of the Buckskin and the mule. The dog was big as dogs go: one hundred ten lean pounds of gristle. When a dog is that big he doesn't have to get out of the way, nor does he have to change his direction or give up the road. He, by definition, has the right of way. Most sensible folks just naturally give it to him without objecting.

    Passing a buckboard going in the opposite direction, the driver nodded a greeting. The rider returned the salutation, not knowing who it was that said hello, but what the hell. It had been a long three weeks and he was tired, needed a bath, and a good night's rest. He turned on Sheridan Avenue, guiding the Buckskin toward the Big Horn Hotel, thinking it was the only accommodation he'd seen and he'd take advantage of it.

    The Buckskin walked past the blacksmith shop and approached State Bank on his left, the Big Horn Hotel coming up on his right. The one-eyed dog and the mule kept walking because the Buckskin did. A wagon sat in the shade of the State Bank's false front. Riles noted the girl and a smaller boy standing on the tailgate

81

pretending they were going to jump into the powdery dust that was the street. Seeing the long-haired dog, the girl pointed, squealing in delight. Riles could feel the Buckskin tense ever so slightly. The dog stopped, staring at the excited girl. The girl waved but the boy, who was younger, perhaps two, threw a rock that hit the Buckskin in the middle of the forehead. The horse immediately dodged left, threw his head to the ground, shoved his hind-feet into the air, and then frog-walked across the street. Having done that, he got serious and gave the rider a major shakedown. First, he sunfished, then he damn near belly flopped in the middle of the dust laden street, frog-walked, sunfished again, and went straight up, landing hard on all fours, jarring the rider to the core. He started again. It was one minute and five seconds before the Buckskin came to a standstill, stopping suddenly in a cloud of grey-red dust, breathing deeply as if nothing had happened. A crowd had gathered, mostly on the boardwalk, clapping, stomping, and cheering.

The unbridled mule had turned around and come back and was standing in the shade between the buckboard and the State Bank. The one-eyed dog was sitting on the boardwalk. Folks were walking around him, sidestepping his stationary body, stopping when confronted by the mule. The dog didn't move. The mule didn't move. Folks turned around and went back the way they came or stepped inside the State Bank to wait it out.

Once the Buckskin stopped his temporary rampage, the rider stepped down, tired, angry, hatless, pissed off, and bent on spanking a little butt until it turned red, making it unusable for a month of Sundays. *The little turd.* He picked up his hat, slapped it against his leg, knocking the dust off, and started toward the buckboard. The boy, sensing his vulnerability, retreated to the other side of the wagon box; the girl stood looking at the man approaching. There was no fear in her.

"Jeez, mister," she said to him, "you're pretty good sittin' on that horse. Do that again! That was fun."

The boy, in his effort to get away, was crowding the man resting in the back of the buckboard who had his eyes on the rider striding directly toward him.

"Now, Mister," Peter Stockton started to say, "you got every right..." He stopped mid-sentence. "Lordie," Peter exclaimed. "Where the hell did you come from?"

The rider looked at the girl, then the boy, still calculating how he'd reach across the wagon bed and grab the little runt, when his eyes fixed on the other occupant, the man with the bum leg, sorely in need of a hair cut, a well worn felt hat bent down at the edges hiding green eyes. His hand rested on a scarred Winchester rifle butt. The rider stopped, staring at the occupant.

"Pistol!" he exclaimed. "I'll be damned." He grabbed the side of the wagon and reached across the wagon box, taking Peter by the arm, shaking it. "Pistol," he said, "what the hell are you doin'? Didn't recognize you sittin' here in the shade like some tired, worn out, useless, featherless rooster."

The one-eyed dog jumped into the back of the buckboard. The girl screamed and ran toward the seat, stepping past Riles Stockton. The boy, giggling, started toward the dog who didn't move.

Riles glanced at the dog. "Take it easy, dog," he directed. "You ain't that hungry. Lie down." The one-eyed dog complied. Not to be left out, the mule stretched his head over the side of the buckboard and started sniffing at the boy. The child went wild with delight, laughing like he'd been tickled.

Peter Stockton was visibly moved. "Riles," he said, "how are you? It's been awhile. Diana's been goin' crazy wonderin' if you was ever gonna show up. I told her to relax, that you would, though I was startin' to wonder, myself."

The rider glanced at the girl who was now standing beside Peter on his right side, trying to avoid the outstretched moist nose of Cecil. "Damn it, Cecil, give it a break, would you?" The mule turned away fixing his eyes on Riles.

"Are you gonna do that again?" the girl asked Riles. "Does that horsey bite? Will he bite me?"

"I don't reckon he's that hungry, girl. You're quite a mouthful."

"You gonna ride the horse again?" she asked.

"You'd like to see me do that again, would you?"

"Yes. I'd like to see it. That was somethin'. Is that your dog? He's very big. Will he bite me? Somethin' is wrong with his eye. It's cryin'. What's wrong with it? Does it hurt? Can I pet him?"

"He only bites rabbits. You're safe. And who is this rock thrower?" Riles Stockton said, looking at the boy.

"That's Josh," Peter answered. "Sorry 'bout that, Riles."

"It is, is it? And who are you, girl?"

"Katie."

"Katie, huh? Named after your grandmother, I'll bet."

"Both of 'em," Peter said. "Katheryn Suzanne."

"Both of 'em? That's a lot of name for a little girl to carry around."

Katie Sue nodded. "Both of 'em," she said. "My mom's mom and my dad's mom."

Riles looked at Peter. "They're pretty nice, Pistol. Yours?" he said. "Didn't know you had it in you."

Peter nodded. "They're mine. I don't have it in me. Their mother does. Her name's Diana. She's in Brackstons. You know her. She was just a kid when you left. Maybe seven or eight."

"The oldest Stafford girl? She mentioned her name in her letter."

"Yes. Well, I don't know what she said in her letter. She sorta snuck that one by me."

"Said the Old Man was dead. Someone killed him. She did say that. Somethin' you failed to mention. Keepin' it a secret? Is he buried with Ma? I suppose so. Yes?"

Peter shook his head.

"No? Which one? Y'all keepin' it a secret?"

"All right." Peter said, emphatically. "I did put off tellin' you. He's taken care of. Black Wolf and the Old Man together."

"Where's that?"

"Up on Dry Head Creek above the buffalo run."

"He still there?"

"On a scaffold erected inside a lodge."

"Best bring his bones home 'fore the coyotes drag him away."

"What do you care, Riles? It ain't like the two of you got along."

Riles stared at his brother. "Pistol," he said, "he was my old man. Like it or not."

84

"All right. All right."

"All right, what?"

"All right, we'll bring him home. What about Black Wolf? They were kilt together."

"Bring him home, too, far as I'm concerned. Ma deserves to have her husband beside her. She don't deserve to be alone, even if he was a hard to get along with so n so who ain't never considered the word 'no." Riles paused, shaking his head. "Where's your woman? I know'd who she is but I ain't seen her in like twenty years."

"Brackstons."

"All right, Pistol. I'd like to be meetin' her. Let's forget about the Old Man and get on to what needs to be done. Her letter said you broke your leg. Said someone was borrowin' your cows. Makin' life some difficult."

"Yeah, I was tryin' to solve the cow problem when I got my leg broke. Just a string of bad luck."

"If it weren't for a little bad luck you wouldn't have any, huh? Can't move around, I gather?"

"It's gettin' better. Have to be careful. Diana won't let me move. It's been more than three, four months. Doc says I need to stay off it for six."

"Si? Far? They show up?"

"You're the first."

"Your woman's inside the store. How you fixed?"

"We're not. With me bein' laid up, that rascal fate kicked the hell outta me. I ain't sugar coatin' it. It's bad. Add to that all of the two year olds, all of 'em, disappeared. All of 'em. Every damn one: cows, calves, two year olds, bulls. You name it. Left us needin'. Frankly, I'd never told you about it. I didn't want your help. I didn't want nobody's help."

"Especially mine."

"Especially yours. It's the way I feel. There you got it. It's horseshit and gunsmoke."

Riles smiled. "And you can't do a damn thing 'bout it."

"That's right. I can't do a damn thing 'bout it. That's how I feel. You gonna stay or not?"

"I'll give you a hand. Help you get on your feet." Riles

glanced at the girl standing next to him. "You are certainly a cutie," he said.

"Riles, I.... Why? Why you gonna do that...knowin' how I feel. You just ran off. You didn't say shit to me. I got up and you was gone. I really don't want your help. Diana had to write a letter. She just had to. I didn't tell you 'bout Pa cause I didn't want you to know."

"Pistol," the tone of Riles voice changed; his eyes were squinted, his voice like gravel rolling around in a tub. "Get your shit together, boy. The Old Man made me promise a thousand times that if you, or Si or Far got in trouble I'd bend heaven, hell, or a shovel around your head and help you. I'm here. I'm gonna help. I don't wanna have this discussion again. Ever."

Peter stared at Riles; he nodded his head.

"When this is over, we're goin' fishin'."

"I don't wanna go fishin' with you."

"I don't care. You go fishin' with me or I'll throw you in the damn river and you don't get out 'til you go fishin' with me."

"You ain't changed a bit, Riles."

"Neither have you."

Peter looked at Riles, swallowed hard, nodded his head.

His daughter sat down in his lap. Looking up at him, she said, "Pa, are you all right?"

Peter nodded. "Riles," he said, "thanks for comin'."

"You're welcome."

"I'm sorry."

"You ain't sorry. I ain't sorry. We're Stocktons. Now ,let's get on with what needs to be done. I'd like to meet your woman. You said she's in Brackstons?"

"My mom is in there," Katie Sue reiterated.

"She is, is she?" Riles laughed. "Brackstons. It's been awhile since I heard that name. Had a couple of boys, the way I remember it."

Peter smiled, nodding. "Two boys. Both work for their old man. Diana won't be long. She don't have a lot of money to spend. She'll probably pass out seein' you. She's been waitin' and waitin'. Holdin' her breath."

Riles looked at Katie Sue, her hands clasped in front of her, twisting about, rocking back and forth on her legs, swaying like she was listening to someone plucking a banjo. "You wanna come with me, sister? I'm gonna go see your mother. See how she is. Help her out if I can."

"Help her out of what?"

"A tight spot. You comin' or are you stayin'?"

The girl looked at her father.

"Go ahead, Katie," Peter said. "This man's your uncle. He's my big brother."

"Your brother? And you don't like him much?"

"Yes. That's right. Not much."

"Like Josh?"

"Like Josh, only a lot older."

"Okay," she said. "If it's all right."

"Sure thing, Katie. It's all right," Peter said.

"One other thing. You said, Black Wolf, too. Both of 'em. Kilt same time?"

"Yes."

"That have anythin' to do with your broken leg and those cows?"

"No. I don't think so. They went huntin' up on Layout late September. When we found 'em they was dead for a while. Hard to tell exactly what happened or who did it. Still don't know, really. I didn't get my leg broke 'til the first of April, last of March. In a helluva snow storm."

"Well, you got one thing right. It's horseshit and gunsmoke. If it ain't one thing, it's two others. There ain't nothin' I kin do 'bout that."

"No, there ain't."

"Si and Far? Do they know 'bout Pa, Black Wolf?"

"No. Well, maybe. Diana wrote 'em, too."

"If not, you'll have to tell 'em."

"I will."

Riles reached over the side of the wagon and picked Katie Sue up, holding her in his arms like she was weightless.

"Damn, girl," he said. "You're light as a turkey feather. You

87

gotta start eatin' 'fore you blow away in the first winter storm that comes along."

"We don't have much food 'cause Papa got his leg broke. Momma says we're sufferin' hard times. Says everybody does it. We're gettin' over it. Papa will be walkin' soon. We gotta find our cows or we're gonna be eatin' deer, rabbits, and prairie chickens."

"Deer and rabbits, huh? She's a pretty smart hunter, I'd say. Maybe you can tell me what else she's plannin'."

"I can. I'm pretty smart, you know."

"You certainly are pretty."

With the child in his arms, Riles grabbed the Buckskin's reins, wrapping them around the brake lever. "Pistol, watch the Buckskin. Don't worry 'bout the mule; he'll stay with the Buckskin and the sorrel. Your lovely daughter and I are gonna find her mother and do some shoppin'. Seems she ain't eatin' proper. She might need some rock candy to tide her over 'til things get better and her pa's leg ain't broke." He laughed. "Hell's fire, girl. Things are better all ready." Riles turned back to look at Peter. "Be back in a moment, Pistol. Her name's Diana? I do remember her. She's the good lookin' one."

Peter nodded. "She is that. Her sisters ain't hard to look at, but Diana is the one that caught me lookin' twice."

Riles hesitated, turned back to the man sitting in the back of the wagon bed. "Pistol," he said. "I believe your woman wrote all three of us a letter. Assumin' they got it, they'll be here. If they ain't already. I'm here. We'll get this situation handled. Get you put together. You take care of your leg. In the next ten or fourteen days, you'll be wishin' she hadn't done all that writin'."

Riles paused. He turned to look at the dog lying in the back of the wagon, Josh patting him on the head. The dog didn't move. "Stay here 'til I get back."

Riles Stockton strode across the hot July street, the girl sitting on his right arm, dust puffing up with each step. "Damn hot, ain't it, girl?"

"Yes."

When Riles moved, the dog followed behind him, jumping from the buckboard bed.

"You all right, sis?" Riles asked, glancing at the girl in his arms.

"I am, thank you."

"Good. This the store? Brackstons? Reckon your ma's inside?"

"Yes."

"You'll need to point her out. I ain't seen her in twenty years. She was just your size the last time I remember. Probably don't look the same. She was just a bump on a log. Maybe five or six. All knees and elbows if I remember right. How old are you?"

"A bump on a log? My mom's a bump on a log?"

"Yes, a bump on a log. That's what I said."

"I'm five." She held up her hand to emphasize the number.

Riles Stockton stepped inside the Brackston General Store with Peter's daughter in his arms. Behind him the dog followed, jumping up onto the boardwalk then walking though the door. Once inside, Riles Stockton hesitated, letting his eyes adjust to the inside of the store and the dimmer light. He didn't see anyone, not immediately. He looked around until he found a clerk earnestly talking to a woman.

The one-eyed dog was behind him. He laid down when Riles stopped.

"That your Ma?" he asked Katie Sue. "Talkin' to that man?"

"Yes. You talk funny. Did you know?"

"I do, don't I? Tongue gets all tangled."

"What's your dog's name?"

Riles turned to see the one-eyed dog sitting on his haunches looking up at him, his tongue hanging out the right side of his jaw.

"That damn dog," he said. "He never listens."

"What's his name. Does he have a name?"

"Dog. I call him Dog."

"Does Dog know he's a dog? He came into the store like he was a person."

"I don't reckon he's altogether sure."

The woman saw Riles Stockton with her child in his arms and immediately excused herself, walking toward him.

"Who are you?" she demanded. "Put my daughter down. Where's her father?" She paused, her mind racing. "Oh my God," she

89

said. "Is he...?"

The dog growled menacingly, stepping forward.

"Easy, Dog."

The dog continued to growl.

"Damn it, Dog."

Diana stopped dead still, her eyes on the dog.

"Dog, knock it off. You're scarin' the hell outta everyone."

The dog retreated a couple of steps, whining.

"Damn dog." Riles looked at the woman. "Pistol's all right, Ma'am," he said. "There's nothin' wrong with him other than his leg's broke and he ain't eatin'."

"Who?"

"Pistol. That's who you are askin' after, ain't it?"

"Who, who are you?"

"Excuse me, Ma'am. I done forgot. Last time I saw you, you was like five or twelve. I forget. Pistol's my little brother, though he ain't so little no more. I'm the oldest. You wrote me a letter."

"Riles?" She paused. Her hand went to her mouth; her eyes began to mist over. "You're Riles Stockton?"

"Yes, Ma'am. That'd be me."

An emotional storm raced across the woman's face. She started to cry, then hugged the man holding her daughter, sobbing into his shirt. "I didn't think you'd come," she stammered. "I was givin' up. It was such a long shot. I didn't know where you was. Not really. It was an old, old address. Oh, Riles," she said, "we're in so much trouble."

"So I hear."

Suddenly embarrassed, she released her grip on him, backing up, looking at the lean, hard man holding her daughter in his right arm.

"Thank you," she stammered. "I'm so sorry. I didn't.... I mean...."

"My pleasure," he said, cutting her off. "All the women I know, see me, give me a big hug, and start crying. I'm used to it. Damnedest thing."

Diana laughed, covered her mouth again, and tried to wipe her eyes. "Petey says that, too. I'll bet you do make all the women cry.

90

Thank you, again," she said. "Thank you so much. I mean you're here." She glanced at her daughter. "Come, Katie Sue." Diana reached her hands out for her daughter but Katie made no effort to move.

"You're gonna wear this man out, darlin'."

"I don't think so, Mama. He's strong like Papa. He does horses like Papa."

"He does?" Diana replied, stepping back.

"Mumuh," Katie said.

"Mumuh? What does that mean?"

"Yes. It means yes."

"Good. I'm glad that's what it means."

Riles Stockton glanced at the clerk standing politely behind Diana's shoulder, waiting. "How are you, Fredrick?" he said. "Long time. Been keepin' yourself busy, I see! How's your old man?"

"Fredrick's my brother. I heard you say your name is Riles? Right? I'm fine, thank you. Thought you was dead. I heard that. Fredrick, as you call him, told me. He's just plain old Fred to us. We're not so formal."

"Not dead, far as I know. Not yet. Help me out, would you. Your name? I'm forgettin'."

"Jim."

"Oh, my goodness," Diana exclaimed. "I forgot my manners. Oh, please excuse me, Riles. I need to finish orderin' what we need and pay for it."

"Things you've purchased?" Riles said.

"Yes, I...."

"Ma'am." Riles raised his left hand and looked at the clerk. "Well, little brother of Fredrick. I figure you're a little brother 'cause Fredrick's the oldest."

The clerk smiled. "Jim. James Brackston." He extended his hand. Riles took it.

"James." Riles smiled. "Once Diana's through orderin',I'll need to add to her list."

Riles looked at Diana. "Ma'am," he said, "your turn."

"Thank you." She looked at James Brackston. "As I was tellin' you, I'm gonna need a fifty pound sack of beans, flour, corn meal, ten pounds of salt, five of baking powder, baking soda, and ten pounds of sugar. If you have it. If you don't....well, we'll do without."

"I'm sure we can fill your order, Ma'am. It shouldn't take long. Your wagon is outside?"

"Buckboard, yes."

James looked at Riles, as if to say what else would you like to add.

"Jim, we'll need two hundred pounds of beans, two hundred pounds of flour, as well as two hundred pounds of corn meal. Need a gallon of molasses, a gallon of maple syrup. I'd like a thousand rounds of 44-40, a hundred rounds of 45s. I'm thinkin' I need a hundred rounds of 44s. We'll need shoes for Katie, here, and Josh. Make 'em a little big. As you can tell, we're expectin' company.

"James, how are you fixed for horse shoes? Black Beauty? We're gonna need a couple of cans," Riles added. "Ma'am, horseshoes?"

"We don't have any. But, Riles,--"

"Jim, we'll need fifty pounds each of number 3 through 6. You got any salt pork? If you do, I need fifty pounds."

Diana interrupted. "We have some hogs, Riles. Just need to butcher 'em."

"James, fifty pounds, if you have salt pork."

"Riles, I can't pay for these things."

"Understood, Diana." She nodded, her eyes growing larger.

"Jim, I'm thinkin' we need ten boxes of ten gauge shotgun shells. I'm thinkin' four tins of Black Beauty Grease instead of two. You do that for me, James? Soon as you get that together, we'll be right outside. We'll bring a freight wagon around and a buckboard, so you and your boys can load 'em up. We'll need to go over our list to make sure we have what we need."

"All right," James Brackston responded, perhaps a little surprised.

Riles turned to Diana. "Now, Ma'am. There anything else you're forgettin'? Now's the time. We're here."

"I... I can't pay for this, Riles."

"I ain't askin' you to pay for it, Diana. Your money don't spend here. I'm askin' you, you forgot anything? That's what I'm askin'. I've added shoes for my niece and nephew. This girl ain't wearin' shoes. Neither is her brother. It'll be comin' winter in four or five months. See to her shoes, would you? Your boy, too. Diana, anything else? Do they need winter coats? The snow on Sage Creek ain't nothin' to laugh at. Will they be needin' coats?"

"I..."

"Please."

"All right, it's just...."

"Diana, we won't be comin' this way for a number of months. Get what you need. I read your letter. If I remember right, you and Pistol are lookin' up to see the bottom. Time to stock up. You certainly know better than I what should be on that list and that you ain't ordered. Tell James here. It ain't the time to be holdin' back. When you're needin' a coat ain't the time to be orderin' it."

"I, I..."

"I, what?"

"I could use an ax handle. And a handle for the pitchfork. Maybe just a pitchfork. Some staples. Some tenpenny nails, some spikes. You don't have to get all this stuff for us, Riles. We got four dollars and forty-four cents. You can't...."

"Your money don't spend, Diana. Put it in your pocket. Get what you need. In an hour or two, we'll be headin' north."

Diana turned to the clerk. "Well, James," she said, "we're in need of a pitchfork, a couple of 'em. An axe handle. And I'm thinkin' we're a little short on nails, fencin' staples."

"You got all that, James?" Riles asked. "Better make that four oak axe handles, four pitchfork handles, a couple of claw hammers."

James Brackston smiled. "I'll put your order together. We'll need a little more time. If I have any questions, I'll ask. Nice to see you again, Riles. The Stocktons haven't changed much."

Riles smiled. "James, you have any questions, just ask away. While you're thinkin' on it, Katie Sue here tells me she's a little light on hard rock candy. I'm thinkin' she'll be needin' a nickel's worth."

"I think I can handle that."

"See that you do and thank you. We'll be outside across the street in front of that bank, you got any questions."

"Yes. Thank you."

"Before we leave, if you could help this little gal out with her rock candy. I'd be grateful. I'm thinkin' those red and white sticks too...that taste of peppermint. She has a sawed off brother out front with her father. Both Katie Sue and Josh have had a rough day bakin' their brains out there in the sun. Don't wanna leave 'em high and dry and without."

"If you'll wait? It will take me but a minute."

"Good. Yes, we'll wait."

Riles turned to Diana and smiled. "Ma'am," he said. "Think it over. Add whatever item you're light on. James is gonna be a little busy."

Diana glanced at the clerk then back at her brother-in-law. "Riles," she said, "I... I, as long as you understand we can't afford this. We didn't sell the yearlings and we ain't got no yearlings to sell."

"I reckon they're somewhere. We'll find 'em. Right now, I'm hungry. So's Mary Sue, here. She ain't ate, either. I'm feelin' a might famished, myself. I 'm guessing the Calico serves beans, elk steak, cornbread, and sassafras tea. You interested?"

"I'm Katie Sue," the child interjected.

"Excuse me, Miss. Katie Sue, it is."

He turned to Diana. "Ma'am," he said, "I'll cover it. If we're a little light, I'll rob a bank. Been doin' it for a livin'."

"You what?"

"Diana, for hell's sake. Let's go find a eatin' place. I'm hungry. Pistol's hungry and Katie Sue, she's hungry. I'll pay for it. It's best we not leave here hungry."

"Pistol? You call him Pistol? I didn't know that."

"Yeah, that's what I call my sawed off, half pint, little brother, broken leg and all. Please? Let's get outta here. After you, Diana."

Diana didn't move.

"Come on, Carlie Sue. Your ma wants to watch the rest of us eat. I ain't figured her out yet."

"Oh, I do not. I just can't figure the Stocktons out. No patience. It's always now. Now. Now."

"Katie Sue. I"m Katie."

"You are? You sure?"

"I'm Katie Sue."

94

"You sure as hell are. I forgot."

"You're funny."

"That's the rumor."

Riles looked at Diana. "Ma'am," he said, suddenly turning sober.

Diana interrupted him. "Really," she said. "Really, I don't understand you Stocktons. None of you listen. I tried to tell you we's limited on what we can spend and you won't listen to me at all."

"You're out of money, I'll spend mine. You wrote me a letter sayin' you need help. I'm helpin'. What's there to understand?"

"I...."

"Diana, I'm tellin' you we're about to spend the hell outta this place. You're not to worry. Get what you need. Ain't like we can't use it."

"Really?"

"Really."

"But you wanna eat first?"

"Yes."

"All right. I'm not fightin' with you. I'm not fightin' Petey. I'm not fightin'. Really, I'm not."

Riles smiled at her. "Well, that's good," Riles said, looking at James who'd reappeared, holding two small sacks of rock candy.

"For the girl," he said, "and the boy." He handed one of the sacks to Katie Sue.

Riles glanced at Katie Sue. "Well girl, better tell the man thank you. He just made your day."

CHAPTER 12

There are different kinds of injuries, different cures, different levels of endurable and unendurable pain. A man can, on a Spring morning, step into the saddle of an old, cantankerous barn horse, one that has never hurt a soul, and get turned inside out and thrown through the chicken coop for his efforts. In the process, he can get stepped on, stomped on and wind up with a broken leg, a broken arm, or a broken neck. As a result of this Spring morning exercise, he may end up on the couch for six months while the bone mends. His life is put on hold; he gets nothing done, while wasting away, consumed by frustration. And it hurts.

Suffering a different injury, the same man can have his heart broken by a lady saying "no," she would not marry him even if he was the Pharaoh in Egypt and was worth ten thousand dollars standing before her in his stocking feet. Sometimes the injury is not physical. Something as simple as not being able to say goodbye can be just as traumatic. In either case, the heart and soul can take ten minutes or ten years to heal. It may never heal. This pain can be neverending, the wound open and bleeding. Recovery from either may never occur.

When Myrtle May Waggoner entered Brackston General and saw Diana talking to a strange, unkempt man, holding in his arms a five year old girl that was obviously Diana's, she hurried straight to her. Without saying a word, she threw her arms around her and wept, her heart breaking.

Diana knew Myrtle. She'd known her as a knobby-kneed girl, known her as a child dressed in an ankle length blue pinafore, her hair put up in curls. As children, they'd attended grammar school together. They'd played kick the can, tag, steal the bacon, and hopscotch. They'd gone to each other's weddings at the First Presbyterian Church, had been with the other at the travail of their first born child. Diana, without thought, wrapped her arms around her friend, extending comfort, not knowing the cause of her friend's deep sobs or the depth of her pain. Clearly, she was suffering.

"Mud," she said softly, "what's wrong? Are you all right?"

"I'm so sorry," Myrtle answered. "I'm so sorry." And she wept, tears running down her face, an unending torrent of inconsolable sorrow. "So very sorry."

"Sorry for what, Mud?" Diana asked, patting her on the shoulder, concern emanating for her friend, schoolmate, and fellow traveler. "What's wrong, Mud?" she asked again. "What is it? Who hurt you so?"

"Your sisters…."

"My sisters?" Diana said, repeating her friend's words. "What do you mean?"

"And your father."

"My father?" What about my sisters, my father? What are you saying?"

"Oh my God, you don't know?"

"Know what?" Diana asked.

"Oh, my sweet, sweet friend. It shouldn't be me telling you this. I am so sorry, Dee, but they are dead. They've passed. Killed. You poor thing. Oh, what have I done? You didn't know, you didn't know."

"Mud? Mud. What are you sayin', Mud? Are you talkin' about Claire and Betsy? Sally? You must be mistaken. Slow down. Explain to me what you're talkin' about."

"Diana, some monster shot your father in the back. Killed him, oh so dead. But that was six or eight weeks ago. I thought you knew. Your sisters found his killer. Ten, ten days later. Sally shot him with your Pa's shotgun. Killed him dead, the bastard. The Sheriff hung your sisters two weeks ago, sayin' it was murder killin' that man like they did. I'm so sorry. I thought you knew. It was horrible."

Diana, the oldest child of four, a woman always in control, covered her mouth with her hand, her eyes blinking in disbelief. Diana, standing in Brackston General, lost her grip on Myrtle. She lost her grip on herself, turned to Riles Stockton without seeing him. Her daughter was staring at her. They both were. Diana didn't see her daughter, either. She turned, looked around herself in shock and saw nothing. She took a step toward Riles, hesitated, stopped herself, wordlessly shook her head. She opened her mouth to speak, then collapsed. The floor reached up to catch her as she fell into a heap at

97

Riles' feet, falling between stacks of Pendleton blankets, winter coats, shovel handles and muskrat traps. Her head slammed against the wood with a dull thud, bouncing twice. Diana Stockton did not feel the pain; she didn't know she'd passed out. She was gone. She suffered injury, not only to her head, to her body and soul, but to her heart, from which she never, ever would recover.

Katie Sue screamed in alarm, struggling, fighting Riles' arms to get to the floor and to her mother. Myrtle stepped back, staring at Diana sprawled on the floor.

"What have I done?" she exclaimed.

Riles Stockton set his barefooted niece on the hardwood floor and reached for his sister-in-law, seizing her, lifting her from the floor, her body loose and limp in his arms.

Katie Sue was crying. "Momma, oh Momma, what's wrong, Momma? Please don't leave me. What's wrong?"

Riles Stockton took control. It was his job. It was where he lived and had lived since he was ten years old. His father had insisted upon it. "Myrtle, Mud," he said, "whoever the hell you are, get hold of yourself. I need you to take Katie Sue by the hand. Pick her up. We're goin' across the street. I'm takin' this woman to Pistol. I need you to bring the child. Do you understand? We'll sort this out across the street. Follow me. Follow me now."

Myrtle Wagoneer did as she was told. Moving directly to Katie Sue, she picked up the delirious, inconsolable child and followed Riles Stockton out of Brackston General into the street. Riles Stockton bore the limp body of Diana. He didn't stop. A buckboard was forced to avert running over him, causing the driver to stand up, pulling back on the ribbons, cursing as Riles passed in front of his horses. The one-eyed dog was at his side carrying a deep growl, looking this way and that, sounding like he was about to kill, flay, and eat a horse. One of the horses that Riles cut in front of reared up, started prancing, side stepping, pulling his mate with him. Stockton paid no attention. The one-eyed dog stopped in the street, stood his ground. The horses backed up. The driver was still standing in his buckboard, cursing, pulling on the reins, trying to settle his team. The one-eyed dog took a step forward, growling at the man and his animals.

Peter, seeing his brother with Diana in his arms, started to stand up, broken leg or no.

"Sit," Riles directed. "I'll bring her to you."

"Is she, she...?"

"Passed out," Riles explained.

"Passed out? What happened?"

Riles lifted Diana's body over the sideboard, her husband receiving her, gathering her in his arms, pulling her limp body to him.

Riles Stockton glanced toward the street, seeing the one-eyed dog holding the traffic at bay. He said, "Over here, Dog. Get over here. Let him go." The dog hesitated, then walked toward Riles, leaving the man in the middle of the street, red faced and shaken.

Riles turned to his brother. "She just found out that her sisters and her Pa are dead."

"What? What did you say?" Peter Stockton asked incredulously, full of shock and disbelief himself.

Riles turned to Myrtle. "Ma'am," he said, "set the girl in the wagon next to her mother. She'll be all right. Then explain to Pistol what you told Diana a few minutes ago."

At first a flummoxed Myrtle didn't say anything. Her mouth didn't work.

"Mud," Peter said, "what? Tell me what you told Dee."

Myrtle set the sobbing, sniffling girl in the wagon bed. "I didn't know she didn't know, Pete. I told her that her sisters are dead, that the Sheriff hung her sisters for killin' the man who shot their Pa. I thought she knew. I didn't mean to upset her. I was trying to tell her how sorry I was. I didn't know she didn't know. I really didn't."

Riles said, "Ma'am, you're doin' fine. Pistol, did you know anything about this?"

"I still don't."

"Ma'am, when did this happen?"

"A little more than two weeks ago. July 2."

"You said the sheriff hung them?"

"Yes."

Suddenly Riles Stockton produced, seemingly from out of nowhere, two SAA Colt revolvers, their hammers pulled back and no longer sitting on an empty chamber. The one-eyed dog at Riles

99

Stockton's side, started growling as if they'd both been attacked. Cecil turned his head to the Buckskin. Time froze like water when the weather turns forty below and a gale is drifting dry snow through the cottonwoods and pine.

"Sheriff," Riles said, his voice ugly, hard, and raw, "you've got some explainin' to do, sir. You got five seconds to do it. I'm unaware of any excuse for hangin' three girls for killin' some son of a bitch that killed their Pa. I'm unaware of any excuse for hangin' three girls at all."

Peter and Mud turned to see who he was talking to, unaware that the sheriff for the city of Kane had suddenly made an appearance and was standing next to Mud, a step behind her, peering over the top of the wagon box at Diana.

Diana moaned. Normally, she would be the sole and immediate object of Peter Stockton's concern, but his wife lying passed out in the back of a buckboard wasn't normal. Not at this moment in time. Not with Riles suddenly on attack. Peter's hands were instantly full of a Winchester 44-40 pointed directly at the star on the man's chest. He was a fraction of a second late to the party, his arms no longer steadying his wife.

Peter heard Riles say in a measured tone, "Sheriff, the only issue here is which of us is gonna kill you: me or my brother."

Sheriff Wesley Bufford was surprised, shocked, for he'd just walked up to a man carrying what looked like a dead woman. He hadn't said a thing. He took a step backwards. Two pistols and a rifle centered on his chest. He opened his mouth. Nothing came out. He had that sense that he was a dead man if he didn't do something. And he wanted to. "Want to" sometimes just doesn't get it done. Bufford was lucky that hot July day that Myrtle Waggoner was there; she saved his life.

"Not him!" she screamed. "Not him, Mr. Stockton! The sheriff in Basin City. The County Sheriff. Jason Gilson. Not Sheriff Bufford. This one, he didn't do anything. I didn't mean him."

Diana groaned again. Peter's right index finger was still tight against the trigger, the grooves pressing against the calloused flesh, waiting for any excuse.

"I," Sheriff Bufford stammered. "I...."

Peter interrupted him. "I, what? Did you or did you not kill my wife's sisters? Hang 'em by the neck?"

"Did not. I had nothin' to do with that. Nothin' at all. I came over here because I saw the woman. Just now. I wanted to...."

"Don't need help," Riles stated. "Sure as hell we don't need help from you. We do our own killin'."

"I..."

Riles interrupted. "Get the hell out of here. You listenin'?"

"I..."

"Did you hear me?"

Bufford heard him. It was crystal clear. In further response, Bufford raised both hands, palms out, fingers up, a sign of submission, contrition.

CHAPTER 13

Sometimes its best not to kick the sleeping dog; sometimes it's best to walk away. Sheriff Bufford started backing away: four steps, then five, and turned, walking across the dusty street, heat waves bouncing off the street, the boardwalk, and the store fronts. He moved straight ahead, imagining the rifle in Peter Stockton's hands still pointed at his back. Later, he realized it wasn't the rifle that bothered him but the two pistols, the voice that cut him to the quick telling him to leave, stating he wasn't needed or wanted. Sheriff Bufford walked away without looking back.

An hour later, after making his rounds, he climbed up the steps in front of the Shoshone Bar. Taking a deep breath, he let it out, considering himself fortunate to be alive. Then he made his way inside, found his corner table, and sat down, his back against the wall. A few minutes later he was joined by Rich Larson, all fifty six years of him.

Rich Larson was an odd man. Everything was a production with him, even sitting down. First, he pulled the chair away from the table, placed his hat on the edge farthest from him. Then he pulled a sack of Bull Durham from his shirt pocket and set it on the table in front of him followed by six or ten wooden matches. Now he was ready to sit and did, resting his elbows on the table. Leaning forward, he took a deep breath, then pulled one off-white sheet of tobacco paper from a little blue packet he carried in his right shirt pocket.

After all of that, Sheriff Bufford said to Larson, "Let me buy you a beer."

"Be my guest, Wes. You look like you had enough for one day. What's botherin' you? Some law-abidin' citizen stomp all over your fresh dug grave, not knowin' you ain't dead yet?"

"What's not botherin' me? Not more than an hour ago I saw these folks carryin' a woman's body across the street. Out in front of Brackstons. She looked dead: her hands, legs, and arms danglin' uncontrollably, her head all the way back, rollin' 'round. I hurried over to see what that was all about. See if I could help. I just got there lookin' over the wagon box and this fellow palmed two pistols. They was pointin' right at me, hammers back. And the other fellow sittin' inside the wagon box--he pulled a Winchester. I was a dead man every which way but Sunday. So yes, somebody stomped all over my grave that ain't been dug yet."

"Hell's fire, Wes. I ought to buy you a beer."

"You should. That fellow holdin' the pistols…it was the eyes," he told Rich. "I've never seen such hatred, such contempt, such willingness to kill in all my life. He wanted me dead like yesterday. He wanted to snatch the life right outta my chest. I'm tellin' you, he would have killed me except for that woman, Myrtle Waggoner. She saved me. I swear. I never wanna feel that feelin' again. Ever."

"Know who it was? Seen 'em before?" Rich Larson asked. He'd folded the cigarette paper around his index finger and was pouring tobacco into it, spreading and smoothing it out the length of the paper.

"Yeah, I do. The one in the wagon? The one with the rifle? That was Peter Stockton. Broke his leg a while back. Remember? Myrtle called the other one Mr. Stockton. I ain't never seen him before today. I've been here goin' on six years and he was new to me. Can't say that I wanna see him again. I'm tellin' you he just didn't care."

"A Mr. Stockton? Myrtle Waggoner? A woman passed out or dead, and a fellow with a broke leg and a rifle?"

"Yeah."

"You're right, the fellow with the broke leg was Peter. The woman you was lookin' at, bet she's a Stafford."

"The story gets better, Rich. I got a telegram. I should say Mrs. Eleanore Olson got a telegram. Elle. Know her? Martin Olson's wife. She brought it to me to read. She said it was from her brother. He lives in California. The telegram warned me of a Syrus Stockton. Said he was comin' to Kane bringin' his guns, expectin' a gunfight and a funeral. Said it was really someone named Rodney Brooks who calls himself Stockton sometimes."

"The shootist?"

"You heard of him?"

"I've heard of Rodney Brooks. Lives down in Texas. A backshooter, is what I heard. There is a Syrus Stockton. Two different people, though. Syrus is the second oldest brother. Peter's the youngest. His brothers call him Pistol. The oldest is Riles, which is who I think you was discussin' life over pistols with. The other brother is Forest Stockton. Goes by Far. Nice fellow. Met him when he was about nineteen. I'd have to say that Syrus--he's the worst of the lot. That's what I'm told anyways. I don't think you met him. If you had, we'd be buryin' you 'bout now. The Stocktons--they're a rough outfit. They keep to themselves as a practice. Don't wanna be bothered. There's a rumor I heard recently that someone stole Stockton MT cows. Did it after Pistol broke his leg and was down and couldn't do nothin' about it."

"You don't say?"

Rich Larson rolled the cigarette paper and licked it, twisting the ends to keep the tobacco from falling out. He stuck the cigarette in the corner of his mouth and offered the Bull Durham sack to Wes. Wes declined.

"Listen, Wes," Rich said, "if that rumor is true, I'd stay as far away from them Stocktons as you can possibly get. If someone puts a burr under their saddle, folks will start dyin' 'round here. You can count on it. Like hell's on fire. I'm tellin' you. That town sextant might as well hire three or four fellows and start diggin' graves. A passel of 'em. Within ten days, he'll have plenty of bodies to fill 'em. With what Gilson did to those Stafford girls, I wouldn't give a rat's ass for his life. I'd say his life is numbered in hours, maybe days: not weeks, or months. You see, the Stocktons and the Staffords, they're related. Pistol married the oldest Stafford girl. But it's more than that I'm thinkin'."

Billy Bangor, the Shoshone bartender, stopped by their table. "How's it goin', gents?" he asked, sittin down in the extra chair and picking up Rich's Bull Durham sack without asking. Rich handed him his blue pack of cigarette papers.

"Billy," Rich said, "Wes here just ran into Riles Stockton. Heard of him?"

"Jeez, Wes, you ain't havin' a very good day. Yeah, I've heard of him. Everybody's heard of him." He smiled. "Except you, Wes."

104

"Now I have."

Billy Bangor leaned over the table, lowered his voice. "You ain't heard this from me but folks are sayin' the whole clan is gettin' together. Rumor is they's related to those Stafford girls they done hung in Basin City. People think that them Stocktons, once they find out, ain't gonna be takin' kindly to it. That's the word lately."

"I don't know if it's all that bad, Billy," Rich Larson said, laughing. "Though it's probably worse. It makes me laugh. In my younger day, time 'fore I got religion, I was stealin' horses from the Crow over on the Dry Head and Arrow Creek."

"You mean 'fore you got married, don't you?" Wes said.

Rich looked at the Sheriff, smiled, and said, "That, too. Mostly that. You never heard this from me, Wes. I'll deny it straight up. Anyway, that's where the Stocktons live. Run their cows there. My old man knew those boys. I'd bring them Indian ponies home to work the green out of 'em. He told me a half dozen times if he told it to me once: don't go stirrin' up the Stocktons."

Rich struck a match on the sole of his boot and brought the fire to the end of his hand-rolled cigarette. He took a long draw, blew smoke off to the side, and looked at Wesley Bufford. "That's good advice, Wes. I never took no Stockton horse. Never borrowed, never ate no Stockton cow. You best believe it."

Rich Larson paused. "I don't mean to bore you none, Wes. You got somewheres to be? I'm just runnin' off at the mouth. You wanna hear the rest of that story? This ain't no rumor, either." He took a drag on his cigarette.

The Sheriff and Billy Bangor looked at him, waiting.

"All right, I'll tell you," Rich said. "Ain't gonna make no difference and you ain't got nowheres to be. My old man lived a good, long life. The way he told it, he knew Carl Stockton and Jake Stafford. Came up the trail from Texas together. Settled here. When Ma got sick, Carl and Jake was standin' on our porch; they put a couple of their steers in our horse corral. Told Pa to eat the sonstabitches. They worked our cows in the spring, put our brand on the ribs of every steer, every heifer. When the yearlings and two year olds was ready to sell, they took 'em to market and gave the Old Man the money. Didn't keep a cent. Didn't ask for nothin'. Carl Stockton

105

was those boys' old man. That ain't no rumor. That's the Gawd's truth. I saw thet, myself. When those folks from down on the Popo Agee started rustlin' Pa's cows, they showed up, run 'em down, and hung every one. Two of those Stockton boys you run into across the street done it. Not the youngest. The second--Syrus, he's probably comin'. That means Far ain't but a couple of days out."

No shit. Think they're all comin'?"

"No shit, my friend. It's the Gawd's truth. You best be a believer."

"Oh, I'm a believer, Rich. I looked down the barrel of those pistols and I got all sorts of religion, myself. You can take that to the State Bank and spend it. I'm a believer."

"Good. Let me add to your sheriffin' worries. I was over at Calico an hour ago."

"So?"

"There was a feller over there I ain't never seen before."

"And?"

"Thin man, narrow face, big ears, dressed in black like a sextant ready to bury some soul, or a preacher ready to preach hot hell. Hair was long, straight, all pulled back like the Crow did from time to time, 'cept it wasn't braided. Had it tied so it fell down his back. He wasn't playin' no pool. He wasn't eatin'. He wasn't drinkin'. He wasn't playin' cards. Everything you do over at the Calico, he wasn't doin'. Carried a hideaway, right sleeve, and a knife in his left boot. Odd combination, for he was right handed. Ol' Bucko was askin' around. Seemed real interested. Know what he was askin' about?" Rich paused, staring intently at Wesley Bufford. "Guess."

"I can't guess. How's I to know?"

"Riles Stockton."

"No shit?"

"No shit."

"Wonder if this Riles knows 'bout him?"

Rich Larson laughed. "I grew up within fifty miles of here. Lived here most of my life. I know'd everybody. It's been twenty years ago, if my remembrance is any good at all, last I saw Riles Stockton. I'm tellin' you, if a buck farts over there on the Pryor, that Riles Stockton knows 'bout it. Damn right he knows. In twenty-four

106

hours all them Stocktons will know. Let me tell you, how y'all will know what I'm sayin' is the Gawd's truth."

"All right, Rich," Wesley said, "I'll bite. How'll we know?"

"Go over there to Brackstons. Ask Jimmy Brackston what those folks bought. If they got themselves more ammunition than flour, you'll know them Stocktons got themselves a burr festerin' under their saddle. Don't believe me? Just go ask little Jimmy Brackston. He'll tell you."

CHAPTER 14

Myrtle Waggonner, peering over the side of the wagon box, stared at the limp figure of her friend. Diana did not speak., made no attempt to move. She lay still, wrapped in the comforting arms of her husband. It was as though someone had hauled off and smacked her with an Abner Doubleday baseball bat, leaving a residue of pain and anguish permeating her heart. Myrtle Waggonner could only imagine the intensity of her grief; a grief so immense that Diana did not move a finger.

Pain and loss are twins that travel together and make idiots of all who suffer a death, mocking us as we struggle to understand the incomprehensible. The question is "why?" It's the same for every living soul. The answer is always "who knows?" It is a proverbial truth, for there is no recovery from a graveyard loss. Time passes and dulls the memory, but there is no recovery. It does not quench the pain that lurks beneath the soft veneer that is the human soul. It is a memory that wanders through our lives leaving an empty cup sitting on the table, never touched, never filled, never used again. No one can replace the loss of three sisters and a father. Not ever.

Diana stirred, moaning and looking up at her husband. Riles Stockton studied his sister-in-law, then glanced at Peter.

"She's gonna be all right, Pistol," he concluded. "In time. Unfortunately, we don't have time. We can't wait for her to get better. Knowin' what we do, we gotta be movin'. Sittin' here ain't safe for anybody, especially her."

"I know. but what can we do? I mean Riles, look at her."

"Yeah, she's in bad shape. But we gotta be movin'. You bring this buckboard around so Brackston's people can load it up. I'll get us another."

"Riles?"

"Pistol, now! You gotta move. Somebody wiped out her entire family. She's all that's left. They, whoever they are, are comin' for her. To keep her and you and your kids alive, we gotta move. Right now."

"Ah, horseshit."

"Yeah, mostly that. Now make her comfortable and bring this buckboard around so those boys across the street can load up."

"All right."

Riles Stockton looked down at his sister in law. "You're gonna be all right, Diana," he assured her. "You're gonna make it just fine. Peter will help you."

Riles Stockton turned away, throwing the rein over the Buckskin's neck. He stepped into the saddle and started the Buckskin down the street, the sorrel followed, his lead rope tied to the straps on the back of the saddle. The dog moved, coming to all fours. Diana forced herself to sit up; she watched him walking away: a broad shouldered, solitary man, followed by an ugly, one-eyed dog, a sorrel mare and Cecil, the mule.

Myrtle had been listening to the exchange. "I'm so sorry, Pete," Myrtle began. "I thought she knew. It makes me so sad just thinkin' about it." Tears started welling up in her eyes. "I wanted her to know how badly I felt."

"You couldn't have known, Myrtle. We sure didn't. Now that we do, we gotta protect ourselves. Thanks for tellin' us. I know it was difficult. We needed to know and you told us. Go home, Myrtle. Best you stay out of it. It's gonna get a bit rough. Best you go home."

Across the street, in front of Brackston General, goods were being counted and stacked on the boardwalk for loading.

"All right, Pete. Take care of Dee, will you."

"I will."

Myrtle turned away and walked across the street.

Diana, sitting up, took several deep breaths, and glanced at Peter. She covered her eyes with her left hand, stifling a sob that seemed to well up inside her. Silence extended from one moment to the next. She tried to muster some relevant words and couldn't. Diana turned. She let her eyes rest on her husband's face.

"Oh, Petey," she said, "what are we gonna do now? I thought with Riles here our problems was solved. That somehow we could get back on our feet. But now, Pa's dead. And my sisters hanged? We can't. It's just impossible." She closed her eyes. Tears ran down her flushed cheeks. She sobbed. "I don't know what to do."

"Right now," Petey replied, "we're not gonna do anythin' 'cept load this buckboard. In three days, we'll be on the Creek and we'll be home. First thing we'll do is get our feet under us. We'll do just what we can do. No more."

Peter stood up balancing himself on one leg. He glanced across the street at the Brackston storefront *Better hurry*, he thought. *Loadin' this buckboard won't take long. Riles will have another wagon comin'.* A sense of urgency began creeping into his being. *Those sonstabitches, he* thought. *This ain't over. It's just beginnin'.*

"Dee," he said. "Sit still, now. Kids, come up here and sit with your mother." Peter looked down at his wife. "I'm gonna move this buckboard around so we can load up. You gonna be all right?" he asked.

Tears streamed down her face. "All right? Petey, somebody killed my pa and my sisters. I'm not gonna be all right. Not ever."

Peter nodded. "I know," he said.

"That's how I feel."

"I understand, Dee. I'm sorry about your sisters. Your pa...."

Peter carefully climbed up on the seat, moving past Diana, grabbing the reins wrapped around the brake. He slapped the bays on the butt with the ribbons. "Hey you," he yelled. The horses lurched forward. "Gee, gee, gee," he called to them, pulling on the left ribbon. They came around slowly, crossing the dusty street in a tight circle, pulling to a stop in front of Brackston General. Peter wrapped the ribbons around the brake, and turned to see his wife and kids crowding into the corner of the buckboard behind the jockey box.

The front door of the General Store opened, and the Wilson boy, whose Dad ran the livery, came out with the fifty pounds of flour Diana had bought. Behind him came the two hundred pounds she hadn't ordered. It didn't take long to fill the buckboard and crowd the space in which she and the two kids were sitting.

Riles Stockton returned half an hour later with a Conestoga freight wagon pulled by two Belgians. The sides were four feet deep without hoops. The wheels were wider, rims thicker. He pulled the freighter in behind the buckboard and alongside the Brackston boardwalk.

"Where'd you get that wagon?" Peter asked him.

110

"Wilson. He owed me. Now I owe him. One of these days we'll get it figured out. By the way, you owe him a couple a steers," Riles said, stepping down from the seat to the boardwalk."

Nodding at Jim Brackston, Riles said, "All right, Mr. James, load this one."

Jim Brackston gave directions for loading the second wagon. Then he and Riles Stockton stepped inside to settle up. When he returned, the men were finishing loading the freighter. The Conestoga freighter had more room and some to spare.

Riles eyed the wagon and glanced at Peter. "You two figure it out," he said. "Either Katie and Josh ride with me on the big wagon and Diana with you, Pistol. Or the other way around. Whichever you like. Figure it out. Let's get goin'."

Diana resolved the issue, if it had ever been one, by climbing out of the buckboard. She reached for her daughter and helped her up on the seat of the freighter. She climbed up behind her and seated herself. She patted Katie Sue on the leg. "You ready, Sugar? 'Cause we're about to go.

"I can do this," she said to Riles. "I ain't helpless. I ain't forgot how to handle a team."

Riles nodded. "Let me know if you change your mind. If you can't, I understand. I can do it. Just ask."

"I will," she said. "One thing I don't want to do is think. I'll be all right. Let's get goin' 'fore I change my mind."

Pete already had the buckboard going, turning it around in the middle of the street. She picked up the ribbons and slapped the work horses on the rump. The wheels began to turn. "Gee, gee, gee," she yelled. Around they came, heading north right down the middle of Sheridan Avenue.

"Momma," Katie said.

"What, Sweetie?"

"Are we in trouble?"

Diana glanced at Katie sitting beside her. She answered, "Yes, Sweetie, we're in trouble."

"Momma?"

"What, Sweetie?"

"What are we gonna do with all that flour?"

111

"I don't know. Make pancakes, I guess." Diana glanced at her daughter. "What's in the bag? Where'd you get that?"

"Candy. Hard candy. Uncle Riles gave it to me. He said I was gonna need it."

"He did, did he?"

"Momma?"

"What?"

"I think he's right."

Diana frowned, looking down the street at the Pryor mountains, two formidable waves of rock and trees forty miles distant..

Riles, riding the Buckskin, came up beside her.

"You all right, sister?" he asked. "You want me to skin that team of horses?

"No," she said. Diana looked over at him sitting his saddle horse. "I can do this, Riles. If I can't, I'll tell you.

"All right," he said. "Take 'em outta here slow. We got a long ways to go. First, stop at Wilsons."

"Got it," she answered.

Watching him ride out front, she knew then why his brothers followed him and she sensed they'd follow him through hell itself. With Riles Stockton there never was any misunderstanding. If there was, someone wasn't listening or they were dead. She sat beside her daughter and stared for a moment at his back. Then she slapped the ribbons on the butts of the horses. They lurched forward. They were moving.

Riles looked back at her, and held up on the Buckskin's reins, holding him in until Diana caught up.

"Keep that rifle handy," he said, "where you can grab it if need be. If we get stopped by anybody, pull her up and get behind the seat with that girl. Got it? We get stopped, you take cover."

"Is that necessary? Really?"

"It is now." he said. "Keep movin'. After we stop at Wilson's, this wagon needs to set the pace. It needs to be out front." Nodding, he touched the Buckskin with the rowels of his Mexican spurs and moved down the street, the one-eyed dog out in front. She watched as he looked at one side of the street, then the other.

112

CHAPTER 15

Standing on the boardwalk in front of the Calico, a tall, thin man, dressed in black--black pants, black boots, black vest—watched two wagons, one after the other, come around in the middle of the street and head north down Sheridan Avenue. He pulled a cigar from his coat pocket, lit it with a wooden match, and drew a breath of smoke, blowing it out into the street, the breeze taking it. A woman with a little boy walked past him; the boy looked up at him. The thin man winked at the youngster, then turned his attention back to the wagons. A horseman on the other side of the second wagon leaned forward. The horse stopped. An ugly dog came back to where he was sitting.

That'd be the Stocktons. Two of them anyway. Heard there were four. That'd be the younger one driving the second wagon, his leg propped up straight out in front of him. He ain't much. Laid up. Ain't seen him move more than a foot. That other one? Ain't seen him before. Can't say that I have. Now that one... he's a different matter.

Suddenly, the thin man realized the rider was staring right at him. He watched as a gloved hand came to his hat brim; two fingers touched it. A grin crossed his face as if he was taunting him.

Lord, how'd he even know I was here? He didn't. He couldn't. I'm jumpy. Too jumpy. What's wrong with me? Like he stepped on my grave. Don't make no difference. Now, he knows. If not, maybe he suspects I'm comin' for him. And the younger one. Him, too. He'll know, too. How can he know? He ain't much, but sure as hell he'll know if he don't already. He don't. No, he don't. But that other fellow? Sure seemed like he did. Hell's fire, that ain't good. Best they don't know. What am I thinkin'? They don't know. I'm a tad jumpy.

CHAPTER 16

Minutes later, Diana pulled the Belgian horses to a stop in front of Wilson Livery. She turned to see Riles stepping down from his Buckskin and walking towards her.

"Diana," he said, "tie them ribbons to the brake lever. Those Belgians won't go nowhere. Go inside and roust old man Wilson outta his easy chair. Ask him to top your load off with fifty pound sacks of oats. It'll take him and that hand of his five or ten minutes. Already paid for." He smiled. "Oats for the horses," he clarified. "Soon as you're loaded, start movin'. I'll be back before then."

"What are you gonna do?"

"I saw someone who I believe was lookin' for me three, four months back. In Pendleton, of all places. I'm gonna see how he's gettin' along."

Riles glanced at Peter sitting uncomfortably above the jockey box of the buckboard, Josh beside him, his little fist tightly holding the sack of hard rock candy. "Hey, little brother, you'd better keep a round or two in that Winchester. No empty chambers. Sound familiar?" He laughed. "Told Diana the same. I'll be gone for a minute or two. Got someone I wanna talk to. Thought I'd get the fiddler started whistlin' Dixie." Riles smiled at Peter. "If fiddlers do any whistlin'. Be a minute. Soon as you can, get movin'. Diana should go first. The freighter is heavier, slower. Her goin' first will set the pace. With a little luck, we'll make Crooked Creek by nightfall."

Turning back to his horse, he took the reins and mounted. The sorrel mare was tied behind the buckboard. Cecil was standing beside her, stretching his neck, looking around.

From her seat, Diana watched Riles Stockton as he spun the Buckskin around and walked him south down Sheridan Avenue.

Climbing down, she walked over to Peter sitting on the buckboard. "What's that all about?" she asked.

"I don't know," Peter answered. "Best to get Wilson loadin' those oats. I expect we'll find out soon."

She watched as Peter picked up his rifle, working the lever to

114

make sure there was a live round in the chamber. Josh sat beside him, his eyes big and round, his mouth working on a peppermint stick.

Peter turned to find Diana still staring up at him. About to say something to her, she said, "Okay, Okay. I was just wonderin'."

"Diana, soon as they're finished loadin', let's get outta here. Riles ain't chatty. He means exactly what he says and he'll have a reason for it. I don't know what he has in mind. I do know he's serious. Expect trouble. Plan on it. It will find him. It always has."

"Shouldn't we wait for him? Just in case?"

"No. No, we shouldn't. He'll catch up. Get that wagon loaded. We gotta get out of here soon as we can. Riles, or no Riles."

CHAPTER 17

Riles Stockton walked through the back door of the Calico Saloon and made his way past the wood-burning cookstove, the sink full of dishes to be washed and rags to be cleaned, then out into the barroom. The one-eyed dog was behind him, the claws on his padded feet clicking on the hardwood floor. Riles let his eyes adjust to the dim light, to the layers of smoke that hung in the air like fog. A long mahogany bar occupied the north wall; bottles of rot gut liquor stood on the shelves behind it. Some of the bottles were empty, simply occupying space. He moved forward, nodded at the woman wearing a long apron streaked with bacon grease, flour, and syrup stains. She stepped around the dog and wordlessly proceeded through the back door into the kitchen.

Riles' nose was assaulted with the smell of smoke, on-tap beer, rot-gut whiskey, cigar and cigarette smoke, and unwashed bodies. Closest to him, at the extreme end of the long, heavily polished bar, stood a tall, thin man in dark clothes. It was he that Riles had seen on the street standing alone, leaning against a roof-supporting post, watching him. His back was to Riles, positioned to enable him to watch the front door and the men who came in and out. At his elbow rested a shot glass three quarters full of something akin to Jack Daniels whiskey. It wasn't Jack Daniels. Such was too good for the owner and his clientele. The darkly dressed man kept liquor at hand waiting to be lifted, sipped, and swallowed.

A cowkid wearing a newly ironed red shirt came inside and was immediately recognized by another sitting at a card table, an empty glass in front of him. The red shirt was in the process of building himself a quirley. The stranger found no threat with these two. To his surprise, an ugly, one-eyed dog walked out from behind him, taking a couple of steps down the long bar, acting like he owned the place. The dog stopped and looked back over his shoulder. The thin man stared, wondering what to do, what to think, and what was a big, ugly dog doing in the Calico?

Riles Stockton approached the thin man from behind while

his attention was on the one-eyed dog.

"Mister," Riles said, his voice soft, a sound easily lost in the quiet chatter.

Doubly surprised, the tall, thin man turned to the voice. Riles slapped him across the face with his leather gloves. Coming back the other way he slapped him again, only harder. It was a quick, stinging blow. The thin man didn't have the opportunity to throw an arm up to protect himself. It wouldn't have helped him. The sting of the gloves was followed with the sight of the round bore of an SAA Colt 44 staring unwaveringly at the man's nose.

"I know you," Riles said. "I know all about you. Hear you was lookin' for me. I know who you work for and what he's payin' you. It ain't near enough. It ain't nowhere near enough. You ain't that good. You'll never be that good. I want you to take that SOB a message. Hear me? Tell him I'm comin' for him. Tell him I'm gonna hang his ass from a cottonwood, watch him die slow. He done stole the wrong cows from the wrong folks. And you? I'd better never see you again. I'll drop this hammer on you right now, you ain't respectful of your betters. Hear me?"

The thin man nodded.

"What'd I say?"

"Take a message."

"That's right, and I mean right now."

"I heard you."

"Good. Now reach down and pick up that shot glass between your thumb and index finger. Drain it."

He did as he was told, unwittingly leaving some in the bottom of the glass, mystified as to how he'd allowed someone to come up unnoticed behind him, how he got the drop on him. The bore of the SAA 44 Colt didn't waver. He noted that small fact, as unsettling as it was. The face behind the pistol was dark, weather beaten, unshaved for a good week or ten days. Odd: the fellow holding the pistol didn't blink. The voice punched at him, made him wonder if he was still going to be breathing and alive at the end of the next ten seconds.

The voice said, "Now walk really slow to the other end of the bar. Don't turn right or left. Don't look back. You do, and I'll have to get some other two-bit hustler to deliver my message. Hear me?"

"Yes." He started to move toward the far end of the bar.

"I said slow. One other thing. You deliver the message and you better head south clear to the Mexican border. Hear me? You don't, and I'll kill you sure as water is wet."

"I hear you. I'm movin' slow."

"Damn right you are."

The thin man moved slowly, really slowly, exaggerating each step, feeling his feet touch the floor from inside his boots, the spurs ringing softly, conscious of every move of shoulder and hand. When he reached the end of the bar, he stopped, staring at the door because he didn't have anywhere else to look, certainly not wanting to look back, fearing it might be the last thing he ever did. He made it to the end of the bar where the barkeep was standing, watching him.

"You all right?" The bartender asked.

The thin man didn't answer. He turned his head cautiously, looking at the bartender, half expecting to hear or feel an explosion in his head. Down the bar where he'd just been, he saw his cigar standing in his almost empty shot glass; a small wisp of smoke disappeared into the air above it.

He looked at the bartender. "Did you see that?"

"See what?"

"That fellow?"

"I didn't see nobody. You sure you're all right? You look a bit peaked. Want another shot of whiskey?"

"No. No. I'm fine. I'm gonna go outside. Gotta take a walk. You didn't see nobody?" he asked.

"What do you mean?"

"I mean, did you see anybody come up behind me? Holdin' hisself a big bore 44 pokin' it in my face like he was fixin' to use it to dot my eyes? You didn't see nobody? Nobody at all?"

The bartender shook his head, staring at him.

"All right," the thin man said. "You do see that cigar sittin' there in my shot glass?"

The bartender glanced at the glass sitting in the middle of the counter at the end of the bar. "I see it."

"Who put that cigar in my glass? Who did that?"

"I guess you did."

118

"I didn't do it. I sure as hell didn't do it." The thin man paused, staring at the bartender. "I'm gettin' outta here," he said. "Before I lose my mind."

"Hope you're feelin' better," The bartender said, watching the thin man tug at the brim of his hat before turning toward the front door.

"Wonder what's with that fellow," he murmured before walking the length of the bar to pick up the shot glass, a half-smoked black stogie stuck in it like a broken swizzle stick. It was disgusting. *People do the damnedest things.* It made no sense. Cigars cost two bits. He knew. He sold them. He looked at the cigar soaking up the remaining dribs of cheap whiskey, then glanced at the doorway through which the thin man had disappeared in an anxious hurry.

"Well, I didn't see nobody," the bartender said to himself, tossing the cigar in the trash, then setting the shot glass in the tub of warm water he kept under the shiny, varnished wood surface of the bar. He shook his head, mystified, glancing at his patrons, noting that Billy Budd had purchased a new red shirt, double rows of black buttons. The kid looked good.

CHAPTER 18

Forest Eugene Stockman sat his horse on the south rise above Sage Creek; behind him was the timber covered saddle that lay between the east and west lobes of the Pryor Mountains. The two mountains blotted out the lower half of the southern sky. The Absaroka Crow, being superstitious, didn't like the mountain and were careful when they hunted there, not staying long if they could avoid it. They had a name for it: Baahpuuo Isawaxaawuua. According to folklore and their oral tradition it was where the Little People lived and hunted. Those dark timbered slopes were not safe.

Forest stared down the slope at several log buildings partially hidden in the cottonwood trees on the north side of the creek. His father built those buildings using a double-bladed axe and a big Morgan horse nearly forty years ago. Every one of his brothers was born there. It was where they grew up, where in seventy-nine their mother died from double pneumonia.

The noon sun was high overhead, shortening the shadows. Honey bees bothered the flowers that still blossomed on the south slope. The house, with its south side rock wall, housed a large shallow fireplace and supported a chimney reaching eighteen feet into the sky. Its shadow partially fell across the moss green shake shingle roof; small portions of the roof were dark under the shade of an old cottonwood. Forest remembered how he and Syrus had split the shakes from a sixty foot pine tree. They'd pulled it up under a two hundred year old cottonwood with two big bay work horses: Minnie and Sam. It had a thick trunk, a dead pine taken from a burn high up on the slopes of the West Pryor.

They'd used a cross-cut saw to cut the tree into eighteen inch sections; then splitting each section into shakes. Each section was measured against the ideal shake his father had cut before he left. Using the axe head of an axe that suffered from a broken oak handle, they split each tree section into shakes, first peeling the old pitch-soaked bark, keeping some for kindling. Riles had carried the shake shingles up a ladder twenty at a time, laying them in stacks on the

120

roof to be nailed: three nails to a shake: course after course after course. Forest wondered where the Old Man went when the work was was being done, how they got stuck with that thankless job.

It was an uneventful task. They'd run out of eight penny nails three quarters of the way through. They'd broken a hammer handle. Syrus had pushed Riles off the roof. It'd been hot that day and the next; they'd removed their shirts, browning their backs in the September sun. Their mother had made a drink out of chokecherry juice and sugar water, just enough sugar to make you want more. In the evening, clouds of mosquitoes had descended on the creek bottom; they were bad; the boys had reached for their shirts to keep from being eaten alive by the voracious bloodsuckers. They had repeatedly soaked their shirts in creek water. *The damn things never bothered Riles. Why was that? He's lucky that way,* Forest thought. Riles claimed it was "magic sweat."

The Old Man had little sayings he used, like "magic sweat." Riles had that sweat. He dished out wisdom and observations in disjointed sentences:

"A half baked cake ain't good for nothin'."

"Look before you fall in the hole in front of your boots and drown yourself dead."

"Slow down 'fore sunflowers are dried up and the lupine ain't worth smellin'."

"Don't jump in the swimmin' hole 'til you can touch the bottom."

"Know what you're gonna get before you get got."

Forest smirked at his befuddled memory, studying the buildings again, taking note of the obvious: no smoke rising from the chimney: no livestock standing in the corral: no bawling calves, no cows standing along the corral fence line. Chickens were busy pecking at the hardpack in the front yard like it harbored a ton of oats. Below the house, out on the west flat, fifteen or twenty head of saddle horses were grazing; a couple were fighting, rearing, striking with their hooves, baring their teeth. Soon they tired and started cropping grass. He noted three pigs running wild on Sage Creek below the house, shooting in and out of the cottonwoods and clumps of black willow. From the slope he could hear them grunting. He watched them hiding in the shade and shadows of the creek. They'd seen him. *Damn things*. A milk cow and a March calf stood at the edge of the yard in the shady side of the blacksmith shop. The calf was sucking its mother dry, butting, rooting at her bag with its nose, fighting for every drop. The cow grew tired of it and moved away from the calf.

Forest studied the log barn below the corral, noting the pole gate lying on its side, a panel of five lodgepoles on the ground, broken and lying helter skelter like the Gods had hit it with a big hammer. He concluded that the place was falling apart from lack of attention. Diana hadn't exaggerated. Nudging the Appaloosa with the heels of his boots, he started down the incline to the cold waters of Sage Creek. Forest didn't use spurs; he didn't like them.

Across the creek he paused, glancing over the compound, brushing the loop off the hammer of his SAA Colt 45. *Can't be too careful.* He remembered Riles' belief about the danger of leaving an empty chamber in a rifle. He felt the same. He never left the chamber open. Nor had the Old Man. He smiled, thinking about his pa's hoard of wisdom tied up in those catch phrases.

"Too careful leads to bein' too dead."

"What's the point of a six shooter with five cartridges? Wanna tell me that?"

The point was that unless you were very careful, a pistol could discharge because the firing pin rests directly on the center cap if you're carrying six. It could still fire, even if a man was careful. At the edge of the hardpack, Forest stepped down from the saddle, pulled his Winchester 44-40, and left the Appaloosa ground hitched. The milk cow, standing in the shade, chewing to a rhythm only she heard, stared at him. Her calf had given up on sucking her tits drier than they already were. The chickens paid him no mind, moving out of the way as he approached the house. He climbed the five porch steps and pushed the front door open. A surprised pack rat scurried across the floor. Pulling his pistol, Forest shot it.

Damn filthy thing.

Picking the pack rat up by the tail, he tossed it out into the yard for the chickens to examine. Forest started a fire in the fireplace. Smoke would keep the bees and squirrels out of the chimney, and he needed to heat water. Carrying water from the creek, he filled the pot in the fireplace and began cleaning the cupboards and the table. He removed the newly formed rat's nest from under the table. It took him all afternoon to do these simple chores.

The next morning, before sunrise, he shot a young buck, dressed it out, and hung the carcass to cool in the spring house. He cut two steaks and started frying the fresh meat over the soot blackened stove. Midmorning he got started on the horse corral. He found a shovel with an unbroken handle, dug three fence post holes, repaired the corral gate, got the milk cow in, and separated her from her calf.

Tonight I'll have milk, he thought. *Tomorrow or the next day I'll make some butter, bake some bread, kill a fools hen. The way I remember it, quite a few used to live on the creek. Nothin' like baked chicken and hot rolls drippin' with butter. Damn, I'd make some lucky girl a hell of a wife.*

On the second day he followed some honey bees and found a bee tree.

On the third day he put five of the saddle horses into the horse corral, shoveled horse manure out of the horse barn, using a slip scraper for some of the heavier work, storing the horse turds at the bottom of the garden. Each morning for an hour, he weeded the garden rows. When he was done he could see the corn, red stocks of the rhubarb supporting wide green leaves, and the hubbard squash growing along the fence line. His mother's sunflowers still grew tall and spindly, their feathery flowers turned to the sun.

On the fourth day he worked on the hog pen. Fixing the pen wasn't difficult, just time consuming. He had to replace three logs, shore up the rock housing in the rear, and lay additional rock in the wall that had partially fallen in when the sow had dug under it, taking away its support. Once he was finished, the hogs were not interested in living in their newly, remodeled home. He roped the first and smaller of the brood and dragged it into the pen, releasing it after he'd closed the gate. The bay he was using wasn't interested in standing in a pig pen with a hog running crazily around. He cleared the fence in one jump. On the second try, Forest found the bay hadn't changed its mind about hogs. It still wasn't interested in tying into a pig bent on tangling its feet in rope. It took six tries to get the

123

second hog in the hog pen. Tired, Forest left the third hog for another day.

The fifth day he reserved for garden work, pulling bunch grass, sunflowers, and lupine out by their roots, leaving the hollyhocks and rhubarb. Late morning, he heard a wagon make the rise behind the house and start down the incline toward the creek, the horses holding back against the tongue to keep the wagon under control and prevent it from racing down the grade.

'Bout time, he thought. *I was beginnin' to wonder what the hell was goin' on.*

He'd been home five days. Getting off his knees, leaving the garden, he walked to the house and sat down on the porch chair to watch the inhabitants find their way to the creek. It was July 26, 1886.

A dog and a halterless mule bearing a pack saddle were first into the yard. Damnedest thing he could remember seeing: a halterless mule bearing a fully loaded pack following an ugly one-eyed, long-haired dog. The dog saw him, came up the steps, momentarily stared at him, then walked down the long corridor of a porch and laid down at his feet. Next, he saw a rider walking a Buckskin horse across the hardpack, stepping down and wrapping the reins around the hitching rail. Glancing at him, the rider slowly removed his leather gloves and stuck them inside his belt with the fingers out.

Nodding a greeting, he climbed the five steps, made his way down the long porch, sat down, looked at Forest and said, "Hot one, ain't it?" It'd been twenty years since Riles had seen Forest.

Forest nodded, watching the heavy freight wagon ford the creek, the wheels dripping wet, a woman slapping the Belgians on the hindend with the reins, yelling encouragement.

"Done any huntin'?" Riles asked

"Not much. Got a pack rat my first day back."

"Eat it?"

"Nope. Gave it to the chickens. All shot to hell. Got some venison hangin' in the spring house, curin'."

"That's good."

"Some biscuits, I took out of the oven this mornin'. Find 'em inside on the table. There's some butter on the table, too...if it hasn't

124

melted in this heat."

"Mind if I have a couple?"

"Help yourself. It's what they're for."

The first wagon, the freighter, pulled up on the hardpack in front of the house and stopped. Diana, wrapping the ribbons to the brake lever, glanced at the two men sitting on the porch, and climbed down. The chickens were already seeking the shade under the wagon, clucking, pecking.

"That'd be the letter writer?" Forest said.

"Yup."

"Good to see you, Riles. Been a while."

"Same here, Far. Too long."

"See you got the milk cow in."

"I did. Pail of milk is coolin' in the creek down by the Spring house. That your dog?"

"Ugly bastard, ain't he?"

Forest nodded. "Ain't gonna win no beauty pageants. Made himself right at home."

"Eats his share, too."

"Maybe he'll take care of that pack rat. Chickens didn't seem to wanna bother. That one's gettin' a little ripe. Another day and we'll have to move it a little farther away."

Riles laughed, rose to his feet, and went inside to find the biscuits sitting on the table.

Forest watched Peter guide his buckboard to a standstill beside the freighter.

He stared at Forest. "Damn your hide, Far, what took you so long?"

"The letter wasn't in too big a hurry gettin' to me, Pistol."

CHAPTER 19

It didn't make sense to Syrus Stockton. Surely not to the stableman, who, pitchfork in hand, stood just inside the door frame of the big west door to the Mulholland Livery Stable. As doors go, it was big, twenty feet end to end. A long freight wagon, with six foot sides and heavy wheeled iron rims pulled by four big Percherons, could easily pass through it to the other side of the barn. Inside, two such freight wagons could unload oats, barley, fresh cut lumber, salt blocks or molasses cake. The old barn could easily hold both and not crowd the rats who spent their short lives running from Tom, the gawd-awful ugly mouser, a large, grey cat belonging to no one and claiming no one. Mulholland Livery was located at the corner of Fourth and California, one block off Main Street. It was the only livery in Buffalo. Others had tried. But there was no competition that could stand up to Mulhollands. Max Mulholland simply outworked all comers and gave good, lasting service daily for a good price.

Syrus Stockton stood in the shadows of the Mulholland Livery barn and looked down Fourth Street toward Main Street. Traffic seemed unusually heavy with wagons passing back and forth and multiple riders moving along in either direction. Syrus wondered where they could all be going. Taking a deep breath, he let it out slowly. The roan stud he'd bought in Sheridan stood at his shoulder, impatient. He blew air through his nostrils, stretched his neck, and shook his head as if trying to clear his sinuses. He wasn't. A casual observer might conclude the horse was mocking Syrus. He wasn't doing that, either.

"You, lost?" the liveryman asked.

"Well, no, I ain't lost," Stockton responded, turning to the man holding the pitchfork with a broken tine. "Just don't know where I am." Syrus stuck out his right hand toward the liveryman. "Si Stockton," he stated. Pointing to the hay fork, he said, "That thing do you any good?"

"Pleased to meet you," the stable man replied, ignoring the question and not giving him his name. That the liveryman did not share his name with Syrus didn't bother him. Syrus didn't notice. The liveryman then finished answering his question. "And, no, not much good," he said.

Syrus nodded. "You oughta throw it away if it ain't doin' you a whole lot of good. Makes you work twice as hard. Unless, of course, you just like workin' hard."

"Can't say as I do."

Taking another breath, Si let it out slowly.

"What the hell's wrong with you?" the liveryman asked. "You're breathin' like a horse done run ten mile. You got consumption?"

"I'm tryin' to figure out that smell. Keeps sneakin' inside my head. It's sweet but it ain't. Familiar and it ain't. Damnedest thing. Drivin' me crazy. Drivin' my horse crazy." Syrus smiled. "Ah, what the hell. I'm just passin' through. Think I'll have a look around. Get myself some bear sign with thet white powdery sugar. Some vittles would be nice. I'm thinkin' some hot, right outta the oven, cornbread dunked in cow butter. Mother used to make it, slathered in butter somethin' wicked. No, I ain't lost. It's the bear sign that's lost."

"Long as you ain't smellin' smoke. Tell me it ain't smoke. Had some so'n'so in here smokin' a big Georgia cigar. Knockin' them ashes in thet straw. Ran him outta here. The stupid bastard. Full of foolishness."

Si looked at the stableman. "Naw," he shook his head. "You ain't on fire near as I kin tell. It's easier to tell you what it ain't. It ain't fresh cut hay. It ain't that straw you threw in those stalls this mornin'. It ain't horse sweat." Si patted the roan on the shoulder with a gloved hand, glanced at the bay then back to the roan. "It ain't you, horse. Thet makes you feel better?" The roan didn't move.

Syrus took another deep breath. "Smell that? It ain't that pile of horse turds you're buildin' in the doorway, partner. Like I say, it's sorta sweet and tart. I ain't smelled it before. Not that I remember, anyways."

Syrus glanced behind him at the roan standing in the sun, his head down. "Say, Mr. Stableman, would you give 'ol red and that bay a rub down? Treat 'em to a bait of oats? They're all tuckered, seein' how he and the bay come all the way from Sheridan this mornin'.

127

Don't want 'em feelin' under appreciated."

"Surely. I could do that." The liveryman looked from the horses back to Syrus. "Sweet, you say? Tart? Quite a combination. Just got a whiff of that smell that's botherin' you, myself. Not much. That'd be perfume, I think. Some woman no doubt wearin' a dab. Right close though, ain't it?" He took another breath. "Yeah, it's close 'cause I can smell it and my nose ain't all that good. Up close that stuff'd choke a dead maggot. You're right. It ain't that pile of horse turds you're smellin'. Lavender, I'd guess. My woman wore it on occasion. Easter Sunday, Christmas. Went to a weddin' once. She used it."

"Lavender! Damn straight. Is that what that is?" Syrus shook his head. "That's the smell of lavender? Never got a whiff of that before that I can remember. Yet smells oddly familiar."

"That'd be my guess. Pretty sure you could get some over to Hitchcock General, you wanted it. That's where my Jesse got hers."

"Thanks," he said. "Take care of 'ol red for me. His pard, too. I'll be back in a couple of hours to look in on 'em. Appreciate it."

"Got 'er done. Not a worry. They'll be ready time you get back."

"Thanks," Syrus said. Syrus smiled at the skinny livery man with the broken pitch fork. "Couple of hours and I'll drop in on you. Come mornin', I'll be needin' a pack saddle for the bay. You got one you can spare? I aim to pay for it."

"I'll be here. I'll fix you up. Got one used, in good shape."

"Good. Hold onto it for me."

Syrus Stockton turned and took a couple of steps toward Main Street. Reflecting later, he thought he'd taken no more than a half dozen. Main Street was a good two hundred yards in front of him. Absently, he thought about Hitchcock General, about maybe buying a box of Mississippi Crooks. *Damnedest thing.* Places where he'd been, no one knew what he was talking about when he asked for a Crook: a cheap penny cigar soaked in rum, five, maybe six, seven inches long, the body squared, with a sweet taste, a sweet smell.

"Mississippi Crooks?" he once asked a store clerk in Quenton Holler, Iowa. The man behind the counter pulled out a yellow box.

"How many you want?" he asked.

It was the first time Syrus had found those cigars in quantity. "Mississippi Crooks? You got 'em? I'll be damned," he said. "Mississippi Crooks in a one horse town called Quenton Holler."

"Pardon?"

"I'll take 'em all."

"I meant how many boxes?"

"No, you didn't. How many you got?"

"Three."

"I'll take three boxes."

"That's what I thought you'd do."

"Damn right, you did. You just put this place on the map of places to go."

"Naw, Jesse James did that. He rode through here once goin' to rob a bank east of here."

"This Jesse James buy any Crooks?"

"Nope. Didn't. Didn't stop. Didn't ask after them. Don't believe Jesse smoked cigars."

Mississippi Crooks. Besides Bourbon Street in Orleans, he'd never seen them offered for sale, but he always asked after them just the same. Syrus had one unopened box left. He was saving each cigar for a special occasion. Trouble was, every day was a special occasion and he was running low on cigars, but not special occasions. After Quentin, he had a reserve for both. But one box…he was getting low.

Syrus Stockton smiled to himself and glanced toward Main Street and there she was: standing slender, unique, like a beautiful Mississippi Crook cigar in an almost empty wood box, the very last in a tobacco case. Staring at the figure of a woman, he could taste rum smothering the tastebuds in his mouth. Her perceived beauty caught his breath. Not breathing wasn't an every day event and it wasn't healthy, either. *Neither were Mississippi Crooks.* Amazing, finding a woman like that standing on a street corner in this no account cowtown in Northern Wyoming Territory. It didn't happen every day. It was unique, like finding three boxes of fine square, six inch, rum-soaked cigars in Quenton Holler, Iowa.

Syrus felt his shirt pocket, pulled out a Crook and stared at it, then looked at the figure of a woman. "Hell is on fire," he said, his voice barely a whisper. "Is there ever anything better than a beautiful woman and a good rum soaked cigar? Hell is on fire."

Staring isn't polite. Everyone knows that. What Syrus saw was a well-dressed woman standing on a nondescript corner in a nondescript settlement called Buffalo. She was framed by the front of Hitchcock General across the street. She whisked his thoughts away like a wind distributes goose down. Behind her moved a buckboard pulled by a pair of greys, stepping smartly, followed by a rider on a bay horse.

Syrus stared. He dared not blink. She'd disappear. In spite of his fear, she did not vanish, standing stationary as if caught in time. *Special occasion*, he thought. He reached for his pocket and remembered he already had a cigar clenched in his teeth, the sweet taste of rum permeating his mouth. He swallowed. His throat hurt. *She was sure somethin'. Damn straight,* he thought. *Damn straight.* He sucked on the cigar and realized he hadn't lit it.

He removed the cigar from his lips, looked at it again, rolling it gently between his thumb and index finger. Unconsciously, he felt for a diamond blue tip, remembered he wasn't smoking, not that close to a livery. A man walking by nearly ran him over, swearing at him.

"What the hell's wrong with you?" the fellow said. "Get outta the way, you fool."

Syrus heard him, but didn't notice. He was distracted by another whiff of lavender. Involuntarily, he rubbed his thin Stockton nose. "Lavender," he said aloud. The stableman, ten steps behind him, holding the roan's reins and the bay's lead rope, heard him.

"Yeah, lavender," the liveryman responded. "Probably that woman up there. See her? Probably her."

Syrus was intrigued, for this sort of thing just didn't happen. It never happened to him. It amused him that he couldn't take his eyes off her, that he didn't want to. She was five foot seven, maybe a smidgen taller, wearing a long light purple skirt with pleats that ran to the boardwalk where she was standing. She could have been a fashion plate from a Bloomingdales Department store catalogue or a woman from a New York City or Paris catalogue, or maybe the catalogues published by Lord and Taylor. Her hair was dark brown, braided in a similar manner to the style used to decorate a horse's mane: ribbons and bows laced and entwined.

"Damn" was all he could say to himself.

The woman stared east down the winding cow trail that was Main Street. Her profile was stunning. To Syrus, breathtaking. He'd never seen anyone like her. Mostly, he paid women no mind, or so he told himself. He found them all attractive.

Whatever she was looking at, she made a prolonged study of it. Suddenly her gaze was torn away. She turned on the heel of her boot, glanced across the street at Hitchcock General, then behind her, west up Main Street.

Syrus stood immobile. Two men led their horses around him. He took a breath, glanced at the six inch cigar in his hand, completely mesmerized by the woman, by the lavender perfume she wore, by the tilt of her head, by the profile of her nose, brow, and cheek. He was transfixed, noting the manner her braids were woven about her head, the curvature of her spine, the lace gathered about her neck, the way the purple pleated skirts hung from her hips, and by the laced black leather boots that covered her feet. She was a woman adorned in purple lace.

Seeing her made him painfully aware of himself. She represented an impossible dream, as unattainable as the perfect woman in the perfect picture hanging on the wall behind the bank manager's desk. He knew it and felt no remorse because of it. A woman like that did not exist in his social structure. It wasn't her unavailability nor the way he considered her standing on the corner of Main Street and Fourth in the bright Wyoming sunlight. She was a rare creature. The Greeks saw it in Athena, the Romans, in Persephone, and the damnable, incorrigible British, in Victoria, the Queen. She was as rare as a unicorn, something he would never, in his future existence, see again and he found her accidently. Discovering her at the corner of nowhere and nowhere was pure serendipity and he did not want to take his eyes off her. He was captured, not in a weird, lecherous manner. It was more like staring for five minutes at the portrait of the Mona Lisa, hanging on the wall of the Louvre in Paris. She was simply beautiful to Syrus Stockton.

So he watched her, a cowkid from southern Montana. Without thinking, he smelled the air for lavender, considering each passing second precious. As silly as it seemed, he thought that the air she breathed was lavender. It wasn't something she wore or took from a bottle made in France. It was something she was: lavender, a flower.

In the blink of an eye, she turned, starting north on Main Street, disappearing around the corner of the store front that faced Main Street across from Hitchcock General. Unwittingly, she left Syrus standing in the street staring at the space in time that she'd occupied seconds before. She was gone.

As if prodded by a sharp stick, he hurried to where he'd last seen her. Pursuit would be in vain. He knew that. However, the fickle breeze brought the smell of lavender drifting to him. The scent was a hope. *Wow!* he thought. *How lucky can a fellow be?* He stepped out into Main Street searching the passersby. He did not see her; the lovely apparition was gone.

Syrus smiled. Halfway down the block, a tall slender man knelt before a two year old boy wearing a straw hat and bibs. The man was speaking earnestly. A dog, long-haired, mangy, and tired, walked toward Syrus, passing the man and the boy. The woman had passed that way. The scent of lavender hung in the air in drifts, in dabs, here, and as quickly, gone. It wasn't heavy, just a tiny whiff, disappearing, and reappearing like a ghost in evening shadows. The man stood, taking the urchin's hand. The boy talked excitedly, waving his free hand as though conducting the New York Philharmonic. The boy smiled, happily clinging to the hand that had dropped out of the heavens to guide him.

Syrus could not help but be disappointed; the lady was gone. "Damn straight," he mumbled. Resigned to his loss, Syrus proceeded down the boardwalk, freed from the burden. He wasn't following her. Well, maybe, to some extent, but there was no point. He knew that but the experience heightened his senses; he heard creaking boards more loudly, heard more vividly a grease starved wheel hub, smelled a horse moving by.

"I'm not findin' her again, no lavender girl," he said to himself. "Forget that." Both the slender man and boy turned to look at him as they passed.

"Don't mind me. I'm just talkin' to myself," he acknowledged.

The man with the boy half-smiled. Syrus laughed. *Don't have to try to make a fool outta myself,* he thought. *Those two already think I'm crazy. I am. A little perfume and I'm a goner, a damn kid chasin' a puppy.*

Across the street he located a café called Mothers. He wasn't looking for it. He smelled it. Stepping off the boardwalk, he started across the street and another whiff of lavender found his nose. In spite of himself, he looked about but did not see her. Instead of the woman in purple there were a lot of people passing by, a dispersing crowd that never was a crowd. No one wore purple.

Knock it off.

Releasing the memory of her, hurt. He glanced down the block and standing at another intersection, facing the intersecting street, was the woman in purple. Almost immediately, she disappeared around the corner of a two story building. Appearing, disappearing and gone, all in a heartbeat. Syrus couldn't help himself. Stepping back on the boardwalk, he hustled down the street to the intersection, and peered down the corner. She wasn't there. The fickle, fresh smell of lavender was; it came on the breeze, drifting toward him, then fell away, vanished.

What's goin' on? It's all in my head. Better get somethin' in my stomach. Feelin' light headed. Yes sir, I'd better get a bite. Chasin' lavender won't fill the stomach. It's gonna kill me.

A smile came to his lips. Down the street where the woman had disappeared again, a crowd of people gathered around a wagon. A drummer was selling the "Elixir of Life." Even farther down, five or six people had gathered in front of a show window. But no purple woman. *I could do this all day.* He smiled at himself. *Lavender,* he thought.

The Mississippi Crook cigar was hanging from his mouth. He'd bitten the end off. Now he spat the leaf out, replaced the Crook between his teeth, unconsciously biting down again. Sucking air through the lifeless tobacco, he stepped off the boardwalk and started across the street, stopping to wait for a wagon to pass. He lit the cigar, sucked on the end, tasting the rum flavor hidden in the tobacco leaf. It was something he rarely did. Several women walked

133

by. Another whiff of lavender hung in the air. He laughed. They turned toward him.

"Don't mind me," he said. "I'm crazy. Ain't got a lick of sense. Thought I smelled lavender right here in the middle of Wyoming, Main Street, Buffalo. Imagine that." He smiled. They smiled.

A slender women in a red silk blouse and a white skirt, holding a white parasol, hesitated, then sweetly said, "You did," turning to walk away, her skirts swishing.

Down the street someone fired a shot into the air; it was followed by a burst of laughter.

"I did, did I? Figured as much," he said to their backs. "Thanks."

Syrus Stockton stood for a moment, then followed the women south down the boardwalk to the front door of Mothers. His cigar had gone out. He didn't re-light it. Opening the door, he was confronted with the smell of bacon, coffee, hashbrowns, steak, cooked eggs, and fresh bread. But no lavender, or maybe just a hint.

Double damn, straight, he thought. *Does everyone wear that stuff? What if she's in here?* he mused, knowing she couldn't possibly be. *I'll introduce myself. That's what. Ah, come on. She couldn't be. Lots of women wear perfume. Lots of women wear lavender.* He shook his head, laughing. *Where is that gal?* he questioned. *She ain't in here!* For good measure, he looked the patrons over, going from table to table, visually covering the entire restaurant, finding no woman wearing purple and lavender.

"One?" the waiter said, interrupting his thoughts. The man wore a white apron with a red stain below the right pocket. It made him look like someone had shot him. Syrus wondered if folks actually lived through a meal in Buffalo, Wyoming. *Probably! Elsewise everyone would be dead. Ptomaine poisonin'. Graveyard full of 'em.*

"Just me," Syrus responded. "Nobody else."

"Table in back. Follow me. I'll show you."

"Much obliged. Coffee smells good."

"I'll get you a pot."

"Thanks."

Syrus stuck the chewed up cigar in his shirt pocket and smiled at a child sitting in her mother's lap playing with a blue and red doll,

134

flopping it back and forth on the table. The small girl smiled back.

Syrus had a bit of everything on the menu. He ate slowly, wanting it to last. He was tired of his own diet of rabbit, venison or, sometimes, sage hen. He took his time: ordered steak rare, beans baked, coleslaw dripping in sweet sauce, apple pie, hot. It was more than enough. It took him over an hour to eat. Lavender was gone. She had left his mind. Mostly.

Afterwards, he got a hair cut, a shave, and a hot, sudsy bath, exciting the barber and the dentist, who happened to be the same person, by shooting cockroaches off the wall. It pleased him that he didn't miss. Feeling better about himself, he took the tour of Hickoks General. Old man Hickok didn't carry Mississippi Crooks. Although Syrus had no reason to go there, he looked inside the post office, a millinery, and the boot shop. It was late afternoon by the time he stopped to see if the farrier had time for the roan and the bay. He did.

"Bring 'em right over."

Syrus went to get his horses. They probably did need to have their shoes tightened or replaced. He believed it was best never to take a chance. He waited while the smithy worked, thinking about the lady in purple skirts and lace, picturing her on the boardwalk gazing down the street, the breeze playing with her hair. *Wonder what's her story?* He tried to imagine and couldn't. *A woman right out of a Lord & Taylor women's catalogue doesn't have a story. They aren't real. Not like normal folk. Not like him.*

Aw, well, he thought. *Some things ain't meant to be. Like the Easter Bunny and Santa Claus. Gotta say it, though. It'd sure be nice to wake up next to someone like that. Now there's a thought that ain't got a possibility. Well, maybe. It ain't got no possibility. You never know. Someone maybe talked her into marryin'. Guess it does happen. Sure ain't likely.*

Shaking his head in disbelief, he looked up to see the farrier finishing with the roan's shoes, patting him on the behind, talking to him, whispering as if he were sharing a secret.

"Damn the luck," Syrus said to himself. "Someday, someday."

"What?" The smithy asked.

"Nothin'." Syrus answered. "Just daydreamin' 'bout fallin' in love with a beautiful lady. Ain't seen any around here, have you? All

135

dressed in purple, smellin' of lavender?"

The Smithy laughed. "Let me know how that turns out," he said. "I'd like to find one of those, myself. You'd better be careful talkin' to yourself. Folks will be thinkin' you're a bit looney."

"How much do I owe you?"

"For the advice? Talkin' is for free. Don't cost nothin', seein' how I don't know what I'm talkin' 'bout half the time. The horses cost you four dollars. Fifty cents a shoe."

"Sounds fair."

"That's 'cause it is fair."

"Good. You et? Let me buy you a meal over at Mothers. Someone over there makes damn good cornbread that I've taken a likin' to."

"Am I eatin' for free?"

"Ain't no such thing. I'm payin'."

Syrus Stockton paid the farrier for his services in gold coin and took him to dinner at Mothers and never saw him again. What he said, however--the conversation they shared--turned out to be memorable. The farrier was from Pigeon Creek, Iowa by way of Abilene, Kansas and Saw Ridge, Texas. He said he'd spoken to Sam Houston himself. while he was alive. He said he was a cranky old man but folks seemed to like him.

"Where you goin'?" he asked Syrus. "Maybe I've been there."

"Over the mountain, then down the river. Long ways. Got some trouble up in the Pryors. Gotta tend to it."

"Across the Big Horn to the other side, then north?"

"That'd be it. Got a letter from my brother's wife. Said they got some trouble. I didn't know he was married," Syrus said.

"Trouble? Rumor has it there's been lots of trouble in that area. More of late. So the story goes. Hard to tell. Folks tend to exaggerate when they's tellin' a story. A rider was through here not two days ago. He said they'd all gone crazy hangin' a bunch of women for killin' some soul that had shot their Pa in the back with a shotgun. Kilt him dead. Nobody believes it, but that's the rumor." The farrier leaned back in the high back oak chair and sipped his coffee. "Appreciate the grits," he said.

"Ain't no grits here," Syrus noted. "Don't care for 'em, myself less my backbone is wearin' a hole in my stomach. That's a different matter."

"Need brings us all to our knees," the farrier said.

"Rumor has it."

"You know what made that rider's story so unbelievable? He heard the law was involved. Deep. Didn't know how. Said he was gettin' out of there hisself. Goin' where decent folks lived that don't tolerate hangin' no women. Said it was the damnedest thing he'd ever heard. I'd agree. Tallest tale I'd ever heard, too. I wouldn't repeat it, myself except you said you was goin' in that direction. Best be warned. You seem like a decent fellow. I'd avoid trouble. Give it a wide berth. That's what I do wherever I can."

Syrus smiled at the farrier. "Words to live by, friend." He watched as the farrier took the last bite of apple pie.

"I do believe that's a transparent apple pie," the farrier said. "Best pie-makin' apple there is."

137

CHAPTER 20

Syrus Stockton intended to start for Tensleep Canyon early the next morning. He thought that if he left before sunrise and pushed it until dark, he'd be on Sage Creek within four days, maybe sooner. A morning thunderhead changed all of that. It brought heavy rain, dampening the browning mid-July grass. With restless horses and cold rain pelting his face, Syrus was wide awake early, a witness to violent thunder popping against the sky, resonating against the granite cliffs. Flashes of lightning momentarily lit up the hills and the converging pine forest that surrounded him. Wind lashed at everything. He waited for it to blow over.

Eventually the storm did, and in stocking feet, light cotton long johns bagging around his knees, he pulled his Stetson around his ears and began the day. He moved the picket ropes, rebuilt the fire, fixed himself several flapjacks, and boiled some coffee from fresh coffee beans beaten flat with the butt of an SAA 45 caliber Colt revolver. It was good except for the grit that somehow got into the coffee, the red dirt that flavored the flapjacks, and the fire, whipped by the breeze that got into the over-heated frying pan and burned the salt pork. It was okay though, because salt pork wasn't going to last long anyway. He figured he'd get it fried and "gone" so as not to let it spoil. It all made sense, best to get it eaten before the rot set in.

The sun was fifteen minutes from being up when Syrus finished his self-appointed chores and went to collect the roan. The horse saw him, blew his nose, and started chewing wire grass, shaking his head. Syrus sat down on a boulder, rubbing his temples, pushing the tension out. For the sixth time since he'd received it, he pulled his sister-in-law's letter from his denim shirt pocket, opened it up, and read it.

Dear Mr. Syrus Stockton,--

That was how Diana's letter began, except no one called him Syrus. *What's with this, "Syrus?"* he thought. Once in a while, not more than once a day, his mother had called him Syrus. His Pa never did. He always addressed him as Si. So did his brothers, and when they had hired help, the hired help called him Si. The letter continued:

I 'm your brother Petey's wife.

That'd be Pistol. Didn't know he was married. That little runt. Really ought to get back to the old place more often. Fifteen years, or has it been sixteen? That's too long. Fifteen years.

We're in trouble. Petey done broke his leg. Horse rolled on him. I reckon he fell off.

Which is it, girl? Did the horse roll on him or did he fall off?

It's just me, Josh, and Katie Sue. They's young bein' they was born not long ago.

Syrus paused. Pistol has himself a son and a girl child? "Born not long ago." I'll be damned. Ain't that somethin'?

They can't help none. Ain't grow'd enough. Legs too short. Someone's stole the cows. They ain't no more.

Maybe Crow. Could be. Ranch is right on the Reservation's southern border. He tried to think of having any Indian trouble and couldn't. *Too far off the beaten path.*

Horses got out. Corral needs fixin'. Poles fell down. Horses need shoein' anyways. Dog got into the chickens; they's mostly dead. Sucked them eggs. Hay will need cuttin' soon. Four, five weeks. There's just me. Please? Help. Kin you come? I'm hopin' you can. Got more bad news. Pa died last September. He was kilt. Peter was gonna tell you but couldn't bring himself to do it. I'm Diana. I'm a Stafford. You know who I am.

Syrus read the last line again. *The Old Man is dead? Nice of Pistol to tell me. What the hell's wrong with him? Big question is what Riles is thinkin'? Maybe he'll come if he thinks the Old Man is dead. I'd never thought anythin' could kill him. Somebody did. How'd that happen? A Stafford? Let's see--there was four of them girls. Four. When I left the oldest was—let's see—maybe nine, could be as old as twelve, fourteen. Somethin' like that. Diana. It's been fifteen years. How bout' that? Pistol got himself a wife and some young'uns. That girl's done grow'd up an' got herself married to that Pistol. The Old Man--that's the real question. What happened there?*

139

There's somethin' wrong here. Surely. Someone's stealin' Pistol's cows. Now, that ain't right. Ain't neighborly. Difficulty bein' we ain't got any neighbors. Not for a hundred miles. Who'd stole them cows? What would they do with 'em? No place to take 'em. Not like a man can hide a thousand head under a five gallon bucket.

Carefully, Syrus re-folded the letter, placed it in the envelope, and placed the envelope in his shirt pocket, patting it with calloused fingers before buttoning the pocket flap. He stood, looked at the horses cropping grass, then at the mountainside behind them. A gust of cool wind stirred the grass, the leaves in the aspen, then died.

Syrus picked the roan's saddle blanket up and smacked it with the palm of his left hand to knock away the grass and debris. With the blanket in hand he approached the roan, holding the blanket behind him, talking softly, steadily. The roan watched distrustfully. With his right hand he scratched behind the roan's ears, his nose, neck, and shoulder. Quietly, he laid the blanket on the roan's back, smoothing the wrinkles out with his hands. It was Syrus' belief that the roan liked to hear about how pretty the girls were in New Orleans, so he told him all about beautiful, dark haired beauties, girls he didn't know much about himself. The roan accepted the feed bag without much fuss, not reacting when Syrus leaned over the horse's back, resting against him.

Something was wrong with that letter and he worried it as he worked. *What was it?* he asked himself.

Removing the feed bag from the horse's head, the roan watched him, his jaw grinding oats. Syrus led the horse to his makeshift camp. He grabbed the saddle, hooking the left stirrup and skirts over the saddle horn, then the cinch, and deftly seated the saddle in the middle of the roan's back.

What was it? It's just a letter. What's botherin' me? Not that Diana would lie. Doubt she'd do that. So what's she sayin' that's botherin' me? Pistol gettin' rolled? Now that would be a sight.

Syrus tightened the cinch, knowing he'd have to tighten it more, for the roan had puffed up his chest against it. Syrus waited. The horse couldn't hold his breath forever. Syrus left the roan standing, rehung the feed bag over his nose, then went to get the bay.

Pistol never fell off a horse once in his entire life. Never. What happened then? Without lookin', it'd be hard to tell. Still, Pistol never fell off of a horse.

Syrus took up the end of the bay's picket rope and began looping it. "You know, horse...?" He paused, staring at the bay. "I suppose you do." He walked up the length of the picket rope, talking to the bay as if they were old friends, each step, looping the rope.

"You know everythin'? You know that Pistol never fell off a horse in his entire life, not countin' that time he broke his arm and Mother wouldn't let him do a damned thing except gather eggs and feed chickens. Eggs and chickens? Can you believe that? He wasn't on a horse then. Not that time. We thought Pistol broke his arm a purpose, not wantin' to work. That time that horse he was ridin' run under a low hangin' branch. Hit Pistol in the chest. He tumbled off the back end, hit the ground on his shoulders. Couldn't breathe. Thought he was dyin'. Favored his arm and shoulder. Riles gets all excited wonderin' what to do. Lucky he started breathin' so he didn't have to do nothin'. But he didn't fall off his horse. Got knocked off. That was Far ran him under that tree. Raisin' hell playin' milker, horseback. The Old Man sure lit into Riles and he had nothin' to do with it. Pistol didn't even see that comin'. Claimed he was attacked by a tree. Damn tree. That's what he said."

Syrus finished coiling the picket rope, walking to where the horse was standing. He rubbed the horse's nose, patting him on the shoulder.

"I'd say somethin' else happened, horse. What? You disagree? You don't know a damn thing. Just think you do." Syrus put the halter on the horse's nose, slipping it over his head. For a moment, he rubbed the bay's nose, scratching behind its ears, patted it on the shoulder, then its rump. "I figure somethin' else happened, horse. Somethin' smells and I don't like it. How 'bout you? Somethin' smell?"

Leading the bay pack horse to where the roan stood, he left him ground hitched and went to get the pack saddle. He returned; the horse hadn't moved.

"You don't know shit, horse. Case you didn't know, when we was kids we had this game. Silly game. The loser milked the cow. We'd climb up on the corral fence and we'd run the top rail clear to the other side, over the chute corral, down by the waterin' trough,

141

clear to the other side and back. At the end, we'd jump on the horse bareback and get the milk cow from the pasture. There weren't no cheatin'. You fall off, you lost, and you milked the cow. I don't remember Pistol ever fallin' off. That little squirt finished first always. He never milked the cow; that's what I'm tellin' you. He had incredible balance. And some of them poles, they's skinny little bastards. He'd run 'em. Flat out run 'em. Know what I mean? Ah, hell you weren't there. You don't know shit. Do you?"

The bay accepted the feed bag and he ate oats, listening to Syrus, his ears twitching back and forth. Syrus looked at him.

He asked, "You listenin', horse? Suppose you are." Si continued talking to the bay, saddling him, then hanging the panniers on the pack saddle, covering them with the tarp, lashing them down with a diamond hitch. "Point is, that boy ran the top rail from one end to the other. Raced a little mustang to the pasture. That started when he was 'bout eight. He never fell off. Never milked the cow. Damn him."

Syrus popped the bay on the butt. "Let me tell you what you don't know. True story. Pops spoiled that boy rotten, him bein' the youngest. That's not the point? The point is from the time that bugger was a baby, Pa would have him ridin' in the saddle with him. He'd be sittin' up there on the shoulders of Pa's saddle, holdin' the reins. 'Course Pa would be holdin' the reins, too. We'd trail cows forty mile, that Pistol holdin' the reins and Pa holdin' Pistol. True story, horse."

Syrus laughed. Both horses turned their heads to see what he was doing. "When that Pistol got a little older, he'd show off. He'd be standin' in the saddle, the reins in his teeth, that damn dog of his on the horse's back haunches, Pistol peelin' an apple with his pocket knife. Don't know what he did with the apple. True story, I'm tellin' you. Pistol ain't never fell off a horse. Ain't been rolled on, either." He paused. "Diana wouldn't know that writin' a letter.

"One time we brought the rough string in for fall roundup. Twenty head and they's all green. Pistol, he picks himself out a little mustang for a ridin' horse. Nice little mountain pony. Ain't never been rode far as I know. Not once. We gets a rope on him. Riles puts a bag over his head. Far ears him down. That horse ain't goin'

142

nowheres. I saddles him, ties it on him right tight. Pistol, he's maybe thirteen; he crawls up there on the hurricane deck lookin' for the reins. No one put a bridle on him. Far, he's just holdin' him by the ears, the blind keepin' him from gettin' all rowdy. Pistol points out that there ain't no bridle, no reins. No nothin'.

"Riles says to him, he says, 'Pistol, what you gonna do with reins anyways? You're in the horse corral. He ain't goin' nowheres. What you need a bridle for? You some sorta ninny? Bet you can't ride him.'

"Pistol looks at him. 'What's your bet?'

"Riles, he's slow, thinkin' 'bout what to say. Finally he says, 'You ride this 'tang, no reins, I'll bake you a cake.'

'Riles, you don't know how to bake a cake,' Pistol says to him.

'I'll learn. 'Sides I'm sayin' you can't ride him and you ain't gonna 'cause you're a ninny.'

"I say to Riles, I say, 'Riles, Pistol's right. You can't bake no cake. He rides him, you gotta do somethin' more than do what you can't do.'

"Riles asks, 'What would that be?'

"I says, 'Riles you not only gotta bake that cake. You gotta milk the cow. You gotta make his bed for a month, every day.'

"'He don't ever milk the cow,' Riles argued like he always does.

"That one stumped me. So I say, 'All right, you gotta slop the hogs and feed the chickens to boot. That'd make it fair. You good with that, Pistol?'

"'Okay,' Pistol, he says. 'Turn him loose. I can ride him. It ain't nothin'.

"I backs away. Far has his ears and Riles, he pulls the blinds off that horse. For a minute or two that horse just stands there, Pistol sittin' in the middle of his back. I yells and the horse, he turns his head to see what I was yellin' about and for the first time he sees Pistol sittin' up there in the middle of his back. Well, that's it right there. That horse unwinds like the spring on a granddaddy clock. He sunfishes. He frog walks. He goes sideways. He goes up. He comes down. He does it again. I swear, if he could, he'd have turned inside out, flipped himself over and upside down. Now, he didn't do that but if he coulda he woulda. I swear. He was screamin', tryin' to shake Pistol outta the cat-bird seat. We was hootin' and hollarin'. Pops, he comes runnin' over to see what the ruckus was. He climbs up on the fence lookin' at Riles like he always does. He says, 'What the hell you boys doin'?' We didn't need to tell him; he could see. At first, he didn't see that Pistol had no bridle, no reins.

"What I'm sayin' is Pistol ain't never fell off no horse."

Syrus paused; he stopped talking, looking at the bay eating oats from the feed bag. He tightened the cinch on the roan, tied the lead to the back of his saddle, and took a deep breath, letting it out slowly.

"All right," he said. "I'm gonna finish my story 'cause there's my little brother," Syrus smiled, then picked up the reins to the roan saddle horse. "That Pistol didn't need no reins. He kept his hands on his thighs, sittin' in the saddle. And that horse went every which way. Now here's where it gets interestin'. The horse bunches himself up and he goes up so high, he damn near touches the clouds and he comes back down." Si took a deep breath. "You know," he said, "I ain't never seen nothin' like it. Not ever. That horse comes back to the ground; he stumbles. He goes down, rolls clean over, loses his footin', and rolls on his shoulder, kickin' and squealin' in sheer terror. Pops, he jumped clear over the fence tryin' to get to Pistol before he's kilt by the saddle horn.

"Pistol didn't need no help. That damn kid, his hands still on his thighs, just restin' there, kicks the stirrups and steps off as the horse rolls. Pops is standin' in the horse corral whiter than a ghost. The 'tang, he rolls clear over and comes to his feet. No quit in him. Dust and dirt was aflyin', fillin' the air. That damn kid, not a brain in his head, steps back into the saddle as the horse is comin' to his feet. It was as if he never got off, like he was born there, lived there every day of his life. It was the damnedest thing I'd ever laid eyes on. Nobody ever believed it, but I saw it.

"For a moment the horse just stands there. He's eyin' Pistol, gettin' ready for the next go 'round. He sure as hell ain't beat. Riles, me, and Far walks up to him quick like. Far puts a halter on him and he don't move. Not yet. But he's gettin' himself ready.

144

"Pistol, he says to Riles, he says, 'I told you I could ride him. He ain't nothin'.' That's what he said. 'He ain't nothin'.' But it was somethin'. It sure was. The Old Man, he throws a fit and stomps off cussin' Riles. He always was a cussin' Riles.

"Well, horse, what do you think? Bet you a dollar to two dozen biscuits that Diana's got it wrong. Pistol ain't never fallen off a horse. No horse ever rolled on that boy. Not ever. I done seen it, myself. ' It ain't nothin',' that's what Pistol called it. 'It ain't nothin', Riles,' he said. That fallin' off a horse bullshit is a damn lie. Pistol probably told it to her to keep her from worryin'. She don't know. I'm gonna have to look into that soon as we gets ourselves to Sage Creek."

CHAPTER 21

Syrus Stockton stared at the earth in disbelief. His reaction was akin to the surprise suffered from finding the hoof print of a goat on the dark side of the moon, trailing off a crater wall into the shadowed depths. Curiosity would force a man to peer over the edge, not knowing what he'd find, knowing it could not be a goat for there are no goats on the moon. Syrus saw and read the upturned and rearranged pine needles, the broken surface of composite sandy loam and crushed granite, defaced and scarred, and leaves of grass bent, broken where narrow wheels had pressed down leaving a compressed track. The trail led west into the Big Horn Mountains.

A light buckboard, maybe a buggy had passed this way. Whatever it was had narrow wheels and a short wheel base. Syrus looked around, right, left, behind him. This was late July 1886 and there were no roads from Buffalo or Sheridan into the Big Horn Basin. There never had been. French trappers, the seven nations of the Teton Lakota, Cheyenne, Arapaho, Crow--they'd passed this way, but they were walking or were on horseback. Not one of those folks brought a wagon. Between here and west of here were thirty canyons, several dozen streams of various sizes, and an unforgiving mountain: no country suited for a light wagon or a buggy.

Studying the tracks, he thought of Link Hannon living on Davis Creek between the east lobe of the Pryor Mountain and the canyon with his wife and two kids. He'd stolen the sheriff's saddle horses. He'd complained about leaving twenty feet of good rope, the end of which was tied to a picket stake driven into the ground inches from the sleeping law officer's head. Hannon never woke him but did regretfully leave a measure of good hemp rope. It was later, for good measure, that Link removed the four wheels from the sheriff's Democrat, hauled them to the top of the red hill south of Davis Creek and stuck them in a juniper tree. The sheriff was afoot, his horses running loose. Pa had lent him a horse so he wouldn't have to walk back to Red Lodge. It was the damnedest story.

The wheeled conveyance somewhere in front of Syrus was

heading west towards Tensleep or Worland, the latter a small inconsequential establishment in the vast confines of the basin. Not so much Tensleep: that was a place ten days ride from Fort Laramie. No one lived there.

The driver was going to have to stop whether or not he wanted to. Canyon walls would stop him. There were simply no roads that would take him through. But why was he here? It was a two day ride back to Buffalo. It wasn't that it was far. There were so many mountains, canyons, and streams to cross and avoid. That made it far.

Buggy tracks? In the Big Horn Mountains? Syrus wondered what that was all about and, like the made up man riding his horse between craters on the dark side of the moon, he followed the buggy. Syrus Stockton needed to have a look at this curiosity. He figured the fellow was lost, out for a Sunday ride, and didn't have a clue as to what he was doing or where he was going. It wasn't the place for whatever he was doing.

Riding into the mountain from Buffalo, Syrus had followed Clear Creek on the east side; so had the man in the buggy. Farther east was Crazy Woman Creek and the Tongue River. In front of him on the left was the towering Clouds Peak and miles and miles of desolation. No one lived there. No one except for the elk, buffalo, white tailed deer, and the animals that hunted and ate them.

Syrus studied the tracks that he was following. It was, maybe, a buggy, a democrat, or a surrey. It was pulled by two light horses with bad feet. No saddle horse was tied to the back. The wheels didn't cut deep into the soil, so it apparently carried no weight. At first, he figured it was one rider: a small fellow.

The buggy/surrey driver had stopped before crossing Clear Creek, had built a small fire and prepared a small meal. It looked like he'd eaten bread, butter, jelly of some sort. Syrus touched the crumbs with his index finger, touched it to his tongue: Chokecherry jelly. There were three sets of tracks: two small children and one adult with a very narrow foot, maybe a size six or seven. Certainly not an eight. Syrus studied the earth, then remounted the roan stud. It did not make a lot of sense to Syrus and he told himself: *Folks do the craziest things. Mind your own business.*

147

"I ought to, horse. I really ought to but this fellow is in trouble and don't know it. A mountain cat, a bear or wolf, even a pack of mangy coyotes comes along, spooks his horses and he's walkin' with two very small children. This fellow's lunacy will harm those kids."

Sure as hell. I'm tellin' you mind your own business. This is nothin' but trouble. Syrus Stockton thought of Pistol sitting upon the shoulders of his father's saddle, holding the reins in his small fingers, looking like the big man. He'd sit there pleased with himself behind the Old Man's gloved hands also holding the reins, safe. Safe, if you can be safe on a horse. *I'm tellin' you, mind your own business, Si. You have trouble enough. Can't afford no delays. Pistol with a broken leg and all. Stolen cows. Jeez. What am I gettin' myself into?*

"I'm goin' that way," he argued. "I'll follow. Can't hurt."

Sure. Can't hurt.

Syrus Stockton nudged the roan with his knees and stepped him across Clear Creek, listening to the killdeer and meadow lark sing in the morning sun.

Damnedest thing, he thought.

The buggy or surrey was farther ahead of him than he thought. It was late afternoon before Syrus caught up, discovering it was an old buggy. The driver had pulled it under the spreading limbs of an old, old cottonwood that towered high above its closest neighbors. The driver had unhitched the horses, built a small fire in the clearing. Syrus couldn't see him. Two small kids, a younger boy and an older girl, were throwing rocks into the waters of Clear Creek. No adult was visible. Two horses were standing in their harness, heads down, cropping no grass, eating no oats, enjoying the shade, or at least grateful for it. They didn't move. *Tired. Not good. Barn yard horses. Not used to foragin' for feed. Both older.* Syrus Stockton shook his head slowly. *Don't see a soul exceptin' them kids. This surely ain't right.*

Syrus was one hundred yards away when he stepped down from the roan. Casually, he slipped the latch from the hammer of his SAA Colt thinking of his father's repetitive lectures.

"Don't have that latch on your shootin' iron, you steps into a crowd," he said over and over again. Too many times. Syrus smiled, remembering Riles asking, "Papa, how many's a crowd?" His father had looked at Riles, at his two younger brothers, before answering, making sure all three were listening. "One," he said and walked away. "One." Raising his gloved index finger. "One. A crowd of one."

Syrus, reins in hand, started walking down the gradual incline, leading the horses, the pine trees standing dark behind him, clumps of quaking aspen on either side giving a spotty light green color to the forest from which he advanced. Down the gentle slope he walked, conscious of the boy and girl laughing, tossing rocks, knowing he was being watched, feeling the hair stand up on the back of his neck. Someone was gunning for him, sighting down a rifle and his head was the appointed target. He could feel it. *Damn it,* he thought. *What the hell am I doin'? Where is this fellow? A man determined to shoot anyone who got close. Especially in the middle of nowhere. Especially where you don't know who or what you're dealin' with. Can't be too careful. Another piece of wisdom Pa was fond of.*

Syrus kept walking, his horses following. The boy and girl had stopped playing and were watching him, too. The boy dropped the rock he was holding and took a step forward. Looking at the girl, he pointed at Syrus, laughing, giggling excitedly. Syrus continued moving forward, mindful of the hair standing up on the back of his neck. The boy started running toward him. He was, maybe, four years old: no fear. He was coming fast.

There are moments in life. Everyone has them. In retrospect, a man can be thankful there aren't many and they aren't often. It is doubtful that our hearts could handle many. At its easiest, one of these singular moments is difficult. Two could kill a healthy man living on a steady robust diet of baked potatoes, beans and buffalo steak, and getting plenty of sleep. Even then, one such moment can put a man on overload. Syrus' father, when handed a newly delivered, healthy baby his wife called Peter and everyone else called Pistol, said it succinctly. He said it, looking at the dark eyed child looking up at him covered in blood and afterbirth. "Ah, shit." It was an "ah, shit" moment, forever recorded in the minds and psyche of his three older sons, Riles, Syrus, and Forest. Outside it was a cold, miserable December day, snow drifting through the cottonwoods, the creek frozen over. Inside, their Old Man held a new baby up for the world to see and knew he didn't know what to do with it. Such was a moment.

Syrus had himself an "ah, shit" moment in late July 1886, walking his horses to where the pine trees met Clear Creek, a four year old boy running towards him shrieking gaily, happy as if he'd been rescued from death's door. A clear, high-pitched voice from the trees stopped Syrus.

It said, "Keep walking, you. You aren't welcome. You aren't staying. Keep moving."

It was a woman's voice, one he'd never heard before, and certainly never expected. The owner of the voice saw the boy running toward Syrus.

She yelled, "Stop right there, Jed. You hear me? Stop right there."

But the boy didn't stop. If he heard her, he took no notice, stopping only when he was several feet from Syrus and the big roan stud horse standing behind him. He looked up at Syrus, smiling, happy.

"Hello," he said, his eyes bright and shining.

"Howdy," Syrus answered. "How's things?"

"Pretty good," he replied, turning as his mother walked out from the thick brush; behind her a host of young cottonwood trees lined the creek bottom. She was framed by a chokecherry thicket, and the tall, suffocating bunches of skunk brush. In her hands she held a lever action Remington, butt against her shoulder, the barrel no longer pointed at Syrus. Though he suspected that it had been.

Jed brought his attention back to Syrus while his mother yelled, "Jedediah, get over here this instant." Jed didn't move; he stood looking up at Syrus. "Are you gonna eat supper with us? We're lost. We don't know where we are. Do you know where we are? Are you lost? Is that your horse? He's pretty big."

"I have a fairly good idea where I am, boy."

Syrus stared at the woman. "Ma'am," he said in greeting.

The barrel of the Remington was now pointed off to the side, the front sight bobbing as her arms moved and she approached. Momentarily, she stared at her son, clearly dissatisfied with his lack of obedience. She returned her focus to Syrus, deciding there was nothing she could do to the boy right then.

150

"We're not lost," she said. "We know exactly where we are."

Syrus noted that the hammer was pulled back on the Remington. *Wonder if she knows. Damn shame if she don't.* "Do you know where you're goin'?" Syrus asked in reply.

It was a simple question, one which took her by surprise. She blinked her eyes, momentarily preparing a response. She said, "Of course we know where we're going."

"Where?"

"None of your business. You shouldn't be asking me personal questions about things that are none of your affair."

Syrus smiled. "Ma'am," he said, "you're forty miles west of Buffalo in the middle of the Big Horn Mountains. You're travelin' in a buggy pulled by two old horses who can hardly stand on their own. The left one has a sore foot. That'd be my guess. The one on the right pulled a shoe; his foot got stuck in mud that last time you crossed the creek. Sucked it right off. You have two little kids who ain't old enough to help themselves to potatoes and gravy if it was handed to 'em on a plate. In another mile or two, you'll have to abandon the buggy. You've gone as far as you can go on this trail in that buggy.

"So you damn well better know where you're goin' because you're there right now. If a bear or a cat gets into those horses of yours, they're gone and you're walkin'. And those two young'uns might as well be dead because they soon will be. I'm makin' where you're goin' my business. You die up here, I'll never forgive myself.

"Ten years ago Crazy Horse's people lived here and no one bothered 'em. Ten years ago, a hundred miles north of here, he took it to George Custer. I'm pretty sure George was a lot tougher than you've ever been and he didn't make it. Do you hear me? Are you listenin'?"

"Basin City."

"Basin City? That's more than a hundred miles. You got a long way to go if you're goin' to Basin City. Several mountains are in the way. You're gonna have to go 'round 'em. You sure as hell can't go over 'em."

"It is not. That man at Mothers said it was maybe sixty miles from Buffalo. According to you, we've come forty. That leaves us

151

twenty, at most. We're close. Real close. I think that in two days we've come most of fifty. Using simple math, we have ten to go. We're almost there. Four hours and I'm home. We have an odometer on our buggy wheel. It works and it says so. I'm not guessing. I know. You're the one that's guessing. I'll ask you to leave now."

"Ma'am, you're not listenin'. You're in trouble. This here is Clear Creek. Four or five miles east of here is a stream called Crazy Woman. It's named after a white woman comin' out here with her family. Her husband and kids got themselves killed by the Teton Lakota. She lived. Went crazy tryin' to get to 'em. Injuns left her alone 'cause she was nuts. Eventually, she starved to death. A trapper buried what was left of her bones. I can take you to her cabin. You can look at the markers for her husband, her babies. I'll show 'em to you so you know you're in trouble. Afterwards, you can go back to Buffalo and live to be a grandma. Your son can grow up. Your hair won't end up on a warrior's belt."

"I said, leave. You don't scare me."

"All right," Syrus said.

"All right? What's that mean? All right?"

"Ma'am, a slow wagon will make ten to twelve miles a day. You have two old horses, two young'uns, and yourself goin' over fairly rough goin'. Since the day before yesterday, the best you made is about ten, plus or minus, miles, dependin' on when you started, how many times you stopped to rest, and for how long."

"Oh," she said, not having anything to say in reply.

"Tomorrow mornin' you'll start out; you'll go about two or three miles. You'll come to a canyon wall. If you go inside the canyon, you'll be stopped. No way out 'cept the way you got in. You can't go no farther. If you stop before you get that far, you can get out of the canyon by goin' around the wall, but you'll have to ride your horses and leave the buggy. You'll need a couple of saddles which you don't have. That means you'll have to ride bareback. You'll have to know how to get around the wall. Personally, I don't think you know. Ma'am, it's best you go back for the sake of your babies while you still can."

"You're wrong. You're just wrong. I don't want to hear any more."

152

"Okay. I'm so wrong hell won't have it. I'm gonna pull back. Let you rest. Cook some food, if you have some to cook. Tomorrow you can make a go of it. I'll watch. Won't say a word, but I'm tellin' you, you should go back. But like you said, I don't know shit."

"I didn't say that. I wouldn't say that. I'm not going back. Don't talk that way around my son and my daughter."

"Yes, Ma'am. Suit yourself." Syrus stepped into the saddle, swinging his leg over the seat, finding the stirrup with his toe. He smiled. "Ma'am?" he said, "I believe you was in Buffalo three days ago? Yes?"

"What's where I was three days ago have to do with you? Besides nothing."

Syrus smiled. "I was there, myself. Saw a young woman about your age dressed in a purple, lacy dress. She was lovely. Somethin' to look at. A handsome woman. Wearin' lavender. 'Bout choked to death on it. I was taken with her. Saw her standin' on the corner on Main Street across from the Hitchcock General. You remind me of her." Syrus touched the brim of his hat. He said, "Good day, Ma'am, and good evenin'. Wishin' you the best, the finest. Perhaps I have it wrong...jumpin' to a hasty conclusion." Syrus spun the roan around; the bay followed, laying his ears back, aggravated by the sudden action. The man glanced back at the woman. "Be watchin' you in the mornin', Ma'am. I'm sure you'll do fine."

"What?"

Syrus left her standing in the green park, moving away from the idle rifle that she obviously wanted to point at him and squeeze the trigger, if she could. He guessed she hadn't because Jed, the four year old, was standing so close.

That's her. I'm not guessin'. She's so familiar. So familiar. No. No, I've never seen her before. Never, he argued. *Wrong. I've seen her before. She's that woman. It's her all right. Bet that purple dress is in her trunk.*

He hazarded a glance over his shoulder; caught her staring at her four year old, a stern look on her face. Her daughter slowly joined her, looking up at her mother. She presented a profile, bending at the waist, her back straight. Shock washed over him like ice cold water. *It is her.* He thought. *Now she knows who I am..., certainly not the nicest fellow. Certainly not who she'd wanna meet in the shadows of the night at the end of a dark, dark trail. She wouldn't be there. She shouldn't be here. Lord. Who would ever think this could happen to me?*

What was she doin' at the edge of civilization, where the rules fade, where law becomes what a man needs it to be in order to live another minute, another hour, another day? She's so careless, bringin' two babies in harm's way without so much as a backwards glance. Just goes to show you. Folks ain't what you think they are. Maybe she doesn't know what she's doin', where she is. Such a pretty lady.

Syrus rode the roan back the way he'd come, shaking his head, perplexed, remembering again the woman standing on the boardwalk: straight, tall. He glanced back at her again: same nose, same cheeks, different hair. Now it hung over her shoulders instead of being stacked on top of her head. She didn't smell of lavender. *Married. Obviously. Two kids.* He shook his head, perplexed. *Can't have everything. Be nice if I could.*

In the late evening, before midnight, after the moon had set leaving only stars to dominate the sky, Syrus was surprised again. He turned, looked up from his coffee cup and found the young Jed standing at the edge of the firelight, staring at him.

"Hello," the boy said when he realized that Syrus was looking at him.

"Jed. How are you doin', boy? Your mother know you out gallivantin'?"

"I don't think so, sir."

"What're you doin' here?"

"I'm hungry. I want to know what you're eating."

"Rabbit. Want some?"

"I do."

"Come over here. Sit. I'll peel a rabbit steak off the back-end of this jack for you to chew on."

Jedediah willed his short legs to move, walking into the fading light of a fire slowly burning down to ashes, the light of the orange flames flickering off his face.

"Have a seat, boy."

He did, seating himself on a broken cottonwood limb, the bark peeled off, leaving white wood exposed. Syrus pulled the blade of his jackknife out of a decaying log and cut the left hind leg off the

154

rabbit and handed it to the boy, licking his fingers. The boy looked at the meat, holding the foot bone in his hands, then at Syrus.

"Thanks," he said.

"You're welcome, boy."

Jedediah proceeded to chew the rabbit meat off the hind leg bone, concentrating on the task as if it deserved his sole attention. It took six minutes. After he finished, he handed Syrus the bone. "I'd like more, please," he said.

"You do, do you? You got a holler leg?"

"I don't think so."

"All right," Syrus said, cutting the right hind leg off, detaching it up on the rabbit's back, pulling the leg bone from its socket and handing it to the boy.

The boy accepted it. "Thanks," he said. "I'm a little hungry, I think."

"I see that." It was then that Syrus saw another urchin standing at the edge of the fire light, clasping her hands together in front of her.

"Missy," Syrus said to her, "you look a little hungry yourself." Syrus guessed she was two years older than the boy, which would make her six or close to it.

She nodded.

"Cat got your tongue?"

She shook her head no.

"Come over here, girl. Sit by the fire with your brother. I'll cut you a piece of rabbit to chew on."

Wordlessly, she made her way to the fire's edge, sitting beside her brother, the light playing off her nose, her long tresses. She watched him with big, dark eyes, the long skirts of her dress covering her knees, hiding her ankles and bare feet.

Pulling his jackknife from the log, he wiped the blade on his trousers, then cut a slice of golden brown meat from the back of the jackrabbit and handed it to her. "It's pretty good," he said to her. She nodded, watching him lick his fingers, not moving, as if she were waiting for permission.

"Well, get after it, sis, before your brother eats the whole damn rabbit. Brothers are that way, you know. I know 'cause I got

155

three."

Immediately she bit into the warm meat, started chewing, not looking at the amused Syrus. A minute passed. Syrus busied himself cutting another piece of rabbit from the carcass, laying it in the bottom of the frying pan. When she was finished she handed him the meatless bone and accepted the second piece, her eyes remaining on him.

"Go ahead, Sugar. That rabbit's gettin' cold. Can't get any more dead than he already is."

Without speaking, she did as directed.

Taking his eyes off of his guests, Syrus cut an end off a loaf of bread, buttered it, smeared it with apple jelly, bit into it, and started chewing.

The boy watching him stood up, walked two or three steps to where Syrus was sitting , and said, "I'd like some." Syrus tore the slice of bread in half and handed the larger piece to the boy.

"Thanks," the boy said and started eating. This time, standing up. When he was finished, he said, "I'd like a drink of water."

Syrus handed him his open canteen, the lid already off. The boy raised it to his lips and took two swallows, paused, followed them by a third, and returned the canteen to Syrus.

"Thanks," he said.

Syrus nodded.

Holding his hands together, his fingers intertwined, the boy glanced around at Syrus' makeshift campsite, at the two horses cropping grass in the night shadows, then sat down on Syrus' bedroll. Syrus had rolled it out on a bed of old leaves and pine needles. That was hours before, when the sinking sun was minutes above the western horizon, about to become lost amid the dark branches of pine trees. The girl had finished with her second piece of rabbit meat and stood up. Syrus handed her a piece of buttered bread covered with apple jelly. She accepted it, ate it like she'd never tasted bread before. She took a drink of water when Syrus offered her the canteen.

Syrus glanced at the boy and discovered he was asleep on top of his bedroll, his mouth slightly open, a soft breeze playing with his hair. The boy defined innocence. It was an interesting dichotomy in propriety. Syrus wondered if he should remove the boy's shoes and

156

tuck the blankets around him. He decided against it. That, after all, was his mother's job, not his.

The small boned girl in her long dress, barefoot, stepped in front of him, patted him twice on the knee with the fingers of her left hand. She paused, studied her brother asleep on Syrus' bedroll, then made her way to him. Wordlessly, she laid beside him and pulled the wool blanket over them both, snuggling next to him. She fell asleep with a bemused Syrus watching, the fire barely alive, dying quickly.

I'll be damned.

It occurred to Syrus that she had not uttered so much as one word during the entire experience.

It was the two pats on his knee from a child lost in the mountains, and earlier the voice out of the thicket telling him to "move on" that created the bookends to his solitary "ah, shit" moment. Thinking about it years later, he realized that it was the moment that turned his life on end and sent him in an entirely different direction.

Sitting in the flickering firelight, he took another bite of buttered bread, apple jelly sticking to his fingers. Crumbs fell on his shirt. For a reason he didn't understand, he remembered a child's homemade book his mother had read and re-read to him, and to his brothers. He wondered if Pistol still had it and read it to his babies. In the center of a homemade fairy tale booklet sewn together by his mother with cotton thread and a needle, was a map. It showed a road into mystical mountains, a road drawn in black ink. On the map was a hand drawn sign. The sign read, "Beware. Dragons live at the end of this road." Glancing at the two sleeping children, he wondered if he had dragons sleeping under his blankets on the far side, the dark side, of a waning moon, at the end of a long road.

For a time he watched the two urchins sleep, studied the gentle rise and fall of the wool blanket as they breathed, watched the boy move an arm about his sister and sigh: perhaps dreaming. Somewhere an owl was hunting, leaving an echo of its passing hanging in the cool night air. Coyotes were howling, yapping in the starlit night, a stirred up hive of activity. In the cottonwoods, crickets were rubbing their legs together, singing their bizarre, aching tunes. He recalled his Old Man pronouncing that every rug rat was entitled to being born and cared for. He had said it more than once, so many times.

He said, "a kid should never have an empty stomach, never go hungry, ever. Never go thirsty, should always have a bed to sleep in, a kitchen table to get his short legs under, a ma and pa to love him, to tuck him in bed at night. Everything else is secondary. Ain't important, to be exact." Syrus Stockton nodded, thinking how ornery his pa was. Syrus had grown up on the banks of Sage Creek. He remembered never ever being hungry a day in his life. *The damnedest thing, that.*

Two hundred fifty yards away, under the shelter of the limbs of a giant cottonwood, the woman, a night cap pulled over her head and ears, moaned in her sleep. Something changed. You'd never know it. She didn't know it, not yet. For lying under the limbs and leaves of that giant tree, with rings counting two hundred fifty-eight years, she lost her son and daughter to four pieces of jackrabbit and a slice of bread smeared with cow's butter and apple jelly. She moaned, her sleep full of fear and foreboding. On the rise at the edge of the pine trees, Syrus got to his feet, looked for the tarp that he'd used to cover his pack saddle and panniers. Finding it, he made his way to his horses and went to sleep wrapped in that tarp, the pickets driven into the ground inches from his head. He smiled, remembering Link Hannon living on Davis Creek joking about leaving twenty feet of good hemp rope, stealing the sheriff's horse for the hell of it. The sheriff had been sleeping in his blankets, his head inches from the pickets he'd driven in the ground that secured them. *Damnedest thing, that.*

CHAPTER 22

It was early morning. She came running across and up the grassy slope, frantically waving her arms, seeking attention. Midway, she realized she'd forgotten her battered Remington, that one article that everyone seemed to automatically respect regardless of gender, station, or size. The sudden realization brought her to a breathless stop. Lack of air forced her to bend at the waist, pulling as much air inside as she could. The distance she'd run wasn't far, but the elevation quickly separated those in good physical shape from those not; she fell easily into the latter category.

The first rays of morning sunlight caught her breathless and indecisive in knee high grass above the winding, bending Clear Creek. The hem of her skirts was wet with dew. She looked back at the buggy parked under the cottonwood and the two old horses she'd tied to a fallen limb. Both horses turned their heads, staring at her. They were hungry for they hadn't eaten: no oats, no corn, no grass. They waited to be taken to the creek for a drink. All night they'd stamped their hooves, shuffling about, warding off mosquitoes, their hooves steadily chewing up the earth where they stood. It occurred to her that she'd done them wrong. She hadn't thought.

The boy and the girl were gone, their blankets empty and cold. She was frantic, bordering on a hysteria that threatened to bubble up into her heart, distorting feeling and thinking. Again, she hadn't thought. In that mountain moment, she needed help. She needed it right now. She continued running. The man, as detestable and distasteful as he was to her, remained the only person she could go to for it. There was no other place, no other person, no other option. The very idea of a bear, a wolf, coyotes, a lion finding two defenseless children in the open, without protection, slowed her natural cognitive abilities, brought them to a standstill. In this vacuum, she ran as fast as she could, pushing herself as hard as she could.

She arrived at the edge of the man's camp, breathless, nearly falling on her face in her rush to save her children. She was a mother, willing to sacrifice herself, her pride, anything. Gasping for air, she looked for him. To her dismay, he was nowhere to be seen. She tried to cry out "help" but her breath coming in rushes was too shallow to enable her to form that word. It didn't come out right. It didn't come out at all. She glanced at his picketed horses munching oats, the feed bags over their noses, calmly watching her.

She was rescued from her panic by a movement which caught her attention. She saw the man standing like an intruder at the far edge of his own camp carrying a tarp in one hand. In one glance she also saw his Winchester rifle leaning against the tree trunk. Her eyes flitted across it to him, lingering, hesitating.

"It's loaded, Ma'am. Loaded rifles kill people."

"What? I... I... I know that," she said trying to think, to concentrate on the need of her visit.

"Just sayin'."

"My, my children.... I can't find them. I need your help. They're gone. Their blankets are empty. Oh my God," she continued, words tumbling out of her mouth. "Please? Would you help me?"

The tall man did not respond immediately. When he chose to reply to her request, he simply nodded, pointed at the bedroll and blankets that lay on a cushion of dead cottonwood leaves and dead pine needles collected from many yesterdays. "That them?" he said.

She looked. She saw jumbled blankets, a dirty pillow and, for the first time, she saw her daughter lying under the blankets, her head partially uncovered, her hair in total disarray. She was sound asleep. She didn't immediately see her son, but he was there, somewhere, next to the girl. At first, Rebecca was incredibly happy, for what was lost was found. If she'd been in close proximity to the man, she would have thrown her arms around him, shouting "thank you, thank you, thank you."

This did not happen.

A deep, growling anger followed her delirious happiness: anger at waking up and discovering her children missing in the wilderness, at running, sprinting, for their lives, at begging for help when no help was needed. It was a false alarm. Embarrassed and angry at her emotional outburst, she saw the man who had them, standing right before her.

"You stole my...children," she stated. Her voice flat, her eyes, if they could have, would have cut holes in him. She wanted them to. She intended them to. "My God," she said. "What's wrong with you? How did they get here? What are they doing here? I almost died of fright."

"Ma'am, last night," he looked up at the sky, "when Orion was over there. Late. Very late." He pointed at the southern sky. "They dropped into my camp. Held me up. Their tummies growling. The boy said he was hungry. Wanted to know what I was eatin'. I said rabbit. Said he wanted some; then he wanted some more. Then came the girl, standing at the very edge of the fire light. She said nothin' at all. Just stood there, a little girl in the dark. I gave her some rabbit to eat. She wanted more. I gave it to her. She wanted a drink of water. I gave that to her. They ate the damn rabbit whole, leavin' nothin' but bones. The boy laid down in my blankets like Goldilocks and went to sleep. Last I saw of him he was lickin' butter and apple jelly off his fingers. He's in there somewheres. When that girl of yours was finished with the rabbit, she had some bread and butter; ate it gone. Full, she laid down beside her brother, pullin' the blankets over 'em both. Went to sleep without a word. It was a helluva thing. Cleaned me out. I was sure-fired held up, robbed, in the middle of the night by a couple of hungry thieves. That's what they were." He smiled. "Damnedest thing," he said. "Damnedest thing."

"They shouldn't be there."

"Tell that to the boy, the girl, not me. I'd say those two knew who buttered their bread. Went right after it."

"It... it isn't right. I want them back. They're mine. You... you can't have them. Even if they're hungry. It isn't right."

"Ma'am, I don't have 'em. They sure as hell ain't mine."

"Don't talk that way."

"What way is that?"

"The way you do."

"Ma'am, my pa said that young'uns are entitled by birth to a kitchen table to get their short legs under, a bed to sleep in with a stack of blankets to keep 'em warm, and a ma and pa to love 'em and tuck 'em in at night. That's what he said."

"What are you saying? That I'm not a good mother? I am.

You can't say that to me. Really, you can't."

"I didn't say you wasn't."

"You did. How do you do that? Acting dumb as a door knob and smart as a whip all at the same time?"

"Brothers."

"What?"

"I got brothers. That's the answer to your question."

"I'm sorry?" What?

"Don't be. I like my brothers. Though I gotta say Riles, he can be a knot head, sure as hell. Accordin' to my pa, kids are entitled to those things That's all I'm sayin'."

"Oh my God, stop talking. I can't believe this. I don't need parenting lessons from a no count saddle tramp. I just want my kids. They are mine. I'm taking them. You can't stop me. You better not."

"There they are, Ma'am. They're not mine to give to you. I don't want 'em. You're their mother. I'm just a saddle tramp on his way home."

"What? A saddle tramp on the way home?" Rebecca threw her hands up, turning to her kids.

"Ma'am?" When she didn't respond to him, he moved away.

She ignored him, busying herself waking the girl and boy, getting them standing upright, trying to get them moving. "Come," she said. "We gotta go. You're not supposed to be here, bothering this man. Hurry. Let's go."

Syrus stepped farther back, getting completely out of the way, taking the Winchester with him, a slight sort of knowing, awkward smile on his face. To his relief, in minutes she had them moving, walking away, if not stumbling away from his camp. That's when she noticed the dead jackrabbit and a fools hen lying near the fire. He saw her looking.

"What are you doing," she asked, "with, with those?" She pointed at the jackrabbit, the fool's hen.

"Thought I'd cook breakfast," he said.

"You're disgusting. I know what you're doing. Really."

"Yes, Ma'am. I am a bit disgustin'." He nodded his head in agreement, smiled. "Unless I miss my guess, in a few minutes you're gonna hook up that buggy and drive it up that canyon. In about three

162

miles you're gonna come to a rock wall. It'll close in on you. Unless you can scale cliffs two hundred feet high with kids under either arm, you'll be comin' back down that canyon with two hungry kids as well as yourself. Thought I'd be ready."

"You can't help yourself, can you?"

"No, Ma'am. I can't. Not when it comes to a lovely lady all dressed in a purple lace dress standin' on a boardwalk in Buffalo, smellin' like lavender. Now, standin' here with two hungry kids, tryin' their best to get over the mountain. I can't. And, if you don't mind me sayin', you won't be able to, either. Not alone. The mountain is too big for you."

"You can't say that to me. I'm married."

"I know you're married."

"How do you know I'm married? I haven't told you."

"You got two young'un's, Ma'am and I can say it."

"Oh, well...yes. I'm married to a federal judge appointed by President Rutherford Hayes, himself."

"I reckon that's good. I didn't know Mr. Hayes was President. Thought it was Garfield. Just sayin', bein' married to a judge or the President ain't gonna help you out of this hole. His judgeship ain't here. I'm hopin' you'll come to your senses, start thinkin', and take those two kids back to Buffalo where you can get help. This canyon-- it's a dead end. You either come back out of there or die in there. Those are your choices. You need help, Ma'am. I'm hopin' you'll come to that understandin' soon so that I can go on my way. My plate, it's a little full right now."

"Your plate is full? You know I don't believe you."

"Yes, Ma'am."

"You're impossible."

"Yes, Ma'am."

"Oh," she said, in frustration, hands on her hips, hair falling in her eyes.

Her children were sitting on the ground, watching. Turning to her daughter, she said, "Em, let's get out of here. We're going to get home today. You'll get to see your father. It's not far now. It's just over the mountain. Hurry. Let's get going. We're almost there. Buddy, come on. Time to go. Come on now. We've worn out our welcome."

As they got up, she herded them out of Syrus' camp. They were walking away. Sort of, except they weren't. It was another one of those "ah, shit" moments that never seems to be forgotten. Twenty yards down the slope, walking slowly, the boy broke loose. He jumped out front, turning to look back. His mother glanced at him. He started to run back, to return to where Syrus was standing.

"Buddy? What do you think you're doing?" She yelled. "Don't do it. Come back here."

He was gone. His legs carried him quickly back to Syrus who was standing by the breakfast fire, watching. The boy threw his arms around the man's right leg, hugging him, not looking up, not crying. Behind him his mother was in pursuit, determinedly walking up the grassy slope, calling his name repeatedly. But the boy was not ready to leave, not yet. The boy took something the man did not know he was giving. The stranger wordlessly patted him on the head, not once, not twice, but three times, cupping his small head in his large hand.

"Better be listenin' to your mother, boy," the man said.

Suddenly, the boy knew everything was going to be all right. He looked up at Syrus.

"Thanks," he said.

"You're welcome," the man replied softly.

His mother, almost to Syrus, frustrated, angry, and at a loss at what to say or do, reached for the boy, but the boy dodged her hand, running, sprinting, if the legs of a four year old boy can sprint, his little legs carrying him down the slope, laughing as he ran in the damp grass. Moments later, he caught up with his sister.

Rebecca looked up at the man. "I'm...."

"Don't be," he said.

"I...."

"He's a boy," the man said. "So was I once upon a time. So was my brothers. He'll be all right."

She started again to say something.

The man raised his hand, stopping her. "Ma'am," he said, "there's no need."

"All right," she said and turned to leave, walking slowly down the slope, the two kids almost to the buggy. It didn't make sense to her. She absolutely refused to believe that the gaping canyon mouth didn't lead to Tensleep, the basin and then Basin City, that several miles from here it simply stopped. Yet when the man looked down his nose at her through dark brown eyes, she did believe him. "He'll be all right," is what he said and she believed it because she wanted to.

He watched her retreat and their departure, smiled, and shook his head. *Damn,* he thought. *I'm glad that woman is married to a judge somewheres...and not me.* He glanced around, numbered what chores he needed to do. He took care of the horses first, moving their pickets to new grass. Three hours later, he built a fire and started dinner. It was not much: roasted jackrabbit, roasted fool's hen, some bread and butter.

CHAPTER 23

It had been three hours since their departure. The dilapidated buggy slowly made its way out of the canyon's mouth, the old horses plodding carefully through the rocky entrance. The horse on the left moved more gingerly than its mate, picking its way through the boulders and gravel, its right forefoot sore, the frog bruised. There was no shade, no shadow in the cool, heavy mountain air. The sun, hiding behind clouds, had made its ascent to its zenith but it was difficult to tell where it was exactly. Thunder clouds hung low over the canyon walls. They were thick, dark and boiling ominously, hiding the pine forest at the top in a moving mist. Sporadically, raindrops fell, catching the brim of his hat and the shoulders of his shirt. It smelled of rain. It felt like rain.

In the distance, Syrus Stockton noted the driver sitting straight on the buggy seat, the ribbons in her hands, her hat covering her eyes and forehead. He wondered what she was thinking: whether her pride, her anger, would propel her on past him and down the trail, starting the two day trek back to Buffalo. If it did, she'd be gone, carried out of his life like a Cooper's hawk riding the updrafts, a dark, disappearing speck of dust in the sky. *That'd be...awful,* he thought. *On second thought, maybe not. It'd be best. Of all the silly luck I've had. She sure is somethin'. Why am I so taken with her? Shouldn't be. What's wrong here? And what ain't wrong here? She's married with two children. Yes. Yes, she is. But from the very first time I saw her.... This ain't a good situation. Not at all.*

The buggy disappeared behind a stand of young cottonwoods, momentarily hidden by buck brush and chokecherry. He could hear the wheels turning. One lacked grease and squeaked as the wheel moved around the spindle. Moments later the buggy came back into view. Taking a breath of cool, damp air, Syrus put his tin cup down on the log where he sat, then went to move the picket lines again.

This sure as hell is gonna be interestin', he thought.

After he finished caring for his horses, he returned to the fire

166

and sat down on the log, the fire in front of him, and looked after the jackrabbit, the fool's hen. She was much closer, her face flushed, her hair hanging in her face partially concealing her left cheek. The boy sat on the seat behind her, his hand on its back. Several times it looked as if he was almost falling out of the buggy as it caught a rock, rose and fell. He jumped, hitting the grass, rolling, jumping up and racing out in front of the wagon. He gained distance, laughing. His mother called him back but he paid her no attention, making his way straight to Syrus and his campfire. Syrus stood and gathered some firewood.

It was hard not to smile at the boy running through the knee high grass, excited, driven by uncontrolled, boundless energy. Syrus knelt and added broken pine sticks to the fire, seating the coffee pot in the hot coals. *Coffee would be nice*, he thought. Turning, he seated himself on the log by the fire and waited. *What will she say?* he asked himself.

The boy's path took him past the roan stud and the bay pack horse.

"Hello," he said, stopping in front of Syrus, his small hand touching his knee. "I'm hungry," he said. "I'm real hungry."

"I'll bet you are."

"Can I have some rabbit? Like a leg? Would that be all right?"

"It's all right with me, boy."

"That's real good. I'm starving."

"Think you could eat a horse and chase the rider right up the creek?"

The boy laughed. "I think maybe so," he said.

"Well, all right." Syrus reached over and cut a rabbit leg from the roasted jack and handed it to him. The boy immediately seized it, bringing it to his mouth.

"Jedediah Kilpatrick, stop that. Right now. Where are your manners?"

She was standing in the buggy, the reins in her hands, the girl sitting beside her.

"It's all right, Mom. I asked," Jedediah said.

"Did you?"

"Yes, I did. It's all right, Mom. He's a nice man."

Standing in the buggy, the woman was a little unsteady. The horses hadn't come to a complete stop. The buggy endured a herky-jerky moment of rolling back and forth. She nearly lost her balance.

"Sir, I'm so sorry. I'm so sorry. Jedediah isn't normally like that."

What should I say to that? He decided on nothing. *The boy's hungry.*

The girl climbed out of the buggy on the off side and was walking behind it, coming around the back, walking toward Syrus. Her gait did not slow; she walked with purpose, her curls bouncing around her ears.

"Emma. Emma, stop right now," her mother demanded. The child didn't listen; she kept walking.

If I'd of done that, I'd a got a skinnin', Syrus thought. *Interestin'. What was this woman doin' out here with those young'uns anyways? Shouldn't be here. It's a miracle she made it this far. Little girl is a cute kid.*

"Sir, sir, I'm so sorry. Oh, Emma, don't embarrass yourself. And me. Jedediah, please."

Emma stood in front of him, looking up at him through big dark eyes.

"She would like somethin' to eat, Ma'am," Syrus said.

Rebecca stood in the buggy beside the black leather, criss-cross, padded buggy seat.

"I..."

Syrus knelt, pulled a leg off the fools hen and handed it to the girl. She took it. Before biting into the roasted meat she looked at her mother as if to ask for permission.

"Oh, Emma," her mother said in response.

Emma looked back at Syrus, her eyes blinking slowly, hesitating.

"It's a hard one, ain't it, girl: your mother sayin' for you to stop, your stomach tellin' you you're hungry. You'll have to decide what's best. It's my thought that you better get started, girl 'fore your little brother eats the whole damn thing." Syrus glanced at the woman in the buggy and swore he could smell lavender. Taking a deep breath, he sat down on the log and stared at her.

"Might as well get down from there, Ma'am. Join your kids."

168

In response, the woman wrapped the ribbons around the brake lever and climbed down to the sod and started walking toward him with perfect posture, perfect stride.

Only God could make somethin' like that, he thought. As she walked to him, he scooted over and invited her to sit down.

"No, no, thank you. I...." She stared to tear up, her hand coming to her face. "We're in trouble. I've been really stupid."

Syrus pointed at the log and the space he'd vacated. She hesitated. He spread a towel over it. "Please," he said.

She looked at him, at the towel on the log, and then back at him. "All right," she said. "I..."

"Hungry?"

"I...," she paused. "Yes, thank you."

"Rabbit or chicken?"

The question was interrupted. "May I have a drink of water?" Jedediah asked. The boy had returned, a rabbit bone in one hand, unsure of where to put it.

"Toss it in the fire, boy," Syrus said. He picked up his canteen, unscrewed the lid and handed it to him.

Jedediah wiped his fingers on his shirt, "Thanks," he said.

"Damn straight, boy." He glanced back at the boy's mother. "Rabbit or chicken?" he said.

"Chicken, please."

Syrus took out his jackknife, opened the blade, cut the thigh off the roasted bird, and handed it to her.

"Thank you," she said. "You're so kind. I mean, sharing your food...."

"My mother was a woman," he said in reply.

"Your mother?"

"Yes, Ma'am. My brothers and me, we was damn lucky that way."

"Your mother? Where is she?"

"Dead, Ma'am. Winter got her. It can be cold in the foothills."

"Oh, I'm sorry."

"It's all right. She was a helluva woman. Raised us right."

"I would have liked to meet her."

"You would have liked her. She was a pistol."

169

"A pistol? Why do you say that? I haven't heard that before."

Syrus thought about his answer. "I don't know," he said. "She was one, I guess."

"I'm so sorry to burden you."

"You ain't no burden, Ma'am." He noted that she'd finished the thigh. "More?" he asked.

She paused as if checking some treatise on manners and civility. "Yes, please," she finally said.

"That bird has another thigh. I'm savin' the drumstick for Miss Emma. Kids like drumsticks. My brothers...we used to cause a ruckus over 'em. Would another thigh do?"

"Yes. It would be perfectly fine. I'm grateful."

Syrus pulled the thigh and drumstick off the roasted fools hen, separating the bones and meat and handed her the thigh.

"Thank you."

"My pleasure."

"I've decided to take your advice...to return to Buffalo. Do you think, I mean..., is it possible for you to help us get there? I don't know if I can get back without help. I'm so sorry to have to ask. To plead, beg, really. I made a horrible mistake. I thought.... I didn't think."

"Ma'am, I'd love to help. This is one of those times where I can't. My brothers, they're in need. I don't have another four days to get you to Buffalo, and come back here and over the ridge. You made the right decision, by the way. You really don't belong out here. I just can't help you find your way back."

She sat holding the meat very still in front of her lips. Her eyes watered. "What am I to do?" she asked.

"Especially with that rig of yours. That left horse looks to be lame. He ain't goin' nowheres, especially Buffalo, or for that matter anywhere else. You're gonna have to cut him loose or permanently ruin him. Not that he's much good, anyways. He's old as dirt. Maybe older."

She sat staring at him; tears began running down her cheeks.

"Ma'am, best I can do is take you over the ridge, if that's where you're wantin' to go. That's on my way. I can do that."

"You can?"

Joy burst from Rebecca, running over the top. She moved pell-mell across the log, the fools hen thigh still in hand, and hugged Syrus. It so surprised him he didn't say a word. In thinking about it later, he told himself that a hug from her didn't hurt. It felt pretty good, in fact, reminding him of his mother's hugs, the three pats on the shoulder, sometimes for nothing. Just a mom's hug.

Syrus Stockton patted Rebecca on the shoulder. "It's all right, Ma'am," he said.

She broke the embrace, embarrassed. "I'm so sorry. I didn't mean to be so forward."

"Ma'am, I'm used to hugs. Beautiful women do that to me all the time. From time to time my pa said that."

"I'll bet they do," she said.

"Don't put too much money on it, Ma'am. Might not be a sound investment."

"I won't," she replied, biting into the thigh she held in her hand.

"Ma'am," he said, "soon as you got these young'uns fed, we oughta be goin'."

Rebecca stood. "Yes," she said. "We're ready. I don't want to hold you back. You're so kind."

"Ma'am?"

"Yes."

"Take the time it needs. A young'un should never be hungry. Feed 'em while I get ready."

"Are, are, you a father? You seem to know so much."

"I ain't even a husband. My pa said stuff like that all the time. I figure he know'd what he was sayin'. So take care of your young'uns while I square things away. We won't be goin' 'til they're fit as a fiddle. It'll take me a few minutes."

"All right," she said. "Thank you. I mean, really, thank you."

"Ma'am." Syrus Stockton touched the brim of his hat, nodding. Without considering what he was doing, he pulled a Mississippi Crook from his shirt pocket and stuck the end of it between his lips in the corner of his mouth. Rebecca stared at him; her eyes seemed to grow larger. He took the cigar out of his mouth and looked at it. "Ma'am, don't worry. I'll not put a fire to it. Like the

171

weed, myself. Soaked in rum. Has a nice flavor."

"Thank you," she said. "I mean for your courtesy."

"Don't mention it," he said.

She watched as he picked up a bridle and walked out to where the roan was standing. She also noticed the pistol tied to his thigh and another seated behind his gun belt. If she'd looked she'd would have seen a third in the small of his back, tucked behind the belt that supported his bull hide chaps. She heard him talking to the big red horse, low and easy. The roan looked at him, blew his nose.

Syrus glanced up at the threatening sky. A few raindrops hit his hat and shoulders, stinging cold against his face. *Damn*, he thought. *This is gonna get complicated.* Syrus Stockton moved quickly, saddled the roan, packed the panniers to hang on the pack saddle, put the pack saddle on the bay.

The woman watched, impressed, for there was no wasted movement; everything had a place, a time, a function.

Turning to the buggy, he studied it, shook his head in what appeared to be disbelief. Quickly, he unhooked the trace chains, pulled the harnesses from the horses' backs, dropped the hames, removed the collars, and turned the lame horse loose. The horse didn't go anywhere, standing, cropping grass, blowing its nose, switching its tail back and forth, occasionally watching him. It was obvious that he'd lived too long in a corral, sheltered by barn walls, comforted by a stall, a manger full of hay, and a bait of oats morning and night. He noted its limp was more pronounced: what with mountain cats, coyotes and wolves hanging around, he may not live long.

Rebecca and the children joined him. Syrus left the bridle with blinders on the other horse, giving the ribbons to the boy to hold while he threw the harness in the buggy. He folded a blanket and laid it across the horse's back and smoothed the wrinkles out. Lifting the pack saddle and panniers to the bay horse's back, he explained to the woman what he was doing.

"I'm gonna put the boy up there on top of the pack saddle. You and the girl will ride that one." He pointed at the horse with the blanket on its back. "No saddle, so it'll be bareback. Ever ride bareback? Don't make no difference. You're gonna do it now."

172

Syrus returned to the campfire, putting it out. Collecting the remainder of his belongings, he returned to the waiting family. He helped them up onto the horses. Ready, he climbed into his saddle and started the cavalcade across the canyon's mouth and into the pine trees south of the canyon on the other side. Disappearing into the trees, they started climbing. It was an hour before they broke out on top. The thunderhead had moved on; the sun was blazing down and too soon would be setting. They followed it west into the Big Horn Mountains, keeping the peak on his right.

The boy liked to talk, so he talked and talked and talked. When he stopped talking, his mother looked at him to see why and discovered he was drowsy, close to falling from the top of the pack saddle, physically exhausted. Syrus lifted him from the top of the packs and settled him in front of him on the shoulders of his saddle. The boy slept. They kept moving.

"That's amazing," Rebecca said to Syrus. "How did you know how to do that? I mean he's asleep in your arms."

"I had a little brother. Ain't so little any more, but when he was small he rode this way in front of my father. Right up here on the shoulders of the saddle. When he was awake he'd have his hands on the reins. So did the Old Man. He literally grew up in the saddle."

The boy moved in Syrus' arms.

"What was his name?"

"Pistol."

"Pistol? Your mom's a pistol and your brother's named Pistol?"

"Odd, ain't it? Guess we ain't too clever."

He stopped when it got dark, immediately setting up camp, picketing the horses, giving each a bait of oats with what he had left. He built a small fire, set out the bedrolls, the coffee pot, the sack of jerked meat and what was left of the fools hen and jackrabbit.

"What are you doin' way out here, Ma'am? Seems a little on the dangerous side."

"I'm joining my husband, Jedediah and Emma's father."

"How come he ain't in Buffalo to meet you?"

"He would have been, I'm sure, if he knew. He doesn't know I'm coming. It's a surprise. I'm surprising him."

173

"That's some surprise. If he's sleepin', bet he'll wake right up."

"It's been two years since I've seen him. He was made a judge. Jed was two when William came west following his appointment. I don't think he remembers his dad. Barely, if at all. Not much, that's what I'm saying."

"Two years is a long time," Syrus replied. "You told me your husband was a judge."

"I did? I forgot."

"Not a problem, Ma'am. Listen, I'm gonna leave you with those young'uns for a while."

"You are? Why? I mean where are you going? Will you be gone long? I...."

"Gotta round up breakfast. Ma'am, don't mean to tell you what you should be doin', but when those two wake up, I'd feed 'em what's left of that rabbit and fools hen. Help yourself to whatever you can find. You got that Remington, you get yourself into any shootin' trouble. Point it and pull the trigger. You'll be fine."

"I will? I'm sure I will. I'm sure.... Yes."

He smiled. "You don't sound all that sure."

"Well, I am."

"Good."

"My husband, William. He was supposed to send for me once he got settled but he didn't. I decided to come to him. I got tired of waiting. Two years is a long time. Jed and Emma missed their father. I thought I could do it."

"I see," Syrus said. "I'm sure you could of done it, Ma'am."

"No, you're not."

"I did have some doubts."

"How far is it to...?"

"Fifty, sixty miles if you're a crow.

"If you're not a crow?"

"It's still fifty or sixty miles. Just takes a little longer."

"Hurry back," she said. "Please, hurry back."

"Ma'am."

Syrus Stockton went hunting. He rode the roan, walking him into a dark, tempered by moonlight. It wasn't cloudy. There was a

174

moon and some brighter stars sprinkled across the heavens. He could see, but he deliberately paid close attention because it's easier to get lost in such conditions. Landmarks don't look the same. Sometimes the wolf hunts at night. Sometimes the coyote, the owl, the mountain cat. He'd heard them and in the light of day he'd seen their tracks. Night hunting isn't the best of times to hunt. Neither is it the worst.

The need to be alone isn't about hunting. He had enough grub to get by personally, but there were more mouths to feed. He needed to be alone more than he needed something to eat. But it was more than that. Feeding two young ones and their mother was different. Something he'd never done before. If he examined it, he would have found it exhausting, loaded with stress.

In the darkness, he found empathy for his father, realizing that this task was his "always burden," not just a two or three day experience. He and his brothers and his mother ate every day.

Being with someone--a woman–and breathing the same air, eating the same rabbit, trying to figure out what's best in a world of infinite possibilities, was new. He found it different from sitting at a card table in a saloon in Auburn, California, watching folks walk in and out. *Damn straight it was different.*

It didn't help that that "someone" was someone else's woman, someone else's wife.

An hour passed. A waning moon lit the quiet of the forest, the grass parks. Higher up on the sides of the peak it had begun to frost. Up there it was cold after sunset: at best in the high thirties, at worst in the high twenties.

Being alone was good. Syrus shot a small doe he found feeding in the bottom of a park; he dressed it and tied its carcass behind his saddle. The roan didn't like the death smell. At first, he bounced around a bit trying to get away, trying to escape the smell of death. Syrus held him in.

Syrus couldn't help thinking of the woman, thinking how it would be to return to someone like that every day, someone who actually missed you. She'd said "hurry back." He realized that leaving with a "hurry back" wish was something he wanted, that he had a hole in his life large enough to ride a full-sized work horse through that he needed to fill. He wanted someone to laugh with, to cry with,

175

to hope with. Suddenly being alone in his life was like a steady diet of horseshit and gunsmoke. In the quiet of a hunt he discovered he didn't like "alone" much.

Stopping on the rise overlooking their temporary camp, he stepped down from the roan and studied the moonlit landscape: the dark pine trees on the far side, the slopes of Clouds Peak on the right, the moonlit high clouds that hid its alpine summit. For a moment he listened to the coyotes yelping, an owl hunting; he watched the swallows flitting about in search of insects. Below him the woman had a fire burning. *Little late for a fire,* he thought. *Built a little higher, a little bigger than needed.* If it were his, it would have been small, burning low in the dark, if at all. With this woman it was a big fire, flames warming the night, tiring her out carrying wood to feed it.

"Hurry back," she'd said. "Hurry back?" He thought about her words. There is more than one reason to want someone to "hurry back." Fear was one. "I miss you" was another. Which was it? Had to be fear. Her future was tied up, locked and loaded, a known commodity. He took a breath and let it out in the mountain air, listened to the cry of a hunting bird. *Too bad,* he concluded. *Best to get over it as soon as possible.*

Still, he thought, *I'm attracted to her. Those little things: the way she looks at me, the way she stands, how she purses her lips. Damn straight. I gotta get her to her man. Step out of her life. Not that I was ever in it. I'd better get right to it.*

Syrus removed his hat, ran his fingers through his hair, looked at the roan.

"You know, horse, that Judge is one lucky SOB, havin' somethin' like that waitin' for him. Wonder what's wrong with him? Why'd he keep her at arm's length for two years?" *Odd,* he thought. *If it were me, I'd have gone to get her ten minutes after I got here. Bring her west myself, soon as I could, but the Judge kept her away from him.* He rubbed behind the roan's ears, scratched its forehead. *I can't think about it no more. This ain't my problem.* "It's best I forget her and find someone else, get my own little problems. What do you think, horse? Sound like an idea?"

Syrus stared at the roan who was looking for grass to crop.

"Come on, horse, speak up, cat got your tongue?" He

176

nodded. "Nothin' to say? Well, let's go down there and enjoy her company while we can. Can't hurt much. What do you say? Still ain't talkin'? Well, you're right. Talkin' is overrated."

Syrus took the reins in his gloved hand and started walking down the gentle rise through knee high grass and sage, the horse following, no longer bothered by the doe's carcass sitting behind the saddle. It took seven minutes to get to the creek bottom and only a few seconds to start pulling sticks from the fire.

"But why?" she asked him. "I just barely got the fire going."

"Fires attract attention, Ma'am. Folks not knowin' we're here ain't nearly as dangerous as them knowin'."

"I don't understand."

"If they don't know, they won't come lookin'. Won't have to deal with 'em."

"Isn't looking for us good? I mean wouldn't you want them to come looking for you, especially if you're in trouble?"

"We ain't in trouble. Folks bring trouble."

She stared across the fire at Syrus. She said very quietly, "I was in trouble. You came. You wouldn't have if you didn't know we were there. I'm glad you found us, if you know what I mean. I don't know what would have happened if you hadn't insisted. I think you saved our lives."

Syrus thought a moment, holding his tongue.

"Ma'am, I suppose you're right about trouble, but if you don't mind, when I'm doin' the rescuin' we shouldn't invite anyone to that horse race. I'd like to get you home to the Judge and get out of town before anyone knows I was there. Silly as it might seem."

"You're a strange man. You do good things and you don't want a soul to know."

"Yes, Ma'am, that's true."

"It's like you're running from someone or something?" She paused. "Are you?" she asked.

"I do try and stay ahead of whatever is chasin' me. I don't know who or what it is that I might be dodgin'. Best not to invite trouble."

"That's silly. Why run from a shadow?"

Syrus pulled a Mississippi Crook from his shirt pocket. He

looked at her for permission.

"It's all right," she said. "Please go ahead. Indulge yourself. You've been most patient. I'm grateful."

He put the chewed up end in his mouth and felt the sweet taste of tobacco and rum spread over his tongue and lips. He asked her, "Got any of that rabbit left?"

"Oh, yes, yes there is. You must be hungry. I'm sorry. I was fussing over the fire and I forgot."

He looked at her and thought how incredible she was. *She forgot? Damn, why would she remember?* He watched as she cut the rabbit into small portions, put it on a plate, and handed it to him. *A plate?* He only had one plate and she'd saved it for him. He nodded, then answered her question.

"I don't run from shadows as much as I seek 'em. There's a safety in shadows, of not bein' where you're expected. I prefer that safety. I prefer not takin' a chance. Especially if I don't have to. My Old Man was always warnin' against leavin' the hammer sittin' on a empty chamber. If you do, it's for safety. It prevents surprises like gettin' yourself shot. He said that if you needed the rifle and the hammer is sittin' on an empty chamber, the rifle is worthless and you could be dead in that second you take to shove a live round in the chamber. He was of the opinion that to be safe you must be ready all of the time. He said that to be ready you don't use an empty chamber. It ain't safe." Syrus sucked on the cold cigar. He paused and looked at her. "That make sense to you?"

"I guess."

"Ma'am, that old Remington you carry around. Is the hammer sittin' on an empty chamber?"

"I must admit I don't know. I haven't even thought about it."

"Ma'am, you should know. Your life, and that of your brood, may well depend on you knowin'. You should know. Really know. You should fire it every once in a while, often as you can. So you'll know how it feels. So you won't be surprised by the feel of it. If you don't mind me sayin', Ma'am."

"I see. I thought that protecting me is what my husband is supposed to do."

"Protect you?"

178

"Yes. Shouldn't I expect that of my husband?"

"Ma'am, two things: One, he ain't here. I'd like to have a woman of my own some day. Someone to protect. Someone to do what you just did for me. You saved the last plate for me. You didn't have to do that. Someone to give me a reason never to leave the hammer sittin' on a empty. If you was mine--I know you ain't--but if you was, I'd want you to think enough of yourself to have the hammer of that old Remington of yours sittin' on a live round. Just in case you needed it. I'd want you and everyone else to know when you pulled back the hammer on that rifle, someone or somethin' is surely gonna die. And that it ain't gonna be you. I could grow old with someone like that. I could get old with someone like that." Syrus paused. "Ma'am, I saw my mother shoot the eyes out of a weasel at a hundred yards. Knock the little bastard right outta of the tree on his head. One shot." Syrus paused again. "She liked her chickens. See what I mean?" he asked. "She meant everything to the Old Man. Damned if she didn't. She was truly amazin'." He smiled.

Rebecca laughed. "Are your brothers like you?" she asked.

"Pretty much. I'd guess." Syrus said, "Ma'am, it's way past late. You oughta get a little shuteye. Tomorrow is gonna be here before you know it. By that I mean in a few minutes. Why don't you get under that blanket with those kids of your'n?"

Rebecca looked away from him. A cool breeze picked up, bending the grass in waves. She shivered, clutching her arms about herself, her mind somewhere else.

"My husband doesn't know his mind like you seem to know yours."

"Maybe I got less to know."

"Maybe," she said. "Maybe what you know is more important than what he knows. The closer I get to him, the more I worry. I wonder what he'll say. I wonder whether he wants us. Maybe this wasn't such a good idea. In two years he wrote me four times. I think maybe the West changes people. Sometimes it isn't a good change. I'm hoping...."

"He'll welcome you with open arms, Ma'am. I daresay you'll be the best surprise he'll ever get."

She turned to look at Syrus. "I hope you're right," she said.

179

"We've come so far."

"Ma'am, we pretty much ride the horse we saddle." He stopped speaking. "You got this one saddled, ready to throw your foot in the stirrup. I can't see no room to be second guessin' yourself. I can't imagine him not bein' happy to see you."

The fire had burned down to orange embers; it was barely a flicker when she turned in. She laid down on the blankets with her two children, covering herself with the blanket Syrus had draped across her horse. Somewhere, two miles away, several coyotes were yapping excitedly. It sounded like there were forty of them chasing a desperate rabbit through the sagebrush. The coyotes must have lost for they kept yapping. She closed her eyes against the night. Had she been watching, she would have seen the strange man disappear into the night, a mere shadow in the fading moonlight.

It was early, about the time a thin line of light formed along the crest of the eastern Big Horns. He woke her; it was a hand on her shoulder, a voice in the dark.

"Ma'am, time to roll 'er out. Get those youngsters up and movin'. There's some venison roastin' on the fire. Be ready to eat in a minute or two. Soon as those kids have their bellies full, we should hit the road...if we can find one and if it don't rain. Assumin' no one takes a shot at us and hell won't have us."

She would have said something in reply but before she could formulate a thought, the voice and the hand on her shoulder were gone. For a moment she wondered if she'd been dreaming. Holding herself still, she could hear the fire popping, wood burning. She smelled coffee boiling, and wood smoke drifting across her blankets. No, it wasn't a dream. She sat up, the blanket falling away from her. It was then she realized that the horses were saddled, the panniers were packed and hung on the pack horse. The only things left were her bedroll, the blanket, the fire and the coffee pot. She wondered how he did all that. She wondered why. What was the hurry?

To her surprise, she found Jed sitting on a rock by the fire chewing on roast venison, his shirt and jacket wrapped tightly around his shoulders. Only Emma was asleep. She found her lost in the blankets, not wanting to wake up, not understanding why anyone

180

wanted her to be awake.

Twenty minutes later, with Jed still nibbling at roasted venison, they left. There was still no sun, no breeze, a cool air, the smell of sagebrush and pine.

They rode three hours before the first stop to water the horses and let them graze. No one said a thing for most of the first three hours. Even Jedediah was silent. She noted that Syrus seemed to know exactly where he was and where he was going. She found his certainty comforting. Someone should know. The next stop was two hours later. He found a grove of chokecherry trees and let the "yonkers," as he called them, pick and eat the berries, spitting out the seeds. They were so bitter. She wondered how they were able to keep putting them in their mouths. He found some currants and had her pick them. They were so much better, sweeter. He hardly talked, noting once that they'd come fifteen miles, "give or take an inch or two."

He rested the animals at the end of the first five hours of constant walking. They waited an entire two hours. Syrus made sure the horses had plenty of water to drink and grass to crop. During that time he disappeared for an hour. When he returned, he told her they were ten miles from Basin City.

"Ten miles?" she questioned.

"Yes, Ma'am. Ten miles."

The boy asked him. "How far is that?"

The strange man poked the boy in the belly and said, "half a day, four or five hours. See where the sun is?"

"I do."

"It'll be right there," pointing with his finger, "when you get to the town where your father lives. Not too far, really. I should be at my home in two and a half days, if everythin' works out, it don't rain, and hell won't have it."

"Is your pa going to be there?"

"Nope. I don't think so. Just my brothers."

"I don't remember my pa. Do you remember yours?"

"Yes I do. Can't imagine yours not gettin' all excited seein' you. I'm all excited and I ain't your pa. See how it is?"

" I do. Where do you live?"

181

"I live a hundred miles that way." Syrus pointed with his finger. "At the bottom of the Pryor Mountain. Two kids just like you and Emma live there."

"How old are they?"

"I don't know."

"I'm four."

"So, I hear."

"Have you met my pa?"

"I have not."

"Is he a good pa?"

"Your mom married him. I can't imagine he ain't the best. She picked him out of the litter."

Rebecca broke out laughing. "Not quite that way, Jed," she said, "but almost. I married him because my mother and father wanted me to. They thought he could support me and you and Emma. He asked, and I said yes. So far they've been right," Rebecca said.

"Sounds good to me," Syrus said.

"It is good." She laughed, looking at Syrus and smiling. "Besides, I got the Remington and the hammer is sitting on a live cartridge. No. No. I'm just teasing. He's a good man. Graduated from Harvard College in Boston. He's the best. We've been married almost seven years. He was a lawyer in Philadelphia. Made a good name for himself. We've only been apart for a little over twenty-four months. You cannot do all of that and not be a good man."

"See there, Jed, he's a good man. Do you wanna get on the trail? Get there and you'll meet him."

"I do," Jedediah said, no longer sounding reticent.

They started and kept going.

"How close is Basin City?" she asked Syrus.

"Well, Ma'am, Basin City sits on the river. See those trees, the string of cottonwoods? They are growin' along the river. Basin City is on the other side. Once we get to those trees, there's a ferry to take you across the river. I'd say an hour or so, you'll be there. How you holdin' up?"

"I'm getting a little nervous in spite of myself."

"You'll be all right. I know you was just teasin' 'bout the Remington, but you keep the hammer on a live cartridge. You'll feel fine. You'll do fine."

"Thank you for the sermon."

"Hell of a preacher, ain't I?"

"Yes, you are. I was thinking. I haven't told you my name. You didn't tell me yours. At first I didn't want to. I...."

"No need, Ma'am."

"No, it isn't right. It's not. You've been so nice to us, to me. I....my name is Rebecca."

"Ma'am."

"I know you won't, but if you ever come back to Basin City, would you stop and see us? Please?"

"Sure."

"Say my name."

"Ma'am?"

"Say my name. I don't want you to forget me. Please?"

He looked at her from under the brim of his hat for what seemed like a long time. "Rebecca, Ma'am," he said.

"Thank you."

"Ma'am."

He said 'Ma'am' in response to her 'thank you,' then this very strange man touched the brim of his hat with his gloved fingers and she knew that everything would be all right just as he said. She nudged the old horse with her heels. The horse took a step forward, then another, down the long hills to the river, to the ferry, to Basin City and her husband.

She paid the ferryman for passage, and turned to Syrus.

"We can make it from here. You never told me your first name. Please don't. Please don't tell me. I want to wonder what it is."

He nodded.

"Remember," she said. "Please remember. Don't forget me. I don't want you to forget me. You saved our lives. We owe you."

He stepped down from the roan stud, wondering why his remembering her name was so important. It was not likely he was going to forget. He looked at her sitting astraddle the old barn horse, Emma behind her. He nodded, then picked the boy up, lifting him

183

from the shoulders of the roan's saddle and setting him in front of his mother. Then he pulled the Remington from the pack horse where he'd tied it. He opened the breech, found it loaded, a shiny new cartridge sitting in the firing chamber. He closed it, letting the hammer down slowly, carefully. He then handed the rifle to her.

"It's loaded, Ma'am."

He mounted the roan, stepping into the saddle, then, one last time, looked at the married woman who didn't want him to forget her. "Ma'am," he said, touching the brim of his worn, weathered Stetson.

"Bye," the boy said to him waving his right hand.

"So long, pard. Take care of your mom and your sister. Big job, you know." He looked at the boy's mother. "I won't forget, Ma'am."

The ferryman led the old horse wearing a bridle with extra long reins and blinders onto the ferry, leaving her for a moment to release the rope so that he could pull the ferry across the river. From the back of the horse she could see the court house and a green buckboard rolling up Main Street.

"Where's he going, Mom?" Jedediah asked her.

"I don't know, Jeddie."

"Does he have to go, Mom?"

"Yes, Jeddie, he does."

"But why?"

She didn't answer his question.

184

CHAPTER 24

The ferryman led the old horse with the woman and two kids on its broad back onto the dock and solid ground. She appeared to be nervous: brow furrowed, her fingers white around the reins as if she feared she was about to drop them.

"Ma'am?" he said.

She didn't respond.

"Ma'am," he said again. "Ma'am, you all right?"

"Oh, I'm sorry. I was thinking. I didn't mean to be rude. I need to find Judge Kilpatrick. He's my husband, you see. We're sort of surprising him. He doesn't know we're coming." She hesitated. "You don't want to hear all of that, do you? I'm sorry. I'm just boring you. Do you know where I might find him? That would be helpful."

"Ma'am. Judge Kilpatrick? Didn't know he was married." The ferryman tugged at his watch chain and, after some effort, pulled a pocket watch from his pants pocket. He studied its face for several seconds, then looked up at Rebecca. "Ma'am, It's sorta late or I'd guess he's up to the court house. I'm told that's where he is when he's workin'. 'Bout this time of day, he's at Harolds. That'd be the Basin City River Bar and Hotel. Harold Gaudheim, he owns it. Judge goes over there when he's through workin'. I figure that's where you'll find him unless he's gone home."

"He's in the bar? I...I. Did you say he's in the bar? My word!"

"Ma'am, he eats over there. That's where he eats."

"Oh, I didn't know. I was surprised that he was in a bar. I mean he's a Judge. I didn't know.... You know, I didn't know. Do you think I can go in there, I mean with two kids? Will they let me in? Is it... is it, you know, safe?"

"I think they'll let you in, Ma'am. Folks eat there on occasion. Have a drink if they are of a mind. Other things, I'm sure. You know, sleep. It's a hotel, I'm told. I'm not sure you'd wanna go in there. Well-respected women, well they don't ordinarily, Ma'am. I ain't castin' no aspersions, Ma'am."

"I know you're not. No aspersions. I understand. What other things?"

"Yes, Ma'am, other things."

"What other things?"

"That'd be Harolds up on the hill." The ferryman was pointing. "I reckon you'll find him there."

Rebecca looked. "Sir, thank you. I appreciate it." She noted that he'd deliberately ignored her last question.

"You're welcome, Ma'am." The ferryman was turning back to the river and the ferry. Rebecca watched him, then looked up the hill. *This isn't going well,* she thought. *Bill is in a bar? What am I to do? Do I take Jed and Emma inside a bar? Should I do that? Oh no, this isn't going well at all.* She kicked the old horse in the sides. He took a step and stopped. She kicked him again. He started walking. *What am I going to do? I can't leave the children outside. I shouldn't go inside myself, I don't think. Should I? I guess I have to. Oh my. Oh my.*

The old barn horse was tired. He'd come a long way. With urging, he continued walking. He didn't stop until they reached the top of the hill. Rebecca brought him to the hitching rail. She helped Jed down, telling him to get up on the boardwalk. She helped Emma down and got off herself and busied herself wrapping the reins around the hitching rail. She glanced at the closed doorway. *This isn't anything like I had imagined. Not at all.*

She stepped up on the boardwalk, took Jedediah and Emma by the hand and approached the door. Someone came out. He stopped immediately and held the door open. "Thank you," she said and stepped inside. He closed the door. She was struck by the fact that inside it was cool, and smelled of cigar and tobacco smoke as well as alcoholic beverages. *Oh my,* she thought. *Oh my. What am I doing?* The three stepped farther into the room. She surveyed the furnishings: the long polished bar on her right, tables and chairs in front of her and to her left. She located her husband sitting at a round table, eating. He was talking to a woman who sat, listening. He laughed, apparently pleased with himself. Rebecca took a breath and took a step toward her husband, a child's hand in each of hers.

Judge Kilpatrick looked up as Rebecca brought the little cavalcade to a standstill in front of his table. *Oh my God,* she thought.

186

He did not miss a beat. "Well, look at this," he said. "Julie Ann," he said, "I'd like to present to you my wife Rebecca, my son, Jedediah, and my daughter, Emma. This is a surprise."

Julie Ann immediately came to her feet, extended her hand to Rebecca. Rebecca took it. "Pleased to meet ya," Julie Ann said.

"Likewise," Rebecca replied.

"Judge," she said, "this is an occasion. Would you like me to have your buggy brought around front?"

"Please, thank you, Julie. At your earliest, if you would."

The Judge turned his attention immediately from Julie Ann to Rebecca. "This is certainly a surprise, my dear. Are you hungry?" He pushed his plate in front of Jedediah. "Here, Jed, eat up. May I order you something, 'Becca? Emma?" He leaned forward. The chair creaked.

"I don't feel comfortable here, Bill." She noted that he hadn't stood yet, that he hadn't hugged his son, his daughter, or her. "I don't think the children should be here, either. I'm not sure it is proper. I, I guess."

"Nor should you. We'll go to Maggies. She has great food. Milk for kids. We can leave as soon as my buggy is made available which should be soon. Right now, in fact. By the time we get outside it will be available. Do you have horses? We can attach them to my buggy. Did you arrive in a buggy?"

"Yes, I have a horse. We got here on a horse."

"That must have been some ride, the three of you on a horse. Maggies is close, just down the street, in fact."

The Judge stood. "Let's go," he said. Rebecca noted that he still hadn't hugged anyone, hadn't touched her, not so much as a pat on the hand. She wondered what she should to do.? Everything seemed so unsettling, so disquieting, so filled with anxiety. Eating at Maggies was also unsettling. It was enduring an uncomfortable quiet that extended on and on..

As soon as they were seated, Jedediah asked him, "Do you like me? The big man on the big horse said you'd like me. Are you surprised?"

"I am surprised," the Judge said. He looked at Rebecca. "What's he talking about? Who's the big man on the big horse?

187

What's he doing talking to strangers?"

"He's the man who brought us over the mountain."

"You came over the mountain? Lord!"

"Yes, it was some trek. We got here safely, though. Thanks to that man. We're very grateful. Really."

"Man? What's his name."

"I don't know."

"You came over the mountain, from Buffalo, I'm guessing, with a man, and you don't know his name?"

"He didn't give it to me, Bill. Does it matter? I mean he took very good care of us. Fed us. Protected us. Brought us right to your doorstep. He didn't have to, but he did. Jed was quite taken with him."

"I see," the Judge said, leaning back in his chair. He looked at his son and daughter. "They've grown so much," he commented to Rebecca. Then, turning to Jed, he said, "Yes, Jedediah, I'm very much surprised."

After they'd eaten, the old livery horse was tied behind the buggy. The two kids rode in the back, with the Judge and Rebecca on the front seat, the Judge directing a pair of blacks pulling the buggy. He didn't say much, nor did Rebecca. She thought that he'd be happy to see them, but he didn't seem to be.

"Rebecca," he said, "you sure did surprise me. Really. I didn't expect to see you, and there you were."

"Does it make you happy? I mean to see us?" she asked. "We wanted to surprise you. Neither I nor the children have seen you in two years. We were looking forward to it. I would have written you but the letter would have gotten here the same time we did. It was all very impulsive. One day I decided to come to you. It seemed like the proper thing to do."

"Yes and no," he answered. "Certainly, I am happy to see the three of you. Certainly. Though I must say I am not fond of surprises of any kind. I thought you knew that."

"But this surprise? You did like it, didn't you? We took such chances. I did, anyway."

"I must admit I don't like surprises at all. Seeing you and our children though is really nice. How did you get here?"

188

"Horseback as you can see. A kind man brought us from Buffalo; he was very kind."

"And you don't know his name?"

"No. I don't know. He didn't give it. I didn't ask for it."

"That's certainly strange. What did he charge? Hope it wasn't too much."

"Nothing at all."

"Nothing. He certainly didn't overcharge you. Let's come back to the surprise later. I am looking forward to showing you our house. It came with the job. It's a two story frame. Several hundred yards off the river on a small rise. Very pretty really."

To her surprise, two minutes later, they pulled into the front yard of a white frame structure with a pitched shake shingle roof.

"What do you think?" he asked.

"It's lovely," she told him. "Very lovely. Better than I could have dreamed."

"Good. I hoped you would like it. Jed and Emma each have a bedroom."

At the breakfast table the next morning, Judge Kilpatrick mentioned to Rebecca again that he did not like surprises. She told him she wouldn't do any more surprises. He also said she shouldn't have brought Emma and Jed inside a bar. He said, "That is a very bad place for children."

"Bill, I had no choice," she said "I knew no one, had no one to leave them with, and so I kept them with me. You understand that, don't you?"

He said he did. "I don't like the idea of our children talking to strangers. You, either. For that matter. I don't like you coming clear from Buffalo with someone like that."

"Someone like what, Bill?"

"Some, some saddle tramp, Rebecca. It's very dangerous out here. People kill each other for the smallest of things. That's why I didn't send for you immediately."

"You didn't send for us at all, Bill."

"I had my reasons."

"Would Julie Ann be one of those reasons?"

189

The Judge, for the first time in their married life, appeared red faced and shaken, as if his hand had been caught in the proverbial cookie jar.

"You will not mention her again. My acquaintances are my business. Not yours. Do you understand? You will not mention her again."

"And my acquaintances, Bill? Whose business are they?"

William Kilpatrick came to his feet in a roar. A glass that she didn't even know she owned prior to last night, fell to the floor, shattering, sending shards spraying across the room along with water. Jedediah and Emma sat immovable in their chairs, and stared at the man in fear and trepidation.

"What?" Rebecca said quietly. "You'd strike me if the children weren't present? Is that it?"

Just as quickly, the Judge regained his composure. "Of course not, Rebecca. I would never do anything like that. You shouldn't bait me," he said. "It might not end well."

"You mean for me?" Rebecca said. "You've changed, Bill. I don't like it...the change."

"We can speak of it this evening," he said. "Jed, fetch me my hat, would you?"

The boy didn't move.

"Jedediah, please get me my hat, boy."

"It's in the kitchen, Jeddie," his mother said. "Hurry. Your father doesn't want to be late for work. Get it for him."

"Don't coddle the boy, Rebecca."

"I'm not, Bill. Your own son is clearly afraid of you."

She could see the anger boiling just beneath his skin again. Indeed, something had changed. To her surprise, she thought of the old Remington sitting on the shelf in the kitchen, a shiny new cartridge in the chamber, and the words of a nameless saddle tramp admonishing her to always keep it loaded and handy.

"Just in case," he'd said.

"In case of what?" She'd asked, laughing. "I've got a husband to protect me."

"Who knows?" he answered.

She'd never thought she'd need it.

190

CHAPTER 25

It was at noon of the fourth day since leaving Kane when two wagons pulled onto the hardpack that comprised the front yard of the Stockton compound. The house sat snugly under the spreading limbs of the old cottonwood shaded by its leaves in the hot days of summer. Its back yard was the Sage Creek. The house sat on a rock foundation, a short walk from the water's edge. On the other side a spring house had been constructed for fresh meat to hang from the rafters and cool, and for milk and butter to be preserved. A small subterranean spring ran out of the hillside under the spring house providing refrigeration in the summer and moderating the freezing temperatures during winter.

The two story log structure had housed three generations of Stocktons. For Diana it felt good just to see it; and for the recent travelers it was good to return, to feel the familiar, to have the feeling of home soak into their bones once again.

Diana didn't expect much when she and Peter left, more or less in desperation, a week before to purchase a sack of flour, some salt, a red and black can of baking powder and to see the doctor. Coming back...well, she expected to see the horse corral gate open, tilting, practically lying on its side, the screen door to the house removed from its hinges and leaning against the north wall, waiting to be mended, rehung, made usable once again. A dilapidated mess is what she expected, but it was her home, her mess; it was Josh and Katie Sue's home. It was Pistol's home and now one of his brothers had returned. It was their home, worn out or not. It had history, the weight of generations, the expectancy of more.

The twelve foot gate to the horse corral was made of lodge pole pines years ago snaked from the side of the mountain with old Julie and a log chain. Her father-in-law had constructed it using an old wagon wheel hub as an axle to rotate the gate open and closed, boring holes for the slender pine poles to rest inside. He'd used a double edged axe with a hickory handle, and an old brace and bit. He'd bored hole after hole, over and over again until the end of the pole fit snugly. In that long time ago, Katheryn was pregnant with Riles. She'd sat on a stump watching her husband work, dabbing the sweat from her flushed cheeks. That was more than thirty eight years ago: a time before the timothy had been cultivated, cut and stacked, before the hog pen, before the spring house, before the horse corral, before the barn.

Over the years, the bark on the lodge poles had weathered, leaving the poles starkly bare and smooth. Inside the corral the snubbing pole was sunk deep in the ground, where many a green mustang had left its fear and anger, and had bent to the will of the brothers and their old man.

Holding the ribbons in her hands, Diana stood, the wagon edging forward a bit, as the horses came to a standstill. The horses' ears came back, conscious of her not being on the seat any longer. She blinked her eyes in surprise: the horse corral gate was standing in the wheel hub, ready to swing open, ready to swing closed. Inside were four saddle horses: two she recognized, two she didn't.

Sitting down, she urged the Belgians forward, closer to the front of the house, glancing at the Buckskin standing, its reins wrapped around the hitching rail. On the long porch two men sat, along with the ugly, long-haired one-eyed dog. She glanced across the compound: the pigs were in the pig pen, the milk cow was standing in front of the barn bawling, and there was a dead packrat lying in front of the hen house. She heard Petey pulling the buckboard up next to the freight wagon.

"Far," he yelled. Diana turned. "Damn your unforgivable hide. Get over here. It is so good to see you. And before you ask, absolutely not. I did not get throw'd off no horse." Anxious, he stood, and started to slowly climb down from the buckboard, using his strong leg.

Forest laughed, stood up, and walked across the porch, the rowels on his spurs brushing hard against the floor, his hand slipping along the lodge pole rail. The steps he took in two strides, striding across the hardpack, grabbing his brother's outstretched hand, pulling him to him, hugging him.

"How the hell are you, little brother?" he said.

"Good. I'm good."

192

"I can see that," Forest replied. "You've never been better."

Both men laughed. Two years difference in age, they looked a lot alike: Stocktons.

Diana glanced at the long log cabin, well- chinked. The space between each log was filled in and well mudded against the cold of winter, the heat of summer. The new repairs were obvious to even the most casual observer.

Wrapping the reins around the hand brake, she climbed down the spoked wheel to the hardpack. Turning, she helped Katie Sue from the wagon seat, then walked alongside the large horse, who, with its mate, had pulled the wagon over and down the mountain. She reached up, rubbing his back, patting his shoulder. The trace chains rattled. She glanced at the front door. For the first time in months, the screen door was not leaning against the side of the north wall, waiting to be repaired. Now it swung on hinges, a latch keeping it closed. The woodpile she used to feed the kitchen stove had wood in it: chopped and stacked just outside the kitchen door. A stack of deadfall waited to be chopped into usable portions that fit the fire box on the kitchen stove. Above her a small trail of off-white, smoke drifted from the rock chimney, carried down the creek on a gentle breeze.

Diana brought her hands to her face. Laying hens were walking in and out the chicken coop, cackling; the pigs were in the pig pen. Behind her she could hear the hens clucking, pecking in the dirt, the pigs grunting, squealing, snorting, rutting in fresh mud. Somewhere something was rhythmically pounding: Bang, bang, bang, bang. *Oh my God,* she thought, momentarily beside herself. She started to tear up, wiping her nose on her sleeve. The water pump, driven by a windmill, was working, bringing fresh water to the livestock in the outer corral.

"Diana," Forest said to her. She jumped, startled. The man from the porch extended his hand. "I'd be Far," he said, introducing himself. He patted his shirt pocket. "I got your letter. I surely did. Came as soon as I could. I know'd you a long time ago. You was smaller than you are now. Not as pretty."

She reached out, taking his hand. "Thank you, thank you," she said. "Just in time, too," she said. "You Stocktons don't mess

193

around. I mean you fixed the screen door, the windmill, the horse corral."

"Well," Forest said. "I got a little bored sittin' on my hindend watchin' your hens lay eggs. Not to mention the milk cow's calf gettin' all the milk. I was a little jealous."

Diana was a strong woman. No one would argue that. Not now, not today, not ever. Since learning of her father and sister's tragic deaths, she hadn't allowed herself to even think about them. She didn't know what would happen if she did. Day after day, Katie Sue had sat beside her, sucking hard rock candy, her hands sticky, her breath smelling of mint. Inside, Diana felt hollow; disjointed; nothing felt right. Nothing made sense. The reality of her loss was too horrid, too incomprehensible.

Now, looking at a hog pen with pigs inside, and a working screen door, she started to cry. Like a tide, her emotions suddenly rose to the surface and spilled out. She sobbed incoherently. The help she'd so desperately needed was right in front of her. Odd what a hog pen and a screen door will do. They seem so unrelated.

Peter hobbled from the buckboard to the front wheel of the freighter, leaning against it for balance, taking the weight off his bum leg. He watched his wife still holding Forest's hand, tears suddenly running down her face.

"Come here, Dee," Peter said. "What is it?" he said, putting his arm around her. "How can I help?"

She dropped Forest's hand and turned to her husband. "Oh, it's just..." she said, "the horse corral. That's what it is."

"The horse corral? What's wrong with the horse corral? It looks all right to me."

"The gate's closed," she sniffled, wiping her eyes on her sleeve. She tried to regain her composure to no avail. She burst into tears again.

Katie Sue was standing beside her mother, looking up at her, her sticky hand on her arm. "Momma," she said. "Momma, why are you cryin'?"

"The chickens are in the hen house. They can be locked up at night to keep the skunks from killin' 'em, from eatin' all their eggs."

Peter glanced at the hen house.

"The pigs are in the pig pen."

Peter and Katie Sue glanced at the pig pen, a hundred yards away.

"And the front door has a screen...to keep the flies out. I so hate flies."

Forest looked down at Diana."Didn't mean to make you cry, Ma'am." Forest said. "If I'd known you'd start bawlin' I sure wouldn't have done nothin'," he joked.

Peter smiled, looking at his wife. "My brothers are here, Dee, just like you asked. Except Si. If he got your letter, he's comin'. I'm guessin' they all got your letters." He glanced at Forest.

"Thanks, Far. Thanks for comin'. Much as I don't wanna admit it, we do need help. Can't tell you how relieved I was sittin' in that wagon box and Riles looks over the side at me. I didn't wanna see him. I was so glad I did."

Riles laughed from the porch. "That was in spite of himself. Ask him. He'll tell you how much he wasn't grateful to see me lookin' at him. He'll tell you how he ain't goin' fishin' with me."

"Yeah," Peter acknowledged.

Diana suddenly wrapped her arms around a startled Forest and sobbed into his shirt. He glanced at Peter, a little embarrassed at the sudden show of affection. Forest hugged her in return, patting her on the back. He said, "I can't wait 'til Si shows up. He ain't used to women cryin' into his shirt pocket. Probably wants to be. Thanks for the welcome, Diana. Can't say I've ever experienced one like this. I'll have to come home more often and milk the cow every once in a while. I know Pistol won't do it. He ain't never."

Diana laughed, tears still leaking from her eyes. She broke away from her brother-in-law, glancing at Riles sitting on the porch chair. She turned to the house, started up the steps, crossed the porch, grabbing the handle of the newly fixed screen door and pulled it open. For a moment she studied it, the weight and rope that pulled it shut, then disappeared inside, letting the screen door close behind her.

She could hear Forest speaking with her husband. He was saying, "Well, if you didn't get throwed, little brother, what are all these splints and crutches for? New fashion? Need another excuse

195

not to milk the cow? You usin' those crutches to make me feel sorry? You know the Old Man, if he was alive, wouldn't cut you no slack in the dally. Wanna tell me 'bout the Old Man? Sure took a hell of a long time. He died last year. You broke your writin' fingers? Can't say I like findin' out a year later."

"I've already caught all sorts of hell from Dee and Riles."

"Not enough. Not near enough. What happened?"

"He went huntin' with Black Wolf like they did every September. This time they started on Layout Creek. They didn't come back. Wolf, Charley, Johnny and me went lookin' for 'em. We found 'em two weeks dead. Back to back. Spent shells all 'round 'em. Not a readable track. Don't know who killed 'em. They put up a hell of a fight, I'd say that. Don't know who. No readable sign. And we looked."

Forest was somber. Riles was wordlessly rocking back and forth in the rocking chair on the porch. "Where'd you bury him? With Mother? I'd like to see where he's buried."

"No. Both of 'em were put on a frame, a scaffold, in separate lodges, over on Dry Head Creek, above the old buffalo run."

"Well, that ain't right, Pistol. We gotta go get him. He needs to be with Mother."

"I know. I know. Riles already told me that. At the time it seemed like the thing to do. It's what Wolf wanted and his people."

"I can see that it might. It ain't that it's wrong. We'll need to go get his bones, Pistol, 'fore the coyotes drag 'em off. He needs to be with Mother where I can pay my respects. Riles tell you that, too?"

"Didn't mention you payin' your respects."

"He should have."

Forest glanced at his younger brother, hesitated, then changed the subject. "You oughtta get up there on the porch with Riles. Sit down. That's what you should do. Riles ain't gonna cut you no slack, either. You sure let this place go to hell. You got a smart woman. I gotta say that. She had to write us all a letter to save your bacon. Must love you." Forest looked down at the top of Katie Sue's head. She looked up at him. "Who's this rug rat? She belong to you, Pistol? Nah, couldn't be. Too pretty."

Peter burst out laughing, glad that the subject had changed. "I

196

can't say as I missed your non-endin' observations on what's right. Katie Sue is her name." Taking his crutches in hand, he balanced himself, speaking to his daughter. "Katie," he said, "this is your Uncle Far."

"Another one? How many do I have?"

"One more," Forest said softly. "One more. He'll be here if the letter your momma wrote reaches him. Then we'll be together. Like your momma wanted. Damn Si's forgettable hide. I'm hopin' he'll make it even if your momma didn't write him."

Sitting on the porch, Riles crossed his right leg over his left, removed and reseated his wide brimmed hat, took a deep breath, and settled back into the chair. He said, "I'm bettin' sooner rather than later, Far. Can't remember him ever missin' a good fist fight. Not if he could help it."

Forest nodded. "Listen, Pistol," he said, "not to kick the dog too much--he's already whimperin'--I really do think we need to put Ma and Pa together."

"Good idea, Far," Riles said from under his hat. "Let's take care of that soon as we take care of this other business. Case you don't remember, Pistol's missin' a number of cows."

Forest nodded, chuckling to himself. He glanced at Riles. "Horseshit and gunsmoke, huh, Riles? Can't do a damn thing 'bout that one." He shook his head, laughed again.

Riles smiled to himself, barely nodding his head in agreement. "I hope we can do somethin' 'bout this one, Far."

"It's good to be home, Riles. Talk to you and Pistol. Feel like I could lay in the sun down there by the creek on that slab of rock and sleep for a thousand years. Soak it in, the mountain sittin' in our backyard like it does. Funny thing 'bout that."

"Funny thing 'bout what?"

"That mountain. What did you think I was talkin' 'bout?" Forest said. "A week, ten days ago, when I was comin' over those Sheep Mountain Hills south of Kane, I crested the rise so I could see her for the first time in a long time. Maybe fifteen, sixteen years. And there she was, sittin' right there where she's always been. Had to step down for a minute or two, just look at her. Felt like bawlin'. It'd been so long. It was like I was comin' home and she was waitin' there for me. You know, with open arms ready to give me a big hug. She spoke to me. I'm tellin' you, she did."

Riles sat up and turned his head, staring at his brother. "The mountain spoke to you?"

"Don't go sayin' it that way, Riles."

"All right, what exactly did the mountain say?"

"She said, 'Where the hell you been?'"

"What'd you say?' Riles said.

"I didn't say nothin'. She didn't really speak, numbskull. Didn't use no words or nothin'. Just felt to me like she did." Forest nodded, smiled. "Riles," he said, "tomorrow I think you and I should do a little scoutin'. See what's goin' on. Best we be ready, time Si gets here."

"Agreed," Riles said. "Gotta say one thing, Far. I ain't never heard of no talkin' mountain." He seated his wide-brimmed Stetson over his eyes, leaning back. In two minutes he was asleep. Out on the hardpack, Cecil stretched his neck and yawned. He shook himself violently, the packs still on his back rocking crazily. Having done so, he sought shade by the tool shed.

CHAPTER 26

Two days later, Riles Stockton was standing on the porch with his hands in his pockets, taking advantage of the shade. He caught a glimpse of a rider coming down the long slope behind the house, the east and west spine of the mountain rising on either side. He guessed who it was. Riles walked down the five steps when Syrus crossed the creek and rode into the front yard on the back of a strawberry roan stud trailed closely by a bay gelding. Both horses were tired and hungry, the rider, fatigued. Syrus stepped down, started removing his gloves, one finger at a time. He smiled at Riles.

It was early morning; the sun had been up half an hour, the day already hot. Behind the barn in the work corral the milk cow was bawling for her calf, her bag tight, waiting to be milked. Neither man said anything: Syrus chewing on an unlit, Mississippi Crook, Riles looking him over, nodding his head, admiring the roan. Syrus loosened the saddle cinch, pulling the saddle off, dropping it to the ground. He stretched, bending slightly backwards, his hands on his back. He wrapped the reins of the roan around the hitching rail and looked up at Riles, the cigar bobbing between his lips.

Removing the narrow cigar from his mouth, he said, "Riles, you got any cakes grillin'? I'm so damned hungry I could eat a fair-sized work horse and chase the rider straight up the creek." Bending at the waist, he seized his saddle by the horn and started toward the steps.

"Let's see," Riles said in reply, "we got cakes, side pork, fresh milk, chokecherry syrup, butter and some apple jelly. That suit you?"

"Damn straight, it suits me."

"Amen. Soon as you've had your fill, we'll talk. You'll find Pistol and Far inside."

Syrus nodded. "Did you mention cow's milk?"

"All you can drink."

"Double damn. You got the milk cow bawlin' for some attention. Must be Pistol's turn."

Riles laughed. He watched his brother mounting the steps.

199

"Si," he said, "good to see you. Really good to see you. We've all been waitin'. Figured you'd be here. Needed you 'fore we opened the ball."

"Damn straight. Wouldn't miss it for a stack of hot cakes," Syrus replied, stepping onto the porch, the jingle bobs on his spurs ringing with each stride. He noted the ugly, one-eyed dog lying in the middle of the porch as if he'd collapsed in front of the doorway.

"What's this?" Syrus asked.

"Dog."

"Must be yours."

"How'd you guess?"

"One eye."

"At least he ain't blind."

"At the very least. You learn to ride yet?"

"Not yet. Lookin' for a good horse. Get inside; wrap yourself 'round some grub. I'll take care of your animals. They look beat to hell. You ought to rest 'em once in a while."

"Thanks. They are beat. Grain 'em, would you? Stay away from the roan. He'll kick the hell outta you and he ain't for sale. Oh, and he needs a rest."

"All right. Consider it done. Who was your servant last year?"

"Sure as hell wasn't you."

Half an hour later, Riles made his way inside, carrying Syrus' pack saddle and the first pannier. He set both against the wall, then went back outside, closing the front door behind him. A few minutes later, he returned, bearing Syrus' bridle, a hackamore, a Winchester, and the second pannier. He laid them beside the pack saddle, then made his way into the kitchen. Everyone was present and waiting.

He found Syrus sitting at the kitchen table, his elbows resting on the edge, an empty fork in hand, an empty plate in front of him. Forest was standing, his butt against the kitchen counter. Peter was slouched in a chair, his leg propped up on another. Diana stood at the stove.

"More cakes?" Diana asked Syrus.

"No. No, thank you, Ma'am."

"Milk, side pork?"

"No, Ma'am. I'm grateful. Damn straight grateful. I ain't et this good since I was workin' a steady job, someone else burnin' the spuds, and I didn't know no better. Thank you from the bottom of my cold, wishy-washy heart. I'm guessin' thet you must be the letter writer married to my little brother. Him bein' married! I know'd that's a damn lie 'cause he ain't never been that lucky. If I remember your letter correctly, you're the oldest of the lovely Stafford girls. Seems to me her name was Diana."

Diana's face flushed. "Call me Dee. Everyone does."

"Or Momma," Katie Sue said.

"Or Momma," Diana replied, correcting herself.

"Or Momma," Si repeated as he was looking at Pistol. "Or Papa," he said. "I read about Pa, that he died a year ago. I didn't like hearin' about it like that...not a year later. Where is he buried? With Momma, I presume?"

Peter rolled his eyes. "I've already heard that twice. I know. I know. Let me tell you before you ask. He and Black Wolf was huntin' up on Layout Creek last September. They didn't come home. We went lookin' for 'em when they didn't come back. We found 'em two weeks dead, back to back, hundreds of spent casin's all 'round 'em. Maybe not that many. We brought them home, put Pops on a scaffold on Dry Head Creek with Black Wolf. Don't know who killed 'em. No tracks to speak of. That's the whole story."

Syrus nodded. He looked at Riles, standing, leaning against the kitchen wall, and shook his head slowly, hesitating. "Horseshit and gunsmoke, huh, Riles? There ain't nothin' you can do 'bout this one."

"Not a thing, Si. Don't know who to do it to."

"What are you gonna do without someone chewin' on your hindend all of the time?"

"Don't know, Si. Might be hard to get used to."

Syrus turned to Peter. "Probably oughta bring his bones home and bury 'em with Mother."

"That's what Far and Riles said."

"Damn, little brother. You done good. When we takin' care of that little chore?"

"That's to be decided," Peter said in reply.

"Sounds good to me." Syrus, pointing the fork at Diana, said, "Now don't you be gettin' embarrassed, lady. I do appreciate the grits. And I appreciate the letter. Got one bone to pick with you, though. In all my born days I ain't never heard of Pistol fallin' off a horse. Except by you. If that was true, that'd be a sin rankin' right up there with shootin' another man's dog. I just ain't never heard of that." Turning to Peter, he said, "What's the story on that, Pistol? I gotta know. Figured that might come under the category of 'damn lies.' No offense, Ma'am."

"None taken."

"So Pistol, the story behind your leg gettin' broke and you fallin' off your horse?"

"He didn't fall off his horse," Forest interrupted.

"Now all is well with the world," Syrus said. "Had me worried."

"Had me bothered, too," Forest said. "Several days ago, Riles and me rode up Ferrimore Canyon to look the place over to see what happened."

Riles smiled. "What happened was some soul shot a perfectly good saddle horse. Pistol happened to be ridin' him."

Forest continued. "Yeah, in the head. The horse fell off the side of that canyon into the draw. Fall broke Pistol's leg. It looks like somebody was waitin' for him. Far as I could tell it was two men. Been there awhile, waitin'. Found where several horses were picketed. Ground was tromped in. Dry wood cut out of juniper trees for fire. Fire ring. Pistol got himself stove up in March. Middle of the winter. Ground musta been frozen. So the sign wasn't all that clear. That's what we know."

"He was ambushed," Riles clarified. "Once he was laid up, the cows disappeared. In that order."

"I thought somethin' was goin' on when I rode up there," Peter said. "Didn't know what. Cows were all nervous, movin' a lot."

Forest nodded. "Like I said, there was sign of some boys standin' 'round smokin', waitin' in the cold. Sign was hard to find, harder to read 'cause the ground was froze back then. There was a lot of hand rolled quirley butts lyin' around. Someone had tried to push 'em in the ground. Musta built a fire to keep warm and do some cookin'. Found some rabbit bones picked clean. I'd say they was there maybe a week, four or five days anyway, waitin'. Hard to tell.

202

Spring rain, wind, ground squirrels, birds, even ants had destroyed what sign there was. Not all. It's either that or the ground squirrels are smokin' Bull Durham."

Riles started talking. "Let me add to what Far has said. While he was lookin' at the shooters, I climbed down in the draw. The horse that Pistol was ridin' had a broke cannon bone, left front leg. Gun shot to the horse's head."

Peter interjected. "I didn't shoot him. When Wolf and Charley found me and brought me back here, Dee had my pistol. No spent cartridges. Winchester was the same. It wasn't me that shot that horse."

"Here's the point I wanna make," Forest said. "I figure these boys, whoever they was, meant to kill him. Missed. Got the horse. Miracle he didn't die from the cold. Someone meant to take him out of the card game. One hand and done. Right now he's supposed to be dead."

"And I ain't, thanks to Wolf and his cousin."

"And a lot of luck," Forest said.

Riles nodded in agreement, walked to the table, pulled out a chair and sat down.

"Coffee?" Diana said.

"Please."

"Anyone else?"

"I'll have some if you got it handy," Syrus said.

"Thank God Pistol's alive," Riles said. "Tells you how serious these boys are."

"Part of that's good news." Syrus said, smiling at Peter. "Couldn't imagine you fallin' off a horse. How's the leg?"

"I get around. According to the Doc, it's too early for me to be using it. I do anyway. It's mostly healed. Lyin' around caused the leg muscle to shrink somethin' awful. Pants don't fit. Hang on me like a scarecrow. Leg ain't strong."

"You ride?"

"A little. I think I can stay on a horse. It's awful sore."

"That's good. A place to start."

Riles interrupted. "That's not all, and it ain't the worst of it." He glanced at Diana. "Do you want me to tell 'em, cause Si and Far

203

don't know? It has to be done."

Diana hesitated. She wiped her hands on her apron and sat down at the table. She took a breath.

"No, Dee. No, I'll tell 'em," Peter said. "It should be me. I ain't done all that well with tellin'."

Forest said, "Tell me what? I'm dyin' to know."

"Poor choice of words, Far," Riles said.

"You don't know the whole story," Diana blurted out. "It's not as simple as Petey gettin' a broken leg."

"Suppose you tell us," Syrus said slowly.

"Hold on." Riles was speaking; the room grew silent. "Si, Far, there's some bad news that you ain't heard." Riles stopped talking, hesitating. "One reason for that is you, Si, ain't been here long enough to tell you anything. The other is that we really needed both of you here...with your heads screwed on tight. We sure as hell don't need either of you goin' off doin' somethin' crazy. The other reason is no one wanted to think about it, let alone talk about it."

Syrus looked at Diana. He glanced at Riles, waiting. No one said anything. The silence was loud, uncomfortable. Finally, he said, "Well, what is it? Somebody tell us somethin' 'fore I grow old and die."

Tears welled up in Diana's eyes. She hesitated, not knowing where to begin or how. "My sisters," she began, stopped. "They're dead. They killed 'em."

Silence suddenly dominated the room. Outside, the milk cow bawled. Her cry mingled with the sound of children playing in the creek.

"Who? Who killed 'em?" Syrus asked

Riles answered him. "The sheriff in Basin City hung 'em in the name of the county. Best I can tell, someone else put the whole thing in motion. Whoever it was, raked it from shoulder to hindend until the deed was done and they was dead. It was intentional. It wasn't a mistake or an accident."

"How did you say?"

"They was hanged!" Diana said, sobbing quietly

"All of 'em? Sally, too?" Syrus asked.

"All three in Basin City." Diana looked at Syrus. "See?" she said, "This is a lot bigger than a broken leg. All three was accused of killin' the man who shot Pa in the back with a shotgun. He killed Pa. A guy named Mumford."

"Old man Stafford? Dead? Really?" Syrus asked.

"Yes. Really, Si," Pete replied.

Syrus looked at Diana. "But Sally? Lord, she was so, so young. When I left she was just a baby."

"She's sixteen."

"Sixteen years old. Who did this?"

Diana answered Syrus' question. "The Sheriff, a fellow by the name of Jason Gilson, his Deputy, someone called Lloyd. Don't know his full name. And four Deputy U.S. Marshals. I don't know their names. Ain't seen 'em."

Syrus glanced at Riles. "Deputy U.S. Marshals? What they got to do with this? Gilson worked for the county, yes? Who was the U.S. Marshals workin' for? Don't make no sense."

Tears rolled down Diana's face. She tried to hold them back but her efforts only made it worse. Peter stood. up, limped to her, sat down, and wrapped his arms around her."I gotcha, babes," he whispered.

CHAPTER 27

Syrus glanced at Peter. "One thing at a time," he said, staring at Diana. He paused, waiting as if he were developing a thought. He said, "Ma'am? Ma'am, look at me. I wanna see your eyes."

At first she didn't respond. She had buried her face in Peter's embrace.

Syrus spoke. "Ma'am?" he said. "There's questions that need to be answered in order for us to know what we're doin'. Can you get hold of yourself? We need to get to the bottom of this. We all do. Even if we don't know it."

Diana turned. Peter came to his feet. "Si? Si, for hell's sake. Leave her be."

"Pistol, sit down. If we're gonna figure this out, we've got to discuss this. Questions need to be asked. We need answers." Syrus turned his attention to Diana. "Ma'am," he said slowly. "Of your family, you the only one left? Mother? Father's dead? Anyone else?"

Except for the sound of Diana trying to control her breathing, the room had grown uncomfortably silent again.

"What?" she stammered. "What are you talkin' about?"

"Ma'am, it's the bull buffalo standin' in the livin' room shakin' his hairy, horned head. Are you the only Stafford livin'?"

"I... I guess, I am."

Syrus' voice grew cold and demanding. "Ma'am, no guessin'. Are you or are you not the only livin' Stafford?"

"I....yes. There's Katie and Josh. But they're Stocktons."

Syrus glanced at Riles. "There you go, Riles. There's a connection here. See it? I'm bettin' Pistol's cows disappearin' is related to those girls....gettin' themselves kilt. I'm bettin' the Stafford Bar S cows ain't where Old Man Stafford left 'em. I'd guess that Jake Stafford called out whoever it is that shot him. Who'd you say shot him?"

Riles answered him. "Mumford. A man name of Mumford."

"Was he workin' for someone or did he work alone?"

"I was wonderin' that, myself," Riles said. "So, while in Kane,

I was down on the river. Talked to the folks who owned the ferry. I asked about it. The word I got was he was on the Linderman payroll."

"Linderman? Who the hell's that?"

"Some rancher. Big on the other side of the mountain. Clear up into Montana. That's what I was told. Brought cows out of Texas at the same time as old man Lovell. Brought his bunch in from Oregon. 1880, 1879. Spring. Longhorn, mostly."

"So, this Linderman is our man," Syrus said, anger rising in his voice.

Forest looked at Syrus. "You gonna be all right, Si?" he asked.

"No," Syrus answered. "I'm not. I thought this was trouble enough: Pistol and Diana losin' their cows, Pistol gettin' his leg broke and all. But this is double serious! Killin' Diana's family is somethin' different all together. It's bigger. I don't understand it. It makes no sense."

Riles took over. "Si's right," he said, "but this ain't no time to go off half cocked. We gotta start somewhere. Let's look at the cow situation first. Let's start there. Let me explain what I know and why. A couple of days ago, Far and me rode the south and west pastures. Nothin' there. If it was winter when those cows disappeared they would have been on the south pasture, maybe Ballar Flat. Far and I looked. Couldn't find any tracks. Couldn't find sign of any large movement of cattle. As you said, the problem may be the weather. Since March, there's been a lot of rain, snow, ground wind, animals. Most of the tracks would be wore down if they were there. Frankly, there ain't much to see."

Syrus looked at Peter. He asked, "How many head you got'?"

"Last count, eight hundred seventy eight cows, forty bulls, and spring yearlings. A year's worth of two year olds. I don't know how many yearlings. If every cow had a calf, there'd be eight hundred seventy yearlings, more or less, same with the two year olds. I'm guessin' there was about seven hundred yearlings. We didn't do any sellin' last year. We kept all of the two year old heifers. Fixin' to get rid of most of the bull calves. Keep replacements."

Syrus grunted, nodding his head. "Okay. That gives us an idea of what we're missin'."

207

Forest interrupted. "You know," he said, "time is everything in this. If they took the cows sometime in March to damn near the middle of May, they was limited where they could take 'em."

"That's right," Riles said. "Can't say as I had given that much thought. Couldn't go over the mountain. They'd be ass deep in snow. Over the Horn the snow would be fifteen, twenty foot deep. Can't go thatta way. South: they could go that way. They'd go over the Flat around the West Pryor out into the basin. Old man Lovell has a lot of cows grazin' out there. I hear he's got twenty-five thousand head. Not much room for more, but we'll still need to have a look."

"Good point. Can't go east 'cause they'd have to cross the canyon. There's only one place: that'd be Chain Canyon. The river'd be frozen over in the winter. If they went thatta way, they'd have to keep 'em on the Basin Pasture 'til nearly June. No choice. As you say, the Horn is one big snowdrift that time of year. They'd be belly deep in snow until first of June. Especially true in March, April. Up that high it's winter."

Peter grunted, adjusted himself in his chair. "Just leaves north to the Yellowstone, across the Reservation. I'm guessin' if they went that way they might cross the Big Horn River on the other side of Fort Smith. Someone would have seen 'em. The first thing we need to do is rule out everythin' but the river south of Fort Smith. That's easy. The canyon in March and April would be a solid sheet of ice. I figure that would be the last place they'd go, but we need to have a look. There's four of us. We can split up."

Riles nodded. "All right," he said. "Unless someone disagrees, we get goin'. We'll meet back here in two, three days."

"There's five of us," Diana said aloud.

"And two rock throwers," Riles added.

Syrus nodded. He looked at Diana. "What are you sayin'?"

"I'm not stayin' here," Diana said, emphatically. "I got an iron in this fire."

"Ma'am," Riles said. "Someone's gotta watch the yonkers."

Diana was quick to respond. "It should be Pete. He ain't supposed to be usin' that leg. He does, and it'll get broke again. He'll be crawlin' for the rest of his life."

"That's all true, Diana," Forest said. "I appreciate your need.

Both of you should remember that Riles, Si, and me--we got nothin' to lose. Ain't got no wife. Ain't got no young'uns. You and Pistol do. Those yonkers need their mother. I think the only issue is whether or not a woman with a rifle is enough? I'm thinkin' 'bout Pistol, too. He's 'most mended but he needs to be careful. I'm thinkin' the both of you stay back for right now. The next question that ain't been asked is where? I'm thinkin' not here. I'm thinkin' you ought to pull back to the line cabin on the north flank of the West Pryor. Hard to find. Easier to defend. I say we meet there in four days and see what we've learned."

"Sorry, Diana," Syrus interrupted. "This ain't a hard decision. As far as I see it, it's easy." Four heads turned to Syrus. He shook his head, smiled. "Remember what the Old Man said? Every kid is entitled to a full belly, a warm place to sleep, and a ma and pa to tuck 'em in at night?"

Riles laughed. "That decides it. So Diana and Pistol are stayin' for right now, movin' to the line shack. We meet in four day's time at the shack."

Everyone nodded. Diana didn't vote. Neither did her husband. Riles paused, looked at Diana. "Look," he said, "everyone here knows you got an iron in this fire and several dogs in the fight. You got all sorts of reasons to wanna be lookin' for blood. There's no denyin' it. Someone with two legs needs to be watchin' over Josh and Katie Sue, as well as Pistol. It is easier for us to be protectin' you and them if you're here and not out there alone. Both of you might not like it but it's best."

Syrus looked at her, nodding. "Riles is right and I've spent the better part of my youth tryin' to prove him wrong. Like Far said, you're the ma. There ain't no way around that, sister. Can't risk your life. I think all of us agree them kids need their ma more than we need their ma lookin' for missin' cows."

Forest exclaimed. "Well, we certainly got ourselves a barroom brawl. Do you think old man Lovell took a hand in any of this, Riles?"

"Not that I'm aware of."

"Then this fellow Linderman is behind this one. I don't understand why he'd want Pistol's cows. There ain't that many. They

209

probably ain't that good. Ain't worth the aggravation."

Syrus turned his attention back to Diana. "Ma'am," he said.

Peter came to his feet. "What now, Si? Leave her alone. She's dealin' with enough without you givin' her hell."

"Pistol, sit down. I ain't givin' her hell. If I was, she would know. This woman has a big hand in this card game. We gotta know which side of the table she's sittin' on before we start dealin' the cards, pullin' our shootin' irons, and blastin' away."

Peter sat down. "Go easy, will you," he mumbled.

"There ain't no 'easy' 'bout any of this, Pistol." Syrus turned to Diana. He said, "Ma'am? You have a decision that needs makin'. And it's now. There's no way around this. You're a Stafford. You're smack dab in the middle. As you said, not includin' the yonkers, you're the last. This means, unless you don't claim it, the Bull Elk pasture, the Cook Stove, Low Mountain, Little Mountain, Mexican Hill, Duncan--they're all up for grabs. We're sittin' here and I'll bet your milk cow this fellow Linderman has already moved into your folk's bedroom and he's cookin' hashbrowns on your stove. Hear me? I need to know. Are you gonna claim your old man's estate or are you gonna walk away from it?"

Diana was listening intently to Syrus' words.

He continued, without waiting for her answer. "With those kids of your'n in the crosshairs, it's a decision that only you can make. I don't think even Pistol has a word here. I'm pretty sure we could keep you and those kids safe if you wanna walk away. Let her go." He paused, rubbing his eyes. "But, my brothers never in their lives walked away from a fight. So it's a yes or no question. Your answer directly affects what we're gonna do. The way I remember it, your old man ran five or six hundred head. Are you gonna lay claim to 'em? Or not? It's yours or it ain't. That graze sure ain't ours. We'll back your play one way or the other."

Diana looked around the room. Syrus Stockton ceased talking. The silence that followed was uneasy again. Several minutes passed before she spoke. "It's a hard business, lettin' it go, walkin' away. I ain't inclined to let those bastards steal my Pa's place. After what they did to my sisters! And Petey and me, we need our cows."

It was Forest who spoke next. "I'm of the opinion that Si is

210

right. If Linderman's people took MT cows across the canyon last winter, they drove 'em over Stafford pastures, probably in June. If they did, they probably took 'em across the mountain, thinkin' they'd lose 'em with Linderman's herds. The yearlings, anyway. I'm bettin' that Pistol ain't branded the yearlings. Not with him bein' laid up."

"You're right," Peter answered. "We ain't touched a iron since I got my leg broke. Nothin' since the first snow last year. It came early, so we ain't done much."

Syrus let the air escape from his lips like an old horse chewing last year's oats and not liking it. "Damn," he said, "this is some chore. Still, we can't be sure which way they went until we go look."

Forest turned to Diana Stockton. "Just to be sure, Ma'am, before we go, you need to tell us which side of the fence you're gonna do your standin'. Which way is the bear gonna go over the mountain? To be clear, right now that'd be Linderman's mountain. He's got it and you ain't."

Si joined in. "Diana, what do you want us to do? Folks are gonna lose their lives. Maybe me. Or one of us sitting here at this table. If you're askin' me to kill some of them Linderman men, I need to know. We all need to know where you stand in this shootin' war. You and Pistol could well decide to get the hell outta here. Right now, neither of you got a lot to gain by stayin'. Might be best to just give her up. Get the hell outta here. You gotta look at that as an option."

"You're right," Diana said. She sniffed, wiped her nose with her apron. "The Bar S, it's my home. It has been, like forever. I grew up there. I helped Mother plant the roses in our flower garden. I branded half of the Bar S cows. I did that."

Riles interrupted her. "Diana," he said, "that's all well and good. I like flowers as much as the next man. Your commitment: the irons you have in the fire are a little more than me, or Si, or Far. Let's be clear. Sure as hell, this Linderman fellow, he's comin' after you and those two kids. You are all connected. Sure as God made little green apples. They've killed four people that we know of just to lay claim to the Bar S, its cows, its graze. Half a dozen more ain't gonna bother 'em none. This includes Josh and Katie Sue. They're in as much danger as anyone. This is about money, big ranches, lots of

211

graze, lots of cows. I don't see why, but they are riskin' everythin' for that somethin'.

Diana looked at the men in her kitchen."I'm not gonna give it to the people who killed my sisters just, just, to get 'em out of the way. And my Pa. That man shot him in the back with a shotgun. The land is mine. I'm not gonna just give it to 'em. They're gonna have to take it. They're gonna have to pay for what they done." She turned and addressed Riles. "You think Petey and me and the kids are targets?"

"Yes. They don't seem to be troubled 'bout killin' kids neither. Sally was sixteen. Just a kid. You can bet Linderman has hired men to do the job. If not, he had others hire 'em so he could say he knows nothin'. It's still him. I'm guessin' they're on the way right now--even as we're sittin' at this table."

Forest nodded. "Me, too. I expect to see 'em today; tomorrow wouldn't surprise me none."

Riles paused. "You're right, Far. I had words with one fellow in Kane. Told him to tell his boss I'm comin' for him. Unless I missed my guess, they're expectin' us."

Syrus responded. "Well, Riles," he drawled, "you still got the knack. Nice to see the fiddler warmin' up his bow." Syrus Stockton came to his feet. "Any other time I'd be laughin'. But," Syrus paused, choking up, "they killed Sally. I left here, she was like a baby. Button cute. Betsy was maybe four. Claire, six or seven. Claire would tell me these made up stories. She's dead for no reason. The same for her sisters, for their Old Man."

Syrus turned and walked across the room to his saddle lying on the floor. He pulled his Winchester from the boot, returned to the table, and sat down. Taking a breath, he started ejecting the shells from the magazine. When he finished, he began reinserting them, one after another until he knew the magazine was full. Opening the breech, he shoved a cartridge into the firing chamber, brought the lever up, and slowly, carefully lowered the hammer until it was sitting on top of the fresh cartridge. Pulling the SAA Colt from the holster on his thigh, he opened the breech and rolled the cylinder, assuring himself that all six were fresh. Everyone was watching him. Tears were running down his cheeks. No one had ever seen that before.

212

Not ever. No one said a word, knowing it wouldn't do.

Finally, he looked up. "I'm gonna have a look at the canyon, the Basin Pasture, The Bull Elk. Soon as I'm done, I'll ride north, pay a visit to the folks up at Fort Smith. See what I can find out. I need a fresh saddle horse. The roan is all tuckered. So is my bay."

"Take your pick," Peter said. "There's some more out on the flat."

Syrus looked at the individuals sitting in the room. "Listen," he said, "we're burnin' serious daylight. We're comin' to this birthday get-together late, the presents have already been opened. The birthday songs have been sung. The cake is done gone. We best be movin' fast. These boys mean to kill us, the yonkers included. Nothin' is safe. No one is safe." He paused. "We best be actin' like they got our necks in a noose, 'cause they do."

He started toward the door, stopped, turned to Riles as if he'd forgotten something. "Listen, big brother, I can appreciate what you said 'bout me and Far not goin' off half-cocked. Needin' our head in this shootin' match. I'll do my best by Pistol; get his cows home, get Diana's land back. I'll do that. Soon as we've got the job done, I'm goin' after these folks that killed them girls. I'm gonna put a forty-five to their heads and send them on their merry way straight to hell. I'm tellin' you now so you'll know. I'm comin' late to this dance. We all are, but the last diddy ain't been played. The fiddler ain't put his fiddle away."

"Good," Riles replied, standing up. "I'll be there with you, finger on the trigger, myself. All right," Riles said, "we know what Si is gonna do. Far, you cover everything between here and the Big Horn River, north to the Yellowstone River. See what you can spook up. Let's meet in three, no more than four, days from now, at the line cabin. I'll take the Flat and everything south of the West Pryor includin' Ballar Flat. Pistol, you're stayin' here. If I was you, I wouldn't stay here any longer than you have to. Both you and Diana oughta go armed everywhere. If I was you, one of you does the chores while the other watches from a place of cover. Take no chances. Don't leave those kids alone, not ever. Not for a moment. They's everythin' the Old Man ever worked for. May he rest in peace."

213

Riles Stockton paused. He looked at Diana, his voice soft. "Kid," he said, "I'm with Si on this one. Someone will pay for Sally, Betsy, and Claire and your pa, Jake Stafford,... himself. Before this is over, they'll pay in blood. Hopefully, it's theirs and not ours. Somehow this mess is tied together. In the next several days we'll find out how."

"I hear you, Riles. Thank you. Maybe you think I'm gonna change my mind. I know what you're riskin' for Petey and me," Diana calmly stated. "I ain't gonna change my mind on this. I want justice. I want someone to die for this. And I ain't runnin'. Petey and me talked 'bout it. We ain't runnin' nowheres. Someone's got to pay. If we can't get justice, we'll take vengeance."

"Well, sister, you keep your rope coiled 'til we get back. You'll be needin' it." Riles hesitated, then started walking toward the door, followed by Forest.

Syrus gloved his hands, working his fingers into their respective slots, re-holstered the SAA Colt, latching the hammer, picked up his Winchester 44-40. He walked around the table to Diana, the jingle bobs tinkling like small harness bells. She was standing at the kitchen window, head bent over, her hair in disarray. He touched her cheek, the hardened leather abrasive on her skin; she looked up at him. When she did, he said, slowly, emphatically, enunciating each word as if it were heavy. "Like Riles said, they'll pay in blood, darlin', bright red blood. Theirs. You can take that to the State Bank and spend it."

Turning away from her, he followed Forest out the front door, walking across the porch, down the stairs, across the hardpack to the horse corral. Forest had already caught his Appaloosa saddle horse and was leading it through the corral gate.

"Si," he said, "Bay's not a bad saddle horse. Used him, myself a couple of times. You might throw a rope on him if you were of a mind."

Syrus nodded, uncoiling his reata.

The old grandfather's clock standing in the hallway that Katheryn Stockton and her husband, Carl, had hauled from St Louis, Missouri to Fort Bridger in 1849 read: ten forty-three.

CHAPTER 28

It was midafternoon. Riles Stockton followed a meandering Sage Creek along the north flank of West Pryor; above him the mountain towered eight thousand seventy-seven feet. North lay the Reservation of the Absaroka Crow, as extablished by Congress in 1869. At a steady walk he moved through juniper and sagebrush, riding a well rested Buckskin horse. Out front walked a one-eyed, long-haired dog, its bad eye weeping. Cecil, a long-eared dun mule followed behind, sometimes totally disoriented, lost in a sea of grey sage dotted by clumps of juniper. He'd stop and disappear; Riles wouldn't see him for a few minutes. Then he'd catch up, jawing, complaining about being left to wander. Soon he'd be gone again, grazing, drinking, looking around, lost somewhere, looking to find himself.

Once past Indian Springs, Riles held closer to the mountain, traveling west out onto Ballar Flat, the far reaches of the still snowcapped Absaroka Mountains in the distance. Oddly, he didn't see a cow nor the trail of a cow. There were always strays but not here. He did get glimpses of white tail bounding away, disappearing amid the cedar breaks. They'd leap into the brush and, once out of sight, stop, and coyly watch him, feeling safe.

A mile later Sage Creek turned south and he found tracks of what looked like two old cows, one following another, and a yearling, walking off to the side. Behind him twenty or thirty antelope followed him, heads up, staring in unison, steadfastly keeping him in sight, curious, not wanting to miss anything. Down on the creek, he came across three moose standing knee deep in mud and watercress. Fortunately, a warm breeze moving north kept the deer and horse flies at bay.

Moose. That's what the Absaroka Crow called his father. The legend was his father had roped his friend Black Wolf while he was drowning in the Clarks Fork, thus saving his life. A moose nearly killed them both before his father was able to kill him. It was long ago before Riles was born. That was part of the reason they were

215

both hunting together on Layout Creek last September. Both men died as they lived.

The afternoon passed. He kept moving. Both Cecil and the dog disappeared. Evening found him on the far west flank of the West Pryor: the land dry, nothing moving but killdeer, magpie, camp robbers, snowbirds and an occasional rattlesnake. South, the basin opened up. He turned east. The one-eyed dog returned. The mule was out front again looking around, wasting his time.

Riles spent the night on some nameless creek with a hungry mule and a tired horse in saddle high sagebrush. The mule kept arguing with the horse over the oats in the feed bag strapped around the Buckskin's neck. Riles finally spread a saddle blanket on the ground and poured the mule a bait of oats to keep him from bothering the Buckskin. Sometimes the mule was just a damn kid, a nuisance. During the night a cool wind rolled in moving north out of the basin.

Riles was up and moving early. In a deep ravine, he built a small fire that reflected no light. He heated some water, boiled coffee, chewed on hardtack. He sat on a small red rimrock to watch the false dawn develop. Slowly a dull sliver of light appeared along the edge of the Big Horn Mountain which sat dark blue and hazy some fifty miles away. He ate. Hardtack never tastes good. The one exception being when you're starving. For the most part, even the dog turned the crumbs down. That day no one was starving, least of all the dog and the mule.

Midafternoon of the second day found Riles on the south side of the West Pryor, moving east toward the distant Big Horn Mountain. He was a lone figure hidden in a dry land lost in tall brush and juniper. There was nothing living but jackrabbits, an occasional snake, and birds. There was no quick movement to startle the sense of well being, of temporary safety, in an obscure, unsafe land.

He found a large spring bubbling up from under a slate of granite rocks. Its edges were trampled with tracks of wild animals. To his surprise, he also found some rough looking livestock, cows wearing the MT brand. There were sixty or seventy head of older cows trailing large-boned spring calves. There were two year old light heifers, and as many two year old bull calves. He figured that it was

216

the spring that had attracted them and provided them cover: a shelter of sage, cedar, and juniper.

He kept looking but soon discovered it wasn't the eight hundred, but livestock the rustlers had missed. These cows had flourished, hiding in the chaparral and brush, watered by a large spring bubbling up from under a rock face. He left them. They weren't going anywhere.

Where Riles Stockton rode the weak always fail, die; the strong mostly prevail, survive. The land insists upon it, taking no prisoners, showing no mercy. It was a place where something out of the ordinary, something not normal, is an alarm: birds no longer singing, an animal running, tracks moving in a straight line. Those who listen and watch are warned. A traveler expects the chatter of birds, expects to cross the trail of mulies, antelope, perhaps a moose, elk, and even a bear or two. Those are hardly worth mentioning in a daily dialogue unless they are missing. Smoke is worth mentioning, as is a horse walking in a straight line. Such an event declares you are not alone. Birds are quiet when someone at the top of the food chain is in close proximity. The quiet tells the listener that death is at hand. Count on it.

Animals hear better, see better; they feel trouble. As a caution, Riles watched the dog, aware when the dog stopped, started growling--a growl that ended in a whine--then stared into the brush that surrounded him. He turned and walked back to Riles, whining, looking over his shoulder. Suddenly, the Buckskin pointed his ears forward and Riles popped off the back of the horse. A rabbit shot across the game trail, disappearing into the brush on Riles' left. The dog didn't move. There were no birds singing; if they had been singing before, they'd given it up. Even the camp robbers and the magpies were silent. One flew overhead, abruptly turning south and disappearing into the brush and clumps of juniper. There were no meadow larks, no snowbirds flitting about, no piercing cries of the killdeer.

Riles removed the leather loop from the hammer on his SAA Colt, then pulled his Winchester from the scabbard, carefully cocking the hammer, his index finger lying along the trigger guard. Riles listened, felt the warm breeze blowing across his exposed skin. The

217

breeze was in his face; his scent drifted through the trees behind him. He waited. The silence was pervasive. He did not move. His father's rule number three: The first to move is the first to die. Patience. His father insisted upon it.

The breeze picked up. Behind him the one-eyed dog growled again.Taking the fallen reins, Riles wrapped them around a convenient juniper limb, knocking several juniper berries to the ground. The Buckskin watched him. Riles waited, noting the horse's attention. Suddenly the horse turned its head north towards the mountain, both ears cocked forward. The dog did the same. A low deep throated growl rumbled through its throat.

"Quiet," Riles whispered. The one-eyed dog disappeared into the brush on Riles' left. Riles detected an indistinct whiff of smoke: small, barely noticeable. He wondered what Cecil was up to.

Crouching, Riles moved slowly ahead. Ten steps brought him to the edge of a long, shallow ravine, forty feet across, hidden. Below him, to his right, covered in brush, a small ravine opened onto a narrow canyon that took Crooked Creek to the Horn. It was then he saw what the dog had smelled: camp smells, a lean, well-used horse tied to a limb, a small fire emitting little smoke.

Riles did not move. He crouched, partially hidden from anyone's sight behind a high, olive green stand of sagebrush. He conducted a slow visual inspection. He removed and reseated his hat. He used the sage, juniper, and cedar to conceal himself, bunchgrass to soften his footsteps. To his left grew a clump of prickly pear cactus.

He asked himself, who and what could bring a person to this dry, arid, inhospitable countryside? Certainly he wasn't up to any good. Riles watched and waited. His patience was rewarded when someone stepped out of the junipers on the far side carrying some dried firewood. The man Riles watched bent to feed the flames with small sticks, turning from his knees to collect some more for later. He bent down again, pouring a cup of coffee. Something was familiar. Riles noted the bedroll, laid out nice and tidy: panniers under a juniper tree, a scoped rifle, disassembled, being cleaned. He saw a can of Maxine's gun oil sitting atop one of the panniers and a long barrel with a Sharps-like firing mechanism. This fellow was a hunter

218

with a big rifle.

Up here? Hunt what? Oh, this fellow is huntin' men.

There was nothing to hunt that needed that rifle in the saddle between the two mountains. Nothing. In fact, a common 44-40 would be a better choice; as would a 30-30. It was the difference between hunting a griz and a house mouse. There was lots of brush for a slow moving hunk of lead to blow through. *No, this rifle is not meant for that kind of shootin'.*

Riles came to his feet and moved behind another taller stand of sage. Behind him the Buckskin raised his head watching, his ears pointed at Riles. Every time the man turned his back, Riles moved closer. In eleven minutes he was less than twenty-five feet from the skinny man. Riles recognized him. *Not good, not good at all. It's the man standin' on the corner of Sheridan Avenue and the Calico Saloon. This one carried a hideaway, right sleeve.*

A breeze picked up.

The man, dressed in grey, rose, glanced down at his fire, stretched, pulling at his shirt sleeves. He turned away, walked to his bedroll, and looked inside the pannier closest to him. After he'd rifled through his things, he stood, working something with his hands, then turned to the fire. To his surprise, he found a dun mule smelling his coffee pot, trying to eat the potholder.

"Hah," he yelled. "Out, out! Damn you." Suddenly the skinny man stopped dead still. The dun raised his head to look at him.

He stood stock still, not turning his head or his body. "You might as well show yourself," he said in a high pitched, gravelly, voice filled with resignation.

Riles Stockton complied, stepping into the clearing behind the assassin, tall sage to his right and left.

"Remember me?" he said. "Thought we was clear, Buster, on what you was gonna do once you delivered my message to the gent that hired you. Did you tell him? Or did it slip your mind? Don't recall anythin' about you showin' up on the dark side of the moon. Especially not here."

The thin man remained frozen, caught, both boots on the ground. He did not turn. Riles imagined the storm racing through the man's head: what to do? He watched as the killer came to a decision;

219

his face grew calm as if he could foresee turning, throwing himself to the side, firing, hopefully killing his adversary.

Probably use the hideaway in his right shirt sleeve, Riles thought. He saw the shudder of the skinny man's shoulders as the hideaway fell into the palm, his fingers working it into his hand. Riles smiled. *So this is how it was gonna play out.*

Riles studied the solitary figure, watched as he readied himself, tensing, time rapidly shrinking. It does that when a man no longer controls the events moving toward him. It was right there: feeling like he was packing a couple of one hundred pound bricks, one in each hand, wearing boots made of pure lead, heels so heavy they sunk into the rock he stood on. Time for action, time for living or dying. Which would it be?

"Guess not?" Riles concluded, receiving no answer to his question. "Except you're packin' a fancy shootin' rifle. That's an answer, I suppose. I'm wonderin'? Maybe you're deaf? Maybe you don't hear worth a damn?. Maybe some fool paid you a lot of money, not knowin' you're as incompetent as a rusty door knob?"

Riles noted the skinny fellow wasn't wearing black. *Guess he's not dressin' up for this occasion.* His garb had a faded, worn look: mostly grey. His face was elongated and he had long ears. His hands were gloved. *Odd combination, that.*

"How much?" Riles asked.

"How much what?"

Riles could see it. The killer wanted to turn around, but he hesitated, didn't for it was safer not to. "Don't play stupid, Buster," Riles said to the skinny man. "You know, damn well, what I mean. This ain't no time for bullshit. Think I done caught you dead to rights. You ain't supposed to be here. You know it. I know it. You're bein' paid to do a shootin'. How much?"

"Five thousand," he said.

"Five thousand dollars? Damn, that's a stack of five dollar gold pieces."

"Cash."

"You have five thousand dollars cash? Your employer must feel pretty confident in your skills. That whole Stafford place ain't barely worth that."

"More. Five a piece. Ten. He wants me to be discreet."

"What's that mean, discreet?"

"Bury the bodies so they ain't never found."

"Bury the bodies so they ain't found? Lord, what's the world comin' to?"

Riles Stockton took another step away from the saddle high sagebrush, stepping down to where the earth was level; the Winchester butt was snug against his shoulder. The skinny man stood still, not moving.

"I noticed your shovel. See you're thinkin' about the buryin'. Who you contracted to kill?"

"A woman and her husband."

"And the two kids?"

"No. Not them."

"What happens to them?

"Don't know. Let's bargain. Let's cut a deal. I'll give you fifteen thousand, you let me live. That's a lot of money. It would solve your problems. Let me go, you won't see me ever again."

"I did let you go. All you did is get a little closer. Besides, I can just put a round through your head and take it all."

"It's not here. Do you think I'd bring money up here? That wouldn't serve no purpose. I need to know you're gonna let me go before I give you fifteen. You must think I'm stupid."

"The thought occurred to me."

"I'm not."

"Do you have any idea what your boss has in mind? What have we got that he wants?"

"Don't know."

Riles nodded. "Don't believe you do," he drawled.

The one-eyed dog emerged from a clump of sagebrush fifteen feet in front of the killer and a few feet to his left. It carried a struggling rabbit in its mouth. One eye was weeping, its lid was mostly stuck shut; but as the killer noted, one eye worked and it was staring at him like he'd stolen a venison roast. His.

"I need a name. Who paid you?"

Without hesitating, he said, "Linderman."

"Linderman? Who is that?"

221

"The man with the money."

"He pay for those Stafford girls, too?"

"Don't know 'bout no girls. Linderman paid for a hangin'. He did that. Ten thousand. Bought a judge. He ain't paid me for no girls." The killer swallowed hard, his mouth dry, but he didn't dare turn to see who was speaking to him. He wanted an edge, something to create an advantage. It didn't matter. He knew, and he knew the very gates of hell were yawning open after him, threatening to snatch him from the ground where he stood.

A small breeze picked up, tugging at his shirt, playing with the trouser legs hanging loosely on his thin frame. The short crowned felt hat he'd bought in Orleans almost blew off as the wind picked up, gusting. It gripped the edges of the hat brim, catching it like the wind does a sail, loosening the sweat band from around his head. In front of him he could see the canyon that took the waters of Crooked Creek down the canyon to join that of the Horn and Shoshone Rivers. His mind was blank, not wanting to think.

Down the side of the mountain toward the Shoshone River, a mile away, a string of five or six mule deer bolted and ran as if being chased by a pack of wolves. They ran quickly, cutting, gracefully leaping, disappearing amid the tall sagebrush and clumps of juniper. The one-eyed dog looked up at the skinny man, the rabbit struggling to be free. The dog bit down hard. The struggle stopped. Dribbles of blood trickled from the sides of the dog's mouth. The dog sat down, the full length of him lying sprawled in the red dirt. He bit at the rabbit's head; it came off in his mouth and the dog started chewing, working his jaws.

The visual image slapped at the killer's sensibilities as this scene played out before him. To save his sanity, he turned his attention back to the voice.

The voice asked, "This Linderman fellow got my message? You're here. I figure he must not of believed me? Maybe he thought I was teasin'?"

The killer said nothing, apparently deep in thought, calculating his odds. He watched the one-eyed dog chewing on the rabbit's head. He wondered if the hammer was pulled back on the pistol the speaker was bound to have in hand.

222

In front of him the dog set the rabbit carcass on the ground, staring up at him as if he were waiting. One of the dog's long front legs was draped over the rabbit's limp body, making sure it didn't go anywhere.

"Friend," Riles, standing behind him, asked, "I gotta know. Did you do as I told you to do? Did you give this Linderman fellow my message?"

"Yes," the man replied, "I did. I said I did."

The dog rose to his feet growling, a menacing hulk. The killer jumped backwards, at the same time turning toward Riles. He saw him, he was ready, he'd palmed the hideaway, he was bringing it up, pulling back on the hammer.

At that moment, something hard, unyielding, a giant fist, struck him, knocking his hat off. The hat hit the packed earth, rolled in a semicircle for a few seconds, and stopped on its crown. The blow shoved him backwards. For a millisecond, the image of his hideaway crossed his mind. The quiet. Water dripping over rocks. A snail. A second slug struck him and he lost all thought, giving way to oblivion.

The one-eyed dog mouthed the dead rabbit and rose to his feet, shaking himself. He carried the rabbit carcass to the skinny man to examine him, unguarded and without interference. Setting the limp rabbit down, the one-eyed dog sniffed the dead man from his head to his chest to his sprawled knees. He wagged his tail, remouthed the rabbit's carcass, and started into the juniper trees by way of a faint, unused game trail.

"What do you make of that?" Riles said aloud, speaking to himself. "Didn't expect him to go for that hideaway. Didn't think he'd do it. Thought he'd drag it out. I'll be damned."

CHAPTER 29

The line cabin sat on the north slope of the West Pryor at an elevation of fifty-two hundred feet. It was built with its back against a solid rock face, sixteen feet from a spring that bubbled out of a split in the rock and ran ten unobstructed feet and dropped back into the fissure. A clump of aspen grew where the spring dropped back into the mountain, their leaves shading the cabin in summer; pine timber covered two sides. The front opened to the north, overlooking one hundred miles of Absaroka Crow Reservation. Unless you were looking for the cabin, you'd never see it.

The Reservation, before there was a Reservation, and the mountain had been the home of the Absaroka Crow for as long as the living could remember. In 1869 the Federal Government, sitting nineteen hundred miles away in a swamp called Washington, D.C,. recognized what had always been. The Crow didn't care much about some well-dressed high-toned men wearing black hats gathered in the Capitol Building to give the Crow what had always been theirs. The long-haired drunk, sleeping in the trees outside of Harden, Montana, awakened to receive this good "Reservation" news, said it best. He raised himself up on his one good arm, crooked from birth, studied the bearer of this news, and said, "Who gives a damn?"

It was to the line cabin on the north face that Peter and Diana made their way with their two children, leaving the evening of the day on which the others left. They left a small candle stub burning, sitting on a small slab of rock in the center of the kitchen table. Someone from afar might see it burning and think nothing of it for someone was home. They were gone long before the sun set. It was summer.The light disappeared a little after ten in the evening. Peter Stockton brought his wife and kids through the pine that grew along Sage Creek then up the ridge.

Fort C.F. Smith was constructed on the Big Horn River in 1866 by the U.S. Army. It was built on the east side, a short distance downstream from where the Horn emerged from the canyon. It was constructed as a protection for immigrants traveling the Bozeman trail, enabling folks to get to the Montana gold fields and the Oregon territory. Its existence was clearly a violation of the treaty of 1851. The trail was named after Johnny Bozeman. Bozeman was a German name that was said to describe an evil, hard to get along with, ornery bastard. It is also said to be one who complains incessantly about his fate. Maybe he was all of that. It's difficult to get a solid read on Johnny Bozeman for he was killed on the south side of the Yellowstone River in 1867. The Blackfeet thought they were cleansing the Yellowstone River Basin of lying, cheating, murdering invaders who sure as all billy hell needed killing. Folks back east thought it was a savage murder and attributed it to the Blackfeet being Indians.

Rumor had it that Bozeman's partner, Tom Cover, shot Johnny Bozeman in the back. It seems Tom got drunk on rot gut whiskey one evening and talked about it. People said that Tom was the guilty party, that the Blackfeet never were that far south. Tom Cover blamed those "murderous" Blackfeet warriors. Unfortunately, there is not a living soul to say differently.

The life span of Fort Smith was two years--from 1866 to 1868. In 1868 the Teton Lakota, during negotiations in Laramie, loudly proclaimed that Fort Smith was a clear violation of the treaty signed by the U.S. Government in 1851. Caught red faced, red handed, the U.S. Army abandoned the fort in 1868, the very year the Laramie Treaty was signed. A band of "mad as a hornet" Oglala Sioux, one of the seven tribes of the Teton Lakota, burned it to the ground. Perhaps the most famous Oglala of them all was a man named Crazy Horse. He was named after his father, and his father's father before him. He was twenty-eight years old when the Oglala Sioux torched Fort Smith.

On June 26, 1876, forty-eight miles north of Fort Smith, he met George Custer on the west side of the Greasy Grass. At that time, Crazy Horse was thirty-six years old. George, one year older than his nemesis, didn't fare well.

On August 5, 1886, midmorning, before his youngest brother left for the line cabin, Forest Stockton rode his Appaloosa gelding north, crossed East Dry Head Creek, traveling the Bad Pass Trail. He put his horse into the river, swam it, and continued until he reached the rise overlooking what was left of Fort C. F. Smith. It wasn't much more than charred adobe brick.

From there, Forest turned east, looking for a cabin of log construction, fifty feet long and twenty-five feet wide. It was hidden several miles east of the remains of Fort Smith, behind a grove of pine and aspen, its back secured against a granite rock wall. The cabin wasn't far, but it was a little tricky to get to it. Even Indian officials working in Crow Agency left the place alone.

Upon reaching his destination, he sat his Appaloosa for a few minutes, studying the scene that lay before him as if it were a bee tree, a hive hidden beneath bark and rotting wood. Forest counted seven horses tied to the rails out front; more were in the back, standing in the trees, waiting.

Bars and saloons are outlawed on the Reservation. This fact was a known truth in all of the parlors, bars, and saloons on the Washington, D. C. drinking circuit. An Indian Reservation was, by federal law, a teetotaling place, if ever one existed, anywhere. That didn't mean bars didn't exist. This one had been where it was for twenty-seven years. As far as anyone knew, it was there before the government built Fort Smith. It was there before the government so graciously gave the Crow back what had always been theirs. It was the regional and local watering hole that didn't exist: not as far as everyone knew. Bad Pass Bar was its name. The bar was named after the Bad Pass Trail. The trail existed before the Absaroka Crow left the eastern Ohio woodland, before there was a Medicine Wheel on top of the Big Horn, before the Little People lived and hunted in the Canyons of the Pryors. It was old.

CHAPTER 30

Forest Stockton dismounted, worked the knots out of his legs, and loosened his SAA Colt in its holster, flipping the latch off the hammer. He waited, standing in the late afternoon light. He looked. He watched. Finally, he walked the short distance to the hitching rail, leading the Appaloosa, and wrapped the reins around the pine pole resting on top of two, belt high, posts. Pausing, he scratched the horse's forehead, ruffling the hair on his shoulder, deliberately taking his time. It'd been over fifteen years since he'd visited the Bad Pass Bar. The last time was with Syrus.

Slowly, he walked to the battered door whose lumber was hewn out of pine with an ax and swung on two broad metal hinges. That'd hadn't changed. Maybe the broad metal hinges had. He didn't know. Someone abruptly came through the doorway, glanced at him, then stepped out in front of the building. The man was staring at Forest like he expected something to happen. Forest grabbed the open door to keep it from closing and stepped inside.

The interior was lit by three oil lamps at one end and one wide open window at the other. The center was dominated by a cold wood burning stove, the ceiling soot black from ten thousand fires over many, many winters. The ceiling itself was made of logs overlaid by timber hewn flat, then covered in shake shingles. Several men were standing at a shiny mahogany bar: shined, shined and re-shined. Others were sitting at tables shuffling cards, drinking, swearing and minding their own business. Most of them did not look up. Several did, however. Forest pulled his pistol, firing it into the ceiling, then replaced it in its holster. Everyone looked, many as soon as he'd pulled the hammer back. His Old Man had told him once that "a deaf man can hear a rat's fart if the rat's packin' a Colt." Once a man has heard that clicking sound of the cylinder rotating, the hammer being drawn back, locking, he never forgets it. Ever. Forest never had.

Burnt black powder gunsmoke lifted in the still stagnant air and seemed to get stronger as the seconds passed.

"I'm lookin' for Black Wolf," Forest said loudly. "A real ugly critter with red eyes and bad breath. Evil disposition 'cause his mother don't love him."

A pregnant pause followed. Finally, a familiar voice said, "What do you want with him?"

"He owes me a drink of fine whiskey. I'm here to collect what's due."

There was another long silence. The same voice said, "I don't owe you no drink, Far. I ain't never owed you no drink. I was the last one that bought. You're the one. You know damn well you left just so you wouldn't have to buy your turn. A chicken shit thing to do if there ever was one. Owin' like you do."

Smiling, Forest walked towards the familiar voice not yet able to make out the speaker, his dark face hidden in shadows and layers of cigarette smoke.

The bartender started moving down the counter, wiping his hands on an old rag, his apron a mess of stains. Forest winked at him. The bartender smiled. He was short, a prickly man with a shuffling gait, his long grey hair pulled back and hanging over his shoulders. As Forest approached the corner of the room and the dark that hid the voice, the bartender had walked the entire length of the bar. He didn't stop when he reached the end of the counter, studying Forest without speaking.

Forest maneuvered around several empty chairs to a table sitting behind another table with four men seated around it and one empty chair. All four were staring at Forest. One was scowling.

"I forgot how ugly you were," Forest said to him. "You'd scare your own mother."

"I do scare my own mother."

"That's what I said."

Black Wolf nodded his head in agreement. He smiled. "Far, whatever got you out from under the flat rock where you was hidin'? Musta been somethin'. Talk about ugly."

"I should lie and say I came to see your father," Forest responded. "Can't stand this abuse."

Black Wolf raised his arms, turning his face away as if a crime were about to be committed and he didn't want any part of it. "No, Far. No. Whatever you do, don't mention his name."

"Why not?"

"He's dead. It's not good to say his name. He makes his way to the land of the dead, the place of the dead. I'm tellin' you 'case you've forgotten. Speakin' his name may cause him to stop his journey and return. This ain't good."

"Damn. I knew that. Sorry, Black Wolf, I know. I heard from Pistol." Forest's voice changed from an easy banter to serious. "My condolences to you and your family. Bad joke. Shouldn't have said that."

Wolf paused, thinking. "The place of the dead, it's a bad place. Every man knows this."

"What's wrong with it?"

"No whiskey, no cards, no huntin', no shootin' white men."

"I suppose there's no women, either?"

Black Wolf leaned back in his chair and stared at Forest. "Especially no women," he said. "What's wrong with you? You know that. Women ain't permitted."

"Nothin's wrong with me, other than someone stole my cows. I'm lookin' for 'em, need to find 'em."

"What? You've been gone for twelve, thirteen winters and someone stole your cows? You should try stickin' around, watchin' 'em yourself."

"Pistol's watchin' 'em."

"You got a woman?"

"No, I ain't."

"That's what's wrong with you. You need a woman. I know one that's lookin' for you. You're in deep trouble."

"I don't need a woman. I need cows."

"MT cows?"

"Yes. MT cows."

"Those are your father's cows."

"He's dead. You know that."

"I didn't say his name. I won't say his name. That'd be real trouble. If both return...I don't wanna think about it. Real trouble."

"Probably a good thing. So, answer my question. You seen my cows?"

"Are you missin' 'em?"

"You're damn right, I'm missin' 'em. That's why I came to see you. I wanna find 'em."

"I ain't got 'em."

"I know you ain't got 'em. You'd have given 'em back."

"Looks like you're fixin' to cry."

"No, I ain't fixin' to cry."

"Well, I'm gonna cry. You ain't bought me a drink."

A big man wearing a red bandana around his neck, no hat, the pocket torn on his oversized shirt, was standing next to the table where Forest was talking to Black Wolf. He spoke in Absaroka Crow to another man leaning against the mahogany bar. Forest glanced at him. The words were familiar. It had been so long. Fifteen years. It sounded like he was discussing stealing his horse.

"Buy me a drink," Black Wolf said. "I'll talk about cows, you buy me a drink. All this talkin' about cows makes me thirsty. Did I mention it was good to see you?"

Forest looked at Black Wolf with an appraising eye. "You know you shouldn't drink that stuff." He reached out his hand. Wolf took it. They shook hands.

"I know. The bartender, he knows. My wife, she knows. My mother, she knows. My mother-in-law won't speak to me. She knows. Everybody knows. Even you, you know. But you want me to remember cows. How many do you want me to remember?"

"Eight, nine hundred stock cows, Their calves. Last spring's calves. They'd be yearlings this comin' winter. Two year olds. All of 'em."

The big man wearing the red bandana was still talking in Absaroka to someone at the bar. It sounded to Forest like he was giving instructions to a companion across the room. *Stealin' my horse? What the hell's goin' on?* he thought. *I'm gonna have to put an end to this.*

Black Wolf glanced at the red bandana, scowling, shaking his head, then at Forest. "That's a lot of rememberin'. Maybe you should be buyin' me two drinks or three."

"Two? That's a lot. You won't be able to remember."

"Maybe you ought to buy me the bottle."

"I saw the bottle Johnny Bad Crow is carryin'. It's half full."

"That should do it." Black Wolf paused. "But it's only a start.

230

A mere beginning."

Forest waved at the bartender and asked him to bring the bottle. He said, "Johnny Bad Crow, my friend sittin' here has decided he wants a half a bottle of the finest, cheapest rot gut liquor you have." Forest paused. "How you doin', Johnny? See you got yourself a payin' job. Almost time to go huntin' you know."

"Good." Johnny said. "I'm doin' real good and I'm ready for the Bull Elk, the Basin Pasture. You talkin' this bottle?" He held up a dark bottle that appeared to be half full.

Of a sudden, Forest pulled his SAA Colt from his holster and struck the man with the red bandana standing next to him, knocking him backwards onto the floor. The man, surprised, shocked, tried to catch his balance, failed, and hit the floor. Immediately, he rolled away from Forest, not springing to his feet, yet possessing a raging anger. He found himself staring at the bore of the SAA Colt 44-40.

"Why, friend," Forest said, "are you tryin' to steal my horse? I heard what you asked that feller to do. Everybody heard. You think I'm stupid? I wanna assure you I love my horse and would be angry and unforgivin' if I walked outside and found he's mysteriously disappeared."

The man on the floor didn't move, clearly stunned. Certainly the bore of the Colt pointed directly at his nose caused some delay.

Forest said to him, speaking slowly. "I could blow a hole in your head and kill you dead or I could let you live. But you look familiar. I ain't placed you yet. Why are you workin' so hard stealin' my horse?" He stopped, thinking. "Here's the deal, if you and I walk out through the door I just came in and find my horse gone, I'm thinkin' dead is the answer for your short, worthless life. Who are you anyway? Do I know you?"

Forest took a step closer, bringing the barrel closer to the fellow's nose. "What's it gonna be? You wanna be a horse thief? Steal someone elses horse."

Black Wolf laughed. "Far," he said,"Far, slow down. I'd appreciate it if you didn't shoot Charley Slow Dog. So would my aunt. Charley is my cousin. He don't know you speak his language. Forgive him his sin." In Absaroka, Black Wolf then said to the room, "Check on Far's horse. It'll be a bay. It's the only color he likes."

"Charley Slow Dog? Really? You don't look like that ten year old kid I knew what, twelve years ago? Wolf, you sure this is Charley? Don't look like him. It's an Appy, Wolf," Forest corrected. "I'll be damned. Charley Slow Dog and I just hit him over the head." He looked at the big man on the floor. "You don't look like you, Charley. You grew up. You musta forgotten. I don't like folks stealin' my horse. Best you remember."

Black Wolf interrupted. "An Appy? Not a bay? You are sick. A pretty boy's horse. All right. Everybody, my pretty friend here owns an Appy," Black Wolf repeated. "Look for an Appy. Please!"

Someone in the front got up and walked to the door. A moment later he came back. He said something to the room and more specifically to Charley Slow Dog who was still staring at the bore of Forest's pistol from the floor.

Black Wolf said, "He said your horse is out there, Far."

"I know what he said. I heard him. What do I do with Charley Slow Dog here? Do I help him up? Do I hit him again? He looks too big to let go. He might not wanna be let go. He might not let me let him go."

Black Wolf shook his head. "Last man that let him go got the hell beat out of himself."

"That's what I'm thinkin'. I don't want that happenin'."

"Charley," Black Wolf said, "Far here is scared to let you go. If you don't let him let you go...he might shoot you. You look to him like you could whoop up real good on him."

"I could whoop up on him. That's what I'm fixin' to do if he lets me up."

"That's just it, Charley. He ain't, if you ain't. He will if you will. So what's it gonna be? You wanna get yourself buried today?"

"No."

"So it'll be all right he lets you up?"

The big man with the red handkerchief nodded slowly. "I don't like this much, Wolf."

"You think you can get over it if Far lets you live?"

"Yes, you put it that way."

"I put it that way."

Another voice entered the discussion. The voice said, "Lord,

Far, why you got this fellow on the floor? Are you gonna shoot him?"

"Si? I was wonderin' when you'd show up. In answer to your question, he was stealin' my horse."

"Well, he ain't stolen it, not yet. He's out front. I, myself and three other gents looked him over. I'm here just in time 'cause your friend, Wolf, owes me a drink."

"Seems Wolf owes everybody a drink," Forest said.

Syrus said, "Your nag is standin' right next to mine. I did have to interrupt his departure. Seems he was bein' led down the street." Syrus glanced at the man on the floor covered by Forest's pistol. "Why, Charley Slow Dog, you done grew up. What you been eatin'? It's treated you good. Did that brother of mine just catch you stealin' his Appy? You know better."

To Forest he said, "Put that iron away, Far. Charley Slow Dog ain't gonna hurt nobody. Wait a minute. I just saved his life, didn't I? That makes it his turn to buy. Last time I was here he wasn't old enough to drink. Still, ain't." Syrus extended his hand. "Get up, Charley," he said, "and get your money out. I'm plenty thirsty. I swear I can drink all you can buy. How much are you buyin'?"

Charley Slow Dog took the extended hand and rose to his feet, staring at Forest, then speaking to Syrus. "I don't owe you nothin'. And I didn't steal no horse. I just thought about it."

"Thinkin' 'bout it will get you in trouble," Syrus laughed. "Stealin' Far's horse? You ought to know he don't like walkin'."

Charley Slow Dog shook his head. "Si, I ain't seen you since...."

"Since you was ten or eleven, the way I remember it."

"I didn't know who this one was. So I thought about it. Si, you know I didn't mean it."

"You know, Charley Slow Dog, you go to hell for lyin', stealin' and bein' ugly. Looks to me like you're bound to get there, soon or late. I'm guessin' you don't remember Far."

"I don't remember him. Really, I didn't."

Syrus nodded at Forest. "Brother," he said, "bet you're surprised to see me this soon."

"A little," Forest replied. "I figured tomorrow."

"I got to thinkin' that the man who'd know about those cows, if anybody knows, would be the Wolf himself. They ain't 'cross the river. I can tell you that. Some strange cows over there. Not ours."

"Black Wolf," Black Wolf interjected. "Black Wolf."

"I plum forgot. How are you? It's been awhile."

"Fifteen or twenty winters."

"You look good."

"I'm good. Far is about to buy me a drink. So far he's just talked about it."

"What's that bottle Johnny Bad Crow has in his hand?"

"That's Far talkin' about it."

Syrus nodded, smiled. "All right, what d'you say, Johnny? A glass for everyone? Three thirsty friends, plus Johnny the Barkeep. How come you ain't pourin', Wolf? It's your bottle. I'm thirsty since it's free."

"Ah, shit, Si. I let you do this to me every time you show up. It's never you buyin'."

"True." Syrus glanced at the bartender. "Well, Johnny Bad Crow, we need five glasses. Wolf is pourin' ain't you, Wolf?"

Black Wolf wound up and threw a shot glass at Syrus, narrowly missing him and looked at the half full bottle in front of him as if he was considering throwing it.

Forest noted, saying, "Now, Wolf, I know you'd like to nail him hard but I am not buyin' you another bottle. Just sayin'. You might wanna reconsider throwin' that bottle."

"Damn," Black Wolf said, standing up, taking the bottle from Johnny Bad Crow.

"Good idea," Forest said. He looked at Johnny Bad Crow. "Line'em up, Barkeep, before the Wolf changes his mind."

Johnny Bad Crow lined up five shot glasses.

Syrus smiled. He said, "Good to see you, Johnny." Syrus looked at Black Wolf. "Everyone's here. Must be goin' huntin'. Ain't even October yet."

The drinks were poured. Each picked up his glass. Johnny Bad Crow raised his glass, glanced at his associates. "To old friends," he said, "who finally come home. Welcome, even if Si ain't payin'. Again."

They raised their glasses to his, took a sip and swallowed.

234

"Damn straight," Syrus said. "Johnny Bad Crow, you slipped in the good stuff." He stretched his hand out. Johnny took it. "Johnny, as I said, it's always good to see you. You know I'd rather owe it to Wolf, than cheat him out of it."

Charley Slow Dog grunted in agreement. "That don't clear you, Si. Far bought the first round."

"No truer words has been spoken, Charley. None at all. But I gotta keep my wits about me. Bet Far has told you we got problems. And they're stackin' up. Gettin' hard to breathe."

Black Wolf nodded, took another swallow and sat down. He said, "In answer to your question, Far, it's been six months, maybe less, maybe five months as I think about it. I wasn't here. Huntin' buffalo. A large herd of stock cows was driven north in the middle of the night. Crossed the river on the ice a couple miles below Fort Smith." He stopped speaking. "It was in the month the buffalo begin to drop their calves. That herd came through under the long yellow hill. Same time me and Charley Slow Dog found Pistol. Bad shape. Cold. Frozen. Leg broken. We got him on a horse and took him to his woman. He never said anything. No talk. He didn't know what happened to him. He was lucky that day."

"The cows? Where are they?" Syrus asked. "Do you know?"

"I do. Yes. Charley Slow Dog and Johnny Bad Crow followed 'em."

"Where?" Forest asked, looking at Charley Slow Dog.

Charley drained his glass. "On the Yellowstone River this side of the Tongue. Many cows. Many men. There is much trouble." He paused. "That was then. We ain't been back. They may not be there now. Probably are, because they ain't left, not on the railroad anyway. No Crow has been hired to gather and load them. Not that I've heard."

Forest nodded, lookin' at Charley. "Stolen before or after Pistol got his leg broke?"

"Don't remember seein' any MT cattle bein' where they should be before we found Pistol in Ferrimore Canyon. So, probably before. Very good on a horse, that one. Pistol."

Black Wolf laughed. "Pistol, the horse rider. I gotta tell you a Charley Slow Dog story. They'll like this one, huh, Charley? We was huntin' and Pistol wanted to give Charley a present. It was Charley's birthday, sorta' because Charley don't know when he was born 'cept maybe the month. So Pistol bets Charley that knife Charley carries around, that he could ride Charley's worst horse without a bridle, without any saddle. Nothin'. Charley takes the bet. Brings him a horse belongin' to Johnny Bad Crow. Nobody has ridden him. Johnny keeps him around for bets. Charley here, thinks he's trickin' Pistol. Pistol rides him, rides the green out of him, rides him to a standstill. Good joke. So Charley gives Pistol his knife and Pistol gives it back to Charley for a present. So that there is Charley's knife that Charley lost, that Pistol gave him for a birthday present."

Syrus looked at his empty glass. He said, "That's true. Pistol is very good on a horse and you found out Pistol is also a pain in the ass. Listen, there is one other thing I'm hopin' you boys might know somethin' 'bout. Long time ago, twenty years or thirty years ago, the Old Man had friends lived over on Little Mountain on the other side of the Canyon. They built a log house on Deer Creek. Went by the name of Stafford. Had a few head of cows. You know anythin' about those folks? A man, his wife, and four daughters?"

Johnny Bad Crow answered the question. Before he did, he took the bottle from Black Wolf and slowly, carefully refilled all five glasses. He said, "It's a bad story, Si. Many come in here and tell it. In time past, Stafford hired many Absaroka Crow for cows, for fall round up, and to work their calves in the spring. No more. Many of those men who worked for Stafford come here. Much talk. They say a man named Mumford killed Stafford. His girl found Mumford. Killed him with a shotgun. Men came in the night and took all three girls away, three day's ride. Killed them. Very strange."

Black Wolf stared at Syrus. "It's not good," he said to him. "There's more to it. Pistol's woman is a Stafford woman. It's said that a man across the big mountain seeks her life. That man has many, many cattle. Like buffalo."

Forest cleared his throat, drained his glass, and set it on the table, his hand covering it. "Do you know who this Mumford fellow worked for?" he asked.

Johnny Bad Crow looked at Forest to see if he wanted any more to drink. Forest shook his head. Johnny Bad Crow glanced at

Syrus. "His name's Linderman. Hires many guns. Takes Stafford cows north of Sheridan. He's the one who takes Stockton cows. Drives 'em across the Big Horn where the river comes from the canyon. Trailed 'em four, five days north to the Yellowstone and Tongue Rivers."

For a moment there was silence.

Black Wolf looked at Syrus. He asked, "What are you gonna do?"

"I think I'm gonna shoot holes in some folks, Wolf. Big ones. Some people out there are tryin' real hard to get theyselves killed."

"Killed? Your father and mine once went to find cows. Stolen cows. Your father, he said, 'Let's go kill some folks, send them to hell before they know they're dead.' He said it will be a big shock for them to be home that quick. Is that what you have in mind?"

Syrus smiled. "You hear 'bout that?"

"Everybody heard about that."

It was Forest who answered the first question. "This Linderman ain't leavin' us no choice. We're cow people. And hunters."

"And hunters," Syrus said. "Gotta feed the people." He smiled.

Black Wolf nodded. "Since we were able to walk. Since we were boys walkin' in our father's shadow, that's what they did. Hunt is what they did," Black Wolf said. His voice was quiet. "In the fall, every fall since I can remember, they hunted deer, buffalo. Your pa was a great hunter. He gave all the meat to my father. Filled the parfleches of the old, those without men in their lodge. After the hunt, your pa brought steers, old cows to my father, told him to give 'em to those who needed meat for the winter."

Syrus said, "The Old Man kept some of those steers for himself. Didn't give 'em all away. He made us boys cut some into strips and dry it in the sun like women do. It was my job to keep the dogs away and bring the racks inside at night so the critters wouldn't get the meat. Bring it out again when the sun came up. I asked him once how come the women didn't do it like the Crow. He said I was an old woman."

Black Wolf laughed. "Those two. No mercy. Once your

237

father said to mine, 'I cursed you.' And He Who Cannot Be Named said 'how is that you cursed me?' Your pa said, 'I've told all of my young to come to you should I be dead and they find themselves in trouble.' And here you are...in trouble." He turned to Syrus. He asked, "When are you gonna make your little war, Si?"

Forest handed his empty glass to Johnny Bad Crow. "He's gonna start right now, Wolf."

Black Wolf stood up. He smiled, looked at Forest, and said, "I figured." Taking his time, he made a big show of pulling his revolver from his waistband, opening the loading gate, checking the loads, and tucking it back in his waistband. "You boys see that before?"

Everyone nodded.

He asked, "Did your pa tell you not to keep an open chamber if you're expectin' trouble? Did he say keepin' an open chamber was plain stupid? Nothin' safe about it? Remember him sayin' something like that?"

Forest laughed. "All the time, every day, all of our lives. Every time he said it, I wanted to ask him what if he shot himself 'cause he didn't have the hammer sittin' on an empty chamber. I never did. I was too scared."

Black Wolf smiled. "Well, Si, it's dark in four or five hours. We'll leave in the mornin', if it's okay with you. I've got horses to get in and provisions to gather and load. Sun up sound good?" Black Wolf started walking toward the door, a tall man with broad shoulders, full of purpose, confident in who he was.

"Wolf," Forest said. "Better make that the day after tomorrow. We need to ride to get Riles and Pistol."

"That's what I meant: the day after tomorrow. That's what I said." Black Wolf smiled. He said, "Riles, he's here, too? It's gonna be a big party. A whole lot of killin', I think. And countin' coup. Be here in two days: Chokecherry Creek. You know the place."

He turned and continued walking toward the door, stopped to talk to someone wearing a big hat, then left.

Forest looked at his brother. "Let's get some shuteye, Si. Tomorrow, I'd appreciate it if you'd get Riles and Pistol. They'll need to be here. I got some fences I need to patch."

238

"All right," Syrus said. "Go patch fences. I'll get big brother and little brother--the brothers two--and I'll bring you back a whole lot of trouble." He smiled. "You go ahead. I'll catch up. You goin' to that spring above the rock face?"

Forest nodded.

"All right. By the way, what's her name? The fence you're gonna fix?"

"Who said anything about a woman?"

"It's always 'bout a woman. Not to worry. I'll get Riles and Pistol. I'll bring 'em all."

"Good. Tomorrow I'll help Wolf, Johnny Bad Crow, and Charley get ready. We'll leave as soon as you return." Forest paused. "You know, Si, I do not remember Charley Slow Dog. I remember the name but he sure don't look like the snot nosed kid I remember taggin' along."

"He grew up."

Syrus put his arm around Forest's shoulders. "Far, now don't go off half cocked. That's somethin' I'd do. Not you. Wait for us before you cut the dog loose. If for no other reason, Riles would never let you hear the end of it."

Forest laughed. "You sure got that right." Forest stared at his brother. "Don't worry, Si, I won't do a damn thing 'til you get back. Don't be draggin' your heels."

"No heel draggin'. Not that I'm worried about you, Far. I am wonderin' though. Didn't know you knew how to patch fences. You'll have to show me. I need some fence fixin' tips."

"You?"

"It's about Willow? Yes? Figured as much."

"It's been ten or twelve years since I've seen her. I didn't think it'd be that way when I left. I think she's gonna be upset. She should be."

"Fences are what they are."

"Yeah, whatever that means."

CHAPTER 31

Forest rode to upper Chokecherry Creek in the early morning. Per his arrangement with Black Wolf, he was to meet him there. Two days later they'd leave for the confluence of the Yellowstone and Tongue Rivers. It was on upper Chokecherry Creek they'd meet Riles, Peter, Syrus, and Diana as well as Black Wolf's cousin Charley Slow Dog and Johnny Bad Crow.

He was a little anxious, worried. Black Wolf assured him in the language of the Absaroka Crow that he should be anxious; he should be worried. His twelve year prolonged absence was not a good thing although it didn't bother Black Wolf. His sister however, didn't have the same feelings on the subject.

"She's married, right, Wolf?" Forest had asked. "She has some kids? Her husband? He's a good man, I'll bet. Yes? What storm am I riding into here? Will she even talk to me?"

Black Wolf, standing by his horse, outside the Bad Pass Bar, a single rein in hand, looked at him for what seemed a long time. *Just like his father,* Forest thought, for his father always considered his answer before he shared it. He always reviewed what the response would be to his words before he shared them. Watching Black Wolf develop his response, Forest wondered if Black Wolf was telling the complete story or enjoying, instead, jabbing him in the ribs for fun.

"She waited," Black Wolf said. "Some fool said he was returning…soon. You see," he said, "she believed him. I told her. He Who Cannot Be Named, told her. We said you could be dead. I told her you were dead. We told her not to wait. She waited, anyway. She refused to listen. Many suitors came. She turned them away, one after another. She listened to them but she kept shaking her head no, no, no. They keep coming. Good men. Strong warriors. Good hunters. She said no until she didn't say no any more. Afterwards, she married. She bore a daughter, then another. Her husband was killed. Big fight on the Platte River. She married again and had a son. She also lost the second husband. Horse rolled on him. Recently, she was getting closer to saying yes again, but He Who Cannot be Named

240

died. Your pa died. The past year has not been a good time for her. She is mourning. Soon that time will be over. Maybe tomorrow. Maybe next month. I do not know. Many are waiting for her." Black Wolf smiled at Forest. "She doesn't know you're here. Until today, I didn't know you were here. My best guess…she won't be happy to see you. Do you want me to tell her? I will, if you want this. It could be interestin'."

Forest Stockton shook his head no. "No," he said. "I'll meet you on Chokecherry Creek tomorrow mornin'. I'll help with gettin' ready, catchin' up your horses. If you tell her, she might not be there when I get there. She may leave and I wanna tell her I'm sorry. I wanna get this over, so I can have my old life back. If that's possible."

"I'm thinkin' she don't wanna hear it, but suit yourself."

"I think I should offer my regret, say I'm sorry. I'm the one that brought her grief. I made it worse by makin' promises I didn't or couldn't keep. I don't expect her to understand, but I was young. Stupid. I didn't know and I should have known. She did. She knew. She told me what would happen." Forest stopped. "It is good that she married. Very good. I am glad she had some babies. Hopefully, she was happy."

Black Wolf smiled. "Personally," he said, "I'm glad to see you. Huntin' will be better with you here. I don't need to understand. You need to explain it to Willow. Not me." Black Wolf grinned at Forest. "No foolin'. I'd like to hear your explanation. It's gotta be good. Real good. I'm guessin' you found a woman. Made some babies yourself. Stayed drunk, hunted some buffalo."

"It ain't that good, Wolf. I ain't thought an explanation up yet. I can imagine how George Custer felt ridin' into that valley, all of them people not likin' him, wantin' to kill and scalp him. Not too pleasant."

"Yeah, she probably will wanna kill you. Count coup. I might enjoy this, I think."

"Thanks, Wolf. Good to know."

"Oh, you're welcome."

It had been fifteen years, give or take a month or a day or a eek. Memory had faded on the latter. This isn't to say that Forest Stockton didn't remember leaving.

"You're not comin' back, are you?" That's what she said to him those many years ago.

"Of course I am comin' back. I just got to get away from here for now, a little while." That was his response. He remembered well her tears.

"Why don't we go together?" she'd asked. "Let's both go."

"No, no," he said. "All I have to my name is this horse, this saddle. I'll come back for you. Soon as I find a way. We have to eat," he'd answered. "I gotta figure that out."

"Yes," she'd said. "You hunt. We eat. That's what men do. That's how they have always done. My father, and his father and his father and your father. They hunted. Their women ate. Bore them children for happiness. It should be this way with you, with me. It would be good."

"I'll come back. It'll be a short time. It'll be good again. I'll hunt for you. Just like you said."

"Why? Why don't we go together, like always. Like we talked. Like we dreamed someday would be?"

"We will. I will. It's just for a month or two. You'll see. I'll be back. I promise."

"It won't happen that way," she'd said. "It never does. It won't happen the way you think or expect it. If we don't do it now. It will not happen."

"No. You're wrong. It'll happen. Trust me."

That morning, he'd left her there on the rise above upper Chokecherry Creek, crying, begging him not to go, asking him to come back even before he'd left. His last words to her were: "You'll see." Only she hadn't seen. His words had been untrue. One day led to the next and he'd never returned, just as she'd said. Somehow Forest had slid down the slipstream of time, unaware years were passing; it was too easy to continue working for someone else, too hard to saddle his horse, too hard to turn his head and point himself homeward. Too hard, too easy, too many days, too many months, too long. He'd wronged her.

His father had said in simple English: "Own up to what's

yours." Now he was here. First to do that; Peter's cows were secondary.

Forest Stockton knew he had no right to expect anything from this girl he'd known so long ago. She was no longer a girl. She had babies. He didn't have any expectations. He'd convinced himself it was like stopping to see an old friend, to put this whole thing to bed so that he and she could get on with their lives. Courting wasn't what he had in mind. Neither was marrying. He just owed it to her. He owed it to himself. What he hadn't done was wrong. There was no repairing it. There was no excuse for his conduct. He knew that, too. The fact of the matter was it all came back to rest at his feet. He accepted the fact that his absence was his fault. It needed to be aired out. He was here to make it right as much as he could. He was here to do just that. Knowledge didn't make it any easier.

Forest crested the hill above Chokecherry Creek. Below him sat the lodges of the Absaroka Crow, of the mother of Black Wolf and his sister, Willow. He watched the smoke rising from the campfires: seven columns rising above a windless settlement of seven lodges. Since the death of Black Wolf and Moose, they'd been pitched here. That was last October. Soon it would be October again. It was a time of mourning. Mourning wasn't over. It would be next month, in September, the time for hunting, for filling the parfleches with the dried meat of the buffalo, elk, moose, and deer.

Below him Forest recognized the lone figure of Black Wolf standing near a fire pit. It was warm. He wore no shirt, dressed in leggings, and a breach cloth. Forest waved at him, and started his descent into camp. Black Wolf waved back. This had been done many times in the past, more than was counted. The only thought in Forest's mind was, *All right, let's get this over. Right now.*

The Appaloosa picked its way down the slope past boulders fifteen and twenty feet high. Forest let him pick his way. He knew as much as Forest did about getting down the hill to the creek. Five minutes later, Forest was standing next to Black Wolf feeling the heat from the flame, smelling the smoke drifting upwards, the venison roasting.

"You sleep in?" Black Wolf said, laughing. "Thought you'd

be here early looking forward to getting your butt whipped by an angry woman."

"Can't say that I was lookin' forward to that when I woke up. Sun's only up an hour, Wolf. Thought I was doin' well gettin' here when I did."

"Wolf! Look." Forest pointed. A herd of twenty white tails were wandering up the creek in and out of the Chokecherry brambles, up the slope of the hill, disappearing in the aspen. Three head stopped to look back, then disappeared into the trees. "You ain't got far to go to hunt. All you got to do is invite 'em over here to get themselves shot."

"Not this year. They're safe. You and I, we're goin'to the Bull Elk, the Basin pasture next time the moon turns full. You ain't gettin' out of that."

"I don't wanna get out of it."

Suddenly, right then, Forest knew someone was standing behind him. His whole body knew; his soul knew. He was in trouble. He thought what Riles always thought in times like these: *Horseshit and gunsmoke. There's absolutely nothin' I can do about this, nothin' at all.* Forest turned to face her. Black Wolf also looked to see why he'd stopped talking.

She stared at Forest. It was a long moment; then she looked at her brother. "You knew he was here."

"I did."

"You didn't tell me."

"I didn't."

"Why?"

Black Wolf stared at his sister standing five foot nine inches tall, one hundred twenty-eight pounds, wearing a doeskin dress, kelchi on her feet, wrapped to her knees, braids hanging over her shoulders and down her back. "You know why," he said. "You know very well why."

Among the Willows turned her attention back to a very miserable Forest, her eyes ablaze with anger, with hurt, with frustration, with resignation for what might have been.

Before she could say anything, Forest said, "I've come to apologize. I've come to tell you I'm sorry. I have no excuse. I wish to

244

be forgiven for being..." he paused..."stupid."

"You didn't," she said. "You didn't come to apologize."

How did she know? "You're right, Willow. I didn't. I came because Pistol broke his leg, because his wife, Diana, wrote me a letter sayin' that my pa was dead, that all the cows were gone, that she needed help."

"What about me? I needed you. Before Pistol broke his leg, before your father died, before your cows disappeared. Before all of that, I needed you."

"I have no excuse, Willow. None at all. I'm sorry. I was stupid. I have come to apologize. I don't deserve it, but please...please forgive me. I didn't mean to hurt you. I wish I hadn't."

"If you didn't mean to hurt me, what did you mean to do?"

"Oh, jeez," Forest said. "You're asking all the right questions. What I did was hurt you. I come to apologize, to tell you I'm sorry, to beg for your forgiveness. I only ask for that, nothin' else. I don't deserve even that. I've been tryin' to return. For fifteen years I've been tryin'. The more I tried, the more difficult it became. I deserve nothin' else. Please forgive my lack of thought, for bein' entirely wrong. Forgive me for hurtin' you. I didn't mean it and that's no excuse. I do not offer it as an excuse. Believe me when I tell you I'm sorry."

Black Wolf interrupted. "Far," he said, "stop it. I'm goin' to start cryin'."

"Shut up," Willow said to him. "This is not your concern." She turned back to Forest. He'd removed his hat.

"Your excuse words that are not excuse words--they are supposed to make me feel better?"

"No. I don't know how to do that. If I could I would."

In the middle of his words, a girl of maybe eleven winters, walked up behind Willow, followed by yet another. Maybe the second was nine winters. The first touched her mother's arm. She said, "Mother, you're yellin'. Who is this white man who makes you so angry?"

Forest looked and discovered the two girls, one after the other. Then before Willow could say anything, he turned his attention

245

to her, momentarily hesitating. "Yours?" he asked. "These two?"

She nodded her head.

In Absaroka Crow he said, "They're beautiful, so very beautiful, just like you. They look just like you when you were twelve winters. They are so beautiful. You must be terribly proud."

His words snatched the air from her lungs, words from her lips. Of course she was proud.

"Don't say that. You can't say that. I want to be angry with you. You left me standing right up there." Willow pointed with her left hand. "I want to be angry at you. I need to be angry at you."

The first daughter stared at him. Both did. Forest spoke to them in Absaroka Crow. To the first, he said, "You are beautiful like your mother when your mother was as old as you now are. She is angry with me because I left her and never came back."

The first girl, surprised at his use of their language, demanded, "Who are you?"

Forest hesitated, looked at Among the Willows, and said, "Who am I, Willow?"

Forest heard Black Wolf swear in English. He turned to see why. Black Wolf was looking at a formidable man, dressed much like Black Wolf. He had a large Bowie Knife stuck in a sheath behind a wide belt that held his leggings around his waist.. He was standing close to Black Wolf's lodge, which was also the lodge of his Black Wolf's mother and Among The Willows, as well as her daughters.

The visitor was gruff, insistent. His voice was low but the pitch was rising. "Who is this white man?" he asked Black Wolf. "What is he doing here?"

"It's not your affair, Dog Man," Black Wolf said. "He's a friend of mine. Leave us. We have business together that is not your concern."

Forest heard the disdain in Black Wolf's voice. Everyone did.

Dog Man looked at Among the Willows. "Come here," he demanded. "Get behind me. Get your daughters behind me. I will take care of this."

Forest was watching him carefully. His right hand knocked the latch from the hammer of his SAA Colt. The man was big. He moved well. *This ain't goin' away*, he thought.

Black Wolf had pulled his Colt from behind his belt. It was pointed at the ground. Forest heard the hammer being pulled back, locking.

Suddenly, and to Forest's surprise, Willow put herself between Forest and the man with the knife taking a step toward him. "No," she said. "No. You are to leave. This man is the son of Moose. He is welcome here as his father was welcome here. He is my brother's brother. For all time. That is the way this is. That I do not like him is my business. You are to leave. It is for me not to like him. Not you. Me. Understand? I want you to leave."

This is goin' to the dogs quick, Forest thought. *Real quick*. "Willow," he said. "Willow, I'm not worth it. Get your daughters to safety. Please. Please, Willow, I beg you. This man can't be reasoned with. He's gonna try to kill me. That's what he's thinkin'."

"Shut up, Forest. For once, do not speak. I am not reasonin' with him. I am tellin' him to go. He's goin'. Stop sayin' those things. I want to be angry with you. I am very angry with you. I want you to be quiet."

"Willow, please." Forest begged. "Please take your daughters and go. I do not mean to anger you. I do not mean to hurt your feelings. Please get them to safety. Get them out of harm's way. Please. Before it's too late."

Willow turned to Forest, taking her eyes off Dog Man but Forest's eyes did not leave Dog Man. "Forest," she said. "Please stop saying nice things. I am angry with you. I want to tell you about my anger. You hurt me. I, I didn't deserve that from you. Not what you did."

"You didn't and I was stupid. I will trade my life for your daughters. Please get them out of the way. Please."

Four additional men had gathered with Dog Man. One asked, "What's goin' on?" No one answered. Each appeared to be moving forward, following Dog Man's lead.

Willow, aware of the sudden movement, took her eyes off Forest for a split second and he stepped around her. "Save your daughters," he said, both hands full of revolver. Her brother was moving with Forest. Among the Willows was shocked at the speed at which these actions transpired, leaving her behind her brother,

247

behind Forest. It was one of those moments, offering no time for thought, consumed and defined by action, deadly and permanent, relentless and totally unforgiving.

Among the Willows screamed to her daughters, "Get down!" She charged at Forest's back, grabbing the revolver that he had stuck in the small of his back, tucked behind the belt that held his chaps in place. Pulling it, yanking it free, she turned, pulling back on the hammer and ran around and in front of him, screaming, "No, no, no!" In front of her was Dog Man, his knife drawn. On either side of him were his friends with revolvers drawn, all charging forward, firing.

"No, no. no." Beside her, her brother was firing: bam, bam, bam. She was in front of Forest running toward Dog Man, pulling the trigger on the pistol she held in both hands. It seemed to explode in her hands "No, no. no!" she screamed. Something struck her; she went flying to her right. Silence. Less than five seconds had passed and her world was black as midnight in a starless, moonless sky. Dog Man, on the other hand, a man who brought a large knife to a gunfight, was simply dead, as were three of his friends.

Among the Willows opened her eyes. For a moment she didn't know where she was. She heard her oldest daughter crying. She was aware of her second daughter blocking out the sun. She was saying, "Momma, Momma, Momma" over and over again.

She heard Black Wolf, his droll voice saying, "You might wanna loosen up a bit. She ain't breathin' with you huggin' her like that.."

Whoever had her in death's embrace did not loosen up. That voice was saying "Oh my God, my God! What have I done? What have I done?"

Her brother's voice was laughing. He said, "I don't think you did a damn thing. You didn't even fire a pistol. Not one shot. You're worthless. You might want to loosen up though. She's suffocatin'.."

The arms did loosen but not much. The voice said, "I told her, Wolf. I told her over and over. She just ignored me. She wouldn't listen."

Black Wolf's voice came back. "Like that's a surprise, I've

been tryin' to get her to listen for fifteen years. She ain't heard a word."

Then there was the voice of a little girl, her youngest. That voice said, "Who are you?" Silence followed.

Her brother's voice answered. "This, Winter's Wind, is your momma's boyfriend. He's lost. Your momma is fixin' to beat the hell out of him. Soon as she wakes up she probably will. It'll be fun. I can't wait."

The girl's voice said, "She just killed her boyfriend. He's dead."

"No, not that one and not your father and not the one after that. This one, here. He's the first one. She was about three winters when she picked him out. He came back so your momma could shoot him. He's crazy that way. "

"He thinks I'm pretty."

"Yeah, he does. And you are. Makes it all even more crazy, doesn't it?"

There was no response.

"You know my momma?" she asked Forest.

"Yeah, I know your momma."

"What's my momma's name, if you know her?"

"Willow."

"It's not really. It's Among the Willows."

"Yes, Among the Willows."

Ten minutes can be a long time. It can seem like forever. Through these counted minutes, Among the Willows began to remember and she remembered. She didn't know whether to get up or lie still. His arms about her felt really, really good.

She said to him, "I'm really angry at you, you know this?"

"Yes, I know."

"I didn't tell my daughters about you, nor my son. I am so angry. I hurt so much."

He nodded. "That's all right that you didn't tell 'em."

"Right now, I don't know whether to get up or not. I am afraid if I do you will stop hugging me."

"Willow, you just killed a man to save my life. Can you explain that?"

249

"I can't."

"I can't, either. You have beautiful daughters."

This time she didn't object. Instead, she said, "I do, don't I."

"Yes, they look just like you."

Among the Willows did not respond, not immediately. Finally, she asked, "Do you want me to get up?"

He answered, "Not very badly."

She started crying.

CHAPTER 32

On the third day after he'd left Sage Creek to explore the winter pastures, Riles Stockton returned, arriving at the line shack about four o'clock in the afternoon. He turned his Buckskin horse into the horse corral with a bait of oats poured in an old water bucket. He didn't bother with Cecil. Once having taken care of his horse, he went inside to get something to eat, to rest, and to wait in the shade for Forest and Syrus.

"What did you find?" Peter asked as Riles sat down at the table. "Anything?"

"Petey, honey, cut the man some slack in his rope. He just got in. He's tired, hungry, could use a drink. Let him take a breath."

"Thanks, Diana," Riles said, "but I do have some good news for the both of you. Found about sixty, seventy head, give or take. Older cows, their spring calves, and some two year olds. That ought to make you smile. You ain't entirely broke. Just mostly."

"Where? Where did you find 'em?"

Riles glanced at Diana. "You got any more bread?" He looked at Peter and said, "Found 'em around that big spring on the southwest side of the West Pryor. Couple of miles from the end of the mountain. Looked fat and sassy."

"That's incredible," Peter said.

"It is, ain't it? Thought it'd make you two all sorts of happy."

Riles bit into a slice of buttered bread. "Love eatin' fresh bread and butter. Cures what ails you or is 'bout to ail you."

Syrus arrived at the line cabin the next day, a few minutes before noon. He immediately informed everyone that Forest wasn't coming.

"That ain't good news," Riles said. "That ain't good news at all."

"He's fixin' fences and waitin'."

"Fixin' fences? There ain't no fences on the Reservation."

"That's what I said to him. He's got a girl. I'm just sayin'."

"And waitin'?" Riles asked. "Waitin' for what? You find the cows? He ain't got no girl. How could he? He ain't been here in fifteen years. What about the cows? You find 'em?"

"No," Syrus answered. "Wolf's people did."

"Where are they?"

"Where the Tongue meets the Yellowstone."

"That's to hell and gone."

"Close. Real close. Probably a little over a hundred miles, give or take, from Fort Smith to where they was five or six months ago. Plus thirty, thirty-five miles from here to Fort Smith. No wonder I'm tired."

"So, Far ain't comin'. You're here. Everybody's here thet's gonna be here. Let's put together what we know," Riles said. "Let's figure out what we're gonna do."

"First, let me say what I gotta say," said Syrus. "I think that it will answer a lot of questions. Save some time. We ain't got a lot of time."

Syrus found a ladle hanging on a nail and got a drink of water from a five gallon can. He smacked his lips. "Good stuff," he said, taking a breath. "Okay. Where are we?"

For a moment there was silence. No one spoke or even attempted to break into the quiet of the line cabin. Outside, a breeze rattled the leaves in the aspen. The one-eyed dog was lapping spring water. Cecil was scratching his back against the horse corral poles. Josh and Katie Sue were building mud and rock dams across the trickling spring before it disappeared back in the ground.

"Well,"Syrus said, "I found no sign of MT cattle goin' 'cross the canyon over to the Bull Elk. I took a look at the Basin Pasture, too. Saw no MT cows, no Bar S cows, either. That's where I'd expect 'em this time of year. There was some Lazy W cows. Ain't never seen that brand before."

Syrus removed his hat, pressed the crease, scratched his head, then reseated it on the back of his head, leaving a strip of white forehead exposed. "Afterwards, I rode the Bad Pass to Fort Smith. Met Far and Wolf at the Bad Pass Bar. You know where I mean. Far was visitin' with Wolf and some other folk there. Wolf told me that maybe five or six months ago, ten or fifteen riders pushed a herd of

252

cows down the river from Fort Smith. He didn't see the brand. No one did. It was the middle of the night. They crossed the Horn on the ice. It was that place where the Horn straightens itself out for a mile or so. Wolf said it wasn't Crow riders. Horses were all shod. Moved quickly. He guessed maybe a thousand head. Maybe more. That's what he was told. Couple of fellows, Charley Slow Dog and Johnny Bad Crow, followed 'em. That's how I figured where they are now. If they are still there. They may not be."

Syrus glanced at Peter. "Pistol, how many did you say we got? Could that be them?"

Peter answered. "We have a little over eight hundred fifty head of cows. That many yearlings. We have two year olds 'cause we didn't take them to market. Would have done that in April, May. There'd also be forty or fifty range bulls. Maybe a few more. We ain't sold no bulls for a couple of years, either."

Syrus nodded. "So it could be them. That would account for most of what they saw. Others at the bar agreed with him. Said it was a big herd. Didn't know exactly how many. All the boys I talked with said Linderman's boys pushed 'em across the river on the ice in the early morning. Kept goin' north from what I can tell. I never saw the tracks, myself. So far, I ain't seen one head of MT beef."

Riles nodded. "You sayin' they crossed the Horn on the other side of Fort Smith? Only question is whether they is MT cows?"

Syrus shrugged his shoulders, took a drink of spring water from the ladle. He said, "Some tracks ought to still be there, if we was to look. A thousand head would tear the hell outta the countryside. Hard to hide their passin'. It's been five or six months. It was winter then. Ground was frozen. Still the trails could be deep, that many cows. When I was in Sheridan not ten days ago I took a look at the stockyards. I didn't see any MT or Bar S cows. Bought the roan and that bay. Didn't see any cows standin' in the corral. I'd notice the MT brand. There was about twenty head with that Lazy W on the hip. Interestin' that some of those was also on the Basin Pasture. Don't figure they belonged there."

Peter said, "We ain't got no choice. We gotta follow 'em to the Yellowstone to see if those are MT cows over there."

"Well," Syrus said, "right now, Far is waitin' for us at Fort

253

Smith to do just that. On my trip back here, I got to thinkin', tryin' to put this mess together. That kind of operation, comin' in, knockin' Pistol on his butt, killin' his horse, takin' them cows off the flat in the middle of winter--someone had to plan it real well. They had to know Pistol wasn't gonna stop 'em before they started. Needless to say, January, February, March it'd be cold. Snow on the ground. River froze over. Ice over a foot thick." Syrus looked at Riles, stood up and walked to the door and stared out over the Reservation. "The question, then, is who stands to gain? This Linderman, what's he get out of this?"

Riles nodded. "I agree. Whole deal was planned. Nothin' just happens. That's what Mother liked to say. If she said anythin', she said that."

Syrus turned and glanced at Riles. "I think it's interestin' that I found no Bar S cows on the Basin Pasture or the Bull Elk. Where they should be. No MT cows, either. Only that Lazy W brand. Let's assume that the MT cows was driven across the river forty miles north of there, above old Fort Smith. It is a good assumption 'cause there ain't any other possibility, not if you think about it."

"It could mean," Syrus said, "several things. First, we're no longer guessin'. Pistol nearly gettin' himself killed ain't no accident."

"Yes," Riles agreed. "That's true."

"It means, along with our cows disappearin', that Claire, Betsy, and Sally gettin' killed wasn't just the law tryin' to get itself right. Lotta plannin'. Bought and paid for. Mumford shootin' ol' man Stafford in the back was no accident. I'd say these folks have been workin' on this for a long time. We best be takin' no chances, ourselves. I can't figure out why, though."

"Lordie," Riles said to no one in particular. Sitting down on a chair, he glanced at Syrus. "All right," he said. "let's look at the obvious. Get into this slow. As you say, we can't afford mistakes. Who stands to gain from the girls dyin', from the MT and Bar S cows disappearin'? From old man Stafford gettin' himself cut in half by a two-bit drifter carryin' a shotgun? I agree with Si. That's the question."

Syrus nodded. "I thought about that, too," he said. "Everythin' points to Sam Linderman. Even Linderman points to

Linderman. It just puzzles me why. It really makes no sense."

Riles leaned back in the kitchen chair. "Hearin' it for the third and fourth time makes it no easier. Why? From what I understand that man owns or controls everythin' from Buffalo to Sheridan and has the graze north to the Musselshell for a hundred miles."

Syrus interrupted. "He's a big fish in a big pan. He's got money. He'll have an army of hired guns. Won't be ordinary riders workin' for thirty a month, room and board. He wasn't here when I left fifteen years ago. I ain't even heard of him. To control that much graze, that many cows, he'll have a hundred riders if he's got one. We're four men, a woman, and two kids."

"Speakin' of Josh and Katie Sue," Syrus said, "Far made arrangements with Wolf for them to stay with Wolf's people out on the Reservation. He lives on Chokecherry Creek. Nobody will find 'em out there. Even if they was lookin', nobody will know where they are because it's the Reservation, because no white people go there. Too risky."

Diana looked at Syrus, "On the Reservation? Without me? I don't know if I could leave 'em. I don't know if I could leave 'em anywhere."

Syrus stared at her for a moment. "You can stay with 'em if you like. Watch 'em yourself. You made noise about wantin' to shoot your gun. Wolf wondered what you wanted to do so he could make arrangements."

Riles stood up, removed his wide-brimmed Stetson, pushed his hair off his forehead and reseated it. He said, "Wolf's people resolves where to put the kids. Let me take it further on a different subject. To do what Linderman did he'd have to control a federal judge, four federal marshals, not to mention the county sheriff and his deputy. This fellow knows who he is. He's used to doin' what he damn well pleases. He paid a judge ten thousand dollars to have Claire, Betsy, and Sally taken off the table."

Syrus' eyes narrowed. "Ten thousand dollars? How do you know that? First I heard of that figure."

"Yesterday, I run across a fellow on the South Side of the West Pryor, over there at the head of Crooked Creek. We had a discussion. He told me that he'd been paid five thousand dollars apiece to get rid of Pistol and Diana. I asked 'bout the girls. Said he didn't know anything 'bout girls but that Linderman had paid a judge ten thousand dollars for a hangin'. I don't figure he had any reason to lie."

Syrus was staring at him, as were Pistol and Diana.

"Not to worry," Riles said. "He's dead. Tried to pull a hideaway on me and I was forced to kill him."

"Additionally, there's this," Riles continued, "some of what I'm gonna say we've already chewed on but it's beginnin' to add up. I know you all don't wanna hear this again but consider this. Betsy, Claire, and Sal was helped to their deaths by four U.S. Deputy Marshals appointed by the only federal judge in northern Wyoming, and two from the County Sheriff's Office. Think about it. This supports what Far and Si are sayin'. What's four U.S. Federal Marshals doin' at a county hangin'? That's territorial. I heard that the Sheriff—what's his name--Jason Gilson, was tellin' everybody there wasn't gonna be no hangin', that he was gonna turn the girls loose. Before that happened, on the last day, those deputies showed up from the U.S. Marshal's Office. Soon as they got there, the hangin' that wasn't gonna happen, happened. A local hangin' that wasn't supposed to happen turned federal. How's that even possible? There's only one federal judge and he was, according to the skinny fellow that tried to shoot me, paid ten thousand dollars by Linderman for his services."

Peter stared with a new respect at Riles. "How'd you know that about sheriffs and Federal Marshalls? I thought they was all the same thing."

"I was a Deputy U.S. Marshal in Injun territory for six months. Didn't like it. Didn't like lookin' for a man like he was a elk or a moose, and I was hungry. Didn't like how it made me feel, so I quit. That's how I know what's federal and what's not."

Peter stared at Riles. "You a Marshal in Injun Territory?"

"And New Orleans. Texas Ranger for a while. Then I came back, first to Abilene, then Dakota. First, pushin' a herd up the Goodnight-Loving, up from Texas to Abilene. Didn't like the Rangers. Bunch of straight laced bastards. That's what they are. Think they're better than they are. I knew some that weren't any good at all. Me, mostly. I wasn't any good. Last fellow I got down there in the Territory was just a kid. Judge wanted him to hang for robbin' a stagecoach over in Arizona. If I remember it right, it wasn't him that done the robbin'. Just the fellow he was with. So I let him go. Told him to change his name and move to California. That's the bear state, you know. Those folks sure like bear. Have one on their flag. Been there, too."

"Don't tell me you was a peace officer in California?"

"California? Oh, no. No. They got the biggest trees I ever did see. I swear I saw one surrounded by fifty men holdin' hands. It was big. Never seen anythin' livin' that big. From there, I went up to Oregon. That's where Diana's letter found me."

"You're lyin'."

"I ain't. Bible swear. I ain't lyin'. On Mother's grave." Riles smiled. "Let's keep to the point. What are we doin'?"

Syrus cleared his throat. Everyone turned to him, waiting to see if he had something more to add. "I think the MT cows come first. We can't stay here with no cows. Pistol can't. Diana can't. So, that comes first. I'm suggestin' we ride for Fort Smith tomorrow. Far's waitin' for us. The fact is, we're goin' against some well-heeled folks. Another thing we should keep in mind: Pistol's cows may just be gone. Not now, but later we might have to ask ourselves what we do if we have no cows. I say that once we know the score about the MT cows, once we have 'em back eatin' grass where they are supposed to be, I suggest then we cross the river on Linderman."

No one spoke. Riles finally broke the silence. "Si's right," he said. "There is four of us, five, if you count Diana. She and Pistol have those two kids to look after. Kids put a damper on whatever we do. We have to keep 'em safe. As much as we don't wanna talk about it, Pistol has the problem of his leg. It ain't healed. Not yet."

"Well," drawled Syrus, "there's also Wolf, Charley Slow Dog, and Johnny Bad Crow. They're ridin' with us."

"Diana, you have another difficult decision to make," Riles said. "Whether you stay with your young'uns with Wolf's folks or leave 'em and come with us. It's far too dangerous to have them kids with us goin' after those MT cows You can either leave 'em with Wolf's people and come with us or you can stay with 'em. Think it

257

over."

Riles looked from face to face. "Anythin' else?" he asked. There was nothing. "All right, it's settled. We leave tomorrow, sun up. I figure we'll all need an extra saddle horse or two. We'll have to stop at the house to pick 'em up. I'm also takin' Cecil and the dog. There ain't no leavin' 'em. They're with me."

"Cecil? You mean that damn mule?"

"Yes. That damn mule. We leave early tomorrow; he'll follow. Sold him once. Tell you that? Left him in this fellow's corral. He wanted a mule and thought Cecil fit the ticket. We weren't gone ten minutes and Cecil kicks the corral fence down. Caught right up. Didn't bother takin' him back to the fellow that bought him. Anyhow, he caught up with me before I could. I gave him back his money. Didn't have the heart to send Cecil back. Never had an ounce of trouble with that mule 'cept I can't leave him behind. Can't sell him. He does pack a load."

"Keep the mule, keep me. I don't wanna be left behind," Diana mumbled. "I understand exactly how he feels. Look at what happened to my sisters."

"They weren't left behind, Dee."

"No, they weren't, but look what happened."

Riles glanced at his sister-in-law. "Rest assured, girl. Some heads are gonna roll 'fore we're done. Those girls dyin' don't sit. You can decide for yourself what you're gonna do. It's up to you and Pistol. You two know what's best."

"I know I can't rightly leave my kids. But I still wanna go. To see it through. Don't know why I'm throwin' such a fit 'bout not bein' included."

"One way or the other, Diana. We'll set it straight. That's what we do. We ain't leavin' you behind. We're recognizin' you got other irons in the fire."

Diana took a deep breath. "I know what I want. I want them men killed for what they done. It's the right thing to do," she said. "It's what they deserve."

Syrus smiled. "Well, there are consequences to everything— right or wrong. Bad things, too. You gotta be ready. Let me walk you through a hypothetical situation. Let's imagine that several days ago, a

258

week or ten days, I met the most beautiful woman, with two kids. Jed, he's three or four and his sister, Emma, a curly haired little gal, button cute--she's five or six. They don't say much. Real nice folk. Couldn't ask for any better 'cause they're the best. Just bein' near 'em made me feel good all over. Trouble is, she's married."

"Married? Jeez, Syrus, you shouldn't even be thinkin' about her. I mean, if she's married."

"I know, Diana. I know."

"Trouble is, she's...."

"No. No. No. Don't tell me. It's the saddest story I've ever heard. No. Don't tell me."

"All right. I won't."

"No. No. Tell me. Go on. What else?. I have to know."

"You sure?"

"Yes, I'm sure."

Riles stood silently in the doorway, staring out over the hazy Reservation. A deer watched him from the aspen grove, taking a step, looking, taking another step looking, taking a step.

"Trouble is she's married to a federal judge."

"Oh, my God."

"Yes, your God. Yes, that Judge. Your God will never forgive me for what I am about to do to him. In a week or ten days, I'm gonna put a round through his head and another in his brisket. I am gonna kill him dead for killin' the three most beautiful girls I ever met. Dead. Do you understand dead? I'm gonna leave his body for the vultures to strip, for the magpies to pick and feed on, for the coyotes to haul off to wherever they take a dead man's bones. Yes, Diana, your God. Your God is never gonna forgive me for what I am gonna do to this woman's husband.

"Think about it. In a few days this beautiful woman will have no husband to protect her, no one to bring her food for herself and those two kids, to put shoes on their feet, clothes on their back, to saddle their horses. No one to turn down the covers and tuck 'em in at night. Diana, that's what I'm gonna do. I'm gonna turn her life upside down and sideways. I'm gonna take those two kids' father away from them. Damn straight."

Syrus stopped talking. He looked at her, watched her eyes

blinking back tears. "Diana," Syrus said slowly. "I've told you a story about justice and the law. A hypothetical story. It's just a story. It's about makin' things right. And consequences."

They were suddenly interrupted by a noise. It sounded like a branch scraping against the roof. Diana turned and looked in the direction of the doorway. Riles had disappeared.

"What was that? Did you hear it?" she said. "It wasn't just me, was it?"

"Nah," Syrus said, smiling. "It was the Little People."

"Yeah, it was them Little People again," Peter said.

"Little People?" Diana asked.

"Yeah," Peter said. "When we was kids the Crow would scare the hell outta their kids by tellin' 'em about the Little People that lived in the Pryors. Scared 'em good. Told 'em if they warn't good the Little People'd haul 'em off and eat 'em. Stories like that." He laughed. "Hey, Si, remember when we was over there by Fort Smith. Remember them kids. Remember?" He turned to Diana. "We was over there chasin' 'round, bein' kids. I can't remember why. The Old Man liked goin' over there visitin' Black Wolf. That'd be Wolf's dad. We was playin', horsin' 'round with these kids. Did that a lot.

"One little girl asked Riles, she said, 'Riles, do you ever see any Little People?' We didn't know what they was talkin' 'bout. Riles shakes his head, says no. He ain't seen none except the Old Man. He says that the only Little People we ever saw was the Old Man. He was teasin'. The Old Man was always givin' Riles hell. Riles told them kids that and they went off cryin'. Scared as hell...like they'd been chased by a bear or somethin'. First time we'd ever heard of Little People. Found out we was livin' in their backyard."

"Did you ever...?"

"Nah, we ain't never seen nothin' like that. Just a fairy tale to scare the hell outta kids. Like the boogeyman or somethin'." He laughed again.

Syrus nodded. "Them kids was scared that day. They went home cryin'. Sure let the Old Man be. Thought he was one of the Little People 'cause Riles said what he said."

"I didn't know that," Peter remarked.

"Yeah, Black Wolf told me that. Johnny Bad Crow, he told

260

me that, too. Said a lot of the people thought the Old Man was, you know, haunted. Like the Little People. Swore they was real."

"Sounds scary," Diana said.

"Them kids was scared, that's for sure."

Peter nodded. "Wonder why they believe in that stuff so much? Ain't like we ever seen anythin' like that."

"Do you remember that little girl that was cryin', Pistol? Do you remember her?"

"One of Black Wolf's kids, wasn't she? She'd be 'bout twenty, twenty-five now. 'Bout that?"

"She's a sister to Wolf." Syrus smiled. "I'm thinkin' that's who Far is keepin' company with."

"You're kiddin'. He tell you that?" Peter said.

"Course not, but why else would he have sent me back here? She had to be the reason."

"She's a looker, too." Peter said. "Pretty girl."

"That's what I'm thinkin'," Syrus said.

"Thought she'd be married by now."

"I don't know." Syrus said. "Guess not."

Diana looked at her husband. "How come you know all of these good lookin' Indian girls? I'm thinkin' about gettin' jealous."

"Raised with 'em. You ain't got nothin' to worry about, Dee. You're first on my list."

"Better be."

Diana glanced at the empty doorway vacated by Riles. She didn't see him again until long after the moon set over the Absarokas and dawn began to creep along the western rim of the Big Horn mountains, bathing the Bull Elk and the Basin Pasture in the soft light of early morning.

CHAPTER 33

In August, first light comes early to the West Pryor. It always has. When it starts, it comes in a rush. And so it did. Morning started with the smallest of sounds: naked feet touching the cold, bare wood floor, big toes, small toes. Someone softly swore; someone, most everyone, was looking for their hats in the dark. A match was struck, a lamp lit. Hats were found right where they'd been hung the night before. The odd aspect of this scene is that everyone except for the four year old and six year old heard that first small noise, of toes touching the floor. It was clear. It was loud. It was unmistakable. Within minutes all but the two children were awake, dressed or dressing, pulling their saddles and bridles out the door, and walking toward the dilapidated horse corral.

They heard the woman opening the fire door to the kitchen stove to see if any hot embers remained in the fire box. If there were any, she would start a fire. If there weren't, she would still start a fire; only, it would take longer. One way or the other, she was starting a fire. Eggs needed to be fried. Potatoes needed to be browned, coffee needed percolating. Cakes needed to be plated in stacks, ready to be eaten. Men needed to eat as soon as their horses were caught, grained, and saddled, their cinches tightened, not once, but twice.

The youngsters were not awake when Diana began peeling bark, collecting kindling, building a flame, cracking eggs, mixing flapjack batter. She prepared to dress them. She found their shoes, socks, their long pants, their hats, then woke them, handed them a stack of clothing. She sat them upright in kitchen chairs with a glass of cold spring water within reach. Instead of taking a swallow they laid their heads on the table surface, closed their eyes, and wondered what was happening. Why were they awake in the middle of the night? Why were the grownups hustling about? It was dark outside and the cool damp was cold on their skin and they didn't want to eat. None of it sounded good.

His Uncle Riles ruffled Josh's hair as he raised his head from the table. "Wake up, kid," he said. "Get somethin' in your belly. Noon is a hell of a long time from now."

The boy groaned. "Oh," he said, returning his head to the table where it was ruffled three more times by passersby. Katie Sue sat wordlessly next to him, eating pancakes, buttered, drowned in currant syrup. The boy looked at her and wondered how she could do that. *Eatin'. Early in the mornin'? Was it even possible?* Someone ruffled his hair again, laughing as they passed the kitchen table.

Diana glanced at Riles. "Every time I start thinkin' 'bout this Linderman fellow, the worse it gets."

"Amen," Riles agreed. "All of us need to be lookin' and watchin' all of the time. We don't know who, but whoever they are, they're lookin' for us and, especially, you two. That dead fellow did say he wasn't paid to shoot Josh or Katie Sue. If that makes eatin' eat your pancakes any easier."

"Oh boy, oh man," Diana exclaimed. "I'm sure glad he's dead! Well, that's a relief! For a moment, I thought you was tellin' another tale about them Little People."

"Little People?"

"Yeah, last night Petey was tellin' me 'bout the Little People livin' on the mountain. Stealin' kids and stuff."

"Oh, those Little People. That fellow, he ain't one of 'em. He's still up there and he's dead. He ain't takin' nobody's kids." He paused, smiled. "You know, Diana, some folks believe in them Little People. I swear. If they happen to be passin' through the Gap, they sometimes leave 'em a little somethin' as a gift. True story. Seen it, myself. Supposed to be mean little bastards."

Syrus nodded in agreement. "Well," he said, "I think Riles shot this one dead. No one here believes in Little People. Ain't never seen one."

He glanced at Riles and, changing the subject, said, "Suppose you're thinkin' about headin' west off the mountain, out on the Reservation and through the canyon country?"

"Unless you got a better idea?"

"I don't. You lead out."

"All right," Riles said. "You spell me from time to time and where you know the country better than I do."

Syrus nodded. "All right," he agreed. "We'll switch as

263

needed." Turning, he spoke with Diana. "Ma'am," he said, "Pistol picked out that little buttermilk horse for you. I threw your saddle on him. You'll wanna tighten the cinch a jag before you step up there. You'll be sittin' on the ground, you don't."

Diana nodded. She said, "Katie Sue will ride behind me. Josh with his father. That will be easiest and best."

"Good. In a few minutes, I'll bring Buttermilk up to the door. If I were you I'd ride him around a bit. Work the kinks out. Soon as you're finished, I'll hand the child to you."

"Thank you."

"You bet."

"You eaten yet?"

"Almost. I'm 'bout ready to sit down. So you'll know, Buttermilk has been grained. She's standin' in her bridle. I checked her shoes. She's got 'em and she's good to go."

"Good. Thanks again."

"I'll take care of these dishes. Soon as we're done and you're ready, we're gone. You got the door, girl, the last spoon, the last fork."

Peter came through the open door, brushing his pants leg. "Hate those wood ticks. Makes my skin crawl. We're 'bout ready," he announced.

"How's the leg?" Diana asked him.

"It's been better. It's sore, but better. It's 'most five months."

"Almost means four months. So be careful."

"Thanks, Dee, I will."

"Petey," she said, "I have some misgivin's. How far are we plannin' on goin' today?"

"It's 'bout seventy miles," Peter answered.

"Seventy miles? That's a long ways. I'm not sure Josh and Katie Sue can do that. They're so little."

"No doubt it'll be hard. If it starts wearin' on 'em the trip will just get longer. Whatever is needed. Don't fret about it, Dee. Risin' up out of bed and ridin' seventy miles ain't impossible. We can do it. It's the same for kids and horses. Horses are flesh and bone, too. Some, deeper. Some with more stayin' power. Some have better blood lines and last longer than others. A travelin' party is only as

264

good as its weakest horse and, in some respects, horses are like people. People need a breather. So do horses. They demand it. They need a drink of water. And, like people, they demand it. Durin' the day, horses also need sufficient time to crop grass, fill their stomachs. They need to stand in the shade and simply rest. Like men, they need these things often. Horses and men can't go forever. Like the fuel reservoir on an oil lamp, they'll run dry and won't be good for anythin'. Josh is ridin' with me. Katie Sue is ridin' behind your saddle. I'll have my arm around Josh all of the time. If we need to stop, we'll stop."

"Wow. That's some speech," Diana said, smiling at Peter.

Syrus laughed. "It's not his. It's the Old Man's," Syrus said. "You're forgettin' the last part of it. The good part." Syrus lowered his voice half an octave. "I know you boys know this," he said. "Assume a horse is out to kill you. Remember horses cannot ever be trusted. Ever. Ever. Assume they are cantankerous. Assume they're ill tempered, then when they are, you won't be surprised. You'll be ready. It's when some cowkid don't expect it that the unexpected happens. It's gonna happen and that's when folks get hurt. Folks gettin' hurt is gonna happen. Gotta be careful. Maybe if we do, no one will be. Ain't likely, but maybe." Syrus stopped. "Did I forget anythin'?" he asked.

"Nah, I don't think so, Si."

"On another subject," Syrus said, "Riles and I figure it's best if you two ride together. That way we keep the kids in the middle. Close to you. Close to all of us in case somethin' happens. I'll take drag. Riles will take point. Where we can cover our trail, we will. Oh, one other thing, Diana. I know you've already thought of it, but since the girl is ridin' behind you, we better get a blanket to throw over the saddle skirt to keep it from wearin' holes in her legs." He paused. No one said anything. "Any questions?" he asked.

There were none.

Riles looked at Diana. "Let me do the one other thing, Diana." He paused. "If, I was you," he began, "I wouldn't mention those "Little People" 'round Wolf and his folks. Especially his kids. They sorta get all riled up 'bout 'em. Scares them kids pretty bad."

She nodded. "Okay," she said.

265

"We'll stop at the house. Take us about twenty minutes."

Two hours off the ridge of the west mountain they took their first rest break. Josh was asleep in Peter's arms when they dismounted. They let the horses drink and picketed them.

Diana settled herself under a cottonwood, close to the creek, with Katie Sue lying on a blanket. Syrus approached; he sat down beside her.

"Assumin' you haven't already decided, when we get to the creek, you're gonna have to decide if you're stayin' or goin', girl. We'll probably be where we're goin' by sundown. I know it ain't easy. Nothin' ever is."

"Lord, Si, would you stop callin' me girl? I'm twenty four and a mother twice over."

"What would you liked to be called?"

"Diana."

"All right, girl."

She picked up a rock and threw it at him. Missed.

"No matter what I call you, you're still gonna have to decide whether you're stayin' or goin'."

"I know. Don't you think I know? Petey's been tellin' me the same thing."

"How many times?"

"Okay, once. It seems like a hundred times and it ain't gotten any easier. Don't make it any easier."

"What's the problem?"

"I wanna go. I ought to stay. That's the problem. And they are people I don't know. You were raised among 'em. I wasn't. I'm not sayin' anything bad about 'em. Not at all. Wolf and his cousin saved Petey's life not six months ago."

Syrus smiled. "I know, I know what you're sayin'. I understand. Damn straight, girl, I understand. It's just the problem ain't a problem. Those are the best people ever. And don't let Riles hear you talkin' any differently."

"Why? What's wrong with him? Besides, they ain't his kids. They're mine. I know I should stay with 'em. So should Petey, to be truthful."

"Yeah, those kids are yours."

266

"That's right. So what's wrong with Riles that I can't talk to him like I'm talkin' to you? Don't tell me there's another story. A long one?" When he didn't say anything more, she finally said, "Well, are you gonna tell me?"

"It's sorta long. But when Riles was about, I dunno, maybe twelve or fourteen, Pops sent him to the Reservation to do some huntin' for a real old woman. She didn't have nobody. Her son was dead. Killed years before. She was old. Her husband was dead. You know, everyone was dead."

"I get it."

"No, you don't. But I'll try and explain. Anyway, like I was sayin', Riles rode over to the Reservation to hunt for this old lady 'cause the Old Man sent him. He'd never met her. Just knew where she lived. She couldn't get around much. You know...she was old. Riles couldn't find her anythin', hunted for a while. Not hard. Like a kid in the summer not wantin' to be there in the first place. Not wantin' to do what the Old Man had sent him to do. So he came back home. Pop says to him 'You get her anythin'?' He says no, he didn't. Riles gets all ready to argue with Pop, tell him he looked. But Pop gets really quiet, like Rile's done broke one of the ten commandments into a whole bunch of pieces. He says to Riles, 'The old lady is starvin' to death. She ain't got no one and she can't do it herself. She's too damn old. She has you. Just how hard can it be findin' a doe for an old, broken down lady that really needs it? Understand boy, it ain't a matter of are you, it's only a matter of when are you?' Pops really takes it to Riles. Leaves him feelin' plenty bad. So Riles goes back. He hunts until Hell won't have it. Has to go quite a ways. Clear to the Yellowstone River. Gets her a antelope and finally, a buck. He takes 'em to her. She ain't there when he gets there. And he don't know what she looks like anyways. Not quite sure what to do, he hangs both animals from a cottonwood limb. He's already gutted 'em. So he skins 'em, waitin'. To the Crow, that's sort of women's work, but Riles, he don't know no better. Does it anyway. He does it cause it needs doin' and 'cause he don't know what she'd have him do with those two carcasses. Figures he can't leave 'em there. Dogs'll carry 'em off."

Peter walked up and sat down in the grass beside them.

267

"What you two yakkin' so serious about?" he asked.

"Tellin' her 'bout Riles and the Reservation lady."

"Oh yeah."

Syrus turns to Diana. "So," Syrus continues, "he's all busy doin' this and the old lady comes home from wherever she's been. She's standin' there watchin' this white boy skin and dress these two animals, this deer, this antelope. She ain't ate in a coon's age. You can imagine how hungry she is; it's on her mind. Riles, he finishes skinnin'. He's been workin'. He's 'bout ready to catch up his horse and get the hell outta there. He turns around and there's this little old Crow lady standin' right there in front of him cryin' her eyes out. Tears runnin' down her face. She ain't doin' nothin' about her cryin'. Riles, he ain't all too sure what he's supposed to do. She shuffles up to him, a short little lady, all wrinkly, bent over, barely able to move herself around. I've seen her. Now she's all grateful, she plants her wrinkly face in his shirt and cries into his shirt pocket. Riles just stands there. She's a mess. She ain't ate. She's starvin'. This is real food to her. Food that she really needs. Not just maybe. Not just for now. It's important.

"So, end of the story: Riles takes care of her until she dies. He does that 'cause he can and 'cause she needs it. She needs somebody to give her a helpin' hand. He made sure she had fresh meat once or twice a month. He helps her out 'cause she ain't got nobody, her boy bein' dead. Riles has some real strong feelings about little old Indian ladies needin' somethin' to eat. Her tears got to him. The Old Man got to him."

Peter nodded. He said, "Riles got himself a name among those folk. Did you know that? He does."

Diana looked at him. Waited. "Well, what is it?" she said.

"Old Woman Cryin' In His Shirt. That's nice, ain't it?" Peter smiled. "I like it."

"Old Woman Cryin' In his Shirt?"

Both Syrus and Peter looked at her. Peter said, "Dee, don't tell Riles that. Okay? Don't ask him about it. He's a little sensitive. Least, he was. He might not be now. Who knows?"

"All right," she answered. "But that's a real nice story."

Syrus laughed. "I got lots of real nice stories. Your husband ever tell you that Far almost married a Crow girl. She was all sorts of pretty, too. Bet she still is."

"He didn't. Are you gonna tell me that one?"

Syrus said, "Well, I'd tell you all about it, Diana 'cept the boss man is comin'. I'm bettin' we gotta go. Borin' story."

"Boss man? Oh, you mean Riles. I'm sure he ain't in that big of a hurry. And he ain't no boss man."

Riles Stockton walked up to the cottonwood tree, leading his Buckskin. The one-eyed dog was splashing in the creek. "We better be movin'," he said. "Rode back a couple of miles to have a look. Didn't see anyone followin' us. No smoke. No dust. Maybe we've lucked out."

"Riles," Diana asked, "did you know that Far almost married a Indian girl?"

"You mean Wolf's kid sister. She's real pretty, too. That girl could keep a horse from buckin' just walkin' into the corral. Take the squeal out of a boar hog."

"Really?" Diana said.

"Willow. That's her name. Among the Willows. She was holdin' hands with Far, the way I remember it. When they was about five. Got lost together, the way I remember it."

Syrus was rubbing his chin. "Say," he said, "she's Far's concern. Thought she'd be married. Ain't she older than you, Pistol?"

"She'd be 'bout twenty-four, I think. I ain't seen her in a while." She's about Far's age, I think. So that's older.

Syrus smiled. "Good old Far and his fences. Sly, that guy. Swear, you never know what he's up to."

It was late and dark when they rode into Black Wolf's lodges on Chokecherry Creek, and early and still dark when they woke up the next morning, preparing to leave. Not much was said; everyone was busy. No one woke Josh or Katie Sue. When they did wake up, they were lying on buffalo robes in the lodge, with a fire circle in the middle of the dirt floor.

In the growing light, Forest appeared out of the shadows to speak to Diana. "Ma'am," he said, "what have you decided?"

"I haven't decided. I don't think I can leave 'em."

269

"You can't take 'em with you, Ma'am. If that helps."

"It don't help."

"Ma'am. We'll be leavin' in a few minutes. Do I saddle that buttermilk horse? I need to know."

"I...."

"Ma'am, let me introduce you to a friend of mine. She'll make you comfortable. See to your needs."

"You're assumin'...."

"Yes, Ma'am, I am."

He turned away from her, walking a few steps. In the growing light appeared a woman, about five foot nine inches tall. Diana guessed she was about twenty-five. It was hard to tell in the dark.

"Ma'am, this is Willow. Among the Willows is her Absaroka Crow name. She will show you around. Answer your questions. You need anythin', ask her. She's a wonderful person. Wolf is her brother. That's who she is."

He turned to the woman again. "This is Diana, Willow. She is Pistol's wife and my sister-in-law."

"Hello," Diana said. "Thank you for helpin' me. I appreciate it. I'm so sorry for the inconvenience I'm causin'. Really, I am. Thank you."

The woman smiled at Diana.

"I have heard about you," Diana said to her. "All good. Riles said you was very pretty. And he wasn't lyin'."

The young woman glanced at Forest. Forest translated for Diana, then for Among the Willows.

"She said, thank you," Forest said. "She understands some English. Just go slow."

"All right," Diana said. "Far, she is so very pretty. Is she the fence Si said you was busy fixin'?"

"Damn," Forest said, smiling. "Si talks too much. I sure don't know anythin' about any fences, Ma'am."

Forest turned to the woman and said something in the Crow language. The Indian girl responded by touching his hand, looking up at him, nodding. She said something to Forest that Diana also did not understand. He nodded, then turning to Diana he said, "Ma'am, we'll be back soon as we can. You'll be safe here. Keep your rifle handy all

270

of the time. There ain't no such thing as too careful, even here."

"You better hurry, Far. I have a feelin' you'll be missed a little by more than just Josh, Katie, and me."

He smiled, turned, looked at Willow then went to check on his Appaloosa.

Among The Willows said to Diana in English, "Come with me."

Diana nodded.

Then, she asked Diana, "What is a fence?"

"Oh, you understood me. That's really good. Really good." Diana smiled at her as she spoke. "Fixin' a fence is where your fellow, your man, he ain't done all he was supposed to and needs to make it up. Needs to patch up you and him, so you don't fall apart. That make sense? A fence is that part of you and him that's the same."

Willow smiled at Diana. "Make a patch up?. A good thing? He's been gone a long time. He just came home. I don't know."

"Yes," Diana replied. "I wouldn't know, either. It's mostly good. It can be. Sometimes it's a real good thing...a very good thing. Sometimes it just makes things more difficult. Sometimes the fences shouldn't be bothered at all. They should be left alone. Do you know what I mean?"

"Yes, I do," Willow said. "and so does Far. He's been gone many, many winters. Things do not stay the same. I can't expect it. He can't expect it. To do so is expecting too much."

Expectations are dangerous, if not elusive.Sometimes they lead to the unexpected. Riles sat the Buckskin, waiting. He watched Peter. He watched him saddle his horse: watched him lead it to where the others were gathering with Black Wolf, his cousin Charley Slow Dog, and with the bartender, Johnny Bad Crow. Riles watched him bend at the waist to check his horse's shoes, watched him thinking. Riles imagined Peter going down the mental check list of necessary supplies: Colt revolvers, rifle, rope, extra cartridges, bedroll, gloves. Leaning against his horse, Peter rested his sore leg, wiped the sweat from his forehead, finally sitting down on a rock, his breath coming in short gasps. He was tired, exhausted and twenty-eight years old. It occurred to Riles that Peter literally could do no more, that he'd

271

pushed himself as far as he could. Four idle months and his body muscles had atrophied due to the movement restrictions caused by a broken leg. He'd grown weak, probably for the first time in his adult life. *I'll bet he's afraid and ain't sure of what to do.*

Riles nudged the Buckskin forward until his horse towered over Peter. He stared down at him; not saying a thing. Just thinking. Peter looked up at him sitting in the middle of the Buckskin, leaning toward him. Riles' left arm rested on the saddlehorn, his bull hide chaps covering his right leg down to the toe of his boots, the silver of his right side spur.

"What?" Peter asked "I'm all right. Just need to rest a bit. Don't look at me like that."

"Like hell, you are. You ain't close to all right."

"So, what's it to you?"

"Everything. You can't go," Riles said. "Given the circumstances, you're needed here. Your leg ain't healed. You can't walk a hundred yards without passin' out. I just watched you. You're stayin' here. That's all there is to it."

"Like hell, that's all there is to it. You can't tell me. You ain't that person no more. The Old Man's dead."

"I just did."

Forest, seeing Riles speaking to Peter, rode his Appaloosa to where they were talking. He looked down at Peter, saw his face in an angry, fit to be tied, grimace

"What's goin' on?" he asked.

"Riles thinks he can tell me what to do. He thinks I can't go."

"That right?" Forest asked. He glanced at Riles, his expression stoic, then back at Peter.

Peter continued."I belong with the three of you. I belong, I tell you. It's where I should be. This ain't even up for question. I belong. I'm one of you."

Forest looked at his younger brother, then glanced at Riles. "You're right," he said. "You do belong. You are one of us. It is where you should be. Everyone here knows it. No one here is debatin' it. But Riles is right. You shouldn't be takin' this trip. You should be stayin'. Takin' care of you with a broken leg and everything else is too much to do."

272

"Like hell, it is. He doesn't have to take care of me."

"Yes, he does."

Syrus, sitting on the back of the strawberry roan stud, had ridden up on Peter's right. Peter hadn't moved from the rock where he was sitting. Syrus pulled his hat off his head, ran his fingers through his hair, and reseated his hat. He blew his nose, wiping it with his gloved hand as if it were itching. He glanced at Peter, then Forest. "What are you people talkin' 'bout so seriously?" he asked.

"Riles is tryin' to tell me I can't go, and that's wrong. I belong with the three of you. Those are my cows…or they used to be and will be again if we get 'em back."

Syrus glanced at Riles. "Lord, Riles, you tell Pistol that?" Before Riles could respond, Syrus looked back at Peter. "That what's got you all worked up?"

Before Peter could respond, Syrus looked back at Riles. "What kept you, big brother? Why did you take so long? I thought you'd lost your grip on the ax handle and didn't know how to lower the boom."

He saw the surprised look form on Peter's face. "You're right, Pistol. Is this what Far told you? That's all good and fine. He's right, too. You do belong with us, but in case you ain't noticed, you got a broken leg and ain't even half healed. You can't walk across the yard without taking three breaks and fallin' on your face, all to spite your nose. Hell's fire, Riles, what took you so long? You can't go, Pistol. Riles is right. It's as simple as that. We'll see you when we get back. Stay here and make yourself useful."

"What?" Peter exclaimed.

Forest glanced at Riles. "What took you so long to tell Pistol, Riles? No wonder he's all disappointed. If the Old Man was here, you'd have to leave home again. You'd never hear the end of it."

Riles shook his head in disbelief and turned his horse around, riding away from his three brothers.

Syrus looked at Peter. "That's it, little brother. The word from on high. You need help gettin' back to the camp fire?"

"No, I don't," Peter said angrily.

"Good. I didn't wanna get down from the back of this horse, myself to give you a hand. While we're gone, take care of Far's

273

girlfriend, would you? He don't seem to be able to do that."

Forest looked at Syrus, turning his horse to follow Riles to the top of the hill. "Si, give it a break, would you?" He didn't wait for a response, nudging the Appaloosa forward, shaking his head.

"What?" Syrus asked innocently. "I say something?" He glanced at Peter. "Sorry, Pistol," he said. "Not this time. Normally, you'd be right there with us. You need to get better. And don't push it. We'll take care of this problem. You watch out for trouble. You may think you're out of it, but it's just a rock throw from the top of the ridge. Stay focused. No empty chambers. Hear me? We'll be back." Syrus turned the roan about. "Hopefully," he added, and followed Forest to where the pack horses were being loaded.

CHAPTER 34

The motley group forded the Big Horn River two miles downstream from where it exited the canyon. It was August. It was hot. It was dry. It was normal. The river was not only the warmest it would be all year, but at the lowest depth. Low did not mean the river was shallow. It was deep enough that the horses had to swim most of the crossing. It ran clear, the sun's rays reflecting brilliantly off the rippling surface. The riders could see the rocky bottom as they slipped out of their saddles, grabbed their horse's tails, and allowed themselves to be towed to the other side. Once there, they stopped, removed their boots, poured the water out, and wrung their socks dry; dry meaning damp. They remounted. It was noon before their clothing drip-dried enough to be comfortable, and their boots stopped squeaking when they walked. Walking didn't happen often. Still, every once in a while,they dismounted for a stretch, giving their horses a needed rest.

They rode north and east, toward the confluence of the Yellowstone River and Tongue River. The country was broken up, a maze of twisting ravines and canyons, their bottoms lined with cottonwoods watered by springs, melting snow, and spring rains that fell until midsummer. It was midsummer. The ride was one hundred miles, more or less. The "more or less" adjusted by their being forced to go up, down, around and through the breaks, draws, ravines, and small canyons. The farther they were from the mountains, the flatter the land became until they reached the twisting, turning Yellowstone River, then the Tongue.

There wasn't much conversation among the riders for several reasons. They rode into a vacuum of knowledge. No one knew who they'd run across or what their temperament might be. A mistake could lead to being shot or killed.

Stealing another man's cows is a hanging offense. In 1886 guilt required no judge, no jury. It was an assumption which reduced the matter to a shooting affair; on one hand, there were riders who did not want to be hanged for their crime and would rather shoot it out than have a discussion. On the other hand, cows were their livelihood; without them, kids didn't go to school, folks didn't get a new pair of shoes, kids didn't have new pants to wear. They didn't have cartridges for their rifles, a handle for their pitchfork. Folks starved. Dying's never a good idea. Taking cows was like stealing a man's horse, leaving him afoot. In the desert, he was surely going to die. In the mountain country, he was surely going to die. If a bear or lion didn't get him, an Indian would. It took years and years to build up a viable herd. For the thief, it was a quick dollar. For the rancher, it was the destruction of difficult, unending work. The rule, whether written or not, was the rope for a cattle thief; same for a horse thief. Stealing cows or horses was taken seriously. It was a life or death proposition. The question was whose?

Everyone was busy watching, hoping to stay alive. They looked for something out of place, something out of the ordinary: a startled animal running, smoke rising, a noise or the lack thereof. Birds suddenly quiet, a horse's' track where there should not be one, a rifle shot, dust rising. It was a party of six riders: two rode the flanks a half mile out, one rode out front; the remainder watched and listened. Every hour, or close thereto, the riders switched.

The country changed slowly. Sage grew less dominant, grass more so; sporadic bunches of pine, juniper, aspen, cottonwood, and cedar littered the hills. Aspen generally grew at higher elevations. Cottonwood generally followed streams, choked springs, and waterways. There was plenty of elk, deer, and buffalo sign. Songs of snowbirds, killdeer, magpies, camp robbers, and meadowlarks broke the silence. Once in a while, they'd see a fools hen sprinting through the undergrowth only to stop, cock its head, and watch the watchers.

On the third day, they came across the first MT branded cow. There was more. Their calves, however, wore a double X brand on the left hip. The double X brand, whenever it showed up, was new.

It had taken three days to ride from what remained of Fort Smith to the confluence of the Tongue and the Yellowstone Rivers. Arriving midafternoon, they stopped, dismounted, letting their horses drink from the waters of the Tongue. Afterwards, they gave each a bait of oats and rested them, allowing them to stand, swishing their tails in the shade of the cottonwoods that choked the river bottom.

276

"We've seen no one," Forest commented. "Not a single livin' soul. I'd expected someone to be watchin' the breadbox. But, no. There ain't one fresh horse track to be found. It's been days, if not weeks, since anyone has been here."

Charley Slow Dog grunted, nodding in agreement. "You're right," he replied. "Not only have we not seen anyone but they ain't been here recent. Not a track: somethin' that says, 'I'm here. I'm watchin'. Come a step closer and I'll kill you.' Somethin' friendly like that."

"It's odd," Riles said. "Looks to me like whoever gathered and drove the MT cows did it like someone was chasin' 'em. They brought 'em to the Tongue and just let 'em go. I'm wonderin' if the cows we've seen is all of 'em? I didn't get a good count. How many do you think we've rode through, last fifteen, twenty miles."

Syrus threw his right leg over the shoulder of his saddle and slid to the ground. Taking the reins in hand, he said, "I don't know. I didn't get a good count, myself. Makes me a little angry, the MT spring calves have the double X brand on the left hip. The bull calves have been castrated and branded. The castrated part is good. We don't have to do it. The cows' brands, on the other hand, for the most part, ain't been touched. Why? Do you reckon they was short-handed? Why didn't they finish the job? Maybe they didn't wanna get caught runnin' the brand."

Forest studied the toe of his boot, then looked at the river current drifting by, the swirling, gurgling water. He said, "I've seen some double X cows here and there. Not many. Mostly MT. It'll take some time to cut the double X cattle out, but we better do it. When we move 'em I don't think we should be drivin' anythin' wearin' a double X brand unless it's ours and we can prove it. It smells. Somethin' we don't want any part of."

"It just smells," Charley Slow Dog said.

"Yeah," agreed Forest.

"Where's Johnny Bad Crow?" Black Wolf asked.

"He was here a minute ago," Forest said, looking around.

"Over there," Syrus said, pointing with his right hand.

They all turned to see Johnny Bad Crow walking out of the brush leading his horse.

277

"Old campfire over there a hundred yards," Johnny said. "Pretty big one. A lot of ashes. Looks like a lot of wood burned in it. Used large river rock for a ring."

"I wanna see this," Riles said. "Beyond those trees, you say?"

Johnny Bad Crow nodded.

With his bay horse in tow, Johnny Bad Crow walked back into the brush. "This way," he said. Riles followed.

Just as Johnny Bad Crow described, it was a big fire ring. Whoever had constructed it had used large river rocks. The ground around it was well-used, packed hard. It had been a while; weeds had started growing up through the hard pack.

"What do you think, Johnny?" Riles asked.

"Nothin' to think. Nobody's here. They ain't been here for a while."

Everyone dismounted. Forest pulled the saddle off his horse and laid it on the ground. Everyone except Riles and Syrus followed suit.

Syrus patted roan on the rump. "What do you think, big brother? We're here. What do we do?"

"The first thing that comes to mind, Si, is rest up. Get somethin' in our bellies, drink a hot cup. I'd like to figure these rustlers. But there's not enough information. Makes me nervous not knowin' where they are. Who they are. What they're thinkin'. The fact is we ain't caught no body in the act. Being in the same County as a stolen cow doesn't make you a theif. Without kowing, we're half-cockedand I'm nervous. They ain't show'd their hand."

"You're nervous? We all are," Black Wolf agreed. "Makes the hair stand up on the back of my neck."

"Why don't we build a big fire in that pit?" Syrus suggested. "At night a man could see it for a hundred miles. They might not see it now, but if they're lookin', when it grows dark, they will. Especially, if they're anywheres close. If they're the people we're lookin' for and they see a little fire light, maybe some smoke, they'll come to see what's goin' on."

"It's possible, "Johnny Bad Crow agreed. "And they might not. Especially if they have no interest. If they don't, we should start gatherin' cows soon as we can. I think tomorrow mornin' first light,

278

we start. That's why we came here. That's what we ought to do."

"And if they come tonight?" Riles asked. "If they do?"

Charley Slow Dog responded. "We be ready. I'm guessin', but if they come, there's gonna be ten or fifteen of 'em. When they rustled them cows that's how many there were. If they are the ones, we'll be out numbered from the get go. So, we better shoot to kill and often. They're gonna do the same to us. The problem is proof. Did they rustle these cows in the first place or was it someone else?"

Syrus said, "We have no proof they stole our cows until they give it to us. Right? Anything else?" Syrus asked, looking at Riles. "Besides that, I mean?"

It was Black Wolf who answered. "Yes," he said, "There is somethin' else. I'm thinkin' we ought to make a trap for those boys. Trick 'em in to showin' us their hand. I'm thinking they are who we're lookin' for. No one else is here. So a trap."

"A trap? What sorta trap?"

"It's just a thought. But I think we should be layin' a trap for those folks layin' a trap for us. I ain't seen 'em and we don't know. So we ask 'em. That's what I'm thinkin'."

Charley Slow Dog rubbed his hairless chin. "Well," he said, "Someone don't rustle eight hundred cows and as many yearlings, last year's comin' two year olds, without goin' to the trouble of keepin' a eye on 'em. They're here. We can depend on that. We should plan for it. They'll show up. Someone will. They'll be ready so we better be ready."

"Sounds reasonable," Syrus said, laughing. "Damn, Charley, where'd you get all of these ideas? Plan on it, you say. Catch 'em up and hang 'em? What you got in mind, my friend? I am gonna owe you a drink, you doin' all this thinkin'. Keep doin' this and you're lible to pass out from the mental strainl"

"Everybody hear that?" Charley Slow Dog said. "Si's gonna buy me a drink. He's payin'. You all hear that? You're my witness."

"Okay, okay," Riles said. "I'm thinkin' that we build a fire in their old fire ring that Johnny found, and like Si said. There must be some good reason for those boys to pick that spot. It's been used a lot. Startin' a long time ago. What do you think, Johnny, within the last month? Six weeks? How many times? How long ago?"

"Sooner," Johnny Bad Crow said. "Judgin' from the deer bones, the growth of weeds in the hardpack, three weeks, outside. Last time someone was here."

"Good," Riles said. "We build a fire in the ring. Light this place up just before the sun goes down. That way it'll be castin' light come dark. If they see that fire I think they'll come runnin' to see what the hell's goin' on. If they are the rustlers, they'll come in wired tight, rakin' their horses, ready to dance, ready to show us who they are and who we ain't. They won't want anyone foolin' around with those stolen cows. It'll make 'em nervous. When they get here, I'll ride in and ask 'em. Have a word or two. See what their intentions are. I'd say they'll tell me. I won't scare them none. If they're goin' south on is, I'll start shootin'. You boys join in. They'll expect it but they won't. If they're Linderman's men they'll jumpright in. Once it starts, get as many as you can. That's where we start."

Riles looked at his companions. "When you're up against a superior force, you gotta use your head. It's the only way you can succeed. Any thoughts?"

"Depends on what they do," Black Wolf said. "How many there are. If we shoot 'em up, we could build another fire a ways off. They come. It'll spread 'em out, confuse 'em. Maybe they have someone smart tellin' 'em what to do. Sounds like as much fun as a buffalo hunt without buffalo."

Johnny Bad Crow built himself a cigarette, rolled the makings, wet it with his lips and tongue. He looked up to find everyone watching him.

"Need some help?" Forest suggested.

"No. I got this one." Johnny lit a match, touched it to the end of the cigarette, sucked on it, blew white smoke into the air. "But be careful," he said. "Let's not outsmart ourselves. They'll know it's a trick the second the second fire is lit. It's just make-work."

"He's right," Syrus said. "I agree with Johnny. A second fire ain't smart. I say no to two fires."

Syrus pulled a Mississippi Crook out of his shirt pocket, stuck it between his lips, felt the taste of rum and tobacco on his tongue, the flavor leaking into his mouth, spreading. Forest struck a match, offering the flame to Syrus, who took it. Syrus sucked in, pulling the smoke into his lungs. He blew it out into the evening air. Johnny was staring at him. Syrus handed him the Crook. "You'll like this better, Johnny. Try it. Tastes like candy."

Johnny Bad Crow took the cigar, stuck it between his teeth, and drew in. He smiled when the rum started spreading on his tongue. "Tastes like candy," he said. "I ain't never."

"Thought you'd like it," Syrus commented, glancing at Black Wolf. "We'll have to play it by ear, Wolf," he said. "See if they'll take the first bait. Last time I hunted buff," he paused, "it was with you. Gotta be like twenty years ago. Maybe not that long. Seems long."

Black Wolf nodded. "Yes. With our fathers. You, Si, and Far were still here; they were with us. I'm not sure about Riles."

"Yeah, Wolf, over on the Bull Elk."

"Long time ago when there were buffalo."

Johnny offered Syrus the cigar back. Syrus shook his head no, remembering. "Riles was here. That was when he damn near drowned runnin' from an ol' momma bear."

Riles nodded. "And here we are," he said. "Damn near drownin' again."

Forest laughed. "You two are gonna have us all cryin'. I do remember the Old Man gettin' a burr under his saddle, givin' Riles hell for leavin' Pistol on the bank while we went swimmin'. He said when one of you swim, all of you swim. What the hell's wrong with you? Ain't you got a lick of sense?'"

"I do remember that mother bear scared the hell out of me. I 'bout walked on water tryin' to get away from her."

"Scared everyone. She was pretty hot."

"Wolf climbed outta the river to get a rifle. He was gonna be our savior. The damn thing misfired. I thought you had the hammer on an empty, but it was a dud. The bear chased lucky boy into the water. Everyone was yellin'. Next time your rifle popped right off. Missed her but it scared the hell out of that momma bear. And we all got the lecture on the value of an empty chamber. Riles got the lecture for leavin' Pistol on the bank. Lucky him. He got both lectures."

"Pistol was right out in the middle of the river bobbin' up and down, scared of water, blowin' bubbles each time he went under."

"He was short. His feet didn't even touch the bottom."

"I wanna go huntin' again," Black Wolf said. "Over on the Bull Elk."

"Let's do it. Next month, end of the month," Forest said. "It'll be September. We're supposed to hunt end of September. It's our right. It's why they made the mountain. So's we can hunt."

"If we live that long," Charley Slow Dog said.

"No two fires, then?" Forest asked.

"No two fires," Black Wolf said. "Everyone agreed? Unless someone's got a better idea?"

No one said anything.

"Well," Riles said, "one fire, then. If they come and if they start the fight, we shoot like hell for five minutes. Then ride like hell to that knoll 'bout a mile south of here.

"All right, let's do this," Riles said. "Come dark, I'll be waitin' for 'em right here. We'll see if this fire gets some attention. If they're around, they may show. The dog will know. The mule, on the other hand, will let his curiosity get the better of him. I'm dependin' on him introducin' himself. If there's more than a couple, he'll be lookin' for an apple, some sugar cubes. If they're here, he'll flush 'em out. Can't stay hidden with a mule lookin' right at you. Maybe one of 'em will try to ride him. That ought to be interesting."

"How's that?"

"Cecil ain't never been rid. He don't take to it. All we gotta do is throw a saddle on him, let him walk around mindin' his business. They'll be safe as long as no one gets on him. Someone gets on him, he'll go plum loco, crazy. In the ruckus, try and put as many of those boys afoot as we can. Slow 'em down. If Cecil gets goin', the dog will be raisin' hell. He's a joiner. Don't know any better.

"What I'll do is ride down there 'bout then to see what's what. Now, everybody, if someone starts shootin', cut the dog loose. But let me talk to 'em first. All right?"

"All right," Black Wolf said. "You sure that's the thing to do?"

"No, I ain't but it's somethin. I'll ride to the fire ring when Cecil starts lookin' for a sugar cube."

Black Wolf nodded. "All right, the mule is the key," he said.

282

Everyone turned to him. "We wait for Cecil to make friends."

In the coolness of the river bottom evening, Riles sat his Buckskin, watching the mule standing just outside the yellow light cast by the burning fire. It was a good seventy-five yards to the fire from where Riles watched. Night birds were flitting about in the darkening sky snatching insects from the damp, muggy air. Riles waited, the leather latch no longer hooked around the hammer, the empty chamber no longer empty on either Colt. Beside him, resting on his haunches and to the Buckskin's left, was the one-eyed, long haired dog. The dog, too, was watching the mule standing just inside the light of the slow burning fire. Riles was a shadow hidden in the tall cottonwoods, difficult to see unless someone was actually looking for him. No one was.

Riles was aware of where Syrus was sitting his red roan horse. Neither spoke. The others he could not see, although they were about and he knew it. No one slept. No one rested their travel weary bones for they, too, were watching the mule, his tail knocking mosquitoes off his rump, once in a while lazily shifting his weight from one hoof to another. The mule was as tired as anyone and the mule had habits. In the evening he was attracted to the calm, mesmorizing flicker of firelight. Because of this habit, Riles could depend on where he'd be come night fall. He did not doubt Syrus: he'd be ready. He'd be dependable. Syrus was involved from the first breath and never haphazardly. Syrus had his back. Riles took comfort in that. Suddenly, the mule's head went up, his long ears pointing across the fire circle at the growth of cottonwoods on the other side.

They're here. Riles thought. *They'll be comin' into the light.* The mule took a step forward, turning his head back toward Riles, scratching his shoulder. The dog whined.

"Quiet, Dog," he said.

There was movement back in the trees beyond the fire. Riles thought he could see a horse and rider in the shifting shadows. The dog whined again.

"Quiet, Dog," Riles said again.

The dog licked his chops, his tongue lolling outside his mouth. He looked up at Riles then laid down.

"That's it. Be patient, Dog," he said.

Cecil, head up, started walking around the fire circle, looking steadfastly into the darkness. He disappeared into the shadows beyond the fire.

Riles listened.

Someone swore. "What the hell is this?" the voice said.

"A mule. That's what it is."

"He's got a saddle. No bridle. Belongs to somebody."

"What's he doin' here?"

"That's what we're here to find out."

"I don't like it."

"No one's askin' you to like it."

"A trap?"

"Could be. The question is, is it? There ain't nobody here that I can see."

"Why you so worried about it?"

"I ain't."

"Why'd somebody build a fire and leave? And saddle a mule and let him go? But without a bridle. Damn thing musta slipped his bit or lost his hackamore. Got himself loose somehow. What do you wanna do? I don't see nobody."

"I wanna wait and see. Whoever it is they're here. Must be close. They wouldn't just leave a saddled mule. We wait."

"I don't like it."

"You said that already. I know you ain't happy. I know you don't like it. Will you please shut up? I'm tryin' to look and listen. I'm tryin' to hear. I can't do that with you talkin' constantly."

A silence followed. Riles heard someone yelling.

The voice said, "Hello the camp. May we come in?"

Riles did not answer.

"Hello the camp," the voice said again.

Again, Riles refrained from responding.

"What's goin' on?"

It was a different voice, a third voice that posed the last question.

"Don't know."

"Other than that mule, there don't appear to be anybody. At

284

least, they ain't answerin'."

"Think it's a trap?"

"Don't know. Could be."

"Roilson?"

"What?"

"Throw a rope on that mule. Lead him out into the firelight. If you can stop talkin', do it sometime today."

There was no response.

"Roilson?"

"What?"

"Did you hear me?"

"I heard you. Hold your horses, Boss. Gotta get my rope before I can throw it."

There was no response. A minute later a man walked out into the firelight, leading Cecil.

"What do you see?" A voice asked.

"I don't see nothin'."

"Nothin'?"

"I see a fire and a mule. That's what I see."

"Get a civil tongue, Roilson."

"I got a civil tongue. What I ain't got is patience with a boss that sends me out here in the open to get myself kilt. Get your ass out here, you yellow bastard. Show me somethin'."

A heavy silence followed those last words like night follows day.

"Roilson?"

"What?"

"I don't wanna see your face when we get back. Hear me?"

"I hear you. Have my wages ready. I ain't got no use for you, myself. Now get out here. I wanna see what you're made of. Cluck, cluck, cluck," the rider said, sounding like a chicken.

The voice from the dark sounded. "You son of a bitch."

"But I ain't a coward. Cluck, cluck, cluck."

A rider showed himself and his horse, riding out into the firelight.

"Didn't think you had it in you."

"I have half a mind to get down from here and beat the hell

285

outta you."

"Go ahead, you think you can."

Time to move. Riles nudged the Buckskin forward. He could feel Syrus moving on his right. Riles walked the Buckskin into the firelight.

"What are you boys doin' with my mule?" Riles asked. "Hope I'm not interruptin' anythin' important." Riles sat his horse, holding the reins tight. The dog was a little in front of him.

The two men's attention was immediately redirected to Riles and the large one-eyed dog in front of him. Roilson spoke first, seemingly not at all bothered, not startled by Riles' sudden appearance.

"Nothin'," Roilson answered. "Found him. Seein' he had no bridle, I caught him up before he got away again. And yes, you interrupted me fixin' to beat the hell outta this two bit, good for nothin' excuse for a man pretendin' to be a boss."

The man on the horse stared at Riles Stockton. "What are you doin' here?" he asked.

"Keepin' you from stealin' my mule," Riles said.

"I ain't stealin' your mule," Roilson assured him. "He's got my rope on him. I just caught him up, seein' he was loose and saddled. You got a rope you'd rather use, give it to me, or if you rather not I'll just turn him loose. Your choice. He sure as hell ain't mine."

"Shut up, Roilson. He ain't said why he's here."

Riles answered Roilson. "Just turn him loose. He ain't broke to lead."

"I'll be damned. Ain't broke to lead and you got him wearin' a saddle. Bet that's some story."

"Roilson, you turn him loose and you can draw your pay."

"You already fired me, nitwit. Twice won't make me any happier. I ain't workin' for you." Roilson loosened the lead rope, turned the mule loose and started recoiling his rope. He stared defiantly at the Boss. "I catch him up. I turn him loose," he said. "You cowardly, worthless piece of shit."

Riles smiled. "I'd say you two ain't gettin along."

"You got that right," Roilson said. "What you doin' out here in the woods, anyways? Hell of a long ways from a good bed and three squares."

"Huntin' my cows," Riles said, his eyes resting on the man in charge.

"Cows? You got cows out here?"

"I do. Anythin' and everythin' wearin' the MT brand on the left hip belongs to me. 'Bout a thousand head of stock cows."

"You don't say."

"No. I do say. You know anythin' 'bout how they got here?"

Roilson answered him. "Can't say that I do. There's quite a few, though."

"I hope so. Been missin' 'em."

"Shut up, Roilson."

"Bossman, you fired my ass. That means I ain't gotta listen to your bullshit at all. To tell the truth, I'd rather hear less of you."

To Riles, Roilson said, "I can't tell you how they got here. I've been here two weeks. They were here before me. That's 'bout all I know."

"That's plenty." Riles stared at the horseman who appeared to be in charge, realizing as he did that Forest had shown up on his left, on foot with two pistols, one in either hand pointed at the ground. He didn't know about Syrus, although he suspected he was sitting his horse on Rile's right, his Winchester rifle butt resting on his right thigh. "You plannin' on stoppin' me from gatherin' my cows?"

"Damn right, I am. They ain't yours."

"Then you'll understand me callin' you a rustler and announcing my intention of stretchin' your neck from yonder cottonwood."

"Like hell, you will. Fitzgerald," the Boss yelled, "put a rifle on this man. Hear me?"

"I got a rifle on him, Boss. What do you want us to do? You want me to kill him?"

Riles heard Syrus' drawl. "Better not, Bossman. You so much as twitch, I'm gonna drill you clean through." Syrus was loving it, which was bad. Riles could hear it in his voice.

Four more riders appeared in the fire light, all horseback. A

287

fifth was back in the trees riding a light colored horse.

"Boss," a voice said. "Boss, on your left. Two, maybe three, Injuns. Maybe a hundred and three. I can't see 'em clearly. Surrounded. We're surrounded. Shit."

Riles smiled: Odd how, in the dark, three Indians can appear to be one hundred three. The imagination is a great multiplier.

The Boss hesitated. He said,"Fitzgerald. Fitzgerald,you hear me?"

"Yeah, I hear you."

"He moves, the one in front of me, I want you to shoot him dead. And you, Roilson, get out of my sight. I'll take care of you later. You worthless son of a bitch. I'll kill you first chance I get."

Perhaps it was being called a son of a bitch, or perhaps it was being called worthless--whatever it was, "I'll kill you," set him off. Roilson went for his gun. A nanosecond later, it was pointed at the Boss, the hammer pulled back and the trigger squeezed tightly, the recoil instanteous.

At the same time, Riles came off his horse, a Colt in either hand as he walked forward. He pointed at the Boss, yelled, "Dog!"
All hell broke loose. The night lit up with a cacophony of explosions, sustained for a good fifteen seconds before there was a momentary break.

The dog went for the Boss in one leap. Roilson shot at him missing both the dog and his "used to be" Boss. The Boss was dragged from the right side of his saddle, a one hundred twenty-five pound dog latched onto his shoulder. Whether Roilson shot and hit the Bossman or not, was the source of debate. The Buckskin backed away, its reins dragging the ground. It was dark. What actually happened was hard to see.

The man, Fitzgerald, either fired his rifle and missed or didn't fire his rifle and was shot for his trouble. Riles didn't see him. Syrus did and Fitzgerald caught a 45 slug in the chest. No one knew whose pistol delivered the death blow or who shot who. There was shooting from all sides, all at once, and then it was quiet.

There was a noise from back in the trees. Syrus shot at it.

"What was that?" Forest asked.

"I don't know," Syrus answered. "It's dead."

288

Syrus heard Black Wolf laugh from somewhere on the other side of Forest.

"Good to know," Riles said. "Good to know."

There are countless stories told by soldiers, by men involved in combat, fighting for their very lives, for the lives of their fellows. Those stories, the good ones, the true ones always start out with "No shit, there I was...." In Auburn, California, Syrus had been sitting at the back of a narrow bar with an oak floor and no windows. The bar sat off E Street. He overheard two men talking. They'd both served in the Confederate Army in the late war. One said to the other, "We, me and my buddy, were sent out as a forward outpost to listen and to report to the Cap if the Yanks came upon us. Cap wanted to know where the Yanks were. We hid ourselves in this clump of brush, diggin' ourselves a little hole to hide in. My buddy went to sleep. Somewhere in the middle of the night this Yank horse patrol came upon us. Fifty or sixty of them.

"Thank God, we were hidden in thick brush. But they were all around us. Everywhere. We weren't gettin' out of this one. We were good as dead. I woke my buddy up, my hand over his mouth to keep him from yellin'. We spent the night with Yanks and their horses all 'round us, them boilin' coffee, eatin' hog meat, writin' letters to their wives and girlfriends. I swear they were so close I could hit 'em with the end of a short stick. Early in the morning they moved on. Thank God. Left without discoverin' we were lyin' there in the brush barely breathin' right in the middle of 'em. Sometime after they'd left, both sides opened up, droppin' five, ten pound balls on top of us. Somebody sure as hell was lookin' out for us, I swear. The two of us made it clear 'til Lee met Grant at Appomattox and it was over. No shit," he said. "True story. There we were. No shit."

At the confluence of the Yellowstone and the Tongue Rivers, in the shadows of cottonwood trees that ah shit moment was upon them. The firing was intense. How many men there were, no one knew. According to Johnny Bad Crow, it was eleven but no one saw all of them. Some got away by jumping their horses into the Tongue River and swimming to the other side. Some didn't get away

289

and if it did it wasn't far. The Boss didn't, nor did Roilson or Fitzgerald, nor did a fellow wearing a dark blue shirt with two rows of black buttons. In the morning those men received a river funeral, their bodies floating away on the slow moving current. Forest, out of respect for the dead would have buried them, but no one brought a shovel and the ground was hard.

Starting early, after a breakfast of coffee and beans, they started to gather MT cattle. They began on the foothills of the Big Horn Mountains to the south, to the Yellowstone River on the north, from the Tongue River on the east. As a precaution, Riles hung back, moving from rise to rise with a pair of glasses and a rifle, looking back, watching, insuring that the roundup would not be interfered with, ready to sound an alarm should the need arise.

Round-up is an activity that commences on the outside and works toward the middle. Cattle are gathered by pushing them toward that middle: one, two, three, and ten at a time. At first, some will try to break back, but soon the few are many, and the herd instinct begins to prevail, and they, as a herd, will move in the direction of no resistance. Eventually, they'll line out, in a long bending line, moving steadily forward. Invariably, one cow or two will take the lead; her calf, if she has one, will follow her. Another will join that one; ten will become fifteen, fifteen, thirty, thirty, one hundred thirty. The trick facing the drover is to keep that one cow in the lead going in the direction desired. Hence, the need for at least one rider to ride point, to keep that singular cow pointed in the desired direction.

From point to drag, it is hard, unending, dusty, dirty work that wears out drovers and their horses. Resting, watering, feeding, eating has to be planned and executed. It has to happen. Otherwise, the drive will stall, the herd disburse, and the cattle will inevitably return to where they were when the operation began.

Five days later, the Stockton Crew put nearly one thousand head of mother cows into the Big Horn River, three miles north of the Horn coming out of the canyon. With those cows was a mixture of yearling calves, two year olds, and nearly fifty range bulls. The old moss-back cow who insisted on being in the lead, was directed toward the summer pastures under the northern shadows of the Pryor Mountain. Two days later they were turned on familiar grass, where they'd spent their lives. The Linderman riders did not appear to follow them and if they did, they did not make their presence known or felt.

CHAPTER 35

Finished, relieved, and yet, angry, the Stocktons met on Chokecherry Creek with Black Wolf, Charley Slow Dog, and Johnny Bad Crow. The purpose was to get their bearings. The creek was Black Wolf's winter home, as it had been the winter home for his mother and father. Peter, Diana, Joshua, and Katheryn Suzanne had stayed there, waiting for the return of the men from their trip to the confluence of the rivers. It was mid-August and the dog days of summer had turned the grass brown, brought the locust out of the ground. From here Johnny Bad Crow returned to the Bad Trail Bar. Charley Slow Dog returned to Arrow Creek where his father, Two Bears, lived with his mother. Two Bears had lived for fifty-six winters.

Riles and Forest were walking together, talking, making their way to the place their father came annually with the steers and old cows he delivered to Black Wolf's father. It was early morning; the sun was barely up. What remained to be done was still in front of them. It wasn't going to be easy. Neither wanted to wait. Neither wanted to "rest up." Nothing good was accomplished by waiting. The task was taking the fight to those who had brought it to them.

In the course of their walk, Riles told Forest that he meant to speak with him but had been busy.

"That don't sound good, Riles. You wantin' to talk to me. Sounds like the Old Man. You ain't got Pistol squared away, so don't start on me. We got a lot of work to do. We need to brand the mavericks, get the sheriff to come and look at those calves branded with that double X. Better do that soon. It'll take the four of us over a month to take care of these matters, even if Pistol was whole. And he ain't. I think the sheriff needs to be contacted soon. The sooner the better. Right now we need to take care of Mr. Linderman before he returns the favor. No one is safe right now. And Pistol has got himself thinkin' he has to be with us. Riles, that ain't gonna happen."

"Gotcha scared, huh? It ain't like talkin' is gonna hurt. Not likely I could cause you any trouble. I ain't seen you in fifteen years."

292

"Twenty."

"You been gone that long?"

"Not me. You. I've only been gone maybe fifteen at best. You started this whole thing by leavin' one mornin'. I remember. You woke me and Si up. You was dressed, pullin' Si and me outta the sack. The Old Man didn't know. Mother didn't know. You was plenty mad. You left me with the job of breakin' your leavin' to Ma. Sometimes your help does cause me trouble. It sure as hell wasn't easy. Pistol ain't never forgiven you. To this day, he ain't. You oughta talk to him. He's got a burr the size of a walnut under his saddle. Mostly 'cause you didn't tell him you were leavin'."

"Ain't that the truth. He's let me know he's pissed. And me talkin' to you? It's nothin', really. Somethin' I've been thinkin' 'bout since Si returned to the line cabin without you a few days ago. Said you weren't comin' 'cause you was fixin' fences."

"Fences? Horseshit. Damn that Si. He never stops talkin'. I swear. Mostly he don't know what he's talkin' 'bout. Riles, I don't need to talk to you 'bout the women in my life. That ain't none of your damn business. I'd really like to keep it that way."

"Sounds fair. And it ain't none of my business. Besides, Si's got his own problems. Believe me. Listenin' to him tell it, I figure he was talkin' about Among the Willows. Now that ain't logical at all."

"Riles, she ain't none of his damn business. It's none of your business. I really don't care to talk 'bout her. If it helps any, I've got that problem solved and he's wrong. Dead wrong. I ain't fixin' any fences. If anythin', I'm takin' 'em down. She and I musta talked all yesterday mornin', part of the night tryin' to fix our lives. We both agreed that fifteen years is just too much time to jump across. Can't do it. That's what she said. I agree. So yes, in answer to your question you ain't asked, that's over. Done. Now change the subject. We got bigger fish to fry. Believe me. Gotta say though, I sure didn't handle that right. I never should have done what I didn't do. You know what I mean. Not comin' back was just wrong."

"Willow? I'll be damned. I'd practically forgotten about her. It's been twenty years you know. Last I saw her, you two were teenagers. What? Like fourteen? You were really young. You remember when you were fourteen? Now that's a forgotten

293

memory." Riles smiled at Forest.

Forest looked at him to see if he was serious or not. Riles was staring at the Pryor Mountains, not seeming to want to talk at all. "I'm sorry, Riles. I thought you was wantin' to talk to me about her. I don't. We got more serious things to be doin', and don't need to be wastin' time." Forest smiled. "Sorry, really."

"No problem, you brought her up."

"Yeah, I did. I did? I've been gone a long time, myself. Time changes things. She's a lovely lady but you can't just pick it up like leavin' never happened. I ain't seen her in like ten, twelve years. I was eighteen and she was almost nineteen when I left. You and Si was gone. I followed. The Old Man went crazy. I finally had to get away from him, from this." Forest motioned with his right hand.

"That must of been difficult. A hard bronc to ride."

Forest looked at his brother again to see if his comment was sincere. He didn't appear to be making a joke. "It sure wasn't easy. Willow was cryin' like she was never gonna see me again. I wasn't thinkin' I'd be gone forever. I was just tryin' to get away from the Old Man. It was hard as hell. One thing led to another and I never came back like I thought I would. What I thought would happen didn't. I figure it just ain't meant to be. You know? Time passes. Things change. People change. I changed. She changed. You'd never believe it. Yesterday morning, she got in front of me and shot this fellow to keep him from shootin' me. Yanked my spare and shot him with it. Damnedest thing. And she's got two daughters. They are so pretty. You wouldn't believe it."

"Know the feelin'. All that history. You probably were 'fraid to come back here after all that. I was."

"Probably. The longer I was gone the longer I wanted to stay gone."

"Until Dee wrote you that letter. Then you couldn't stay away no longer."

"Yeah, until I couldn't. Even then, Riles, I kept wonderin' if I was doin' the right thing." He paused. "Somethin' happened. You'll never believe it. It was weird is what it was."

"You rode over the rise south of Kane and saw the mountain."

294

"Yeah. How did you know?"

"You mentioned it."

"I did?"

"You saw the mountain. It spoke to you. Said somethin' like 'Where have you been, fruitcake?' Somethin' like that?"

Forest laughed. "Don't know 'bout 'fruitcake'. But I did come over the rise for the first time in a long time and I saw the mountain. It felt like it saw me. Not possible I know, but it felt like it. Me sittin' on the Appaloosa. I swear it said to me, 'Where you been, huckleberry?' I was so glad to see it sittin' there, a thunder cloud coverin' it, dark, forbidding. It was home. 'Bout started bawlin'. Damn horse turned his head to get a look at me. See what was goin' on."

"Comin' back makes leavin' a little difficult, don't it?"

"Lord, Riles. That's just it. I don't know if I can. Exactly the opposite of where I was before I saw the mountain. I don't know if I want to. I can't remember why I left and that mountain that mornin'….. 'Where you been?' it said. I didn't know the answer."

Riles chuckled. "I have a "rememberin'" question for you. See if you remember--let's see--I was eleven. I think I was. That'd make you about seven? Don't think you can remember it, but you brought it up. You was seven years old and sittin' on the top rail of the horse corral on Sage Creek. You was watchin' the boys take the green outta the rough string. Maybe you'll remember. Every fall, Black Wolf and Pa would round up fifteen or twenty mustangs, ride the green out of 'em. Black Wolf would take seven or eight; the Old Man would take seven or eight. Then every fall they'd go huntin', take us with 'em when we was old enough. Do you remember who you sat with on that top rung?"

"Yeah, I do. It was Willow. I remember. I ain't forgotten, if that's what you think. She was my friend. We had fun. She and I."

"Willow, yeah. I'm surprised you remember. Remember what you told her?"

"I told her somethin'?"

"She was afraid of one of those green ponies comin' over the top rail and gettin' her. Afraid she'd get hurt somehow."

"That's right. That's right. I remember. I told her she didn't have to worry."

"Yeah. You said she didn't have to worry 'cause she was with you. All seven years of you."

Forest laughed. "I was one confident seven year old."

"You sure as hell was. You sat up there seven or eight feet off the ground holdin' this little Absaroka girl's hand tellin' her not to be afraid 'cause you was there."

"Maybe she was holdin' mine."

"Maybe. That's sorta what I'm worried 'bout."

"What?"

"Do you remember the next year–Spring?"

"Not really."

"You'd of been eight. She might have been nine but maybe not quite."

"Why you bringin' this up, Riles? I told you it's over between us. We're just good friends. That's what we are. Took us all day to work that out."

"Just shut up and listen to me. You brought it up. I didn't. I've already forgot why I wanted to talk to you. Answer my question. Do you remember? You'll see where I'm goin'."

"I said not really."

"Couldn't find you. Remember? The boys had been bringin' the cows up, gettin' ready to brand and castrate the bull calves. It would have been the first, middle of May. You and Willow turned up missin'. You was just little kids and lost. Mother was beside herself. Took all mornin' 'fore we found you and that little girl. You were up on the side of the hill behind the house. Halfway up the first rise where that first bunch of pines are still growin', parks on both sides. It wasn't like you was lost, mind you. You two knew where you was. Nobody else did. Got everyone all excited. Especially the Old Man."

"I remember. It's pretty up there. You can see forever across the Reservation. And the flowers...that time of year are very beautiful."

"We found you. The Old Man was mad. Course he was always mad. Nothin' new there. Willow was all decked out in mountain flowers. Especially those blue lupine, yellow sunflowers, and orange paint brush. She had 'em in her arms, holdin' 'em in her

296

hands. Somehow the two of you had worked 'em into her hair. I don't know how the hell you did that but you did. The Old Man was fixin' to beat the hell out of you for scarin' everybody half to death. But he saw Willow all decked out in those flowers, holdin' 'em in her hands, lookin' incredibly innocent, incredibly beautiful. And you standin' beside her dumb as a rock. All he could do was stare. Remember? He looked at Black Wolf, shook his head like he didn't know what to do, didn't know what to say. Finally, he threw up his hands and walked to that grey horse of his and went back to work. When the Old Man didn't know what to do...he always went to work."

"I remember. I remember. Yeah, Black Wolf sat us down on the side of the mountain on a big old granite rock: Willow and me. Him, too; he sat down with us. We looked over the entire world. It was lyin' there before us. He spoke to us like we was somethin' special. I remember that."

"What did he say?"

"Don't think I don't know what you're doin', Riles, but she and I, we're all over. We've done decided it."

"You're ahead of me. I don't know what I'm doin'. What did he say, Far? I wanna see if you can remember. I wanna know if I remember, myself."

"He told Willow she was a beautiful flower, how much he loved her, that she was like her mother. He told me that it was my job to take care of her, that she was a flower like the flowers we picked for her hair. That mountain flowers were best when their roots were left in the damp ground to grow and be nourished by our mother the earth."

"Wow! You remembered. And you? Do you remember what you said?"

"This is the kicker, ain't it, Riles? What you're lookin' for."

Riles stared at his brother without responding. He waited for Forest to remember as though he had nothing else to do in the entire world.

"I said, 'yes, sir, I'll do that, I'll take care of her.'"

Riles smiled. "'Yes sir. I'll do that. I'll take care of her.' That's what you told me you said to him when you was eight and she was almost nine up on the side of the mountain in May. The mountain that spoke to you, by the way. Seems to me you told Si you had fences that need fixin', not fences that needed takin' down. Promises to keep. Ain't that what you told Si?"

Forest stared at Riles for an extended moment without saying anything. "All right," he finally said. "Damn you, Riles. Then we gotta address the needs of some men that need killin' so that we can get to livin'."

"Yes." Riles paused, nodding. "So we can get to livin'. Hurry, Far. We ain't got much time. Do you know where she is?"

Forest nodded. "I do," he said. "Pickin' chokecherries. It's that time of year." Forest looked at Riles. "I wish you hadn't done this, Riles. We had it all worked out. We understood, and now I gotta remind her of this?"

"Maybe you ought to learn how to pick chokecherries."

"I already know how."

"Good, listen, I'll find Si. Talk to Pistol. We need to leave soon. You ain't got much time."

"She's gonna think I'm crazy."

"Yes, she is."

CHAPTER 36

Peter approached Syrus, carrying a Winchester 44-40 lever action rifle, limping, favoring his bad leg more than normal. "Riles said you was over here. That we was gonna eat and talk. I don't see any food. So what are we gonna talk about? What are we gonna do?"

"Attack and keep attackin' 'til they're all dead. Except you. You're goin' home."

"What? Not again. Nobody told me. Not this time. I can carry my share of the load."

"Nobody needs to tell you, Pistol. You can hardly move. Besides, you got a woman and two kids to look after. You simply can't do this. Soon you'll be whole again. I don't want you kilt. That should be enough of a reason. Plus that, I don't want you to go."

"You can't tell me what to do. Did Riles put you up to this? Sounds just like him. I need to go with the three of you. It's what I need to do."

"No, he didn't put me up to nothin' and you don't need to go."

"Si, Jeez. As it is, we're bitin' off more than we can chew. Let's go slow. Let's organize ourselves. I really need to be part of this. I need to be included."

"You are a part of this, Pistol. You'd be riding with us except you got a bad leg. The other thing you got is a woman and two kids. They are part of us. Someone needs to take care of 'em. That's you. Soon, Pistol,soon as that leg is healed, you'll be with us. We're getting' ready now to leave. We gotta be movin'. And we gotta be movin' now. Someone needs to protect you and yours. You're elected."

"That's horseshit, Si. Riles always thinks it through. Always. He just ain't got it right this time."

"Not always, Pistol. Sometimes he don't think at all. This is one of those times where he's right. Listen, Pistol, " Syrus said, "you do know that you can't bring your wife and kids home until Linderman is taken care of, don't you? You do know that, don't you?

If you do, your woman and your kids are as good as dead. Not to mention yourself. Bringin' 'em home right now is stupid."

"Si, you're yellin' wolf when there ain't no wolf. Besides, you just rolled up with a thousand head of cows and you bet Diana is thinkin' she's goin' home. We got a lot of work to do."

"Work? There is a lot of it. But think, Pistol. Use your head. You two are standin' in Linderman's way. He's already killed four people that we know of. We're all that's standin' in his way. He has to go through us. We done took our cows back. By now he knows it. He's comin' for us. Has to. He's either crossin' the canyon or he's sendin' his boys to follow the cows. He's doin' one or the other or both. You can bet it ain't gonna be as easy this time. He expects us. He knows we're here. You can't just hide those cows. Too many."

"I have been thinkin'," Peter said. "Maybe he'll back off. I don't want anyone kilt on account of me."

"Lordie, Pistol, what's got into you? Listen, go talk to Riles. See if it helps. He ain't gonna let you go, but he'll listen to you. He's gettin' his horse and lookin' for Far. In an hour we're gonna be movin'. Except you. You're gonna go home or somewhere, hole-up, and wait this one out."

Syrus removed his hat, swept his hair back on his neck, and reseated his hat. He looked away, across the canyon to the Basin Pasture and the Bull Elk.

It's gonna be a hot one, he thought.

CHAPTER 37

Riles found Syrus on the hill above Chokecherry Creek, one hundred yards from where his father, Moose, brought steers and old cows each year to help feed the Old Ones. It was the decided place of meeting. Syrus was working with his horses, packing his panniers, making ready.

"What are you doing, Si?" Riles asked. He asked, but he knew the answer before he asked.

"I'm gettin' ready to get ready. Those Linderman boys will be comin' for us, Riles. We can't wait. Pistol is lookin' for you. I already told him he ain't goin'. I told him you wouldn't let him go but you'd listen. So listen and tell him no."

"Tell him no, huh?"

"Yes. Tell him no."

"I hear you. No rest for the wicked. I wish it wasn't this way. We ain't been in the shadow of the Pryors twenty minutes, Si, and we're already movin'. I'll saddle the Buckskin and I'll be ready. I think Far is makin' amends for his wicked ways. He'll be here soon. I don't know where Pistol is. I didn't see him. He ain't gonna like it but he ain't goin'. I'll tell him again.

"I told him. He didn't take it particularly well."

"Thanks for the help and the update." Riles was shaking his head and mumbling to himself.

"What?"

"I said horseshit and gunsmoke. If it ain't one thing, it's another. Half an hour. I need half an hour."

Syrus nodded. "And there ain't a hell of a lot you kin do about it is there?"

Riles laughed. "That, too."

"Good, 'cause we ain't got twenty minutes, Riles. It ain't there. It's been a week since we shot the Linderman boys up. Since then, I'm bettin' they've been movin'. If they ain't already, they're comin' for us. We gotta be ready to meet 'em. That meeting has to be on our terms. The head of the lizard has to be chopped off. So bring an ax 'cause the fiddler ain't puttin' away his bow 'til then."

Syrus paused, looking at Riles. "Riles, you know it. I know it. I'm pushin' too hard. Everybody knows it. I know we gotta eat. I know we just made it here. We've already been here for more than your twenty minutes. For twenty minutes we've been here, sittin' dead in the water. On the other hand, those bastards ain't been waitin'. We daresn't wait, Riles. We can't afford it. Let's get goin'," Syrus said.

"No. We need a short break, Si. A little rest. It ain't gonna be long. I'll get everyone together right now. Before we leave, for a few minutes, we'll share each other's company."

"All right. But we best be takin' that short break of yours while we're movin'. That's my opinion," Syrus said as he threw the stirrup over the saddle seat and grabbed hold of the cinch strap, tugging on it, taking the slack out of it, throwing it under the horse's belly. "We can't afford another ten minutes."

Riles laughed, handing him the reins to the Buckskin. "Watch him. Give me twenty-five minutes, knowin' I'll need a couple of hours to put this all together. Let's get everyone together. We need an idea of what we're gonna do. Who's gonna do it. If either of your brothers happen to walk by...keep him here."

"All right. But we've been together. We've sorted it over and we've sorted it out. We're gonna kill Linderman before he kills us. That's what we're gonna do."

"I know, Si. Give me twenty-five minutes. I'll get my sorrel horse. I'll ask Diana to work on somethin' for us to eat."

"I've said all right three times now. I keep givin' in, Riles, but we ain't safe here. Not even for five minutes. We gotta be movin'. We sit still, those boys will find us. Simple as that, Riles." Syrus looked at Riles. "We gotta find 'em first or we're dead."

"Twenty-five minutes, Si. I'll send someone to find Far."

Syrus turned his attention back to the roan stud. "Twenty-five minutes," he repeated. "Twenty-five minutes. No more."

"Right now, I gotta find and talk to Pistol before he blows a cork or two. Know where he is?" Riles said.

"Like I said, he's lookin' for you."

"That helps," Riles said, laughing.

Riles found Peter catching up his horses, including Diana's buttermilk gelding.

"What's on your mind, Pistol? Si said you needed to speak to me."

Pistol glanced at Riles. "We gotta get some things straight. It's like you've taken over."

Riles stood silently, staring at Pistol.

"Ain't you gonna say somethin'?"

"You ain't said anythin' yet."

"Si says I'm not gonna go with you."

"It's best you don't."

"Riles!"

"Pistol, you can hardly move around. I ain't gotta tell you, but your leg is broke. You're not goin'. You'll be a hindrance. More importantly, you need to watch over those two kids and Diana. Someone's tryin' to kill 'em. Besides, we can't be doin' what we gotta do and look out for you. It ain't fair to nobody. It ain't like you're less of a man. It's just the way it is. Your damn leg bein' what it is. And who's gonna be lookin' out for Diana and those two young'uns?"

"I know. I understand. It's just hard to take," Peter said. "All right. All right, then. I wanna take my family home. I wanna do it now. You got the cows back for us, Riles."

"And you helped, Pistol, the best you couild. You didn't have to be there to help. I understand. You wanna go home."

"It's just that it's not fair, Riles."

"No, it's not. Someone has to do it. What does Diana wanna do?"

"I don't know. I don't even know where the danger is comin' from or who's bringin' it. Jeez, Riles, I'm not even sure what the right thing is. I know it's not over. I know that. Si doesn't let me forget it, either."

"No one knows, Pistol. Does Dee wanna go home? Is that your decision?"

"What decision?"

"Goin' home? Takin' your woman home? Protectin' her?"

303

"Riles, you make it sound like I can decide. I wanna go with you but you're sayin' no, I can't. I wanna take care of my family. I'm not sure how. What if I'm wrong?"

"Parents don't get to be wrong, Pistol. It ain't one of the options."

"Horseshit and gunsmoke."

"Yes, and there ain't nothin' you can do 'bout it."

"I never knew what that meant. You and Si said it all the time. I asked Far once what it meant and he said if I live long enough I'd find out."

"None of us will live long enough, Pistol. Takin' care of Diana and the kids is the responsible choice, frankly."

Peter looked at him. He nodded. "All right," he said.

"Fine, Pistol. But if I was you I'd take everyone to the line cabin. It's easier to defend."

"And if Diana and I decide we wanna go to the Creek, we wanna go home?"

"Then that's your decision. I've told you what I'd do if I was you."

"It's kind of funny. The Old Man would tell me what to do."

"I ain't the Old Man. I don't wanna tell you what to do. I do know you need to watch over your wife and kids. You know the arguments; you know what supports, and what don't. You'll have to make up your minds on what's best.

"Now let's get goin'. Find your woman. Get some food up there on the ridge so we can eat together one last time. I'll find Far. I wanna be gone within an hour. You should be gone, too, Pistol. Do what you damn well please. You don't have to be gone within an hour. But I think you should be, or stay here. That's it. That's all I got to say."

"You sure say a lot when that's all you got to say."

"What?"

"Nothin', never mind."

CHAPTER 38

They gathered on the ridge. The two kids were running around laughing. Riles was checking his horses, the pack saddle on the sorrel, reviewing his mental checklist. Syrus was helping with the fire, heating the coffee pot, overseeing the roast rabbit, the deer meat on a stick. Diana was calming Josh down, making sure he ate.

Peter was sitting on a rock, staring over at the canyon where the Big Horn River passed through it on the way to Fort Smith. "Hey, Riles," he said. "I feel good. We're headin' to the line cabin. Hurry back, would you? I don't know if we can take this sittin' 'round much longer."

"Do the best we can, Pistol. Take care of your leg. Besides your family, it's what's keepin' you out of the fight. We need you. Take care of yourself."

"I will. Where's Far?"

"He's comin'."

Among the Willows walked with Forest toward the apex of the ridge. Diana, upon seeing her, didn't believe she was joining the group. Not after all the things that Willow had told her.

Willow could see the gathering. Beside her, Forest walked slowly, leading his Appaloosa horse. He was talking about cows, his brothers, hunting, and things like that, and what they could do when he got back.

"You all right?" he asked.

"Not really. You're leavin' again. I hate that. It's what you promised never to do."

"Hell of a note, ain't it? I ain't got no choice. I wouldn't leave if I had a choice." He looked at her. "Willow, I…feel like an idiot. Goin' back and forth. I think this is right."

"I do, too," she said. "Let's talk about somethin' else. I don't want to make this decision again." She looked at him. "I don't want you to go." She laughed. "I don't want to let you out of my sight. At the same time, I know it's war. Men make war. Men protect their families."

"Thanks for understandin'."

"Forest, I don't understand. Don't get yourself killed." She stared at him. "Please," she said.

He smiled. "Okay," he said.

Forest had asked her to walk with him for he was leaving. People would die. Many coups would be counted. Forest had said some men had to die for what they'd done. She'd seen this before. She'd heard it before. She wasn't sure about coming with him. The closer she got to the top of the hill, the more unsure she became. Men often did not return from war. She was anxious. Why, she didn't know. She wasn't sure. It made no sense. She wanted to run away but no. This was her man.

She could feel his nervousness as he glanced at the people gathered, waiting for him, for her. He didn't like goodbyes. He told her he wasn't saying goodbye even though he was, that he'd be back as soon as he could be. They were words said to make her feel good, but they didn't. She'd heard them before.

It wasn't as if Willow was afraid of these people. She wasn't. She'd grown up with them. For as long as she could remember, the boys had been part of her life as much as the grass, the mountains, and the buffalo. Still, she was apprehensive; she was conscious of all of the eyes watching her as she climbed the gentle grade to the top of the rise overlooking upper Chokecherry Creek.

Riles Stockton rose from the rock on which he sat, stepped forward. "Willow, it's nice to see you," he said and handed her several orange paintbrush flowers that he'd gathered from among the rocks as they waited, as she and Forest had walked up the incline.

Surprised, she looked at the flowers in his outstretched hand, at Riles, and back at the flowers. She glanced up at Forest, then turned back to the flowers. She accepted them, bringing the buds to her nose and smiling at Riles. "Thank you," she said. "You don't know how much this means."

"Oh, I think he does," Forest stated.

"He does," Willow said. "He's the story teller." She smiled. "We owe you and I to him. He was there. We were so small. I don't remember who was there except my father and you."

Riles laughed and Syrus handed her some venison roasted on

a stick. It was warm to the touch. "Not a flower," he said, "but it tastes better, keeps you goin' longer." He bent over to smell the flowers in her hand. "No," he said, "it don't smell better."

She laughed. The spell was broken.

"Let's eat," Riles said. "Soon as we're through eatin', Si, Far, and I are gonna be goin'. We'll stop at Sage Creek. I understand Pistol and Diana are goin' to the line cabin. I don't know when. I understand soon."

Riles looked at Pistol, paused.

"Soon as we're ready. As close to right now as possible," Peter said.

"Good, let's eat. We'll wait for you. We'll ride with you as far as Sage Creek."

"No. No. Riles. You folks get goin'. We'll be all right."

They drank a beverage made of water flavored with fresh chokecherry juice, bitter, yet sweet. It was bitter, if bitter can be sweet. They ate fresh venison roasted over an open flame, taking their time, laughing in the afternoon sunshine, a breeze blowing in from the mountain. For a little over forty-five minutes they didn't think of their differences; they didn't think of their agreements, or disagreements. They enjoyed each other and the venison steak, a snowshoe rabbit, three fools hens and a variety of jerked meat: moose, buffalo, antelope and venison.

CHAPTER 39

Riles Stockton led the Buckskin and the sorrel to where Syrus and Forest stood waiting for him. Forest patted the one-eyed dog on the head, scratching him behind the ears. "Comin'?" he asked the dog. He found the stirrup and swung into the saddle. He was immediately joined by Riles and Syrus.

"Say," Syrus asked, "do you remember when we got into it down there by Indian Springs? The Old Man sent us out to do somethin'. What was that? It was a cow, wasn't it?"

"That old spotted cow, she'd lost her calf; somehow she got caught up in that tree. I still wonder how she did that. We got her loose, then she run Pistol up the tree. Like she planned it. You left him in that tree cryin', Riles," Far said.

"Sure pissed the Old Man off."

"It was Pistol got her loose, then she ran him up the tree," Riles replied. "I remember."

"She had a rack of horns. I remember that," Far said.

"She was the last of those that Pa brought up from Texas. Old. Probably didn't have a tooth in her mouth."

Far added. "Yeah, Pistol was in that tree most of the afternoon. 'Til Pa came and got him out. He says to Pistol, 'Boy, whatcha doin' up there?'"

All three laughed.

"And Pistol says, 'I'm watchin' that mossy, Pa. Makin' sure she don't get away," Syrus said.

"Boy, whatcha doin' up there?" Far repeated, turning to look back at Pete and Diana, packing their pack horse. "What's he doin' back there? That's the question. I can feel his disappointment in not being with us but he's making the right decision. He's takin' care of family much as he can. Damn leg.

"Can't blame him for bein' upset. He's worried about them damn kids. Got himself a beautiful woman; he's worried 'bout her. Needs to take care of her. And he is. I think his leg is gettin' a little stronger but he's favorin' it a little more than he should. Makes me

308

worry he'll push it too hard.

"And that Diana--she's worried about killin' Linderman. Makin' him pay." Forest paused. He looked at Syrus to see if he understood. "That's all she can think about. Sorta burnin' her up."

Syrus rubbed his whiskered face. "It's all I can think about to tell the truth. Who can blame her? I feel for Pistol myself. Fact is, nobody's safe. Especially Dee. She ain't safe. Hell's fire. We ain't safe and we can take care of ourselves."

Forest chuckled. "Killin' Linderman is all any of us can think about. What with Linderman gunnin' for us like he is. We was damn lucky up there on the Tongue. We surprised 'em." Forest turned and looked at his brothers. "Well," he said slowly, "how exactly are we gonna get this feller's attention now? Now that he knows we're here? Don't look much like he's gonna go broke payin' attention. None of it makes sense. He's comin' at us pretty well-heeled. Got all those gun hands. Payin' out all that money. I can't figure it. If he wanted us out of the way, why didn't he just pay us? Maybe Pistol would move. He's payin' those gunnies more than that whole place is worth, cows and all. It makes no sense. He's got us outgunned, outmanned. It ain't gonna be easy. I'm thinkin' this is a case of how to grab the lion by the beard and yank on it real hard. Gotta get his attention or kill him."

Riles smiled. "Beard the lion? You thinkin' that's the game?"

"Don't let it bother you, Riles. We don't have to play it by the rules. You never did. Why start now? Pa would be rollin' over in his grave."

"If he was in a grave."

"Good. I don't want this to be fair," Riles said.

"Fair? Did you say fair?" Syrus turned to look at his older brother. "Where did you ever get that notion, Riles? Linderman started it. He's sendin' folks to kill us. Steal all of Pistol's cows. We ain't got no choice. We either run like hell, die, or kill him first. Fair? This ain't about fair. It's about survivin'."

"Take it easy, Si," Forest said. "You think you're the only one involved?"

"I just don't wanna hear no fair. This has nothin' to do with fair. If we get the drop on 'em, kill 'em."

"Okay, Si, it ain't fair, but Far's right. The question is how to get to him before he gets to us. I'm thinkin' we better be quick about it. We don't even know where he is."

Syrus nodded. "One other thing," he said. "Now, this means somethin' to me so I want you two to listen. If I don't make it, you two have gotta put a bullet in that Judge's head. Hear me?"

Riles glanced at Syrus. "We hear you, Si. What's got into you? What ain't you tellin' us?"

"You gotta promise. Like I said, it means somethin' to me."

Forest turned in the saddle and glanced at Syrus. "Si," he said, "it's a done deal. The man's already dead. He just don't know it. First, we gotta take care of this Linderman feller. He's the hard nut we gotta crack. For one thing, he ain't never alone. For another, he's got a lot of artillery surroundin' him."

"And take care of his woman, too. Promise me," Syrus said. "I said, promise me."

"What woman?" Riles asked.

"The Judge's woman."

Riles stopped his horse, the sorrel coming up behind him. He looked at Syrus sitting astraddle the roan. "It's always 'bout a woman, ain't it, little brother? What's her name?"

"Rebecca. And she's got two real nice kids. A boy named Jed, a girl named Emma. Promise me, Riles. It means a lot to me. She made me promise I wouldn't forget her."

Riles stuck his thumb in the air. "You got it, Si."

"Far?" Syrus insisted.

Forest stuck his thumb in the air and smiled. "I was thinkin' 'bout Pistol." he said. "Do you have any idea how lucky we are that Pistol grew some responsibility? And he's got a bum leg? For once in his life, he'll be out of the way instead of right smack dab in the middle of it. Waitin' for the Old Man to rescue him."

Riles and Syrus started laughing.

"Damn straight," Syrus said. "That's luck."

Riles glanced at his brothers. He said, "What d'you say we go back to the home place? We'll need some grub to take with us. Wanna hear somethin' crazy? I've been thinkin' 'bout fish hooks lately. I've been tryin' to remember where the Old Man hid those damn things. Had a whole box. A little red box. Remember? Fish hooks? When was the last time we went fishin'? Some ammunition, too. Gonna need that. Ain't done any huntin', either. Next month it'll be September. It's gettin' that time of year. Besides, Cecil needs somethin' to carry."

"Damn mule," Syrus said.

The sun sat overhead in a cloudless sky, beating down with a relentless fury typical of mid-August in southern Montana. Behind the riders and about one hundred fifty feet off to the north side, the mule's head came up. For a moment he stood there watching the Buckskin walking away from him. To his left the one-eyed dog came out of the trees, stretched its long, lanky legs and started walking, following after the Buckskin. He disappeared behind a clump of skunk brush, coming out on the other side with the mule watching. The dog broke into a distance-eating trot.

The mule stood still. He watched, tossing his head, then he decided he was being left behind. He started his legs moving at a steady walk, decided that wasn't fast enough, and began to trot, dust lifting from his hooves. That didn't appear to be good enough and he started running, following the one-eyed dog across the Montana grass.

Riles glanced at Forest. "Far," he said, "we ain't answered the question yet. How do we expect to run this Linderman fellow down? I figure he'll be hard to catch, harder to kill. Especially with what we have in mind. It ain't like he's gonna stand up and yell 'here I am, shoot me dead before I shoot you dead.'"

"I'll tell you. Answer me this," Syrus said. "Where will he least expect us? Eatin' dinner at his dinner table, usin' real dishes and real silverware like Ma wanted. He won't be expectin' that. I know I sure as hell wouldn't."

"Where do you get these ideas, Si?"

"Pick 'em out of the air. Damn straight, I do."

Riles glanced at him. "Do you think those boys from over on the Tongue made it to Deer Creek?" he said.

"Maybe they're still over there on the river trying to figure what happened. Most of 'em are dead," Forest said. "Why would they come clear over here? There's nothin' for 'em. All, or most of,

Linderman's cows are on the Sheridan side, clear to Musselshell. That's what I heard. That's why I'm wonderin' why he'd bother with us. We ain't nothin'. That's got me puzzled."

"I know, I know," Riles answered. "I expected 'em to run us down once we started gatherin'. They didn't. The big question is why are they botherin' us to begin with? We ain't got nothin' they ain't got more of."

"Must be some reason," Forest said. "I've asked myself the same question. If it was me, I'd have come after us as soon as they could saddle a horse. I'd of kept comin' 'til I run us down and killed everyone of us. It'd of been easy. Catch us between them cows and the river. They didn't. Why?"

"I can think of some reasons," Syrus said.

"Yeah, what are they?" Forest asked.

"Maybe they had wounded. That'd slow 'em down," Syrus said. "Maybe they ain't eatin' regular. They had those dead people they left on the river. Course we throw'd 'em into the river. They didn't know who they'd tied into. They was a little gunshy, if you ask me. It might have occurred to 'em that if they caught us, we might hang 'em."

"They got hungry? Could have shot a deer or an elk?" Riles observed.

Forest nodded and said, "Maybe the Boss called 'em home?"

"That Boss was dead."

"Where's home?"

"Sheridan, I guess."

"Maybe, but why? Ain't logical. I think they're still on the Tongue. Linderman's cows are over there somewhere. They ain't here. Home is the Sheridan side of the mountain. Not Deer Creek."

"That's just it," Forest said. "This whole thing don't make a lick of sense. Kill four people, three women for that half-pint Stafford outfit? Old Man Stafford had trouble gettin' out of his own way what with that bum leg of his. He was old, buggered up. The only thing he could do is watch. He wasn't as old as the Old Man. Why would Linderman want that one-horse outfit? I don't want it."

"It ain't that bad," Syrus said. "Maybe he was just greedy. Maybe Stafford told him where he could put it. Got him all upset."

312

Riles asked, "This fellow, Linderman married?"

"Don't know," Syrus answered.

"You don't know a hell of a lot, do you?" Riles said.

"Nope. Knowin' stuff--Pop left that to you."

"Except for what I don't know."

"There's that," Syrus said.

"Let me say the obvious," Forest interrupted. "We're gonna have to ask someone who knows."

"Ask someone?" Syrus said, "Did you say ask someone? Who the hell are we gonna ask? We don't know nobody."

"I'll tell you who to ask," Forest said.

"Well?"

Forest responded. "You two know-it-alls, want me to tell you who to ask?"

Neither Riles nor Syrus said anything. They just stared, waiting for Forest to tell them.

"Ask the cook."

"The cook?" Syrus said.

"The cook. He's always standin' around. Always listenin'. He's never goin' nowheres. If anybody knows, it'll be the cook. I say we ask the cook. Big outfit like that has a cook. Probably more than one."

"What if he don't understand English?" Syrus asked.

"Then we got a problem."

"Talk to the cook? Far, I don't know why I listen to you all the time. Gets me into more trouble. Not a bad idea. The cook."

"'Cause I'm lucky. And it's better to be lucky than good."

"Thanks, Pops."

"You're all sorts of welcome. 'Bout time you remembered."

"How we gonna find the cook?"

"Look in the kitchen. Where do you think you'd find a cook?"

"Means we have to go to Deer Creek one way or the other. We got two ways. Chain Canyon, cross the Horn there, or we ride south, cross at the Narrows, climb top of Little Mountain up there by that cave."

"That ain't a cave. It's a hole in the ground."

"It's one deep hole. Ain't got a bottom."

313

"So the Narrows, it's forty or fifty miles from here."

"They'd never expect that, though. At Chain Canyon, you could stand off all of George Custer's Seventh with a rifle and a picnic basket. We'd be in the open crossin' the river. Ain't too much cover bobbin' around in the river."

"Let's not."

"Agreed."

There is an odd, musty smell in a house where folks haven't been living, sleeping, walking around, washing the dishes, going inside and out, or frying a steak or two. It's an old, dry smell. Dust collects, leaving a thin coating over everything. Mice leave their tracks and trails across the floor. It had only been a couple of weeks since they'd left, but a pack rat had found a way inside. It had begun collecting sticks, building a nest, adding colorful toys in the corner of the kitchen under and around a cabinet. Riles opened the doors and the windows and let the cat inside. Somehow she got onto the roof. Forest got her down. She did not want to be held, petted, or, even spoken to. She meowed and meowed, walking around the various rooms, following Syrus, talking to him, like she was cussing him out for abandonment.

While Forest got a noon meal together, Syrus and Riles packed the panniers for the mule's pack saddle. The packs were ready by the time they sat down to the table. The cat stood right at Syrus' feet, talking to him, alternating between purring and meowing, leaping to the counter, and coming back to stand under the table, rubbing against a chair leg.

They washed the dishes and stayed the night. In the morning they left the kitchen window open so the cat could get in and out. She was on the porch when Forest caught up his Appaloosa, threw one of the reins around its neck. The dog got up, looking at him. Forest grabbed the horse's head by the bridle, pulled him around, and stepped into the saddle. The horse started walking. Forest reined him in as Syrus pulled himself into the saddle. Riles walked out onto the porch, closing the door.

"I should ask you, two, where the hell you're goin' this early in the mornin' but I already know."

314

They waited while he caught the Buckskin. "Is it still 'talkin' to the cook?'" he asked.

Forest laughed. "It's the cook. Talk to someone who knows everythin'. Need some information. It's the cook that's got it. Let's see what he knows."

"Long ways if we go 'round by the Narrows. Could get ourselves in a jam with those Linderman riders. Somebody sees us. Just sayin'."

"Riles, nobody knows me. They don't know Si. No one has seen any of us for over, well almost, twenty years. If they know anyone, it'd be that damn mule and that one-eyed dog of yours. I'm gonna go talk to that cook and see how this Linderman butters his toast."

"Me, too," Syrus said, pulling a Mississippi Crook out of his shirt pocket.

"How many of those things you got?"

"Three boxes. One mostly used."

Forest looked at him. "You never smoke 'em. What you think, they're candy?"

"I ain't learned to smoke yet."

Riles smiled. "You boys ready to get?"

"I ain't sure how smart this is," Syrus said. "Walkin' right into where they live."

Forest smiled. "What ain't smart is stayin' here. Maybe you need some matches," he said.

"I don't need no matches. What we need is to see that cook and not get ourselves killed. Maybe we can get somethin' to eat. Far ain't nothin' to write home 'bout when it comes to cookin'."

'Yeah, well, I can still build a fire. Let's go roust the chickens outta the coop. Linderman have a coop? Old Man Stafford did."

"I hate chickens."

"How can you hate chickens? You're always eatin' eggs. What's wrong with you?"

"Maybe I do need some matches."

CHAPTER 40

By afternoon, they'd traveled around the eastern edge of the East Pryor mountain, crossed Dryhead Creek, Davis Creek, Layout Creek, and had entered the bad land hills that lay between the East Pryor and the Shoshone River. By late afternoon, they'd crossed Crooked Creek and reached the dry hills above the Narrows, where a river two hundred feet across was reduced to a width of twenty-six feet. In front of them was Little Mountain, its grey slopes spotted with cedar and juniper. Once on top of Little Mountain, they traveled eight miles north and east and were looking over the edges of the eight hundred foot walls of Devils Canyon. Below them raced the white waters of Porcupine Creek, unchallenged and unstoppable, as they made their way toward the Big Horn River and the canyon through which it ran.

Half a day later, they followed the old Sioux trail, dropping into the canyon to the confluence of Deer Creek and Porcupine. Thereafter, they stayed on Deer Creek until they found the Stafford ranch buildings sitting in the cottonwood trees, baking in the hot August sun. It was a you-can't-miss- it proposition: follow the creek--run into the Stafford buildings.

Except for chickens scurrying about, clucking in the heat, no one seemed to be around. The area felt deserted, tainted with the faint disappearing echo of the four girls who grew up alongside their father and mother on Deer Creek on these waters, in these buildings. Their laughter, the intimate imagery of their lives: bruised knees, scratches, a bowl of chokecherries, a jar of currant jelly, were only remembered by the shadows cast by cottonwood, pine, aspen, and chokecherry trees.

The main buildings consisted of a long log cabin with chimneys at both ends built fifteen feet above Deer Creek on a foundation of rock, an eighteen foot high horse barn, and a series of corrals. One end of the corral extended across the creek for the benefit of the livestock in the corrals, enabling them to obtain a drink of water. There was a bunkhouse, equal in size to the main house, sitting behind the horse barn. At one time it had been the main house; now it was secondary and housed cowhands during the fall when the round-up demanded the extra hands. At this moment, there weren't any cowboys around. There was another small, cabin-like structure with a column of smoke extending above it, floating, drifting into the calm mountain air. It was built above the creek.

In front of this latter structure were three empty hitching rails and a sawed-off pine block, three feet high, used to chop the heads off chickens and geese. A wooden barrel sat beside the cabin at the corner to catch snow melt running off the roof. Nearby, to the side of the structure, was a stack of firewood for the cookstove and three empty five gallon cans. Above and to the left was a disused garden spot, protected by a pole fence; the moldy earth was flat where the Stafford girls and their mother had planted string beans, corn, hubbard squash, and carrots in the late spring of the year. Hollyhocks grew in a line along the fence, giving it a vivid splash of color.

Down by the edge of Deer Creek, straddling a portion of the ice cold snow water, was a spring house that cooled butter, milk, beef, and venison. The foundational first course was made of granite rock hauled from the creek bottom, welded together with cement and tight bonding. The upper courses were huge pine logs pulled from an old fire-damaged forest on Porcupine with a team of Belgian horses.

The corrals were vacant except for two cows and their calves. As far as the three men could tell, no one was in or about the big house, the barn, and the garden flat above the house. No horses were tied to the rails, nor were there any horses standing in the adjacent horse corral. Except for the buzzing of bees, flies, and mosquitoes, and the tumbling water rumbling through the creek bed, there was no sign of life.

Riles, followed by Syrus and Forest, rode across the hardpack. On edge and cautious, they made their way past the spring house and behind the building that housed the kitchen. Smoke was rising from the single chimney, drifting through the cottonwood, caught by the early afternoon breeze. Dismounting, they wrapped the reins of their horses to the hitching rails, stretched, and looked around. They saw no one, expecting just the opposite. The only immediate, living resident turned out to be the cook. He was inside, busy, preparing for

317

the late afternoon meal. He did not stop what he was doing to so much as look at the intruders. He didn't need to. He was the cook: paid more than an ordinary hand, more than a gun hand. He had status because he could make food.

He spoke to them, watching the oven as he spoke, conscious of the bent needle on the rusty heat indicator. "It'll be two hours 'fore dinner. Wait outside or stay inside and do the dishes. Suit yourself."

Certainly, he didn't expect dish help. He never did. It would have surprised him if someone unilaterally volunteered. In the Fall and Spring when there were extra mouths to feed, extra dishes to wash, he got help: not now, not in the dog days of Summer. Not when, at most, he was feeding twelve to fourteen hands.

In the quiet of the kitchen and crew dining room, Riles Stockton strode across the floor from the front door, his spurs rasping across the pine floor, the jingle bobs ringing brightly. Forest and Syrus stayed at the front, looking out through the windows, watching the horses and looking for signs of trouble. The cook still hadn't bothered to look up. If he had, he may have noted the leather catch latches no longer encircled the hammer of his visitors' SAA Colts. There were no empty chambers with ten dollar bills wrapped and tucked inside them. Even if he had looked, he would have missed that.

He did hear a Winchester being set on the table top. He looked up. Riles was standing at the work table across from him, waiting for his attention.

"Thank you kindly for your time," Riles said to him. "More than grub, we're lookin' for information. Thought you might have it. We'll take just a moment of your time."

"No. No, you won't. Didn't you hear me? Ain't got the time." He paused to look at Riles; from Riles his eyes went to Syrus and Forest loitering at the windows near the front door. Immediately, he recognized that their attention to the outside world wasn't normal, that it bore an expectation of trouble. His attention reverted back to Riles. "You ain't from here," he said casually. "Ain't seen you 'round. Don't know if the Boss is hirin'. Don't suppose it hurts to ask. Try your luck. I ain't got the time to talk right now. Sorry. You're

318

welcome to stay 'til we eat supper. We'll feed you one way or another."

"You ain't from here, neither," Forest said, turning his attention from the window to the cook. "I ain't seen you before."

That statement brought the cook up short, for how would this man know that? He took the time to look the three over much more closely. Riles stood beside the table that the cook was using for holding mixing bowls, pots, pans, utensils, a dishpan almost full of dishwater.

Forest walked the short length of the dining area and looked at the cook, then glanced inside a bowl partially full of what looked like bubbled gristle and fat-fried, puffy corn kernels. He sampled some of the kernels, tasting them, rolling the mixture around on his tongue. He started to chew, making a face, swallowing. He tried a few more.

"Appreciate the grits," he said. "Ain't tasted nothin' like this. Has a flavor I could get used to. Not bad."

"Those ain't grits," the cook said. "Ain't close to grits. Grits are made of ground corn. Soaked. Now, you boys are gonna have to get yourselves outside. I ain't got time to talk. Gotta get supper ready."

Forest nodded, took a few more, put them in his mouth, chewed. "Well," he said, "they sure as hell are good eatin'. Crunchy and gritty. I appreciate that. Someone oughta tell you you done good when you done good. From the looks of you, I'm guessin' you're the cook?"

"One of 'em. The other--he's a bit under the weather. Over in the bunk house. Got a little of the Rocky Mountain quick step."

"You ever make bear sign?" Forest asked him.

"Bear sign?" The cook sounded surprised. "Those things-- they ain't bear sign, neither. I ain't got time for this lollygaggin'. Told you, I ain't got the time. Now get out of here. All of you."

"'Fore you lose your temper," Riles said, "and get yourself shot full of holes, I got some questions I need to ask."

Forest interrupted, pointing. "I know that ain't bear sign. I was wonderin' if you ever cooked up a batch."

"Sometimes. Ain't, lately. Takes flour, sugar, and time. Lots

319

of it. You boys leavin'? I told you to leave."

"And a oven," Syrus observed.

"That, too. Except not so much a oven as a deep kettle to hold boilin' grease. Lard."

Forest reached in his pants pocket, fumbled around and came up with a gold piece. He studied it, then handed it to the cook. "Sir," he said, "I believe you'll find that this here is a five dollar gold piece. I'd appreciate it if you'd make me a batch of bear sign, if you would. I'd be grateful. Not right this moment. I ain't pushin'. But soon. Real soon."

"You want bear sign when I get 'round to it? 'Not right this moment"?' That could be never. I ain't got enough sugar; I got some flour but I ain't got no cinnamon. Sure you wanna do that? Leave your money with me?"

Forest nodded. "'Course I'm sure," he said. "I like them damn things."

The cook looked at the gold piece, bit it with the several teeth he had left in his mouth. For a moment he stared out the window across the hardpack that extended all the way to the horse barn, wondering what the third man was looking at. To his surprise, he saw a dun mule, without a halter, a pack saddle on its back, standing in the middle of the yard, his head down, resting as if he was dead tired, his long ears flipping back and forth. Suddenly the mule started walking purposefully, sniffing at the ground as though trailing something. The cook blinked his eyes and caught a movement on the front steps of the kitchen through the open door. In the doorway was the ugliest, long-haired, scraggly dog he'd remembered ever seeing. In the back of his mind he remembered someone mentioning a mule with a saddle. This one didn't have a saddle. And a dog. An ugly dog. The cowboy who'd mentioned them was from over on the Tongue River.

The cook said slowly, "I suspect you folks didn't come here to talk 'bout bear sign and grits?"

Forest answered him. "Nope," he said. "Not really. Came to ask you some questions. I was told the cook knows everythin' there is to know 'bout what we wanna know. So we're askin' you."

"Suppose I don't wanna talk to you boys?"

320

Riles smiled and said more pleasantly than he needed to, "In that case, we'll have to beat it out of you. Fill you full of holes. Break a few bones. Cut your ears off. Relieve you of a few toes. Set the dog to chewin' on your leg. Stuff like that. We're hopin' to get a few answers without doin' those things. But if you're gonna insist..."

The one-eyed dog walked into the room, his claws striking against the floor. The cook stared at him, noting the drool leaking from the side of his mouth, the long scraggly hair, his swollen, weepy eye. The dog groaned as it laid down on the dirty floor.

"And five dollars worth of bear sign. Don't forget that," Forest interjected. "We'd like that, too."

"What is it you're wantin' to know?" The cook hesitated, sounding unsure, wiping his hands on a damp towel. "I ain't been here long. I don't know much." He saw Riles Stockton's side arm, noting for the first time that the leather loop was not wrapped around the hammer; this man looked older than the other two, a might taller.

Riles was staring at the cook, rubbing his chin. Across the dining area, Syrus was studying something through the curtainless window. Forest sat down on a bench, watching him, waiting.

The older one started asking questions. He asked, "I understand the Boss is a feller name of Linderman?"

"Suppose I could answer that. Can't see it hurtin' him, you knowin' that. Yeah. He came from Kansas City, Missouri. Rode with Quantrell in the war. Was a Master Sergeant."

"Married?" Riles asked.

"Wife and three kids. What do you wanna know that for? How's that your business?"

Syrus had turned his attention from the window. "They here? Sittin' over there in the big house, maybe?"

"No. 'Cross the mountain. Sheridan. Boss has a house over there. Lives over there mostly."

Syrus asked,"He, here? This Linderman feller?"

"I think today he's out with the boys. Workin' cows up around the Falls. On Porcupine. Left this mornin' early. You're the folk that belong to that dun mule and that excuse for a dog, ain't you? Caused all that trouble on the Tongue?"

"Guilty as charged," Forest said and stood up. "When's he comin' back?"

"Right away. Soon. To avoid trouble, you better be on your way."

Riles nodded slowly. "You tellin' us the truth, Mr. Cook, or are you feedin' us a line of bullshit? Givin' us what you're thinkin' we might wanna hear? There ain't no grass up there on the falls. Ain't no cows, either. Never has been."

"No."

"No, what?"

"I ain't tellin' the truth. Just what you wanna hear."

"The truth, then? Before I cut your nose off."

"Said they'd be back 'round nightfall. Two hours or so." The cook coughed. Inadvertently, he knocked a frying pan off the table onto the floor, followed by a pan and a spatula. They made a bang and a clatter. He reached down to pick up the frying pan by the handle. When he rose, he found himself looking at the working end of three pistols. Nobody was smiling. It appeared to him that not one of the three cared whether he was the cook or not.

He paled. "My God, man," he said. "It's just a pan. It fell on the floor. I picked it up. I told you what you asked. What more do you want?" The cook paused, staring at Riles. "You're a Stockton," he said. "Is that your name? If it is, I've heard of you."

"Yes."

"Jesus."

"This Jesus fellow, he ain't got nothin' to do with this," Riles said. "Nothin' at all."

"Listen, Mr. Stockton, I ain't had nothin' to do with none of this. None at all. Three weeks ago, I was just offered a cookin' job at a good salary. That's all. But I'm quittin'. I didn't kill no girls. I didn't steal your cows. Nothin'. Understand me? I ain't interested in your gold, neither."

"My gold? What gold? We ain't got no gold."

The cook stared at Riles. "That ain't what I'm hearin'."

"What are you hearin'?" Forest asked.

"It's in the Porcupine. That gold up there in Old Gold City done washed down Porcupine Creek for thousands and thousands of

322

years. The reason it's not in Old Gold City is it's at the bottom of the falls. Everybody's talkin' about it. The falls is like a giant pan, a natural sluice box. That's what they're sayin'. Said there's so much gold at the bottom of the falls, you have to take a shovel to shovel it outta there. All you gotta do is divert the water outta the creek so you can get in there."

Syrus broke out laughing: laughter that turned to bitterness. "Old Gold City gold?" he said. "There sure as hell ain't no gold there. All of them claims proved to be worthless the year they was taken out. Maybe a little color here and there. A touch. Nothin' worthwhile. I'm tellin' ya: none. There ain't no gold to wash down Porcupine. What a joke. You mean to tell me Sal lost her life for some pipe dream; for gold that ain't there? That's never been there? Oh my God in heaven. Forgive us all." He stared at the cook, letting the hammer down slowly on his SAA Colt.

The cook noted that he did not look happy; if anything, he was consumed with anger.

"Take it easy, Si," Forest said. "You're gonna scare the hell outta the chickens. They'll stop layin'."

The cook gasped. "Si? You're Syrus Stockton?" He stared at Syrus, then at Riles. "Both of you? Listen," he said, "I ain't got nothin' to do with this. Nothin' at all. That's just what they're sayin'. I'm just repeatin' what they're a sayin'. Linderman is plannin' on divertin' the creek so he can haul the gold out in wagons. He's plannin' on usin' Chain Canyon so he can freight it out year round. Winter won't stop him. He's gonna use Sage Creek. Wants to meet the new railroad once it gets in there. Clear to Wade, Montana. That's what he's gonna do. He's got it all figured."

"The hell, you say."

"That's the gawd's truth. I swear I ain't lyin'."

"Use Chain Canyon? Go right down Sage Creek like we don't even live there? He ain't plannin' on askin'?"

"Well, yes. How else is he gonna bring gold out durin' the winter? He can't go over the mountain. Snowed in. Sage Creek is the only way. Can't go over the Reservation. Once the canyon freezes over, he can drive a team right over the top on ice. That's what he's plannin'."

323

"Lord, help us," Syrus said slowly. "Old Gold City? Can you imagine that?"

Forest glanced at Syrus. "You been up to Old Gold City?"

"Yeah, a while ago. Ain't nothin' but a lot of holes in the ground and men with big eyes and bleedin' fingers. There ain't nothin' up there 'cept short grass. Grass is good. You know. It's right on top of the mountain. Only thing taller is Bald Mountain. Sure as hell ain't no Virginia City, no Sutter's Mill. It ain't even a Tombstone. Folks don't live up there no more. Can't. Too damn cold durin' the winter. Gets ten to fifteen foot snowdrifts durin' the cold months, and it's forty below when it's warm. Cows can't live there 'cept in the summer. Shit. Gold. That's a pipe dream only an idiot would believe."

Riles looked at the cook. "How'd this Linderman come across this place here?" he asked. "Didn't know Jake Stafford was in the sellin' mood."

"I don't know. Tell you, I'm new to this outfit. I think you boys better move along. I do. Before someone catches you here. Shoots you dead. I ain't wantin' to talk any more. It ain't my business. As you know, I'm just the cook."

Forest smiled, pulled his knife out of the scabbard, and stuck the blade in the counter surface. "You don't know? You not knowin' don't sound likely to me."

The cook glanced at Forest. "Who are you?" he asked.

"I'm nobody," Forest said. "So who'd Linderman buy this place from?"

"From Old Man Stafford. I heard Linderman had a fellow name of Mumford shoot him. He wouldn't sell. Just a story told 'round here. Probably ain't true. Suspect you boys already heard that one."

"I heard he had the Stafford girls killed. You hear that, too? Seems you have."

The cook didn't respond.

"Did you hear that?" Riles asked, waiting for an answer that did not come. "Did you hear that?" Riles asked again, insistent.

"I did."

"Any truth to it?"

Again the cook was slow to answer. He finally said, "I didn't see it with my own eyes. I heard he paid off a Judge down there in Basin City. I heard a rumor it was ten, fifteen or twenty thousand dollars. Paid a fortune to get a fortune. One of the boys told me that on his way out, not two, three weeks ago. I'd been here maybe a day or two."

Riles' eyes immediately fixed on the cook. "You said, 'On the way out.' What do you mean? Speak up. I ain't got much time to be foolin' with you."

"He was quittin'. Had enough. Said it ain't right."

Riles said, "You put any store in it?"

"He was a good man. A real good man."

"How'd he know?" Riles asked.

"Didn't say."

Syrus interrupted. He asked, "There was four U.S. Deputies in on killin' those girls. Know where they are? Know who they are?"

"They ride for Linderman. I heard one was over on the Sheridan side of the mountain. Rode shotgun for the Mackelvy Overland. That's what I heard. He showed up here last week. All four of 'em are here. The four of them, I hear they're bein' paid to hunt the Stockton brothers down. Heard they are bein' paid a wagon load of money to kill you dead. I see there's only three of you, though. Not four, like I was told."

"How do you know it's them?" Riles asked.

"I know. I got eyes. I got ears. I ain't blind. Saw the fifty dollar gold pieces they carried and the U.S. Deputy badges they was given. Saw the Greeners they was furnished, didn't give back. They was braggin'. Nice new shotguns. The best. If they knew you boys was standin' here in the cook shack, you'd be dead. All of you. They're a mean bunch of bastards."

Riles asked, "What's your name?"

"Frank."

Syrus said, "Frank, do you take friendly advice?"

"Sometimes. When it's good."

"Frank, if I was you," Syrus said, "I'd get the hell out of Dodge City while you can. It's my thought that the wheels are 'bout to come off Mr. Linderman's wagon. The one he's figurin' on haulin' all that gold in. Stupid bastard."

Frank stared at Syrus. "Have you looked inside the barn? Out back? Have you looked on the other side of the barn? There must be twenty-six new freight wagons in there and more out back in the trees. There's a pump to suck the water out of the bottom of the falls. There ain't no wheels comin' off the wagon. This Linderman is serious, I'm tellin' you."

"Twenty freight wagons? How'd he get them in here? No. I don't wanna know."

"Well, boys," Syrus said to his brothers, "you wanna know anything else? Or is that it? The man in the know is standin' right there in front of you holdin' Forest's five dollar gold piece. You know now what this is all 'bout. Twenty freight wagons!"

"Frank," Riles asked, "how many are ridin' for Linderman?"

"Twenty-six."

"Gun hands?"

"Yes. Nobody ordinary. Gun hands. A rough bunch."

"That include those boys over on the Tongue?"

"No. I don't know nothin' 'bout 'em other'n you boys shot 'em up pretty bad. A number quit. Wasn't worth gettin' shot dead over. That's what I heard. They also got word of Syrus Stockton and Riles Stockton gettin' themselves involved."

"You lyin' to me?"

"I wouldn't. Believe me, I wouldn't. You're Syrus Stockton? I can't believe it. No, I can't."

Riles looked at his brothers. "He's right. Let's get outta here," he said, "while we can."

Forest smiled. "Say, Frank," he said, "you hold on to that coin. I'll come back for the bear sign."

Frank looked at him and placed the coin on the counter. "No," he said. "It's best you take it with you. I don't want you comin' back."

Forest picked up the coin and put it in his pocket. "Suit yourself, Frank. I was you, I'd take that advice Si gave you."

"I ain't concerned over your advice or his. Seems there ain't enough of you to make any difference. The three of you is dead, unless I miss my guess. Everyone is huntin' for you."

326

Forest chuckled. "I'd have to agree with you, Frank," he said. "We sure as hell ain't much. What was that you fed us?"

"Cracklins' and parched corn mixed together. And some salt. Rendered pig skin, what you had."

"Well, I'll be damned. I'd of never known, Frank. Listen, we're thinkin' of leavin'. Why don't you step out in front of us. Don't want no surprises. Don't want you standin' behind us, that's for damn sure. Like livin', too much to let you do that."

Frank the Cook stared at Forest, then through the open front door. He nodded as if he was making up his mind. He took a step toward it. It wasn't as if he had any choice. He didn't expect anyone contesting the goings and comings of Riles and Syrus Stockton. Who would? He wondered who the other man was, a pleasant fellow. Didn't matter. He was with the first two.

Frank turned toward the door; he wiped the sweat off his forehead. It seemed to be getting warmer. "All right," he said. "Then you'll go?"

"Down the road, Frank and outta sight," Forest said. "Hopefully, you'll never see us again. You'd be wise to get the hell outta here. You don't wanna see us again, even on an accident."

"Got company," Syrus announced casually, quickly pulling both revolvers, easing back the hammer on each. His brothers joined him. Between the three of them there were six revolvers, thirty six shots in the cool of the afternoon on the back side of Little Mountain.

Riles glanced outside. "Looks like there's five men. Who'd they be, Frank? The five standin' out front across the way? Looks like they're goin' somewheres, they're holdin' the reins on four saddled horses. Where'd they come from?"

Frank glanced through the doorway and across the hardpack. Then he looked at Riles. "Ain't good news for you. I told you to go. That be those men you asked about. The fifth man--the one without a hat, with the baggy trousers, suspenders--that's the Boss, Mr. Linderman. You can ask him those questions. Let me go now. I don't want any part of this fight. It ain't mine. It really ain't."

"Well, I'll be damned," Riles said. "I don't think so. You step right out there, Frank. Introduce us. Can't get any better than this.

Somebody somewhere really loves me. " Riles was waving the pistol in his right hand at him. "Get," he said. "I wanna meet these sonstabitches. I wanna meet 'em right now."

An unwilling Frank stepped through the door, almost stumbled, holding his hands up for all to see. "Don't shoot, don't shoot, don't shoot," he pleaded loudly, hoping everyone could hear. Eyes turned to see him. Surprised to see him. The dog got up and walked by Frank and outside onto the yard. For a moment he stared across the hardpack. Frank was followed by Riles on his left, Syrus on Riles' left. Forest, was on Frank's right, smiling. Frank had to look at him twice to believe it. The fool was humming a catchy little tune, mumbling the lyrics: "...thou are lost and gone forever, oh my darlin', oh my darlin," repeating it again and again and again. And he was smiling.

"I hate that song, absolutely hate it," Syrus said softly. "Damn near drives me crazy every time I hear it." His thumbs rested on the hammers of both of his pistols. *Twelve shots. See if I can take all twelve before I'm out and have to reload.*

"Si," Riles said, his voice soft, "you got one of those bastards hidin' in the barn doorway. Standin' in the shadows to your left. 'Cross the way."

"I see him."

Frank," Riles drawled, "introduce us."

"Mr. Linderman," Frank shouted, his knees weak. "Mr. Linderman, I want to introduce you...to to the Stocktons. This here is...."

"What?" The older man heard him, but he was moving, running for cover as fast as he could run, as fast as his legs could carry him. "Kill them! Kill them, kill them!" He shouted the order over and over.

Someone said, "Ah, shit!"

A shot sounded, exploding in the afternoon air. Syrus shot the man standing inside the doorway to the barn. His was the second shot. The fellow, surprised, raised his pistol to fire and suddenly received a barrage of fire that he had not expected, nor did he recover. The sustained firing lasted six seconds. Not a long time to live, if you're going to live: a short time if you're going to die.

328

Frank tripped; he fell flat-faced in the grit and gravel, kissing the earth. How he didn't get shot was a miracle, or so he told his grandchildren forty-five years later, sitting in his frame house in Sacramento, California watching the American River crest, overrunning its banks, rising as it did to the second floor of his house. He was eighty-seven years old and lived to be eighty-nine, one of the few men to have met Syrus and Riles Stockton and their brother, whose name he never learned, and lived to tell the story.

Syrus and Riles were not talking. They fired away, following moving targets, shooting with one hand, then another. Each took a total of six shots in six seconds, using both Colts. Forest took four shots, moving forward all of the time, presenting a moving target that no one hit. And they tried. He didn't give them a chance. They were surprised from the instant Frank made the introduction.

Riles had shoved Frank the Cook aside, tripping him, shooting the ex-deputy Killmond Jacobson in the chest, forcing him backwards, his heart and lungs a mass of goo, the slow-moving projectile slamming around inside him, ricocheting. Frank fell flat to the ground, the dust puffing up around him, missing Forest's forward progress by inches. Riles sought one target after another, shooting at something, anything that moved, calmly firing. The horses bolted toward the corral, making an effort to get away. *Don't stop firing*, Riles told himself. *Never stop*. And he didn't until he was down six cartridges and could find nothing more to shoot. Six seconds. Immediately, he sought cover and began pulling fresh cartridges from his gun belt, shoving them into the cylinder, replacing those that were spent. *Damn*. His thigh hurt; his arm was stinging; his hat had been knocked off, the sun was in his eyes. He stood up; the wind caught his hair.

It was strangely quiet, except for Frank crying in the dirt, beseeching the blessing of preservation from on high. Linderman was lying next to the barn, alive, quivering in the silence. He started to get up, hesitated, and started again when the firing had ceased, belly crawling for safety. He was trying to make his way to the barn door. The four deputy U.S. Marshals were shot multiple times. Not one survived, taking shots to the chest and head repeatedly. It happened so quickly, they were not prepared; ducking, running, and dead.

Syrus limped, blood dripping from his pant leg, from one man to another, putting a shot into each of their heads. Bam, bam, bam, bam. The percussions were loud, echoing against the mountain. They were dead; in his mind there was no question.

Standing in the middle of the courtyard, between kitchen and barn, Forest reloaded his two SAA Colt Peacemakers. Nothing moved. Syrus also finished reloading. Both men joined Riles. Frank was still not moving, waiting in fear for his life to end abruptly.

"Frank," Syrus said to him. "Get outta the dirt. What the hell's wrong with you? You know better. Thought cooks was supposed to be clean."

Forest said, "Riles, Linderman's over there. He's still alive. Far as I can tell he ain't been shot. What do we do with him?"

"Where?" Riles asked. "Where is he?"

"Lyin' over there by that barn wall. Saw him movin'. He's alive, I'm sure of it. I didn't shoot him."

"I see him."

"What are you gonna do with him, Riles?"

"Hang him."

"Easier to put a bullet in his head."

"Yeah, it would be. Too easy. He don't deserve easy. Not after what he did."

"Si, get that bay horse standin' over there by that horse corral fence. Pull that rope off the saddle. I'll get that weaselly bastard. We'll get this done."

An older man, Linderman, stood under a cottonwood limb in Jake Stafford's front yard, his boots on the hardpack, with a single slip knot around his neck. He wasn't a pretty sight. Frightened, he was bawling, sniffling, sobbing; he peed his pants, expecting no mercy, getting none. Riles wrapped the end of the rope around the saddle horn of the bay horse and walked the gelding forward until Linderman's feet were off the ground and he was fighting for breath at the end of an ever-tightening rope. Riles didn't bother tying Linderman's hands together. Linderman choked to death fighting for air, his fingers struggling with the rope. His neck didn't snap; it took him a good fifteen minutes to die. No one assisted his death by killing him.

Frank the Cook kept rocking back and forth on the heels of his boots, standing in the courtyard. He'd look up and see Linderman fighting for his life, close his eyes, then look again. He kept mumbling to himself. Linderman's pathetic struggles caused his body to swing back and forth, the rope to tighten. A breeze picked up, rattling the leaves in the trees. Inside, Frank's cooking fire burned down, the stove began to cool. There'd be no supper that night.

"We better be goin', Riles," Syrus said, handing him the reins to his Buckskin horse. "Twenty-six gun hands might be a few more than we can handle."

Riles nodded, threw the reins around the horse's neck, and hoisted himself into the saddle, pulling the horse around where he could see Frank.

"Frank," he said, "look at me. Frank, look at me."

Frank looked up.

"Listen," he said. "this outfit, all of it, belongs to my sister-in-law. She's a Stafford. It belongs to her and to her two kids. If you or the bastards that used to work for Linderman so much as pull a fence post outta the ground, I'll hunt you all down and kill you." Riles paused. "Do you understand what I'm sayin'? One staple, one pole outta place. I ain't got no mercy for the likes of you. Do you hear me? Look at me. Look at me. Frank?"

Frank looked.

"Not one staple. Not one spike. Understand? Do you hear me?"

Frank the Cook nodded his head.

"Be outta here tomorrow. All of you. Do you understand?"

Frank the Cook nodded his head.

"Good, Frank. Make damn sure we don't see you again north of the Mexican border. Not ever again. Oh, and you don't bother Linderman. Let him swing. Hear me?"

Frank nodded his head. Frank never saw Riles Stockton again, though he did manage to grow old and die in Sacramento, California, a distance of five hundred twenty miles north of the Mexican border.

"We better get out of here, Si," Riles said.

An hour later they were climbing out of the canyon, following the old Sioux trail to the top of Little Mountain. The mule was out front, the dog bringing up the rear. Once on top, they looked back. In the small side canyon that housed Old Man Stafford's cabin, the horse barn, and the long bunkhouse, a single column of smoke rose steadily.

"Think they're followin' us?" Syrus asked.

"Don't know. Doubt we could be so lucky. If they was comin', they'd be makin' a lot of racket. I don't hear nothin'."

"Maybe not. Those hands might not have made it back yet."

"We ain't that lucky."

CHAPTER 41

It was evening. Peter and Diana Stockton had reached the house on Sage Creek. Josh and Katie Suzanne were exploring the creek, throwing rocks into the whirling waters in an effort to fill it up. It was a job started thirty years ago by a knobby kneed two year old, Riles Stockton.

"Tell me, Petey, what is it with you and Riles?"

"You'll think I'm crazy."

"I already think you're crazy."

"I told Riles we wanted to go home, that we were goin' home. He just looked at me."

"Sometimes I think you don't like Riles. From the way you talk about him, you don't like your own brother."

"He's hard to like sometimes."

"What did he say when you told him what we wanted to do?"

"He asked me if that was my decision."

"Sounds like he ain't tryin' to beat you to death with a club. That ain't bad."

"He suggested that we go up to the line cabin, that we don't stop on the creek. Says the line cabin is easier to defend, that it might be a better place for right now. Said that the yonkers would be safer. You know what else he said? Sorry, stupid question. Of course, you don't. He said bringin' you up there was a good thing for me to do. Said it would be easier to protect what's important. Said he'd handle the Linderman thing. That it was no use me gettin' shot dead with all of these folks dependin' on me. Especially with a bad leg."

"But we didn't go there."

"I didn't want to but I told him we would. I wanted to come home. But I've changed my mind. It is easier to defend. All of us will be safer there. More so than here. He's always tellin' me what to do. I ain't likin' it much. That don't mean he ain't right. Mostly I end up doin' what he tells me. I always do. He's my brother. He's the oldest. The Old Man, he told me to always check with Riles. Said he's a good thinker that way. Said I might not like what he's got to say but that

333

he'd always put some thought into it. I really didn't want you to write him. I really didn't. I knew this was gonna happen."

"You don't always do what he tells you to do."

"Not always but most always. Probably why I don't like him much. The Old Man used to really lay into him when he didn't consider what would happen to Si, Far, or me. That's why he up and left. The Old Man wouldn't leave him alone. Rode him tight. Finally, he couldn't take no more of it and one night he left. As stupid as it may sound, I didn't get to say goodbye to him. That always bothered me. I was eleven. I really, really missed him. He always seemed to make things right. After he left, nothin' was right. He's here again and as much as I don't wanna admit it, things are better again."

"Listen, Petey, speakin' of right. There's somethin' I gotta do. I figure you ain't gonna like it none. I gotta do it right away. I ain't got time to discuss it."

"Think we got enough time to sit down?"

"Yes, I think so."

Peter glanced at Diana, nodded, went to the kitchen table, pulled the chair out, and sat down. Diana put a glass of spring-cooled milk on the table in front of him with two slices of buttered bread. He glanced at the slice of bread, noted the butter, and took a bite. "What's botherin' you, Dee?"

"I agree. You do need to go to the line cabin. Like Riles said, there ain't no better place to keep our kids safe, not right now. I'm sorry, but you're gonna have to watch 'em. I gotta go. It can't wait. I might be too late already."

"What are you talkin' about? Go where? You're leavin' a lot out, Dee."

"I gotta go kill the Judge."

"The Judge?" Peter stood up; the milk-sopped bread fell to the table. Outside, the milk cow was bawling; the chickens were clucking; a magpie was talking from the high branches of the cottonwood trees. Peter blinked, staring at his wife. For a moment he paused, working his jaw as though it needed to be greased, the joint wearing out. He made himself smile.

"What the hell you talkin' about, girl?" he said. "You ain't gonna kill no judge. You can't. It's against the law."

334

"Sit, Petey."

"I don't think I will."

"Sit. I insist. Sit right now. We need to talk."

"No. What's got into you, Dee? You can't kill no judge. Look what's already happened. You're in danger here. The kids are in danger. That SOB Linderman has already sent one killer after us. Probably sendin' an army right now."

"Petey, I have to take care of this first. After I get back...."

"Get back? You ain't gonna be gettin' back. You ain't goin'."

"I didn't think you'd take it well, Petey. I've already packed my saddle bags. I got Si's pistol. I'm takin' Far's rifle. I'm leavin' yours for you. You may need it."

"I ain't takin' it at all. What's gotten into you?"

"It's Si. It's Far. It's Riles. It's you. Mostly, it's me."

"Si? What's he got to do with it? They all can take better care of themselves than you can."

"All right. It's that woman."

"Woman? What woman?"

"Remember, Si told that story at the line cabin. I figured it out. It wasn't no story. He was tellin' the truth. I gotta get to that Judge before Si does. That's all there is to it. He's gonna kill the Judge for me, for my sisters, if not me. I gotta stop him. It's 'bout that woman and those two kids. I asked Riles about what Si said. I asked if it was true...the story. He said somethin' odd to me. He said Si never lies. Said he says a lot of things, but if he tells a story 'bout a woman, there's a woman. That's what he told me."

"Stop it? You can't stop it. It's impossible. That judge is a dead man. Nothin' you can do to stop it. Fact is, after you wrote those letters...he was a dead man. So is that Sheriff and so is his Deputy. They just ain't buried yet. Don't you understand this? This is about family. There ain't no goin' back on this. The Old Man said it that way. Family is the only way. There ain't no other way. Why do you think I didn't want you to write them letters? I knew they'd come. I knew all of 'em would come. Pop said when it comes to family, we either come back carryin' our shields or bein' carried on the damn things. That Linderman fella, he ain't stoppin'. My brothers, they ain't stoppin'. The Judge, he's a dead man."

335

"Shields? What's that mean? What are you talkin' about?"

"How the hell do I know? The Old Man just said it and we said okay. It has somethin' to do with Greek warriors. I don't even think the Old Man knew what it was about. The message is clear. Ain't no doubt. Family is everythin'. There ain't nothin' else. No one and nothin' stands in the way, Dee. I should be with my brothers right now. That's where I should be. And I ain't there. Riles said no. And that's it when he says no. So, we're here."

"Petey, listen to yourself. Family is everythin'. There ain't nothin' else. I gotta go. I love you. I'm a Stockton. My kids are Stocktons. Si needs me and he don't even know it."

"Ah, horseshit. Si has never needed savin'. Not a day in his life."

"Petey, he does now. It's his heart that needs savin'. Family is everythin' and I have to try. I've gotta get there before he does. I figure you can take the kids up to that line shack, stay there 'til I get back. Three days at the most."

"You ain't leavin'."

"Petey, I ain't askin'."

"Dee, think 'bout what you're sayin'. You really can't do this."

"I am doin' it, Petey."

Peter threw his hands in the air. "All right. I'll be on the mountain. If not, Josh and Katie Sue will be with Wolf's people. Find his sister. She'll have 'em. Willow. Her name's Willow."

"I know Willow," Diana said. "We all know Willow. Far can't do no better. Neither can she."

Peter turned to see her disappearing out the front door. Moments later, he heard her yell at the horse she was riding. "Haah, you." And she was gone.

A man on a good horse can ride one hundred miles in a day. To do it the horseman has to get up early. He can't be lollygagging and he absolutely can't be running. It's at a walk. Running will break the horse's wind and he'll be worthless the rest of his days. But a good steady walk will cover the distance. Afterwards, the horse will need a solid break. He'll need to be grained a quart of oats every morning for a week, a daily rub down, his cannon bones rubbed out,

336

and he'll need plenty of good timothy hay to eat, plenty of time to stand around in the shade swatting horseflies. He'll be all right and he'll have traveled one hundred miles. Diana had one hundred miles to go to reach the Judge's home and she wasn't starting early.

She'd ridden eight hours by the time she reached the Shoshone River. She had fifty miles to go. It was midnight. She didn't stop, riding through Greybull with ten miles to go. It was noon when she rode into the front yard of the Kilpatrick house five miles on the south side of Basin City. It sat five hundred yards back from the river.

Diana was dead tired; her horse was dead tired. It was the distance. It was the sultry heat. Mosquitoes and deer flies kept the horse's tail moving. He kept blowing his nose as if he were trying to get something out of it. He'd be all right. He made it. One hundred miles. She made it. Diana Stockton stepped down. She noted two kids playing in the front yard. The youngest came running out to greet her.

Jed, she thought.

"Hello," he said, looking up at her and the horse behind her.

"You must be Jed," she said. "You look like a Jed. Your mother at home? I'd like to speak with her."

The boy nodded. "I am. She is."

"Your dad?"

He shook his head no. "He's someplace. I don't know."

"That your sister?"

He nodded.

"She got a name?"

"Emma," he said.

"Emma. What a pretty name. Is that your mother standin' in the doorway?"

Jed looked. "Yes," he said looking back.

"Do you think I could talk with her?"

"I do."

"Good. Let's go talk to her. Maybe you could introduce us."

"Introduce?"

"Yes, you could tell her I'm here to speak with your father. Would that be okay?"

"Yes, Ma'am."

"So formal. Who taught you to say that? Your mother?"

Jed shook his head.

"Who?"

"A big man who rides a big red horse. He said that to my mom all of the time."

"And now you say it?"

"Yes, Ma'am. He was really nice. I liked him. He's gone."

"Would you like to get him back?"

"Yes," he said. "Ma'am, do you know the man?"

"I do know him. He told me all about you. He's my brother-in-law."

"He did? He told you?"

"Yes."

"Introduce me to your mother. I'll see what I can do."

Upon seeing Jed talking with a strange woman, Rebecca had come to the door. She stood waiting, watching, wary.

Diana walked to the front door leading the bay gelding. Jed walked beside Diana; he took her hand.

Diana said, "Hello." Then turned to Jed. "Are you gonna introduce me to your mom?"

"I don't know your name."

"Oh, that's right. I didn't tell you." Diana turned to Jed, smiled. "Forgive my manners. Jed," she said, "my name is Diana Stockton. I have some business with your father, the Judge."

"Mom," Jed said, very seriously. "Mom, this is Diana Stockton."

Diana turned to Rebecca. "Ma'am, I have some things I need to discuss with your husband. Could I wait for him here?"

"My husband? Oh, I don't know. He really doesn't like to do business at home. I'm not sure that is a good idea. He won't be back for another hour or so. Maybe you should try going over to the courthouse instead."

"Ma'am, I can wait. We've come a long ways."

Jed spoke up. "Mom, she knows the man. You know, the man."

"You'd be Rebecca, yes?" Diana asked.

"Yes, I am. How did you know?"

"I heard from a reliable source that you was a nice person."

"From the man on the red horse? That's who Jed remembers: the man on the red horse," Rebecca asked.

"Yes, that one. He's my brother-in-law."

"Oh. Well this is a surprise. Of course. Where are my manners? Come in, then. Wait inside if you'd like."

"I'd like to drop the saddle, if I could, and let my horse take advantage of your grass. Maybe I could get him some water? He's been workin' really hard."

"Oh, of course. You can turn him loose in the corral; feed him some hay. Jed can show you. Soon as you do, come up to the house. I'll fix you some lemonade and a sandwich."

Finished with taking care of her horse, Diana Stockton brought her rifle and Syrus' 44-40 SAA Colt stuck behind her belt buckle. She knocked on the front door frame. The door was open and Rebecca immediately appeared with a cold glass of lemonade with small chunks of ice floating in it.

"Ice?" Diana exclaimed. "Wow. In August. That's amazin'."

"Yes, isn't it? We have an icehouse and ice from the Big Horn. It is harvested every winter, I'm told."

Diana smiled and took a drink. "Thank you, Ma'am."

Rebecca led Diana into the parlor. "Please, call me Rebecca. I don't get many visitors. Not yet, anyway. We've only been here like ten days. Well, more like two weeks. We're just moving in."

"Thank you, Rebecca. You're everythin' Si told me you were."

"Si?" Rebecca stopped and turned to look at the woman standing in her parlor.

"It's what we call "the man on the horse" when we ain't callin' him late to dinner," Diana said, smiling.

"Please sit," Rebecca said, motioning to the sofa. "His name is Si? I didn't know. He didn't say."

"He didn't tell you his name? What? He was keepin' it secret? What's wrong with that man?"

"I asked him not to tell me. It's my fault."

"You asked him not to?"

Rebecca nodded. "It was complicated. My life…"

"I can see that."

"Did he say anything else? You know he brought us over the mountain. My son was really taken with him. We all were. Jed asks about him every day. He asks if the big man on the big red horse is going to come to see him." Rebecca smiled. "He's a really a good cook. Did you know that?"

"I didn't." Diana looked about the room.

"You have business with my husband? Most people go to the court to speak with him."

"I was told that he might be here, so I came here."

"You said you came a long way?"

"Sage Creek. Maybe a hundred miles. Started yesterday."

"That's a long, long way. Your business must be very important."

"It is. I'm tryin' to save someone's life."

"Would you like to set your guns down? Did you notice I didn't offer to take them? Si was very careful with his weapons. It was like a fetish. I got a lecture more than once on empty chambers in rifles and always in a Colt. He said 'the hammer must sit on an empty chamber.' Did you know he carried a ten dollar bill in that empty chamber? He was very persuasive." Rebecca paused. "You could set them on the table if you like or the floor."

"Thank you. The Stocktons are very insistent about how they care for their rifles and SAA Colts. It'd make you sick how careful they are at not bein' careful, all at the same time."

"No. I don't think so. Si was very persuasive and very insistent."

"I'll bet he was."

"You really must be tired."

"You got that, sister."

Fidgeting and looking out the window, Rebecca said, "When Bill gets here, I'll go out and ask him to speak with you as soon as he can. I don't know if he will. I'm finding that sometimes he's a little short, a little bit hard to get along with when he gets home. I'm just learning that. You know, I hadn't seen him for two years. We're just getting back together. He came West when he was appointed to be a judge."

340

Diana followed her gaze. Jed and his sister were playing tag under the trees out front. "Thank you, Rebecca. I don't mean to cause you any grief. But this really can't wait. I'll be out of your hair as soon as I can. It won't take long, I assure you. You've been so kind. I feel I am imposin', really I do."

"Oh, no. I am glad to meet you. Meeting Si was remarkable. You are most welcome and you're not imposing at all."

Jed suddenly appeared at her elbow, looking up at her with big brown eyes and a shy smile. "Ma'am," he said. "Is the big man on the big horse coming to see me?"

"I think he is. He told me he was. That was about a week ago. So I'm thinkin' yes. Pretty soon."

"Really?"

"Really."

"He won't have trouble remembering me, will he?"

"Not at all."

The Judge made it home forty minutes later, stopping the buggy in front of the house. Diana saw him pull up and noted that Jed looked up and then ran off. He did not run out to greet his father, nor did the girl. *Something is wrong here. If Josh even thought his father was comin' home, he'd be out on the porch waitin' for him.*

Rebecca went out to meet him., immediately telling him he had a guest with important, life-threatening business. He did not look pleased.

"Diana," she said, introducing her, "this is my husband, Judge Kilpatrick. Bill, this is Diana Stockton. Her brother-in-law brought me over the mountain. I will leave you two to your business. Please excuse me, Diana." She started to walk from the room.

"Rebecca, please stay."

"What?"

"Please stay. This concerns you."

"It does?"

"Yes, it does. Please have a seat."

"Who did you say you were?" The Judge asked, setting his briefcase down. He was tired. He'd put in a long day, granting and denying motions, listening to attorneys who didn't want to be told

341

'no', arguing the claims of irate people who felt wronged to begin with. It was clear he resented the intrusion.

"My name is Diana Stockton. That's my married name, sir." Her hands were in her lap under the linen cloth Rebecca had furnished her with the lemonade. The cloth covered Forest's SAA Colt. My maiden name is Stafford. You knew my sisters: Sally, Betsy, and Claire. Quite well, I understand."

Angrily, the Judge interrupted her. "I don't know what you are talking about. I want you to leave."

Diana stood and resumed her accusation. "About six weeks ago you killed 'em. Hanged them in Basin City."

"That's a bald-faced lie," he shouted. "I did no such thing!"

"Diana Stafford--that's my maiden name. Now do you know who I am?"

"Bill? What is she talking about?"

"Rebecca, ask your husband how much he was paid to kill my sisters. If he tells the truth, he'll tell you ten thousand dollars. Ten thousand dollars to kill my sisters."

Rebecca stepped forward. "Bill? What is she talking about? What--"

"Shut up, Rebecca. Get out of the way." Without hesitation the Judge sprang into motion, producing a single action Smith and Wesson from under his jacket. Thumbing the hammer back, bringing the pistol up, the cylinder rotating, the hammer fell on an empty chamber. The safety! He pulled the hammer back again, locking it in place, swearing as he did so, hurrying to bring it to bear on the slightly built woman standing in his living room holding an SAA Colt 44-40 pointed at his heart. His wife was screaming, her hands up trying to ward off what was happening in front of her.

"Shut up," he screamed at her. "Shut up! Shut up!" He stopped talking, his eyes focused on Diana.

Diana Stockton pulled the trigger on Syrus' SAA Colt 44-40. The hammer fell; it did not fall on an empty chamber. She simply missed. The percussion slammed against the walls.

The Judge hurried. He saw a second chance, an opening. He rushed it: pulling, yanking, firing. The single action Smith and Wesson revolver missed, too.

Diana squeezed the trigger a second time; the hammer fell and the lead projectile caught him in the throat. The next one caught him in the stomach; the third caught him in the chest. One after another. The force of the bullets pushed him back, slammed him into the wall, knocking him to the floor. He dropped the Smith and Wesson he held. He struggled to turn over and failed. He was dead, his heart no longer beating. Acidic, black powder smoke filled the room, burning the nose, the eyes. Rebecca was screaming. Diana sat down and immediately, by rote, reloaded Syrus' pistol.

In the confusion, in the cacophony of sound and fury, Rebecca stared at Diana in disbelief, her hands and fingers covering her face. Then taking her hands from her face, she looked at the twitching body of her husband. To her left she was aware that Diana had stood up, shoving the Colt behind her belt buckle, picking up her rifle, as yet unfired.

"Ma'am," Diana said to her, "I'm sorry. Your husband killed my sisters. All of 'em. He was paid to do it. Ten thousand dollars. We Stocktons do not tolerate that sort of horseshit. I'm not goin' to tolerate it. I'm goin' now. I'm sorry for this sorrow I brought you. Are you gonna be all right?"

"You just killed my husband and you ask me if I'm going to be all right? Are you insane?"

"Yes, Ma'am. Ma'am?"

Rebecca sat down in a hard kitchen chair and buried her face in her hands, blinking her eyes, trying to understand what had happened. Gunsmoke burned her nasal passages and the back of her throat. She thought of Jed and Emma outside. Certainly they'd heard the percussions exploding: bam, bam, bam, bam. Her ears were ringing. *They must not come in*, she thought. *They must not see their father. They must not.* She glanced at his body, the blood leaking from the holes that Diana Stockton had blasted into him. *Now what? What am I going to do?*

CHAPTER 42

The top of Little Mountain is flat, grassy; it slopes gently, mile upon mile, west toward the big canyon and the Big Horn River that winds through the bottom of it. High, where the turkey buzzard catches the updrafts and endlessly circles hunting the dead, it is a mere fifty miles from Basin City and the county courthouse, the jail, and the small office where Sheriff Jason Gilson kept his Winchester shotguns hanging on the wall. But fifty miles distance is somewhat inaccurate if you're riding a horse. That conveyance requires a rider to take the winding trail off the mountain, then go through the bentonite hills, the nameless creeks, Sheep Mountain and, of course, deal with the river that bends back and forth on itself. It's a trip that cannot be taken without addressing the land whose design was not meant for ease of travel or for hearts that cannot be broken. In truth, forget about the turkey buzzards drifting in the sky; the trip exceeds fifty miles, easily doubling itself.

From Little Mountain, the three brothers rode steadily south, keeping on the east side of the river, taking care to preserve their horses. A well-rested, a well-preserved, a well-maintained horse can carry its rider out of danger at a moment's notice; it can also get him to his destination. Taking care of one's horse is a dead-on requirement, a prerequisite akin to breathing, sleeping, eating, staying warm in the winter. One noted reason is that walking will never do for a man with a pair of boots with two inch underslung heels and a pointed toe. For another: escaping danger and staying alive depends on a ready horse, a steady horse, one that can carry its rider out of harm's way, one that can perform immediately, without hesitation, without doubt, and with confidence. Added to this dynamic is yet another: a horse has to eat, has to drink, needs rest. A horse is a living animal subject to the vicissitudes of all flesh. Lastly, the impending death of a judge, a sheriff, and his deputy doesn't require a defined hour and minute. It merely requires a finality, an ending. Justice requires it. Retribution demands it.

Late in the evening of the third day, they made their way

down the long hills toward the Cardston Ferry landing situated at the east end of C Street in Basin City. They rode onto the front yard hardpack of the two story Kilpatrick house the next day at 9:30 a.m. No one was about, yet the front door to the house was open, as were the barn doors. Chickens, clucking in the heat, were pecking at the ground in front; some were lying in the dust, fluffing it up into a storm. Several magpies were quarreling in the cottonwoods overhead arguing over who got the chicken eggs.

Riles stepped down from the Buckskin and handed the reins to Forest. "Here," he said. "I'll check the barn." He starting walking toward it; the dog followed him, then trotted past him to investigate the open door and the shadows within. The mule stood in the yard behind the Buckskin, one hind foot off the ground, his head down, resting.

Syrus hesitated, surveyed the homestead, then stepped down, and handed the reins of the roan stud to Forest. Seeing no one, he walked along the white picket fence. An overheated hen scurried out of the way. Seeing no one, he opened the gate and proceeded up the walkway to the open door, flipping the loop off the hammer of his SAA Colt. Before getting on the ferry to cross the river, he'd filled the empty chamber, remembering to do so when they paid the ferryman for passage across the river. Something, everything made him nervous.

In the heat, he walked up the walk, leery, if not fearful, of what he might find. Through the open door he could smell coffee boiling. He overheard the low voices of two children giggling. He peered inside. The living room was a mess; he noted papers strewn all over the dinner table, several stacks on the floor. Someone had been looking for something. He wondered what. A thought ran through his mind that the Judge might be home, that the mess was his. It looked like unfinished business. He listened for a male voice, wondering if things were going to blow up now that he was standing there. He wondered whether there was any way to let the woman down easy and protect the tender kids. There wasn't. He knew it; he'd reviewed the matter a dozen times.

He knocked loudly.

A four year old face appeared through the kitchen door to see who was there. The face lit up in recognition. The boy, gleefully laughing, ran across the floor to the doorway, grabbed him by the leg, and hugged him. Syrus ruffled his hair.

"How you doin', boy?" he said.

"I'm good," the boy answered. "She said you'd come to see me."

"She?"

"That lady."

It was then he saw the blankets stacked on the floor, covering something. Two, three, maybe four of them hiding what looked like a body. It was a body. It didn't take a genius to figure that out.

"Mrs. Stockton," the boy said

A girl's face appeared in the kitchen doorway. She didn't move, watching him through big, round eyes. Behind her, her mother appeared, looking just as he remembered her. He wondered why the sight of her always left him breathless. *Damnedest thing*, he thought. *Why was that?*

Rebecca seemed to glide over the hard oak floor. She hugged him, holding him for a moment, clinging. Syrus returned the hug, patting her shoulder just as his mother had when they were kids. "Rebecca," he asked, "is that....? On the floor there?"

"Yes it is. I covered him up in those blankets."

"How...how did that happen?"

"A woman."

"A woman?"

"Who?"

"She said her name was Diana Stockton. She said she knew you."

"Oh, no," Syrus said. "Wait a minute, will you?" He released her. Syrus stepped to the front door and waved to his brothers, getting their attention.

"Where is she? Is she here?" Syrus asked Rebecca.

"No. She left."

"When?"

"Yesterday. In the evening. She was very, very angry. And she was very tired. She wouldn't stay even for a moment."

"I'll bet. Do you know where she went?"

346

"No."

"Did she...?" He tried to find the proper word.

"Yes, she did. Not like you think. It wasn't like she came inside and she shot him dead. Bill...came inside. Yes. And I introduced them. Diana said I should stay. Bill started shooting at her."

Rebecca shook her head, staring at the blankets. "At first, I covered him with a table cloth. I didn't want...., then blankets, as you can see. He's too heavy for me to lift."

Forest and Riles came to the doorway. Syrus pointed to the body of the Judge hidden under the blankets. He paused. "Yeah, Riles, it's horseshit and gunsmoke and there's nothin' you can do 'bout it." He nodded and turned his attention to the woman.

"Rebecca, these are my brothers. This is Far and Riles." Syrus interrupted himself. "Listen," he said to them, "Diana was here yesterday evening. She shot the Judge." Syrus glanced at Rebecca. She nodded her head in agreement. "I've asked and she doesn't know where Diana is. That can't be good. We're gonna have to find her before she gets herself in trouble."

Riles stepped farther into the room, looked at the blankets covering the body and studied it; then he looked at Rebecca.

"Ma'am," he said. Rebecca turned to him when he spoke to her. Riles touched the brim of his hat. "Ma'am," he said again. "Do you want us to take care of this? Not wanting to sound indelicate but in this heat he's gonna ripen fast. You don't have much time. In fact you don't have any time at all."

"You mean my husband? How... what do you have in mind?" she asked.

"The quickest is the river," he said. "It's close."

"The river? What do you mean, the river?"

"Yes, Ma'am. Haul his body to where it's deep, tie a large rock to it and sink it."

Inititally the thought troubled her. She hesitated, then nodded. "You mean drop him in it. Yes? Oh, I don't know. He's a judge. Doesn't he get a funeral? I suppose that would be all right in this heat but it doesn't seem right. No one knows. He has parents, two brothers. So far I have told no one at all. No one knows.

347

Shouldn't I? Truthfully, I don't know what to do." She hesitated again and looked at Riles, giving him an opportunity to respond.

Riles Stockton nodded. "Ma'am," he said, "It probably ain't all right but we ain't got the time to dig a grave what with Diana runnin' around shootin' folks. We ain't really inclined to do that anyway."

"Yes. I can see that. But I'm really not sure what to do right now."

"Well, it's decision time," Forest said. "It's hotter than hell outside. Inside, too, for that matter. He's gonna be ripe soon. If we don't do somethin', you're gonna have a pile of maggots in your livin' room. He's gonna be stinkin', so you need to figure it out and be quick about it. We ain't gonna stick him in the ground. It's too much work. We'll haul it out to the barn if you like. We could drop him in the river with a rock tied to his body to keep him down. If you want, we'll leave him right where he is. I advise against that."

"Ma'am?" Riles said. "If I was you, I'd get them yonkers out of the room. Might not look too pretty. Up to you."

"Riles," she paused, her eyes watering. "I know what he did. I know why you're all here."

"Ma'am, he's still your husband. He's these kid's father. That's why I asked."

"I know. You're a gentlemen."

"Ma'am, no one has ever called me that. You'd be the first."

"All right, all right." she said. "Thank you." She glanced at the boy. "In the kitchen, Jed. Right now. Emma, take your brother. In the kitchen, both of you. Finish the dishes. Come on, let's go. Hurry." She turned to the three men. "All right," she said. "It's the river."

After the living room was vacated, Riles pulled the blankets off the corpse. Syrus grabbed the feet and Riles took hold of the back of the corpse's jacket collar. Between the two of them they carried the body outside, down the walkway to where the horses were tied.

The smell of death bothered the horses; they tried to get away from it. Syrus grabbed the reins to the roan. The roan stopped trying to bail out.

"Here," Syrus said to Riles. "Hold him. If you have to, throw somethin' over his head."

348

Riles grabbed the horse by the ears and held him down. Syrus lifted the corpse over the saddle. "We'll need a rock, somethin' heavy, and a rope," Forest said.

"Take a look by the barn door," Riles said. "There's a length of rope just inside."

Syrus stepped up into the saddle. Forest handed him both reins. "Let's get this done," Syrus said.

It was a water burial. They used a rope tied to an old grindstone, tied to the body, wrapped around his waist. Syrus released him in the middle of the river, the current taking him down; the rock took him under.

"Now what?" Forest said to Riles. "The judge is taken care of, bless her heart. Wonder where she left Pistol. Bet that's a story worth hearin'."

"Now, we find Diana, before she gets herself into trouble," Syrus said.

Riles smiled. "Yep," he said. "No small thing that Diana gets her tail twisted in a knot."

"Don't think she went far," Syrus pointed out. "Not with the Sheriff in town."

They walked back to the house, leading the roan, not saying anything. Nothing needed to be said. The job was done; the judge was dead. They were ready to move on. As they arrived at the front gate to the picket fence, Rebecca came outside and down the walk, meeting them as they stood together.

"While you were gone I prepared something for you to eat," she said.

"Ma'am, we really...."

"I insist," she said. "You need to eat."

No one moved. "Ma'am, we really...," Riles started again.

"I insist," she said again. "You've actually helped me. I made a mistake coming here."

Forest replied. "All right," he said. "I'll eat. I'm hungry. Diana can wait another fifteen minutes. What's she gonna do? Shoot some poor soul?"

"Thank you," she said. "I didn't know. How could I? I only just arrived. But Bill...the Judge..he had changed. I was afraid of him.

349

We all were." She stopped and looked at the men waiting. "I'm sorry to go on about my troubles," she said. "I just don't want you to go. Please come inside. You can wash at the kitchen sink. There's a towel there. Everything's prepared. Just wash up and sit. Dig in. It's not much. But it's something to tide you over'."

"Thank you," Forest said. "I'm tellin' you we can make good use of it. Been eatin' Si's cookin'."

"Si? Oh, but he's a very good cook."

"Don't be tellin' him. Won't be able to live with him."

"Oh, I already have...told him." She looked at Syrus.

"Damn the luck," Forest said.

Riles laughed. "Nice try, Far."

The three men followed Rebecca inside. Forest and Syrus washed up and sat at the table. They joined Jed and Emma who were already eating mashed potatoes and gravy, some corn on the cob, and green beans: garden produce that someone else had planted.

When Riles started washing his hands in the kitchen, Rebecca approached him. She was holding a clean towel. "May, I speak with you?" she asked. "You'll think this is crazy. Please don't think ill of me. Please?"

"Like that'll be hard. Si says you're a regular angel, Ma'am. My pleasure to be of assistance. What can I do for you?"

"You people are all the same. Ma'am this, ma'am that. My name is Rebecca. It's always been Rebecca. It's never been "Ma'am." Please. Just call me Rebecca."

Riles looked at her, dipped his hands in the lukewarm water, paused, and said, "Rebecca, then. How's that?"

"Thank you."

"You're welcome."

"I want to ask you a favor. It won't make any sense at all. But I need you to do it, please."

"Ma'am?"

She looked at him and pursed her lips. "I need you to put this in Si's saddle bag."

She handed him a flat package wrapped in a cotton cloth. He took it, looking at her.

"Feels like a plate," Riles said.

"It is a plate. Please? Do this for me. If you don't, I'll never see him again. If you do, I might. I don't know. Maybe. I'd like to."

Riles smiled. "Sounds magical. Is it a magical plate?"

"In a manner of speaking. Apparently, he's partial to plates-- the last plate."

Riles looked at Rebecca quizzically. He lifted his right hand. "All right, don't explain it. I'd probably never get it anyways." he said. "But you don't have to worry about Si none, Rebecca. He ain't gonna go nowhere."

"Thank you. I hope you're right. It's so awkward. Your sister-in-law killed my husband. What he did isn't tolerable." She paused. "Si has been the only good thing that's happened to me and it ain't supposed to be that way. He refused to let me, Jed, and Emma die on the mountain. He saved our lives."

"You the lavender girl?"

She smiled. "He's really taken with that scent, isn't he?"

Riles nodded. "Mother liked lavender herself. She said 'angels wear lavender.' We believed her. Si, in all honesty, probably thought it was a flower or somethin'."

Turning, he put his hat on, took the package in hand, and walked through the kitchen to the front door and outside.

He wasn't gone long. Rebecca sat down at the table, but she wasn't eating. Riles returned, smiled at her.

"Well," he said, "did you leave anythin' for me? I'm so hungry my belly done thinks someone cut my throat."

Jedediah laughed. "And you could eat a horse and chase the rider right up the creek."

"How did you know, buddy? Someone tell you?"

Jedediah said, "I just know. I heard that before."

"Someone tellin' my secrets."

"Yes, I think so."

Syrus looked at Rebecca, addressing her slowly. "Ma'am," he said. "I'm sorry to make this all business. But, we're in a time bind of sorts and I've got no choice." She was looking directly at him. He, then turned to Riles. "Listen, Riles," he said. "I gotta go. I have a thing or two I gotta take care of in Basin City. Gotta speak to the Sheriff, tell him a sad story or two; explain my disappointment, how bad it makes me feel. Maybe I'll even get him to cry. You never know. It'd be nice if he'd take responsibility for what he's done."

Riles nodded. "All right. Think you need some help?"

"Nah, I got this handled. Doubt he's expectin' me."

"Suit yourself. We'll meet you on the east side of the river, at the Cardston Ferry landing. When do you think we'll see you?" Riles asked.

"Sometime 'bout noon. Say two o'clock at the latest. That work for you?" Syrus asked. "It could be earlier."

"We should be there before you. We'll be leavin' here soon ourselves. Doubt your business is gonna take long. We'll be movin' right along."

Syrus Stockton turned to Rebecca. He said, "Thank you so much for the vittles. I'd say they was prime. Thank ye kindly."

He turned his attention back to his brother. "Riles," he said, "if you and Far could look for Diana, that would be damn straight of you. I'm thinkin' Diana'll be lookin' for another horse. I'll check at the livery on my way through town. No doubt it'll take a couple of days for that one she was ridin' to rest up; especially she came all the way from Sage Creek."

Riles raised his water glass. "To the good life, Si," he said. "And may your kids be born stark naked, wearin' nothin' but their birthday suit."

"I sure as hell hope so."

CHAPTER 43

Syrus Stockton rode the roan stud past the pillars of rock that announced the southern edges of Basin City. The long-legged roan didn't slow his gait, taking long strides that ate distance quickly. The horse and rider passed the stone yard on the rider's left, surrounded by a white picket fence on all sides. Crosses, and wooden and stone monuments marked the final resting place of a few of the county's early citizens, some young, some old.

The cemetery was new. There were not very many occupants, for folks hadn't been there long. Some of them had just taken up residence. The rider noted the three new white crosses of the Stafford girls: first Sally, then Betsy, and finally Claire. At the front of each cross was heaped an oblong mound of fresh loam. Deep in the earth their bodies lay by side, five foot six inches down, buried under rocks, sand, and sod. Each casket lay protected from the elements, vermin, but not time. Soon the pine wood would rot and the casket would cave in under the weight of earth and stone.

The roan didn't stop; neither he nor his rider gave the newly honored residents any notice. The roan's progress was steady, carrying the rider north up Fourth Street. Stopping at the cemetery wasn't what the rider had in mind.

Syrus Stockton did stop at the Rilson Livery Stable, stepped down, and stretched. Upon meeting the liveryman, he asked, "Got any MT horses standin' around lookin' lonely?"

The liveryman laughed. "Matter of fact, I do," he said. "Lady left him with me yesterday. Rented another. That horse of hers was beat into the ground. Rode hard. I gave him some oats, and rubbed him down. He's been standin' in the shade since, mindin' his own business."

"Well, I'll be damned," Syrus said. "Imagine that. The MT horse would be mine. I'd like to take him with me. You don't mind? What do I owe you? I'd like to pay you."

"Not much. You know the lady that left him here?"

"I do, my sister-in-law."

"Good. I'll throw her saddle back on that horse she was ridin'. She'd put it on the horse she rented from me. The Sheriff brought the rented horse back to me yesterday. Same saddle. That suit you?"

"Damn straight, it suits me. Thank you kindly."

Once finished with the livery, Syrus rode north, leading the bay gelding. He followed Fourth Street north on the right hand side, noting the territorial post office, the flag flying in the breeze above the doorway. Next was Morgans Tack with a MacLellen saddle out front sitting on a saddle stand, Maggies Café with its row of blue and yellow petunias and, lastly, the Basin City River Bar and Hotel. At the intersection of Fourth and C Street, he pulled the roan horse to a stop. For a moment, he stared west, looking down C Street at the County Courthouse.

Finally, he said, "Let's go, horse, I think we're in the right place, least we're where the right place led us to be." *What I'm wonderin' is where that woman Diana can be. Ain't like her to be hotfootin' it.* Try as he may he couldn't imagine what Diana would be doing without a horse.

Nudging the roan forward, he turned west on C, heading toward the three story brick court house and the one level Sheriff's Office sitting behind it on the north. Stopping in front of the building labeled County Sheriff, he noted two horses tied to a hitching rail: one, a grey, the other, a bay. Big horses, they both stood seventeen hands at the shoulder. They'd been tied to the rail a while. The earth was torn up where they'd stomped around. Horse turds were strewn about.

Stretching, Si removed his Stetson, scratched his thinning scalp, then reseated his hat. It was easy to imagine where the scaffold had stood. Heavy wood planking scarred the earth where the four by fours had borne the weight of the men and the three girls atop the scaffold. The street itself was scarred deeply. It would be years before those ruts disappeared.

Anger surged through him. Syrus climbed down, patting the tall roan on the shoulder, dropping the reins. He left him ground hitched, the bay's lead rope tied to the back of his saddle. He walked toward the open door. His right hand casually, yet deliberately,

354

brushed the leather latch string off the hammer of the SAA Colt 45. He lifted it, letting it settle easily back into the holster.

He carried the Peacemaker on his right hip, his calloused palm an easy reach to the butt. Another Peacemaker, a 44-40, was stuck in his waistband. As he moved, the ching, ching, ching of his spurs dragging across the hardpack sounded musical amid the hum of flies, honey bees, and grasshoppers. He stepped up on the first wooden step; the jingle bobs played a crazy, incoherent tune comprised of one single note. Climbing the two steps, he walked through the open door, crossing the threshold into the ill-lit office.

Four men were inside: two seated, two standing, all looking at him. As had been his custom ever since being elected, Sheriff Gilson sat behind his desk, idly drumming his fingers, every once in a while fiddling with a used pencil. Lloyd Canker rested his lanky frame in a tall high-back chair to Gilson's right. He was playing with a three inch stub of a Rally cigar, listening to the conversation. Behind Gilson, on the wall was fastened an oak rack for rifles and shotguns. The other two individuals were standing in front of the Sheriff's desk, their arms folded across their chests. They'd been laughing, talking among themselves. Lloyd deliberately scratched a diamond tipped match on his pant leg. It lit up, bursting into a smokeless flame which he immediately applied to his short, mostly used-up, cigar. Considering Syrus' entrance, he blew cigar smoke into the still air, momentarily eying him. It was going to be a long, hot one. Outside a lone magpie flew across the street.

"Gents," Syrus said, interrupting their conversation, acknowledging their presence with his eyes and a nod of the head. All four turned to consider his voice and watched curiously as Syrus surveyed the room, mentally noting where everyone was standing, sitting, and what they were otherwise doing.

The man closest to Syrus returned his greeting with a nod. Immediately, as if on cue, he turned his attention back to the Sheriff and said, "Jason, looks like you got yourself some law business. Better let you get to it. Can't waste no more time on fish stories, even if they are true. Friday, then?"

"Joe," the Sheriff said, acknowledging the man's comments, "sounds good." He remained sitting at his desk, casually studying the person of Syrus Stockton, noting the SAA Colt stuck in his waistband, the SAA Colt on his hip. It was not unusual for a man to be carrying them both. Neither pistol was odd or out of place. Everyone he knew had one or two. For a second his gaze stuck on the stranger's holster. An alarm sounded dully in the Sheriff's memory but it didn't register: not clearly, not cleanly. However, an unformed thought lingered as he casually noted the stranger's hammer latch. It wasn't draped over the hammer. Instead it hung off to the side, out of the way.

An accident. Perhaps. Perhaps it wasn't. Wonder if this fellow knows. The Sheriff noticed the stranger's index finger on his right hand. It was tapping the top of his gun belt that supported the holster. An alarm was ringing. *Hammer loop? What about it? It's fallen off the hammer. Or this fellow removed it deliberately! Why would he do that? Did it matter? Getting a little jumpy, aren't we?* Gilson noted the quiet patience permeating the stranger's demeanor. It seemed as if he hadn't a care in the entire world. At the same time he seemed alert. It was the eyes. Another bell was sounding in the back of his head. *What?* he asked himself. *Something.* Gilson asked himself what person was ever patient about wanting to talk to him? *Somethin' odd here. It's nothin'. Already it's been a long day and it's nearly noon. Gettin' hot, is what it is.*

Turning to the departing visitors, Gilson said, "Say boys, thanks for stoppin' by. And okay, sure. Let me take care of this gent. Looks like he came a ways."

Odd, the picture that came to the Sheriff's mind right then. It was the image of a blind rattler, smelling the air, tasting it with his tongue, listening, holding itself still, poised. The snake was patiently waiting,without a care in the world. *Ah shit,* the Sheriff thought. The alarm was really sounding now, so loud he could no longer ignore it. *What have I got here?* Gilson questioned.

The second man who'd been talking with the Sheriff when Syrus stepped inside, glanced at Syrus. He said to him, "We're just talkin'," he explained. "Nothin' important goin' on today. I'm sure these boys can help you. Let me get out of the way. Ain't got no business here anyways." He stepped to Syrus' left. His companion moved toward the door that Syrus had just walked through. He smiled.

356

"Surely," Syrus said to him. "You're fine. I ain't in no hurry. Appreciate the courtesy. What I got won't take long."

It all seemed an eye blink to Syrus. The Sheriff's visitors were outside, standing together in front of the small wooden porch, one talking to the other. Neither in a hurry. "Ain't rained lately," the first one said. "Drier than hell, that's what it is. Where you goin'? Thought I'd have a coffee. Wanna join me?"

"Sure."

The Sheriff interrupted Syrus' thoughts, causing him to turn his attention to the two law officers that worked for Big Horn County. "How may I help you?" Gilson said pleasantly, his attention brought to bear on the square shouldered Syrus, whose index finger was still rap-tapping the top of the leather belt that supported his holster.

"Sure," Syrus said. "I was thinkin' I 'bout come full circle. You two are the last on my 'to do' list."

"Glad we can help. What do you need?" The Sheriff was studying Syrus once again, wondering what, if anything, he was missing. *Something? But what?*

"You know what? Listen, let me introduce myself. I'm your personal grim reaper and I've come for you both. I've come to punch your tickets to the next life," Syrus said, his index finger tapping softly, a staccato beat of which the Sheriff was acutely aware.

"What?" Gilson said, incredulous. "What?" The alarm in his head was sounding now, gaining volume. It was thunderous. Gilson sat up, leaning forward in his chair, his hands resting on top of his desk. "Grim Reaper? What are you talking about?"

"You heard me, Sheriff," Syrus interrupted him. "I ain't speakin' French. You're the two SOBs that hung the Stafford girls. Killed poor Betsy, her sisters Sal, and Claire. Right outside, I'm told. A few minutes ago I rode past where they're restin'. Saw those new white crosses. Quite nice. It'd been all right 'cept they shouldn't be dead. Flowers. That'd be a nice touch. They needs someone to put some flowers on their graves. Maybe get a nice stone monument with their names carved into the rock. Some Desert Roses would be nice, to my way of thinkin'."

Gilson didn't feel like he needed to accommodate this

357

stranger. This was twice in the last day. Suddenly he was angry, challenged. "What is it you want?" he demanded.

"Justice," Syrus said. "A smatterin' of justice."

"Justice? What?"

"You know what I mean. You and your Deputy killed those girls. Kids. I mostly grew up with them."

Gilson started to justify himself. "Mister, that was a legal hangin'. I had a signed Order. 'Sides, it ain't none of your damn business. We was followin' the order of the Court. Nothin' more. Wish I could have done somethin'. I really do. Had no choice. It was conducted under the auspices of the U.S. Marshal's Office. All legal, all proper."

Syrus smiled. "Those U.S. Deputy Marshals? All four of 'em? Might interest you to know they're dead. The Judge is dead, too. Told you, you're last on my list."

"What? They're what?" The Sheriff asked, his voice rising in pitch, not believing what he was hearing.

"You hard of hearin', Sheriff? Every one of them deputies is dead. Dead. Damn straight. Top to bottom and sideways. Other'n those four, you and Lloyd here, you're all that's left on my list of bastards that truly shouldn't be alive. What you did wasn't right. You know that. I come for you. The scale has to be balanced. The dead need to rest in peace. They ain't restin' quite yet. They're fixin' to, soon as you two are burnin' in hell."

"Ah, shit," the Deputy Sheriff Lloyd Canker said as it dawned on him that this fellow was a little crazy. "Who the hell do you think you are?" Lloyd started to stand, coming to his feet. He'd heard enough. Pushing himself out of his chair, his right hand reached for the pistol sitting in the holster tied high on his right hip.

Syrus' right hand moved, a blur: his actions not delayed by thinking, not hindered by some convoluted doctrine of right and wrong. For Syrus Stockton things were figured out in transition lightning streaks. His right hand was instantly full of an SAA Colt 45 and he shot Lloyd Canker through the upper ribs, left hand side. The sheer force of the slug shoved Lloyd backwards and up against the wall. Lloyd's fingers were stretching for the shotgun rack. His fingers never got that far. The second "slow moving" slug slammed into his sternum, twisting him about and into a warm heap of flesh on the dirty floor.

The Sheriff was so surprised that he didn't move. The exchange was completely over and he was still in his chair, his hands on top of his desk; Lloyd Canker was dead on the floor. Jason Gilson started to stand. His right hand came up in an effort to stop Syrus from shooting across his desk. "Stop," he cried. "Stop. Stop."

Syrus didn't stop; he shot him anyway, the first slug passing through the Sheriff's right lung. The officer never got his Colt out of the holster. He was falling back as the second shot tore though his abdomen. Syrus pulled the Colt SAA from his waistband, cognizant of the Sheriff trying to reach for the firearm he'd hung on the wall, probably hoping for the ten gauge Greener. It was too far away.

"You're too late, Sheriff. Both you and Lloyd." Syrus spoke softly, his ears ringing from the noise. "You two did the killin'." Deliberately, Syrus took aim and shot Sheriff Jason Gilson through the skull, leaving his body jerking spasmodically on the hardwood floor. "You worthless son of a bitch," Syrus said, enunciating each syllable with care as he moved around the desk for a better look at the Sheriff's body lying on the floor. "You knew better. Both of you did," Syrus said. "Them girls didn't deserve what they got from you. They was entitled to a lot more. Like a helpin' hand. You ought to be ashamed." Syrus grew silent. Gilson was dead.

The two men outside had backed out into the street, shocked and surprised. Syrus filled the door frame, a pistol in each hand, studying them. They were continuing to back up. "I ain't got nothin' agin' you two," Syrus said. "But you wanna join in, feel free. Pull those hog legs.You know what I have in mind. If'n that's your decision, I'll vote on it. You can go to shootin'."

The individual standing farthest from Syrus replied immediately, "Not me," he said. "Deal me out."

The remaining fellow hadn't moved. He was looking back at Syrus. He glanced through the doorway at Lloyd's warm, cooling body, though he couldn't see him well, then at Gilson. He spoke slowly in a measured tone. "What you did, had to be done. Someone had to do it. You ain't got no complaint from me."

"I ain't, huh?" Syrus asked.

"No. You ain't."

Someone, a voice locked in a cell in the back, yelled. "What the hell's goin' on out there?"

"Nothin'," Syrus answered. "Nothin' is goin' on." To the man standing in the street, he said, "You'll understand I ain't turnin' my back on you?"

"I understand perfectly."

"Best you two be movin' along."

"Much obliged," the man last to speak said, nodding, staring at Syrus. His companion turned away; inadvertently the wind took his hat. A twisting gust caught it. He reached to pick it up. The wind grabbed it again. He started running after it, his hat rolling on the street in front of him. He was nervous, unsure of whether Syrus would shoot him in the back. Each step came more quickly than the last. The direct rays of the morning sun struck him in the eyes, causing him to squint, his white forehead glaring in the bright sunlight.

"They'll come after you. You gotta know that," the remaining witness said without moving.

"People will die," Syrus observed. "That ain't changed. You leavin' or stayin'?"

"That's my bay horse," he said, pointing at the horse tied to the hitching post next to the grey. "I ain't leavin' without him."

"There he is."

"You'd better get, yourself," he said starting toward the hitching rail. "This place is gonna be full of righteous folks right soon. They might not be understandin'."

"Reckon so," Syrus replied.

The man with whom Syrus spoke walked past the doorway to the hitching rail and retrieved the bay, pulling himself up into the saddle. Turning the horse toward C Street, he stopped in front of Syrus, looked at him, shook his head. "I didn't think anyone would do what needed to be done. I thought they'd got away with it. You didn't. I'm surprised. Best to you." He touched the bay with his spurs, rode to C Street, and turned west.

Syrus glanced down the street. The first man had made it all the way to the intersection, not looking back, not daring to look back.

360

From the Sheriff's Office doorway, Syrus noted that now only one horse was tied to the hitching rail: the grey. The roan and the bay were still standing ground hitched right where he'd left them, Diana's saddle horse beside the roan. He wondered where she was.

Turning, he went inside, removed the keys to the cells from the handmade nail driven into the wall behind Sheriff Gilson's desk. He glanced at the Sheriff's twitching body and shook his head.

"You're a worthless piece of shit," he said to the body. "All you had to do was let them girls go. That's all you had to do. Worthless. But you know that."

The Sheriff had long since stopped breathing; a death rattle formed in his throat and hissed out into the room. Si nodded, then walked down the dark corridor toward the three cells. He was a little more than surprised to find Diana standing in the middle of the first cell.

"Ma'am," he said. "Good to see you."

"Si," she said and nothing more.

Syrus Stockton opened the door to her cell. She quickly came out without invitation and disappeared down the hall. With the turn of a key, Syrus opened the other two doors, swinging them wide, talking as he turned the key.

"I'm lettin' you boys go," he said, "'cause the Sheriff ain't gonna come back here to help y'all none. Ain't bringin' y'all no vittles. No water to drink. You'd probably starve to death, you stay around here. But stay if you feel you must. I don't give a damn."

"What did you do?"

"Nothin'."

"Who was shot?" The man who asked was in the center cell that had housed the Stafford girls.

"Nobody."

After opening the iron doors, Syrus walked back down the corridor and into the outer portion of the Sheriff's office, his spurs going ching, ching, ching, the jingle bobs sounding a crazy musical tune as he walked. As he made his way to the open door, the Mexican rowels bit into the ragged hardwood floor. Without slowing, he walked through the doorway and onto the graveled street and the hardpack that kept the cheat grass from taking hold and growing.

361

When he came out he found Diana sitting on the bay saddle horse, the reins in hand, waiting. He noted his rifle in the boot. She wore a pistol belt around her waist.

Taking up the reins to the roan, he pulled him around by his bridle, mounting in one slick well-practiced motion. In the bright mid-morning air he walked the stud down the street, east toward the river, followed by Diana on his left. He saw no one else. No one had yet come to investigate. Somewhere to his right, a blacksmith was pounding a piece of iron; a mother yelled at her son to "straighten up."

Reaching the river's edge, they momentarily waited for the Cardston ferry to make it back from across the river. To insure he wasn't forgotten, he waved at the ferryman yet on the other side, letting him know he was a customer: waiting. When the ferryman arrived, Syrus Stockman stepped down and walked the roan aboard, followed by Diana. He gave the man a couple of dimes, paying for the roan and Diana's horse. The ferryman grabbed the pull rope and started the strong arm routine that carried his patrons to the east side of the Big Horn River.

"You see that?" the ferryman said to him.

"See what?" Si asked.

"Catfish. Jumped clear outta the water. Big sucker."

"Naw, I didn't see it. Musta been somethin'."

"It was. Two or three pounder, if it was an ounce. You two havin' a good day?" the ferryman asked.

"Not bad," Syrus responded.

As if in response to the question, Syrus looked down C Street toward the County Court House. There was still no activity. He assumed the bodies had not been discovered yet. *Oh well,* he thought. *Sooner or later.* Diana was looking toward Basin City as well.

Syrus looked away, across the river. He couldn't help himself. He was thinking about lavender: how it smelled, how it felt to have a nose full of the scent, how it felt standing near a woman wearing it. *Damn,* he thought, *I sure like her a lot. I reckon I need a woman wearin' lavender. Sure as hell make it easy to stay in one place for a long, long time. It sure would be nice to have Rebecca bakin' my beans. That would be some luck. I could use some of that luck. I surely could. What have I gotten myself into with*

362

all my righteous thinkin'? Lavender? He remembered what his mother said to him. "Sonny boy, Si," she said, "angels wear lavender."

"They sure do, Ma," he'd said.

Syrus glanced across the river at the diminishing shore line and up C Street. Without thinking, he reached into his shirt pocket for a Mississippi Crook. It was empty. *Damn it*, he thought. Moving to his saddlebags, he undid the latch, pulled the covering up and out of the way. He reached in, found the cigars, and brought out several, saving all but one for his shirt pocket. His fingers found something else. In a cloth? Wrapped tightly. *What?*

Using his fingers he felt around it, lifted it out where he could see it. Whatever it was, it was wrapped in a clean cotton cloth, over and over, neatly tucked in at the edges. *What the hell?* he thought. Carefully, he unwrapped it. It was a plate. Pure, smooth, excellent china. Nothing else.

"What's that?" Diana asked. "A plate? You carry a china plate in your saddlebag?" Her voice sounded incredulous. "Well, ain't you the proper one."

"I guess I do," Syrus said. "I didn't know I did."

"That cloth. Look at it. It's got somethin' writ' on it."

Syrus took the plate and set it inside his saddlebag; he held the cloth out where he could see all of one side of it. Sure enough, it did have a writing on it.

Out of the corner of his eye he glimpsed someone running south on Fourth Street. Syrus looked, wondering.

"Let me see that towel," Diana said. He handed it to her. She held it up to look at the writing. "Si, you wrote on this towel 'the last plate'? You needed to know that? Forgive me, but that's silly."

Syrus laughed. "I didn't write that. That ain't my plate. I ain't never seen it before."

Diana looked at him. "You got a girlfriend, don't you?"

"I didn't know that, either. Say, Dee, what was you doin' in that jail?"

"I don't wanna talk about it. I don't."

Syrus glanced at Diana. They were approaching the east side of the river. He thought of his brothers; they'd be on the east side waiting, looking for Diana. He looked at the towel, read the inscription: 'the last plate.' He thought about Rebecca and those two bright faced youngsters. He wondered where she was. His brothers would be surprised he had Diana, even if she wasn't saying much. He glanced back at the west side of the river, at the street going up a slight grade. The runner had disappeared. No one was visible now.

For a moment he studied the Pryor Mountains sitting in the white clouds, bracing themselves for another round of summer thunderstorms. He remembered Forest talking about seeing them for the first time. *What was that--three weeks ago?* He said it was almost as if the old mountains were speaking to him. *"Where the hell have you been?" they said. "Where the hell have you been? That's right, Si, where the hell have you been?"*

They'd almost made the east bank. Syrus looked again across the river. Still no one. He wondered. He hadn't thought Basin City to be such a slow moving, sleepy town. The words of Riles came tripping into mind. *"Horseshit and gunsmoke. Ain't nothin' I can do about it now."* And there wasn't.

364

CHAPTER 44

From the time Syrus Stockton entered Basin City from the south until he'd gotten on the Cardston Ferry and made the east side of the river, fifty-six minutes had elapsed. If anyone had seen him or noticed the horse he was riding, it wasn't something they remembered or talked about.

To Thomas Gentry it was an event he wished to forget. He'd spent the morning conversing with Jason Gilson and Lloyd Canker. Tired of fishing off the Cardston wharf, he and Jason had planned a fishing trip up Shell Canyon over four or five days, starting the coming Friday. In a millisecond, he found himself staring at the bodies of Jason and Lloyd. The man who'd taken their lives was staring at him and at Joe Johnson. It was clear to Gentry he'd seen enough. In fact, death was seared into his mind. From where he was standing he could see Lloyd's body in the corner of the office, Gilson lying on the floor beside him, a saddle tramp he'd never seen before standing over them, a pistol in either hand. The stranger's words, "They deserved better, Gilson," were stamped in his memory.

Rapid, haphazard thoughts ran through Gentry's mind like a locomotive with too much coal burning hot in the firebox. His difficulty was that the fireman was shoveling in more coal, more, and more coal. Someone, whoever it was, had shot the poor bastards right there in front of God, and everyone, including himself. *It was the damnedest thing*, he thought.

A sharp breeze, a wind devil had caught his hat, sending it flying. He ran after it. By the time he got fifty feet south on C Street chasing his hat, he began thinking of his involvement in this killing. The more he thought, the more he wondered what the man, a pistol in either hand looked like. He was having difficulty recalling him. *Oh my God*, he thought, *I'm losin' my mind.*

The more he thought about it, the more he realized it was better not to know. Another hundred yards and he no longer remembered if he'd even seen the slimly built man or if he'd even been there himself. It was becoming so vague, so hazy. "My God,"

365

he muttered. Maggies was open, so he stepped inside. Walking to the back, he sat down, his back to the door as well as to a wall. Greeting the waiter, he ordered some apple pie. He did not say another word. Each time he heard the door open, he jumped a little. But not a word crossed his lips. It was best not to know.

Joe Johnson knew what he saw. He knew what Tom Gentry saw. Neither one of them went fishing that weekend or for a dozen weekends that came after. Somethings were best not spoken. This? This was one of them. When asked, he did not deny being there or seeing the stranger step inside the Sheriff's office, touching the brim of his hat in greeting.

Later, questioned ad nauseum, Joe Johnson , the man who'd forked his bay horse from the rail in front of the Sheriff's office and left in a hurry, clearly explained what happened. *Never, never dodge trouble,* he told himself. And he didn't. On being questioned, he swore that the man who spoke with the Sheriff that morning was a thin man, wearing a long-sleeved, faded, red shirt, some sort of felt hat, probably a Stetson, that sat oddly on his head. He carried two pearl gripped pistols, tied down on the leg, probably Smith and Wessons.

"Looked it, anyway. Sorta like that feller Bill Hickok. And he rode a lean, grey horse, looked blooded, deep chest, tall. It was a big grey," he said again and again. "Sure as hell was." He marveled that no one talked to Tom Gentry. He, himself, never mentioned Tom's name.

CHAPTER 45

In August, Kane, Wyoming gets hot and muggy. It feels like a swamp. It can be bad that way. It has a fast moving river on the north, a slow river on the east, and a lot of standing water left by the big river winding back and forth in giant loops, leaving channels of stale water. The main event of the day is swatting the blood sucking mosquitoes. It's nearly impossible to be rid of them.

Sheriff Wesley Bufford didn't want to be a blood donor, didn't want to feel the muggy, oppressive heat, didn't want to be baked hot, watching the heat waves rising from the street. He'd been the elected sheriff of the town for two and one half years and had developed certain habits. On Tuesdays and Wednesdays, in the afternoon, a man needing a law officer could find him at the Shoshone Bar, in the northeast corner, sitting at a table, his back against the wall. It was something he liked doing. On those days in August, in the afternoon, no one snuck up on Wesley Bufford. Everyone knew where to find him: the Shoshone Bar. Inside it was cool, the walls well insulated, the back windows small, the front door most always closed.

At two in the afternoon, Rich Larson made his way to Wesley's table, performed his sitting down ritual, then deposited his large frame in the chair, groaning.

"What's goin' on, Sheriff?" he said. "Anythin' interestin'?. Done any serious fishin'?"

"News? Ask Billy. Bein' the bartender, he's in the know. He hears everythin'. It's mostly lies, but he knows. Nothin' escapes him."

Billy brought two mugs of beer to the table, set them down, foam running down the sides and onto the scored surface, then seated himself, taking a breath of smoky, stale air, letting it out.

"Ain't you drinkin', Billy?" Rich inquired.

"Workin'." he stated. "Too early."

"Well, Billy, tell us who died. Someone's got to have died and made the Kane news," Rich said, starting to build a cigarette, folding the paper around his left index finger. "Wanna smoke, Wes? You, Billy?"

Both declined by a shake of the head.

367

Billy pursed his lips. "Heard a rumor," he said. "Heard Gilson died. Heard that this mornin'. Fresh news. Straight from Basin City. Man said he read it in *The Rustler* newspaper."

"Gilson, the Sheriff Gilson?"

"That very one."

"I ain't heard that," Wesley said. "Didn't read it, either. Who told you? Bet it's a rumor. Believe me. This place ain't nothin' but a rumor mill."

"This mornin'. Few hours ago. Fellow from Basin City. Said it was in the paper."

"Natural causes?"

"If three 44 slugs is natural."

"Where did this happen?"

"Died in that little office of his, front of the jail, back of the court house."

"When?"

"Couple of days ago, I guess. I didn't see the paper."

"On a Monday?"

"Yeah, a Monday. Probably. I don't know."

"That don't seem likely, Rich. Not a Monday."

Rich shook his head. "There ain't no 'likely.' I told you boys their life expectancy would be short. Didn't I say it? I told you both, what, two weeks ago? Musta been the Stocktons. Who else? Those mountain boys are a mean bunch of bastards. Hate to say it, but I told you."

"Stocktons? Nobody seen no Stocktons. You just got 'em on the mind."

"They ain't gonna come over here and say, "Sheriff, I just killed the Sheriff in his office, sittin at his desk, in Basin City. They ain't stupid."

"Fellow said the paper described a skinny fellow ridin' a grey horse. That's who they say done it."

"Gilson had a grey. You sayin' he shot himself?"

"Could of, but he didn't. Shot three. Him and his deputy."

"Goodness. Both of 'em?" Wes exclaimed.

"I told you. Remember?" Rich said in a self-congratulatory

368

manner.

"His office? That's in the middle of town. There must of been a witness or two."

"Guess not.

"Well, there was surely someone in the jail. There's always someone in jail over a weekend."

"Nope. Nobody that weekend. Jail was empty. Doors wide open."

"Nobody?"

"Nope."

"That ain't all," Billy said. "With the Sheriff dead, folks went to get the Judge. See what to do. He ain't home. He still ain't home. Neither is his wife and two kids. He just brought them out from the east, you know. All of them are gone. House was locked up, if you can imagine lockin' a house up in the middle of the summer. Fellow said it was real strange."

Rich took another drag on his cigarette. "They's probably just took the weekend to get away. He likes to fish. A vacation. They'll show up in a day or two. Always do."

Rich Larson took another puff on his hand-rolled cigarette. "Anythin' strange 'bout it, Billy?"

"Yeah, well, no woman's clothes was in the closet. Nothin' a kid would wear, either. His fishin' pole was in the barn. So was his buggy, a little surrey, and a couple of horses. One had a brand from over there in Buffalo. It was a livery horse."

"That's odd, I guess."

"Nobody seen nothin'. That's what's odd. Judge leavin' town without sayin' anythin'. And that ain't all. Now, get this. The kitchen table was still set. Just like Sunday dinner. Half-eaten, like someone left in a hurry. Doors were locked."

"How long ago?"

"Couple of days."

Rich smiled. "Well, Sheriff," he said. "Why don't you ride outta here and arrest all those Stocktons? I'm tellin you."

"I ain't jumpin' to no conclusions, Rich. It ain't my problem no ways." Bufford took a sip of draft beer. "Thanks, Billy, for the beer. Right now that goes down real easy. How you been doin'?"

369

"Good. Real good. I wouldn't go, neither, Wes. Don't listen to him. You'd come back dead and no one would hear from you again."

"Those the only killin's?" Rich asked.

"What do you mean only? Ain't like we've had a rash or anythin'. This is Kane. Only thing newsy we get is the Pastor got his foot stepped on by a horse."

Billy nodded. "Had a lady, pretty girl, come to the back door a day or so ago. Said she'd like to order some Mississippi Crooks. Said they had to taste like rum. Birthday present, she said. For her."

"Mississippi Crooks? The cigar?"

"Yeah."

"I ain't never heard of 'em."

"Well, they're the real deal, Wes. They got 'em in Gulfport, Mississippi. I know cause I ordered 'em. I did."

"You ordered a cigar for a lady?"

"No. Not a cigar. Four boxes of cigars. She's plenty serious 'bout smokin'. A happy person. All smiles."

"Four boxes? You're sayin' it."

"I asked her if she was takin' up smokin'."

"She laughed, said yes she was. She always wanted to. Said she was just kiddin'. Had a boy with her. Nice lookin' kid."

Rich nodded his head, blew smoke off to the right.

"I asked the boy if he was gonna be smokin' cigars."

"He laughed, said, 'No thank you' real formal like."

"I asked him, who then?"

"He said the man with a bunch of brothers and a dog."

"A bunch of brothers and a dog?"

"Know anybody like that?" Wes asked Rich.

Rich smiled. "Not a soul. I ain't heard of a cigar smokin' lady, either. That's one for the books."

The saloon door opened and a man stepped inside and walked down the full length of the bar. Billy got up to wait on him. He ordered a shot of whiskey. Billy poured the drink. Turning, the new customer leaned against the bar, took his hat off, and placed it beside his drink, then seemed to change his mind on what he'd ordered. "Hey, barkeep, pour me another, would you while you're at it? My last day or two ain't been somethin' I'd like to remember."

He noted the badge on Wesley Bufford's vest.

"You the Sheriff?" he asked and took a sip, swallowed it slowly. He took a breath of air, blinking, turning something over in his head. He took another sip, drained it, then picked up the second shot glass, staring at the liquid as if it offended him. "You know, Sheriff, I'd retire if I was you. I'd get the hell outta this country as fast as I possibly could. I wouldn't wait another minute if'n I wanted to keep suckin' in and blowin' out like a regular human bein'."

Bufford stared at him. "What's the problem?" he asked.

Rich Larson turned in his chair to get a look at him. "You look like someone that's done walked over his own grave. You all right?" he asked.

"No, I ain't all right. I ain't close to all right. I come from over there on Deer Creek. Been cookin' for that Linderman outfit. You go over there right now, you'll find four bodies, men that claimed to be Deputy U.S. Marshals. Showed me their badges. They's shot full of holes. Ain't a breath left in their lungs. They's dead. I saw them, myself. I did." He looked at the shot glass, then drained it, collecting the last drop on his tongue, swallowing. The man at the bar held his peace for a minute or two. The room was quiet. Rich, Billy, and the Sheriff stared at him, waiting.

"The man I worked for.-- Now, I ain't been paid, but I'm not waitin' another minute--the man I worked for, an old feller by the name of Sam Linderman, he's swingin' back and forth at the end of a rope, hangin' from a cottonwood. Right there in his front yard. He's dead. They's all dead. I ain't never seen nothin' like it. I ain't stayin' to see anythin' more like it. Everybody's dead. I know you think I'm lyin'. I ain't. There ain't a livin' soul over there. I'd get the hell outta here, Sheriff, if'n I wanted to live."

The cook from Deer Creek picked his hat up, rolled the brim tightly in his hands, then seated it on his head. He glanced at the two men seated at the table, then at Billy Bangor behind the bar. He nodded, touching the brim of his hat with his index finger and walked out the door, closing it behind him.

No one moved.

The End

371

ABOUT THE AUTHOR

G. R. Howe was raised in Kane, Wyoming. He graduated from Brigham Young University and received a law degree from John Marshall Law School in Chicago. Illinois. He began practicing in Ventura, California in 1976 and pursued a career in law for the next thirty-four years, after which he and his wife, Joy, retired to Wyoming and began writing western novels.

You can visit his website, "Empty Saddles and Rusty Spurs" at www.emptysaddles.com.